BLUE RIDGE BRIDES

THREE-IN-ONE COLLECTION

LAURALEE BLISS
LYNN A. COLEMAN
TAMELA HANCOCK MURRAY

BARBOUR
PUBLISHING

Journey to Love © 2007 by Lauralee Bliss
Corduroy Road to Love © 2007 by Lynn A. Coleman
The Music of Home © 2007 by Tamela Hancock Murray

ISBN 978-1-60260-413-1

All scripture quotations are taken from the King James Version of the Bible.

This book is a work of fiction. Names, characters, places, and incidents are either products of the authors' imaginations or used fictitiously. Any similarity to actual people, organizations, and/or events is purely coincidental.

Cover Image: Robert Cable/Getty
Cover Model Photography: Jim Celuch, Celuch Creative Imaging

Published by Barbour Publishing, Inc., P.O. Box 719, Uhrichsville, Ohio 44683, www.barbourbooks.com

Our mission is to publish and distribute inspirational products offering exceptional value and biblical encouragement to the masses.

 Member of the
Evangelical Christian
Publishers Association

Printed in the United States of America.

JOURNEY TO LOVE

by Lauralee Bliss

Dedication

To Beth McDowell.
Thank you for your friendship and your listening ear in my times of need!

Chapter 1

Peace I leave with you,
my peace I give unto you:
not as the world giveth, give I unto you.
Let not your heart be troubled, neither let it be afraid.
JOHN 14:27

1650

We now commend the soul of Robert Henry Colman to eternity, through the name of our Savior Christ. Amen.

It was finished. The chapter drawn to a close. The end of a season and the beginning of the next, like the russet leaves that fall from the trees on the first breath of winter. Beth Colman tried to sleep, but instead witnessed vision after vision of the burial in her mind. She could still hear the long droning of the minister who had spoken over the coffin of her dead father. She could see the people huddled together, their heads bent, hands folded, the wind ruffling the drab material of their cloaks. Following the departure of all the mourners in attendance at the gravesite, there came to her the smiling face of her older sister, Judith, who seemed unaffected by what had occurred. Even now, Beth couldn't help but frown at the memory. How could Judith smile? Didn't she realize they had just buried the last of their parents? That only the two of them remained out of all their relatives? That all had entered into the heavenly kingdom, leaving them alone in this world?

"There is no need to be alone, Beth," Judith had said to her, pulling the black cloak she wore close about her. "Come stay with Mark and me. I can't bear to think of you at Briarwood any longer."

Beth considered the request, then shook her head. "No. I will be well in time." After all, she had things to do at Briarwood. Father's effects to go through. Times of contemplation, wondering what new chapter would be written in her life, now that this one was finished. As her Savior Christ had spoken—"It is finished."

What will I do next? Her eyes grew accustomed to the ceiling of wood above her, illuminated by the soft, moonlit glow that filled the room. A week had passed since Father's burial, and still she felt barren in purpose. Her life, for so long, had been consumed by Father's needs—fulfilling the duties, no matter how trivial, that his booming voice demanded. Doing what was required to ready him to face a new morning and then assist him to slumber at night. She watched him try to do the simplest things, only to sit listless in a chair, unable even to clothe himself in breeches and a shirt. He would say strange things, too. Mutter. Groan. Then speak in an angry voice with an intonation that seemed to shake the very foundation of the solid stone house. During these times, Beth often went into hiding until the episode passed. The physicians who came to see Father had failed to diagnose the strange malady that afflicted him. He toyed with madness, they said. Father seemed trapped in a realm no one could enter. Despite it, Beth could not leave him to his mental instability. She had to help him. He was her father, after all. Even when Judith begged her to let him go, to allow others to care for him so she might live her own life, Beth had refused. And likewise, after his death, she refused to leave the house but remained to see what else needed to be done.

Beth lay in bed, half-anticipating Father to call out at any moment. Maybe that's why she couldn't sleep nights, even though he was gone. Before his passing, she hadn't slept through a night without his waking her for some request in the midst of a mindless tirade.

"Elizabeth! Fetch me a brandy!"

"Elizabeth! Open the window and let in the night air!"

"Elizabeth! Tell Mother I need her and to come here at once!"

Beth winced and shut her eyes. Oftentimes, Father would call for her mother, who had died long ago. He would ask where she was and why she didn't answer him. At first, Beth couldn't bring herself to tell him Mother was gone from them, taken away when she was still young and beautiful, a victim of the dreaded pox. She feared what it might do to Father's already tortured mind. And so, much as she hated to speak a mistruth, she rationalized her words as being for her father's greater good and claimed Mother had gone to market, was out visiting friends, or having a new gown made. Father soon realized, however, something was amiss. He had a worried and wild look about him. When she finally did tell him that Mother had left to be with God, Father broke down and cried.

A tear drifted down her cheek. Beth quickly wiped it away. Judith was right. She shouldn't stay here in this huge house, which seemed more like a tomb than a home, with her thoughts consumed by memories. She must seek a new path for herself, but what?

After a fitful night, the rays of morning sunshine proved a welcome sight. While the sun should have cheered her, she felt nothing. If only she didn't feel so unsure, so useless with idle hands and a vacant heart. Looking into Father's room that morning, she expected to find him in bed, his gray eyes focused on the ceiling, a frown painted on his grizzled face, awaiting her assistance. "Help me up, Elizabeth!" his gravelly voice would demand. With the help of the servants, she would escort him to a chair that would become his place of rest for a good part of the day, by a window overlooking Briarwood's famous gardens. She would read him a passage of scripture. Fetch him the day's meals. And pray that whatever ailed him would be gone forever.

And now, her father's mind, body, and soul were brought to peace by the merciful hand of death.

Beth wandered about the halls until she found her personal servant, Josephine, setting out the morning victuals. The lump in her throat quenched any hope of an appetite. She only took a bit of crust from the bread and forced it down her throat.

"I'm so sorry for all this, Miss," Josephine said with a sigh. "How can I help?"

"We will clear my father's room today," Beth announced. "And then I will see if Lord Addington is still of a notion to acquire Briarwood. 'Tis only right and good for us to do what needs to be done. He once loved this place. He will take proper care of it, I'm certain."

Josephine nearly upset the pitcher she was carrying. "Oh, must we leave?"

"You know we can't remain here any longer."

"I suppose I shall seek out my family in London, then. But begging your pardon, Miss, where will you go?"

The words echoed in her mind. *Where will you go, Elizabeth Anne Colman? What will become of you?* "I suppose I shall marry," she said with a half-hearted laugh. "If it's not too late." The chuckle faded away. Again came the memories of suitors who paid visits—the sons of Father's aristocratic friends, even a second cousin, all interested and looking to discover if Elizabeth Colman might be ready to exchange this life for one of marital bliss. And in each instance, she had refused their intentions. Father would ask why all the young men were paying calls to Briarwood. She would tell him they had hoped to find an eligible woman for marriage. Father would take her hand in his, his gray eyes pleading, and beg in a scratchy voice for her not to leave him.

She'd abided by his wishes. . .until now, after his death, when the door had suddenly been thrust open before her. What else was there to do but marry?

"I fear it may be too late for some of the callers, Miss," Josephine said with sorrow evident in her voice. "Many have left England, or so I've heard. My lord master Austin. My lord master Billings. To that new land they are going. The land far away across the ocean, the one called Virginia."

Beth frowned. "As if some new land could bring happiness," she murmured. "Then I suppose I'm too late for everything. . .even for love."

"Nay. I don't believe that. 'Tis never too late for love, especially from our

7

God who knows when the time is right. 'Stir not up, nor awake my love, until he please.' And I know that time is soon upon you, Miss."

Josephine's words proved soothing on a day already filled with uncertainty. How Beth would miss her when she took her leave of this place. They had become more like sisters through the care of her father, even if Josephine was only a servant by status. Yet Beth knew the girl was so much more. While her sister, Judith, had left to marry and set up her own house, Beth found in Josephine a true heart and listening ear as in no other.

Just then, Beth heard a friendly greeting in the foyer. The pleasantry echoed throughout the manor home. She hurried to find Judith there, alongside her husband, Mark. Beth envied her sister for finding such a man as Mark Reynolds. Tall and stout, with golden locks, fashionably dressed in baggy breeches, a ruffled white shirt, and a short waistcoat accented with lace, he was the perfect portrait of a gentleman. Her sister stood with her arm linked through his, appearing content and peaceful, her dream of love and happiness fulfilled—all of it making Beth's heart ache.

Judith immediately took Beth's pale hands in hers. Her sister's were warm and inviting, while Beth's hands were as frigid as the winter snow. They walked together down the cold and dank hall to the sitting room. "I'm so sorry for all you have been through, dear sister," Judith said. "I couldn't sleep for thinking of you."

At least the merciful words brought the assurance that someone cared. "I'm well. You needn't worry about me."

"Oh, but I do worry. I know this must be hard. You were devoted to Father for a very long time. Though we shall miss him, we must think of tomorrow." She paused. "*Your* tomorrow, dear Beth."

Beth looked away, to a tapestry hanging on the wall. It had been one of their mother's favorites, of the English countryside filled with the flowers of springtime. It spoke of beauty and life. Beth hoped to take it with her wherever she went. Suddenly she caught herself. *Take it with me where, pray tell? Where shall I go? What will I do? What will be my tomorrow when I can't see past yesterday?*

At that moment Mark joined them, quietly occupying one of the sturdy chairs nearby. "We have been thinking," Judith continued, acknowledging her husband. "We hadn't spoken of this since Father took ill, but we believe the time has come."

Beth watched the two of them share silent communication through their gazes as it seemed only married people could do.

"My husband and I have decided to leave England."

"Leave England!" Beth repeated. "I don't understand. Where are you going?"

"You know our country is in turmoil right now. Many of our friends have found themselves persecuted for their status and their ties to the former crown. One of my lord's closest friends has even been falsely imprisoned." She drew in a breath. "We can't live under this, nor do we wish it upon our children yet to be begotten. So we have decided to take our leave of this place, to board a ship at Portsmouth and remove ourselves to Virginia."

Beth stared, unable to believe what she was hearing. Leave their homeland? The place of their birth? The land where they had been raised and the land that now cradled the earthly remains of both their parents, though their souls embraced eternity? "But how can you leave?"

Judith stirred in her seat. "We believe it's for the best. And we want to fulfill a dream of Father's."

"What dream is this? He never spoke of going to Virginia."

"You may not know this, Beth, but he wrote often of his curiosity with regard to his own parents. Our grandparents. Where they had gone. What might have become of them."

"Your grandparents were part of the lost colony," Mark added. "The one that settled in the place called Roanoke, in the land of Hatorask. We have the opportunity of finding out what might have happened to them."

"But that was so long ago," Beth said. "No one knows what happened."

"We can try, Beth," Judith implored. "Though Father is gone from us, I know he would approve if we sought to find out what happened. Perhaps even now we have family relations who live in the new land of Virginia. Aunts and uncles we have never embraced. Cousins, even. We must find out if we're truly alone or if there are others we may not know about."

Beth could not help but fly to her feet. "But why? We have just buried Father. How can you leave me and this place?"

Judith stood to her feet as well, her hand outstretched. "We don't plan to leave you. We want you to come with us to Virginia. Beth, consider. There is nothing for you here. Even now our country stirs with rising conflict. Men fighting each other for selfish gain. I don't want us to be here, caught up in the suffering. Virginia is safe. And there we can find the answers to our family, to the mystery that plagued Father for so long, while we make a new home for ourselves."

Beth fell silent. Her mind struggled to understand all of the considerations suddenly thrust upon her. Never had she heard Father speak about a longing to discover what happened to his parents. Perhaps he had, but she had been so consumed by other things—maybe she hadn't listened. And maybe that longing in his heart had furthered the illness in his mind.

Glancing up to see the pleading in her sister's eyes, Beth couldn't help but be stirred by what she said. She wanted so much to know what would happen with her life now that Father was gone. And the adventure would be a welcome change. Could the answer lie with a voyage to some distant land? "But is it truly safe, this Virginia?" Beth wondered.

"Sister, doesn't God lead us to safety, to His strong tower? I believe He is leading us, as He has led others to find life in a new world."

He has led others to find life in a new world. Her gaze traveled to the tapestry. Perhaps buds of hope and purpose were about to blossom, if she could only find the courage to embrace them.

∞

With her knees weak and her stomach still heaving from the tossing of the ship, Beth was thankful to feel firm ground beneath her feet. They had finally completed the treacherous voyage across the ocean to the bustling port called Jamestown in Virginia. All around were the sounds of men toting barrels and exchanging loud chatter. Many stared at her as if she were fresh produce in the market. Animals wandered about in the street. The sharp scents of a foreign place filled her nostrils. Her senses were overwhelmed, sending her thoughts tumbling away. Between the voyage and, now, the activity of this strange land, Beth was desperate to find a quiet place to recover from all she had endured. *Would such a wish prove too difficult to fulfill?*

At least she was thankful to see her brother-in-law take up the reins of leadership, seeing to their comfort by inquiring of a place for them to stay until they could find a place of their own. When Mark learned from passersby of a family that allowed weary travelers to stay among them, he escorted Beth and Judith at once to the Worthington Tavern. It looked rustic to Beth—a mere commoner's dwelling made of clapboards, the thatched roof constructed from reeds that grew thick on the shore. She pulled her wrap tighter as if trying to shield herself from this place. How different it all appeared from the thick stone walls of the manor home of Briarwood framed by the lush English countryside. At least the inn had a solid wood floor and not a swaying ship deck, which had left her feeling dizzy still.

Beth entered the tavern to see a long table and several men slurping down food from wooden bowls. She tried to keep her attention elsewhere but couldn't help noticing a man who sat at the end of the table. His gaze had been clearly focused on her when she entered. Again, she drew her wrap tighter around her. It had been a long time since a man looked at her in such a way. Not since the suitors who paid calls during her father's illness. A very long time ago indeed. But this was neither the time nor the place to think of suitors. This was not her beloved England, either, but a new place inhabited by strange people—and strange men.

Suddenly the man left the table and approached Mark. "Good day, my lord. My name is John Harris. You just arrived on the ship from England?"

"Yes. I'm Mark Reynolds. This is my wife, Judith, and my sister-in-law, Beth."

The man named John nodded to her, but Beth looked away, pretending to stare at the simple, rough-hewn walls that comprised the humble house. When she looked back, he was still staring at her, as if appreciating some marvelous painting. The thought made her blush. She chastised herself for such a vain thought.

"Perhaps you can help us, Master Harris," Mark continued. "We are most interested in seeking out a place called Hatorask. The area where the colony of Roanoke was said to exist. Have you heard of it or know of anyone who has?"

"Hatorask!" Beth could see the fire ignite in the man's blue eyes and his lips upturn into a smile that displayed good teeth. "I know the place well. Why are you interested in the Hatorask region, my lord?"

" 'Tis a family matter."

"I see. I can assist you in your journey, if you wish."

Mark smiled. "Blessed be the Lord! Surely He has guided our footsteps. Very good. We will talk further." Mark turned and whispered to Judith.

"Come, Beth, let us find a place to rest," Judith urged, taking her arm.

"What business does your husband have with a stranger?" Beth wondered aloud.

"My lord is beside himself," she said with a chuckle. "He wishes to find out about our relatives as soon as possible, before we settle here. He seeks a guide to lead us to where the colony once existed."

"But. . .we have only just arrived! And I'm so weary. . . ." Her voice faded away. *Please, dear Lord, just a moment's rest. A small fragment of peace.*

"There will be plenty of time to rest. There are plans to make. It would do us well to accomplish the journey while we can, before we see to a home." She sighed. "And I can't stop the passion within him. When Mark first heard of this mystery within our family, it moved him unlike anything I have ever seen. He will not be stilled until we have found the answers. And I must admit I want to find the answers, too. I want to know if we have relatives here."

"These ideas of a journey and exploration, discovery and mystery seem to move every man," Beth commented, thinking of the way John Harris responded at the mere mention of the Hatorask region. "I even saw it in the stranger's eyes."

"It does. 'Tis what made this place, after all. Men and women with a dream who came to this land despite the great odds. Like our grandparents. And so it is God's will that we come here to make new lives. I believe it." Judith gently squeezed her hand. "He will bless us, sweet sister."

"I hope you are right," Beth said softly. "But can we just sit for a moment and breathe without having to endure another journey?"

Judith laughed. "Only for a moment, until my husband returns. Then we will soon be off on our next grand adventure."

Beth sighed. Just as she feared. If only she could find a place of refuge.

Perhaps she should have remained in Cambridge, even if it was inside the cold stone walls of Briarwood with all its memories. At least it was calm and quiet there. Here, she was at the mercy of her zealous brother-in-law and strangers, such as the man named John, who stared at her with blue eyes that bored into her very soul. "Merciful God, please help me."

Chapter 2

John Harris thought long and hard of the encounter at the tavern last evening. How like a doe did the sister-in-law of the gentleman Reynolds appear. Graceful and purposeful but shy. Unsure of her surroundings. Fearful of strangers. Vulnerable. Try as he might, he could not dismiss her from his thoughts. He wanted to reach out and reassure her, to make her feel welcome and at ease with these strange surroundings. If only he could.

Though he had been here for many years now, he still recalled his own uncertainty the first time he stepped onto this new land. He was just as much a frightened animal of the forest as she seemed to be. But it didn't take long for him to fall into the company of men looking to explore the lands that stretched out beyond Jamestown and the great James River. They were eager to find what existed to the very horizon. The tiny flame of desire to explore soon became a raging fire. Wherever his feet were destined to tread, he would go. And he went. Fast and far to the region known as Hatorask. And on his heels came his brother, Robert, likewise an adventurer, following in his shadow, learning all he could at the tender age of sixteen, even if he was a bit impetuous at times.

There was a great interest to explore back then and little time to contemplate having a home and family. Until now, when John returned to Jamestown to see families sprouting like vegetables in a garden. Hearing the laughter of little ones playing with their balls and hoops in the town square. Watching the farms begin to dot the countryside, the fields fairly bursting with tobacco and corn. Witnessing it all, John decided the time had come for him to likewise plant roots. He would give up exploration and seek a life with the woman God had chosen for him.

John ventured often to the port of Jamestown where the ships docked. Many bore eligible women called "tobacco brides," arranged for those who sought wives through the payment of tobacco harvested from the fields. He had neither tobacco fields nor a home, nary a shilling to his name. But it didn't deter him. Watching the women arrive in the shallops from the great ships anchored in the bay, he prayed for the right one to call his own. *Lord, show me the one You have chosen to be my bride.*

Then the shallop arrived, bearing the graceful doe of Miss Colman. He could still see her so clearly when she stood at the docks. Her hands had been trembling, her eyes wide as she looked about the new land. He wanted to go forward at that moment and offer a greeting to calm her fear. Instead, he retreated into the background and walked to the tavern for his meal, all the while hoping he would see the young woman again soon. And suddenly, she was there, right at the doorstep. His heart couldn't help but leap at such an answer to prayer. She didn't seem to notice him, but that would change once they made their acquaintance. He would make certain of it.

John consumed his drink in the pewter tumbler before focusing his attention on the man sitting opposite him who had introduced himself as Mark Reynolds. Like himself, there was a passion within the man to see beyond the outer regions. And now the man sought a guide to take him to the Hatorask region in the land called the province of Carolana, the windswept land of sand by the ocean, many miles south of Jamestown. John could not believe his fortune at meeting someone interested in the very place he once explored.

"So you are willing to guide us to Hatorask for this price, Master Harris?" Mark inquired, showing him a purse of money.

John nodded. The money was fine, yes, but the journey was even better. At least for now he did not have to think about settling here by the James River. There would be plenty of time for such things. Now it seemed God had sent Mark Reynolds to renew his own fervor for exploration. "And what of the women in your company, my lord? Will they also make the journey?" He could not steady the rapid beating of his heart. *The truth be known, will your sister-in-law be coming along?* He hoped she would be there to brighten the journey with her presence. Perhaps he could have both—not only a trip to Hatorask, but also a woman to one day call his own.

"Of course. We seek their relatives. Is there a manner of difficulty with this?"

"Oh no, not at all." He hoped he didn't sound too eager. He didn't wish to reveal his interest in the fair young woman that was the gentleman's sister-in-law. Like the new land, he wanted very much to discover her true beauty and worth, which now lay hidden beneath a cloak of fear and uncertainty—and to give her a small measure of the confidence she needed to survive in this place.

For himself, he might have been too confident after the time spent here. Too sure of his abilities. And the pride cost him dearly, forging a wound that nothing could heal. John looked away. He didn't want to reveal that aching in his soul. Why it came forth now, he didn't know. He pushed it aside, especially when he saw the gentleman gazing at him as if wanting to discover his personal land of heartache and grief. John would not allow him to find it. Nor any woman either. The matter lay deep within himself, and there it would remain.

"Well, I thank our Sovereign God that we found you, Master Harris."

"Please call me John." He offered his hand.

"And you may call me Mark. As I said, 'tis indeed providential we have met. To find a man that knows this land of Hatorask where the colony of Roanoke once existed and can guide us to the very place. . .quite remarkable."

"You realize that no trace of the colony has been found except for a few belongings left behind in haste and some strange word carved in a tree. They are very much gone forever."

Mark only smiled as if the news proved inconsequential. "I believe there is an answer somewhere, just waiting to be discovered. And with you leading us, John Harris, I'm all the more confident we will find what we're seeking."

John marveled. A cheerful and confident man indeed. No doubt commanded by his Savior. If only John felt such things in his own life.

"And have you found success here in this land, Master Harris?"

"If you mean do I own lands and a home, no. There is more to success than the possessions one gains."

"I agree. We have but a few possessions ourselves as we didn't want to be burdened by them on such a long voyage. We are beginning anew." He sighed. "It is just as well. England has become a den of thieves. There are those willing to squeeze the life out of their brothers because of jealousy. It is good to come here with little, to begin again as if a paintbrush to a clean canvas."

John immediately liked the man sitting before him. Mark offered words of wisdom. He wasn't pretentious. And he was eager to hire John for a trip that fed his desire to explore once again.

"Thank you." Mark stood to his feet and extended his hand, which John shook. "A pleasure doing business."

"Likewise." John offered a farewell and ventured out of the tavern into the bright sunshine. A fine spring day it was turning out to be, although the summers here could be unbearable. He wondered how the fair Miss Colman would take to a new place that proved much different from her native England. He knew that a strange land tested faith with periods of doubt and hoped he might help renew that faith and cast any doubt into the sea.

With the sun shining full in his face, he thought of the time he first stepped off a shallop onto this land, wondering if he had made the right choice. If he would succeed in this place. If he would make the money he needed to pay off his debts. But the exuberance of his younger brother overshadowed any of his doubts. Like Mark Reynolds this day, his brother, Robert, was a cheerful soul, teeming with confidence no matter what lay before him.

"What a fine place this is!" Robert had said, the grin spreading from cheek to cheek, his zeal infectious. "Is it not a fine place indeed, John? Will we see all of it?"

"All of it and more, Robert." *Better to agree,* he thought. When he did say the words, he felt his confidence rise. He believed they would see all of the land. They would lead a victorious life, and they would claim it for God and for country.

But little did we know, this fine place is also an unpredictable place—a place that could birth dreams only to have them taken away. A place of danger and death.

John walked the muddy road between the homes made of clapboard or simple sticks held together with mud. He tried not to dwell on the past until he saw a vivid reminder of it all, standing there before him. He stopped short. They were not often seen in Jamestown after many of the uprisings that had occurred. Now there were two of them. One even wore an English hat of all things. The shiny black hair reflected the rays of sunlight. The skins of animals that clad their glistening frames looked fresh, as did the painted faces. John tried to shift his thoughts to peaceful things, to dwell on the things above and not on the Indians before him, but he couldn't. The mere sight of them stirred up raw feelings within, feelings he had not been able to relinquish eighteen months later. His wound was still fresh, as if it had happened yesterday. He wanted to look aside and continue on but kept staring at the Indians instead. They had goods in their possession. Obviously they had just finished bartering—obtaining pots, beads, and other trinkets for baskets of corn. And that is not all they traded. They traded lives as well—colonist for Indian, Indian for colonist. Lives torn apart. Blood spilled fresh. The faces and voices known so well, gone forever.

John hurried away before the anger he had fought to control rose with a vengeance, leaving peace in the dust. Only then did he hear his name hailed. He turned to see a fellow explorer of the southern regions, Samuel Wright, calling to him from across the street.

"John Harris. And where are you off to in such a hurry?"

He was glad for the interruption and silently thanked God. "Good to see you, my friend. I have great news to tell. I'm going back to Hatorask."

"Are you now? And why, pray tell? I thought you were going to settle here with the bride of your choosing."

"I've been hired to lead a family there. A man that just arrived on the ship yesterday. And two women."

"Two women, eh? Why are you burdening yourself with such travelers?" He paused before a grin spread wide across his face. "Unless. . .could it be? Have you now turned your heart to settling down with a bride at Hatorask? A dream about to be fulfilled?"

John admitted he once thought of settling in the land by the ocean, without another living soul inhabiting the place for miles. But it was hardly the place to put up a home or to bring a wife, unless he could convince his lady that Hatorask would be a fine place to settle. And yet look what he was about to do—lead a family that had an eligible woman among them to Hatorask.

"Ah, I can see it. That is exactly what you wish to do, isn't it? To see if perhaps you may have found what you've been seeking?"

"I'm only hired to guide them there," John insisted. "And I haven't spoken to her."

Samuel shook his head. "Then tell me, why guide them to that place in particular? There are no settlements. Nothing but Indians and a few fools like us, searching in vain for treasure."

"They are seeking relatives lost with the colony at Roanoke."

"What?" Samuel waved his hand. " 'Tis a long journey for a foolish dream. The people there died long ago. Killed by the Indians, they were." He blanched. "Forgive me, John. The words came out in haste. I didn't think. . . ."

"It matters not. But the gentleman, Reynolds, the one who hired me, seems to think there may still be answers left to find. He is like us, Samuel. He wants to explore. Adventure is a part of him. And even if his quest leads nowhere, the fact that it leads to Hatorask is good enough for me."

"And I'm sure a bit of money to fill your pocket makes a good convincer, as well."

John grinned. "Money speaks quite loudly. I have debts left in England that the purse will surely cover."

"Then I wish you Godspeed on this new journey of yours. And. . .be careful."

Samuel's words held an ominous ring to them. John once thought himself the most prudent individual regarding everything he put his mind to—until he threw caution to the wind and tragedy reared its head. John tried not to blame himself, but he did. He was supposed to be the protector, after all. The leader. The one who held lives in his hands. And he let it slip away. His inattentiveness had cost him dearly, more than any money could buy or any exploration to Hatorask could do. Only God Himself could bear the true pain of it all.

Don't do this to yourself, John. Don't or it will destroy you. You know this to be true. Let this rest in the Almighty's care. Cast thy burdens upon the Lord, for He cares for you.

He tried to focus his thoughts on the surroundings—the people bustling about, those sharing pleasantries with each another, the sound of bleating sheep, the conversation of men working the nearby dock—anything to rid his mind of the past and the scenes that plagued both his waking and his sleep.

Then he caught sight of her once more, and everything else left him. He rubbed his eyes to make certain he wasn't dreaming. She was indeed Miss Colman, walking along the opposite side of the street with her sister. He watched the women carry themselves with grace and dignity, careful to avoid the people and the roaming animals. Miss Colman held tight to her wrap as if it were some great shield protecting her. Her sister talked endlessly about something—what, John couldn't determine. He drew closer. Miss Colman looked pretty in what bit of the gown he saw below the wrap—although too fancy for these surroundings. Brown curls rested on her shoulders. She was perfect, if cautious. He inhaled a breath. He must make her feel at ease. After all, they would soon be journeying to Hatorask together. It would be good to make their acquaintance as soon as possible.

He began walking toward them, only to stop short when he heard them conversing in a disagreeing tone.

"If only I knew someone here," Miss Colman mourned. "I don't like this. I would stay here if I could and let you both go on this grand adventure of yours. I have no interest in it."

"There is nothing to fear. My lord has already told me he has found an excellent guide. Don't you wish to discover what happened to our family? Our grandparents?"

John watched her draw the wrap even tighter about her, outlining the curve of her upper arms. Her hands were lily white in color, her face even more so against her large brown eyes as she stared at her sister. Her eyes gleamed with intensity, almost as if tears might be clouding them. John shook his head. This would never do. He couldn't bear to see her cry.

He came up. "Hello, my ladies. Welcome to Jamestown."

Miss Colman cried in a start and whirled about, her hand covering her mouth. "Sir, you should have made your presence known!"

"Dearest Beth, he did," the sister admonished her, then turned to John. "Thank you, sir."

"I just spoke with your husband about the journey to Hatorask, madam," he said to the sister. "John Harris, at your bidding."

"So you are our guide! My husband speaks highly of your knowledge, Mr. Harris."

When he looked at Beth, as her sister called her, her gaze loomed elsewhere. She couldn't look at him straightway—almost as if he had an evil appearance or a face marred by the pox. If only she would look at him, and yes, appreciate what she saw. He very much appreciated her comeliness. "I'm eager to show you the land. 'Tis handsome indeed."

"I hope you can help us with our quest, as well," said the sister.

John readied himself to speak of their quest at finding out about the Roanoke Colony—a rather foolish notion in his opinion. Instead he only smiled and nodded. He was not about to cause a further rift between them all. He now turned to Beth. How he liked her name. "I trust you fared well on your journey here from England, madam?"

"I was ill every day," Beth complained. "The sailors were a vile lot. They cursed and were drunk. I feared for my virtue." She cast him a quick glance as if she were comparing him to such men. He winced at the thought. He wanted only to soothe her fears, to tell her she could trust him. But even if he were to say the right words, she might not believe him. She had to be convinced by deed and not by word alone.

"But God protected us," the sister admonished. "He is our shield and strong tower. And now we are very much anticipating our journey to the southern regions, Mr. Harris." She paused. "Perhaps you would do us the favor of joining us for dinner at the tavern so we may further discuss the trip? I think it would set all our minds at ease to hear of your exploits."

He bowed. "It would be my pleasure, madam." He hoped for a nod of approval from Beth but received none. *Give me but a few moments, Miss Beth Colman, and I will ease all your misgivings.*

"We look forward to seeing you again." With a nod the sister proceeded on. Beth followed close behind, but not before she cast him one final glance. It was that glance that stayed with John, sparking hope in his restless heart.

Chapter 3

"Why did you invite that stranger to eat with us?" Beth moaned to Judith. She held up the looking glass to examine her hair, which she painstakingly arranged in a chignon with ringlets framing her cheeks.

"If we are going on this journey, you do believe it's wise to find out more about our guide, don't you?"

"Don't you trust your husband that our guide is a man of excellence?"

"Of course I do. I only invited him in the hope he might ease your fears. It's not like you hide them well, Elizabeth Anne."

Beth frowned at the utterance of her full name. She had heard from her parents how they named her after the former queen of England, partly for the reddish highlights in her brown hair, but mostly for her fiery spirit to live. Her delivery had been difficult, from what she had been told. The midwife said when she was born, she was small, spindly, and would not live to see tomorrow. And yet here she was a grown woman, healthy in mind and body, if a bit troubled in spirit. She only wished Judith wouldn't make light of her concerns. She had been through a great deal these many years. Was it not proper and right for her to consider these plans in light of everything?

"I do not fear," Beth denied. "I only want to be certain this journey you and your husband are planning is indeed the will of the Almighty and not some vain quest that will only bring disappointment. Consider this. Wouldn't you rather settle down, Judith? Make a fine home in a dwelling that your husband will build for you? Have a large garden? Raise young ones? I very much would like a niece or a nephew."

"Of course I want all that. Every woman does."

Beth leaned closer. "Then why this trip? Why must we go to Hatorask now? You and I can stay here and let the men go on the quest. There is no reason for us to go, too."

"I will not leave my husband. And I will not leave you here alone in this place. So unseemly. How can you even think such things? Can you not bear to consider this one final duty? 'Tis our relatives we seek, after all. Do you not want to know if we have family here? That we are not alone in this world after losing both Father and Mother?"

"I know nothing of our grandparents. Father was but a lad when they left to come here. It was so long ago. What does it matter if we find out what happened to them?"

"It matters to our family. And it once mattered to our father."

"He never spoke of it to me. If this issue lay so heavy on his heart, I'm certain he would have said something. Maybe you dreamed it so you might go on some grand adventure."

Judith said no more but strode over to the trunk sitting in the corner of the room. She opened it slowly, sifting through the few items they brought from England. When she reached their mother's folded tapestry, Beth helped her take it out. She inhaled a sharp breath when she saw it—the symbol of all she had lost and all she had left behind.

"What do you seek?" she asked Judith. "The tapestry?"

"You will see." From the bottom of the chest, Judith withdrew a tattered book, the leather worn, the pages falling out of the thread binding that barely held it together.

"What is that?" Beth wondered.

"You've never seen this, I'm certain. As the eldest, I was given Father's journal from Mother, who asked me to keep it safe. Father wrote in it faithfully when he was young. He speaks of many things on his heart, but especially about a few things I believe you will find interesting." She opened it carefully. A cloud of dust from ages past rose up, bringing with it the aroma of history and the lure of unanswered questions.

Judith began reading. " 'This night I think of my parents taken from me. Yes, I do care for my great-aunt and uncle who have raised me, but I think this night of my parents and their journey to the New World to be a part of the new colony. Uncle William spoke of their yearning to see a new place. But they never returned. I wish I knew what happened to them.' " Judith paused. "There now. Do you see how much this meant to Father?"

Beth looked over Judith's shoulder to examine the pages, the ink smeared and barely legible. She traced the print of her father's hand and his thoughts inscribed on the paper for memory's sake. "But this writing was done long ago, and the intent forgotten, just like this colony that our grandparents helped to found. From what I've heard, nothing was ever found of the colonists but for a few clues after Governor White returned. Some tried to find the survivors, but to no avail. Why should we hope for any greater success?"

" 'Tis the least we can do to satisfy Father's wish. Can we do no less while we have the means? Who knows what may happen? Mark is eager to go forth. And if this man, Master Harris, was brought by God to be our guide, surely the Lord's hand is already on this journey."

Judith closed the book and set it on the chest, urging Beth to hurry and come downstairs before the guide arrived for the meal. Once she left, Beth slowly opened the book, smelling the earthy odor of age. She noted Father's distinct handwriting.

Uncle William says I must bury these thoughts I have for my parents, that they are in a better place, with God in heaven. I wish I could, but something in me yearns to know. When I am older, I will buy my own passage to the New World and find out what happened. They are my flesh and blood, after all. My parents. Even if Uncle William has no understanding of what lies inside me, I must know what happened. 'Tis the only way to find peace.

A strange feeling came over Beth after reading these written words. *'Tis the only way to find peace.* Dare she even consider that Father's tortured mind might have been further burdened by this pain from long ago? Now that he was gone, had God opened the door to make it possible for his children—she and Judith—to seek the answer for him? If only she could know.

Beth sighed and closed the book. Enough contemplation. Their guest would arrive any time now. She peered once more at the small looking glass that displayed her features. Her brown eyes were wide and thoughtful, the sunlight through the small window igniting the strands of red in her hair. Yet fear toyed with her over the thought of traveling to another unknown place. If only she could convince Judith to allow her to stay behind while she went to fulfill their father's dream. Perhaps Beth could still stay here if she found a room with an older woman. Maybe this John would know of someone who would take her in. Or perhaps she could stay and help the family that served as the proprietors of this place. Though the tavern where they remained certainly was plain and not in keeping with the grandeur she was accustomed to, it would suffice as a place of refuge.

Beth set down the looking glass. It was not to be. Judith would never agree. And in her heart, she knew Father would want her to be a part of this family quest. There was no choice in the matter. This journey to Hatorask was also her journey—a journey of the heart and spirit.

They had already taken their seats at the dining table in a small room when Beth arrived. She gave a quick greeting and stiff curtsy, with her back straight and hands folded, before taking her place at the table. She sincerely hoped John Harris would not stare at her as he had during their last meeting. Many men in this place of Jamestown looked at her with interest, as if marriage were foremost in their minds. Judith laughed it away, saying they were but lonely men. Few women graced the new land. It was to be expected, after all. But the attention made Beth uneasy, wishing she knew more about relationships; how she should act, what she should say. No doubt their dinner guest would be more than willing to give a few lessons in such etiquette. She had seen his gaze, both when she arrived and when they met on the street. He appeared overly eager to make her acquaintance.

But at that moment, John was not staring at her but rather the food placed on the table—rarebit with cornbread on the side. When the blessing was said, he eagerly helped himself to a large portion and began eating as if he had never tasted food. She watched in dismay as he held his spoon like a club and shoveled down the food with all the appearance of a ravenous animal. When he looked up and noticed her obvious disdain, he set down his spoon.

"Forgive me, madam. Rarely have I had the chance to eat in the presence of such beautiful ladies."

Judith laughed. " 'Tis good to see a man enjoying the victuals."

Beth was about to make a comment to the contrary, but instead, she picked up her spoon and took a dainty bite. After a few minutes, she glanced up to find a smirk painted on John's face.

"I fear you will be dining most of the evening if you indulge in such modest amounts with each bite, madam."

"But at least I will have the pleasure of tasting my food, sir."

He sat back, the smirk widening into a grin. "You have wit. And here I thought you fearful as a rabbit."

"So long as I'm not someone's intended prey." Beth bent once more over her food but could clearly see that this John no longer seemed interested in eating. His gaze was now set upon her.

"I agree. How do you wish to be seen, madam?"

"As someone of worth, just as the eyes of the Lord see me."

His face relaxed, his blue eyes muted as if a fog had drifted over them. "A wise answer. As you wish."

Beth felt her face grow warm. He had fallen for her very words. Now what was she to do?

The moment was broken by a loud cough. Mark gestured to John with his goblet.

"So tell us about this place called Hatorask, Master Harris. I wish to know everything there is to know."

"Where do I begin, my lord? 'Tis better to see it for yourself than for me to try to describe it. But if you can imagine a land with no homes or people but only the call of the gulls and the roar of the ocean, you would be correct."

Beth put down her spoon to think on the scene he had painted with his words. Cambridge had been far away from the sea. Except for the voyage here, when the pounding of waves against the ship was the common sound, she had not been acquainted with the ocean. "Why are there no settlements?" she asked.

"There was once a charter for settlement set forth by the late King Charles I. But politics within England have changed, as you know. The king is dead and so, too, is the charter he once gave to settle the province called Carolana. For now, men are content to explore the region until there is a permanent charter."

He paused. "But there will be settlements soon, I'm certain. Jamestown is filling with people. Some have established homes northward along the James River. But there are also increasing tensions with the Indians of this land. Settling the southern regions seems to be the open door at the moment."

"Have there been many conflicts with the naturals?" Mark wondered.

"There are times of tension and times of peace, if one could call a cessation of hostilities peace. The last hostility was a few years ago. Still, I do not wish to associate with them. They hold to devilish practices."

"Surely they are but poor, lost souls," Beth commented.

"They may be lost, madam, but they are in command of their weapons and with a will to use them. There have been treaties signed at different times, but none have lasted for very long. Men seek peace only to suffer in the aftermath. 'Tis best to remain on guard, for you never know what will happen while you're looking the other way."

Beth tried to focus her gaze on her meal but found her thoughts adrift like a ship at sea. If he was trying to allay her fears, this description didn't help in the least. Now she had new fears to consider.

"I'm certain one must be on their guard in England, too," John added. "There are plenty of rogues and scoundrels in this world."

"Indeed," Mark commented. "With the change of hands in the English government, we found our very existence threatened in our own country. The common man is seen as the one in need of justice, and those with wealth are seen as a scourge."

"Is that why you left?"

"And our father died," Judith added. "The time for change had come. Not only the political changes in our homeland but also the changes in our families moved us to seek a new life. And since Beth once cared for our father day and night, it seemed good for us to leave and begin again."

Once more Beth felt the gaze of John linger on her. "I'm certain your circumstance must have been difficult for you," he said softly in her direction.

"No more difficult than what we are about to undertake with this expedition," she murmured. All at once she felt a slight touch and jumped at the sensation. John's fingers had come to rest lightly on top of her hand.

"Madam, you have no need to fear while I'm here. Yes, the journey to Hatorask is long. But once you're there, the place will captivate you." He removed his hand and exhaled. "It did me. I was not without uncertainty, but soon the land did enchant me with its wonders. And to know that God wishes for us to be happy, to build our lives, to make this place mighty for His name's sake. 'Tis all good."

Beth couldn't help but lift her gaze to meet his. She saw the crook of a smile form on his lips. He was indeed a good Christian gentleman, speaking words of assistance and hope that stirred up her curiosity. "So you will see to our safety?"

"With my life." He then took up a piece of cornbread Judith passed to him.

Beth could barely eat after this. While Mark and John continued to talk about the land of Virginia and the province of Carolana where Hatorask lay, Beth marveled at John's interesting characteristics. Perhaps a journey in his company might do her good. She could find out more about him and inquire of God whether a blessed union waited on the wings of her future.

When John bid them farewell that evening, Judith immediately ventured over to Beth and smiled. "Well, it seems as though you and Mr. Harris have each made one another's acquaintance. Perhaps too well, if appearances are not deceiving."

Beth flushed at the implication. "He was only trying to reassure me."

"I could see that quite plainly. Every word you spoke, he held it close to his heart. And I must say you also seemed interested in his words."

"Maybe only in that I still hold some manner of attractiveness to men." She was surprised at the tears that welled up. Day after day, night after night, caring for her father while watching suitors come and go with hunched shoulders and sad expressions, she couldn't help but wonder if the status of the unmarried, such as Queen Elizabeth, would also be her lot. Maybe she would be forever married to principle and to place, wherever that place might be. That is, until now, with the attention of John Harris renewing hope.

"I know you have been through much in your young life, Beth. But now is the time to reach out with your faith and embrace what God has planned for you. There are great things waiting for you. Surely you can feel it."

"I only hope I'm ready."

Judith embraced her. "God knows the times and the seasons. Open your heart, Beth, and you will find the season of love when you least expect it."

A season of love, like the blooming English garden woven into Mother's tapestry. She sighed. How lovely that would be. If only she did not find herself doubting the words.

Chapter 4

*E*very word you spoke, he held it close to his heart. And. . .you also seemed *interested. . . ."*

Beth reflected over the words spoken by her sister. Could it be so plain to Judith and everyone else that some manner of attraction was there? She hardly knew John Harris. They had just met and only because Mark hired him. Was he like all the men she had seen walking about the streets of Jamestown, a man desperate to find a wife and establish himself? Or were these the natural bonds of love that only God Himself could bring to light? She sighed, hoping to know in her spirit whether this was the Lord's making or some strange thing conceived out of a desperate mind.

Since the dinner, Beth and John had not spoken, despite the meetings he had with Mark to discuss the journey. Beth immersed herself in gathering what provisions the family would need to make the journey. They could take little with them but the necessities of life. Fingering her mother's tapestry inside the chest, Beth wondered what to do with it. Perhaps Mistress Worthington would keep watch over it here at the tavern during their absence. Besides her father's journal, it was the one material item she and her sister had that reminded them of their beloved parents, now gone. She hoped it would be safe.

Beth looked up at that moment, thinking of her parents and of Judith's confidence in the idea that, perhaps, they had relatives living somewhere in this new land. If they did find relatives from long ago, how would they make their acquaintance? Beth sighed. There was little use in pondering such things until the time came. For now, there was the journey to the place by the ocean that John Harris had described—with a sandy coastline stretching for eternity, accompanied by the laughter of the gulls.

Beth was closing the lid to the chest when suddenly she heard voices escalating in the room across the hall. She came out into the hallway and to the door, recognizing Mark's calm voice. The second voice belonged to an agitated man, the vexation clear in his words.

"Why must you do this?" the man demanded of her brother-in-law. "Now the entire expedition is in jeopardy!"

"I do what I believe is best. Surely you know we need them to help us carry our provisions. And they were most willing to do it for a few trinkets and gold coins."

"You don't understand, do you? You don't understand the danger in hiring people like them."

"There is danger in everything one does. But if we place our hope in Christ. . ."

"I have placed my hope in Christ, my lord. But living here in this place also calls for wisdom. And I can tell you there is no wisdom in hiring the heathen to do one's bidding. None whatsoever. There is only evil and a heavy price to pay."

Beth heard the sound of boots pounding across the wooden flooring.

"If you are determined to hire them, then I will not be responsible for what happens on the journey. I cast the burden into your hands. You will take the risk. Not I."

"I'm more than willing to do so," said Mark. "I have no intention of putting any blame on you for whatever happens. 'Tis my choice alone."

"A choice at what cost? At the cost of the women's lives, for instance? Don't you know these people will kill and steal while you are looking the other way?"

"And have we not also done the same, Master Harris? Truly we have done our share of evil when we came to colonize this land, taking at will their lands without treaty, stealing what belongs to them, making off with food and other sundries."

Suddenly there came a growl, like some living animal of the night, just beyond the door. A chill swept through Beth. She glanced down to find her hands were shaking. Quickly she turned and began stepping back toward her room.

"So you make excuses for their massacres." John Harris spit the words, his voice seething. "Then we have no reason to do any further business. I relinquish my duties as guide. And I do pray you will open your eyes, my lord, and see that I'm right before it's too late."

Beth heard the latch to the other door rise. She hurried inside her room and closed her door, just as the men entered the hall.

"Master Harris, I beg you to reconsider. You know the very land we seek. I'm not certain what it is about the naturals that distresses you, but I believe God's hand is upon us. I know you can lead us there safely."

"I can't bear the responsibility if you insist on hiring them."

She heard the thump of footsteps. Peeking out the door, she caught a fleeting glimpse of John Harris as he escaped down the flight of stairs. Looking back, she found the grim face of Mark, and his sad eyes suddenly rested on her. "You overheard?"

"Yes. I don't understand. What happened with Mr. Harris?"

Mark sighed. "He and I do not agree about the naturals I hired to help us with the journey. I found two Indians today willing to be porters for a price. But when I mentioned my intention to Master Harris, he became angry, insisting I was a fool and calling the naturals 'murdering heathen.'"

Beth's gaze fell once more on the stairs where John had disappeared.

"I don't know what to do," Mark said helplessly. "We need him to guide us to Hatorask. Without him, we can't go."

Beth wondered if Mark was waiting for her to come up with some manner of agreement between them. Nothing came to mind.

He turned on his heel, his head hanging low, and wandered off to the room in which the two men had quarreled, presumably to ponder the events that had just transpired. Beth considered what had happened. Perhaps God was at work through these circumstances by having John Harris refuse to lead them. Maybe they would have met danger had they gone, and John's wrath kept them from making an unwise decision. But then, she considered the words John uttered in their previous meetings. His obvious interest in the land of Hatorask. And his words of comfort, how he would protect her with his life and lead them all to safety. Why then had he chosen to abandon the journey? And why did he hate the Indians?

Beth returned to her room and sat down by her chest. She opened it to gaze once more at the tapestry and the bit of cheerful scenery on the material's surface. It was not a cheerful scene that came to her now but a flood of memories from a sadder time. In them she could still hear Father's angry outbursts that became more frequent as his illness progressed.

"I will not do business with the likes of that man!" his voice roared. "He is out to kill me! Quick, bring the sword. I will deal with him. He will not live to see the sunrise!"

Somehow, Father had found a saber and begun waving it in the air. It chopped a chunk of wood out of a fine chair. Beth stared in horror at the sight. Her father, once noble and wise, now appeared an armed madman with his senses abandoned. *What can I do? Dear God, please help me!*

"Find him!" Father continued to shout. "I will cut him to pieces. I will tell him who it is that refuses to deliver Briarwood to him! Scoundrel!"

The tirade went on. All the servants went into hiding. No one knew what to do. Her father held them at bay with the anger of a depraved mind and a rapier in his hand.

Finally Beth burst into tears and begged him, "Father, please! Please put down your sword before we're all hurt!"

His anger ceased like a candle extinguished. The sword clattered to the ground, and with it her father, crumpled up on the floor, weeping, too exhausted to be moved.

Beth snapped her eyes open, realizing she had been dreaming. But it seemed real—as real as anything—as real as the encounter between John Harris and Mark. She began to shiver. All the fine words John had spoken, of protection and honor, seemed moot after this latest confrontation. She wanted to weep once more. There was no love in her future. No hope. She tried to shift her thoughts to things more pleasant but saw only anger and discontent.

Not long after, she met Judith in the hall. A look of sadness distorted her sister's otherwise chiseled features of firm, pale skin, tight cheeks, and a strong chin. "Judith? What ails you?"

She sighed. "Your wish has come true, Beth, and you had nothing to do with it."

"What wish is this?"

"Your wish not to go to Hatorask. Haven't you heard the news? There is no guide. John Harris's services are no longer at our disposal."

Beth bent her head and nodded. "I'm afraid I heard everything. I witnessed the conversation between Mr. Harris and your husband. Though I shouldn't have. . . ," she added hastily.

Judith drew closer, her eyebrows furrowed. "Please, tell me what was said. Why did this happen? Why is Mr. Harris no longer our guide?"

"Because your husband hired Indians to help us. John doesn't trust them. When Mark tried to reason with him, John told him he would not help, that he could not be held responsible should anything go ill. After that, he told Mark he would no longer be our guide."

Judith sighed. "Beth, you must go and confront Mr. Harris. Only you can reason with him."

Beth started, confused. "What? Why must I be the one to confront him?"

"Because he holds a great fondness for you. Everyone noticed it at dinner the other night. Surely you can change his mind."

Beth began to pace. "How can I trust myself to another angry man?" Suddenly all the pain of her father's care came rising to her lips in a tumult. "You were not there, Judith. You didn't see Father's tirades. Waving his sword, ready to cut us to pieces. Shouting to the bell tower itself. And there I was, trying to calm a tide worse than what the ocean can stir in a storm. I can't do that again. I don't know this man or what his temper can do. Yes, he was a gentleman at dinner, but after what I witnessed, I no longer know. . . ."

Judith stood still and silent, observing her. Nothing was said for several long moments. Then she sighed and nodded. "I do understand what you are saying, my sister. And it's true; we don't know what lies in his heart. All the more reason not to judge him so hastily until we do. And so you must find out. If not, our cause is lost."

"But why must it be me? Why can't you and Mark confront Mr. Harris? This is your dream, not mine."

Judith opened her mouth to reply, then shut it in haste. Again, several quiet moments slipped away, agonizing moments of silence. With it, Beth saw the relationship with her sister begin to slip, too. Would she allow her feelings and the past to destroy her last living relationship with a family member?

"I think it's plain to see why only you can do this. Mr. Harris has taken an obvious liking to you. You can see it in his eyes and hear it in his voice. I think if you go to him and implore him to change his mind, he will do so on your account."

"But what if this may be God's way of revealing His will? That we need to remain in the safety of Jamestown? That we may be placed in mortal danger if we go?"

"I don't believe that's true. Think of Father. The words he wrote. The longing in them. And somewhere deep inside of you, isn't there a longing, too? To know what happened to our family? To wonder if we are truly alone or if others exist? Ask yourself this, Beth. Seek out your true heart and see what it says."

Seek out my heart when right now my heart doesn't know what to believe? At first Beth had thought the whole venture foolish. Then she saw with her own eyes Father's writings, before the madness overcame him and the true reality of the world left him. He talked of seeking the truth about the colony at Roanoke and his parents' whereabouts. Then came the memory of John's words—the description of this land of Hatorask, of windswept beaches, seabirds, the ocean, and land unfettered by the growing masses, ready to be claimed for the Lord. She considered all these things, comparing them with what lay in her heart. *Not my will, but Thine be done, Lord. Guide me and lead me for Thy name's sake.*

Beth spent the afternoon by the river James. She watched the ripples on the water fanned to life by a steady breeze. At that moment, she desired a change in her life. Since coming to this land, fear ruled everything. Now she earnestly wanted to do away with such feelings and stand firm and decisive. She did not want to be that ocean wave talked about in the book of James, tossed back and forth, full of doubt. She wanted to step forward in faith, just as her grandparents had done when they embarked on that fateful journey long ago, not knowing what would happen. They likely had fears, as well. . .fears that they might not survive the journey by sea. Or when they arrived, fears of the new land and the new inhabitants they faced. But somehow they had overcome them to be a part of the colony. Wasn't their fortitude embedded in her, their granddaughter? At least she had picked up roots and come here. She had begun the walk. Now it was time to continue the journey. And the only way she could find out if her road led to Hatorask was to talk with John Harris.

Beth stood to her feet, whispering a prayer, hoping for God's grace and guidance. It seemed ironic that she would be the one to try and convince John to lead the expedition, but such was the leading of God in these matters. In His will she must trust.

She had not gone far when she discovered John Harris in the main thoroughfare leading to Jamestown, conversing with another man. They talked boisterously as if they knew each other. She heard a brief mention of the Indians.

"And that's the way it's going to be, Samuel," John said sternly.

"You're a fool, John Harris. You can't let the past do this to you."

"This is not foolishness but wisdom. How else does one plan for the future without learning the lessons of the past?"

John turned then, just as she approached. Their eyes met. Suddenly Beth was overcome with timidity. She withdrew, turning aside and striding for the opposite end of the street. Despite her willingness, she didn't have the confidence to confront him, not with his anger still so fresh.

Suddenly she heard her name. "Miss Colman! Beth! Please wait!"

Somehow she managed to stop. He came forward, hesitant himself, his eyes wide with obvious concern. "You overheard?"

"I did not mean to pry, Mr. Harris. I was planning to meet you, but the occasion doesn't present itself to a friendly meeting."

"Please don't think wrong of me." He paused. "I—I didn't want you to hear."

"But I have, Mr. Harris. I've heard everything."

He appeared startled. "What do you mean?"

"I overheard the conversation at the tavern with my brother-in-law. Who couldn't help but hear your angry words? I know all about anger, you see. I saw it every day in my father. And I must say I'm glad you won't be our guide. I couldn't bear to come under it all again." She began to walk away, only to sense his presence behind her, confirmed by the sound of his footsteps.

"Please don't leave like this. I wish I could make you understand."

"Then why don't you?"

He shook his head. "There are some things that must be put aside for another time and place."

"Then we have nothing more to discuss." Again she began to withdraw, and again he followed her like a shadow cast upon the ground. She turned. "Mr. Harris? Why are you following me?"

"Please, let me make amends. I don't want you distressed over this." He sighed. "'Twas wrong of me to say what I did to your brother-in-law. Surely you can forgive me as our Savior Christ has done, as He implores us to do even now, when we have been wronged. Even to seventy times seven."

Beth could see his internal pain in the way his forehead crinkled and in the tense lines that ran across his face.

"If it will help, I will go right this moment and ask your brother-in-law for his forgiveness." His expression seemed to say—*I will do all that and more, only please don't be unhappy with me.*

Beth sighed. "Do whatever you feel you must, Mr. Harris."

He said no more but left with only a cloud of dust in his wake. She shook her head, wondering more and more about this man. He held to some deep-seated unhappiness within, especially where the naturals of the land were concerned. Though she did want to know where it came from, she feared the answer. And yet he was willing to relinquish everything, for her sake. That spoke a far greater volume than any angry words.

∞

Later, as Beth was sitting down to do some mending, Judith hurried in, her face all aglow.

"Oh, Beth! Whatever did you say to make him change his mind?"

She glanced up, startled by the greeting. "I don't understand."

"Mr. Harris, of course. He went and told Mark how wrong he was, that Mark could hire whomever he chose, but that he would be most humble to accept the position of a guide if Mark would agree to take him back. Oh, 'tis a miracle from on high!"

Beth stared, dumbfounded. "I said practically nothing," she admitted. "I did mention Father and his periods of anger. I told him I was glad he wasn't our guide." She chuckled. "As if that would make him change his mind!"

Judith marveled. "Whatever you said, he did change his mind. God was with you." She embraced her. "Oh Beth, you don't know how happy this makes me."

Beth was glad for her sister's joy but could only wonder if she'd done the right thing and what would come of it all in the end—especially where she and John Harris were concerned.

Chapter 5

He had been fool, just as Samuel had said. Blind and deaf, too, but certainly not dumb, for he had spoken his mind openly. He had unleashed his tongue like some venomous serpent insofar as what the lovely Beth Colman had witnessed at the tavern. If only he had known she was nearby when he spouted the angry words to Mark Reynolds. He would have bitten his tongue, swallowed down his indignation, and refused to allow the past to grip his actions. Now it was too late.

John sighed. How he wished Mark hadn't hired Indians, but the man felt he was doing what was right. Mark had no notion of the past. John should have realized it from the start and not cast his discontent upon the man. And certainly he would have never lashed out had he realized Beth was in the other room. Now she had witnessed an angry man, unable to bridle his tongue, full of vengeance and hate, a grim reminder of her past.

If only I could take it back. I'd tear up every word. Or better yet, cast it into the fire. He felt no better after confronting Mark, offering the sincerest of apologies and grateful that the man had reinstated him to the position of guide. But it was Beth's reaction—her wide brown eyes and drawn face—that marked his dreams at night. Her unhappiness with him. Her sadness the day when they met by the river. He must bring himself back into her good graces, but how? Soon they would be leaving for the southern regions. The possessions were all but ready. He had seen the Indians Mark hired, hovering near the tavern, though John tried his best not to think about them. He had met with Mark once more to discuss the route of their journey by way of a crude map. But he did not feel right beginning this venture without restoring Beth's confidence in him. The idea that he would protect her and give her honor, as he once told her at the dinner table, seemed fruitless unless this changed. He wanted her to cling to his promise of safety. To trust him. To cleave to him, especially as they began this trek into unpredictable regions. But first he must mend the breach.

"You're looking quite sad again," commented his friend Samuel. John looked up from the small stick he had been whittling, even as his mind sorted through these many thoughts. "I thought you would be in good spirits, now that you have rejoined the journey to Hatorask. What is ailing you this time?"

John wanted to convey the situation to Samuel but feared the man might scorn his reasoning. . .or ask once more when he planned to resolve the past that

33

still dictated his actions.

"You have made peace concerning the naturals that are coming on the journey, yes?"

John shrugged. "As much peace as one can muster, considering the circumstances."

"Then is it the woman you prefer?"

He stepped back, amazed by the man's perception. "How did you know? Is it that obvious?"

Samuel laughed. "I have eyes, my friend. It isn't hard to see. I always believed you should find a good woman and settle down. You need to put aside that rest-less nature of yours. You have found such a woman, haven't you?"

"The sister-in-law of the man who hired me to guide them. But she no longer accepts me."

"What have you done?"

He twisted his lips. "Need I say? You know about the confrontation I had with Master Reynolds concerning the Indians. She overheard me speak about it and in a tongue not in keeping with a gentleman, I fear."

"Ah. So now she thinks you're some untamed beast."

"Or worse. What shall I do?"

"Have you told her about the past?"

He shook his head. "I can't burden her with my troubles."

"But it seems you already have. No doubt she knows that some unrest lurks in you. You will have to tell her."

John shook his head. "I refuse to speak about it. You know it, of course. To do so again would open the wounds."

Samuel plunked himself down on a rocky boulder beside John. "My friend, you must show her you're not a man of stone but one with a cheerful counte-nance, able to defend her and help her. You can be cheerful, yes?"

"When I'm with her, I am." John sighed once more. He felt renewed around Beth as if he were embracing the warm wind, flying high like one of the gulls that soared above the shores of Hatorask.

"Then go to her. Charm her. Convince her there is nothing to fear con-cerning you, that you made a mistake. Assure her it will not happen again." He nodded at the tiny cross John had whittled. "You may even yet hold the key in your hand."

John looked at the cross and grinned. "I cling to this more now than ever, I must say. Though I can do without its suffering. 'Tis too heavy a burden for any soul to bear."

"But Christ bore it for you. You needn't keep bearing it." Samuel nodded. "You will one day need to reconcile the past, John. 'Tis the only way there will be light for the future. You have seen for yourself what the past can do."

Oh, to reconcile the past. To have that peace that surpasses all understanding. Yes, it would be good to sit beside Beth, stare into her lovely eyes, and confess to her all the trouble he carried. But he could envision the look as she thought of her own pain concerning the deaths in her family and her father. Maybe she didn't wish to revel in further sorrow. How could he inflict more on her than what she had already endured? No, he couldn't tell her. Not now. He vowed before God to restrain his grief, to keep hidden his past, to allow God Himself to rectify the situation. It must be this way.

Looking at the cross, he found a piece of leather twine and looped it through the small hole he had made at the top. A crude type of jewelry, in a way, but symbolizing much power. Perhaps Beth would accept the gift as a peace offering and, in turn, change her opinion of him. He'd found her of interest from the moment he laid eyes on her, looking lost and in need of a friend. And he wanted to be that friend, that confidant—the one who would supply every need, if he did not allow his own needs to overshadow all else.

John stood to his feet, holding the cross, walking the length of the road to see that another ship had come to port. From the shallop came more women, looking as fearful and uncertain as Beth had the day she arrived. But none of them matched her beauty or her spirit, even as he saw them cling to their belongings, searching around, hoping for a friendly face. At one time, he might have been there to help them, looking for that special woman with whom he could set up a home. Instead, he would travel to Hatorask, perhaps with the very woman he would one day marry. That is, if God opened the door between them that had been shut tight by his heedless actions.

Wandering back to the Worthington Tavern, he found Master and Mistress Reynolds lingering in the main room, organizing their meager belongings for the trip. Both of them looked up and smiled when he entered, as if they were pleased to see him.

"Are we soon ready to depart for the southern region, Master Harris?" Mark inquired.

"Very soon. 'Tis a pleasant time to travel. In the summer there are known to be fierce windstorms and wicked heat." He glanced around, hoping to find the delicate form of Beth thereabouts, but caught no glimpse of her. He panicked. Had she decided not to be a part of the expedition after all? Had she turned aside from him and embraced another life? "Pray tell, where is Miss Colman? She isn't ill, is she?"

Mark and Judith exchanged glances. "Not at all," Mark said. "She is quite well."

He hesitated, wondering how he should broach the subject of a meeting with her before their journey commenced. He felt the cross he had whittled, nestled in the palm of his hand. The key, as Samuel had called it, and one he prayed would unlock her heart. "I—I have something I would like to give her."

"I can call for her," Judith announced, hurrying to the stairs. John said nothing, even though he could sense Mark's questioning glance, wondering what might be happening. He did not wish for another confrontation with the man but ignored his inquiry to think of the meeting to come.

After a time, John heard footsteps on the stairs. Beth Colman appeared, as radiant as always, dressed in a colorful gown of forest green and a shawl about her shoulders. She did not look him in the eye but stared at the floor. "Yes, Mr. Harris?"

He drew in a sharp breath. How would he begin, and with Judith and Mark watching? "I have something to show you, Miss Colman. Something I believe will put to rest all your questions."

Her gaze lifted to meet his. Her eyebrows narrowed. "I have no more questions, Mr. Harris. You have answered them all."

He swallowed hard, wondering what she meant. Could it be the meeting the other day proved more fearsome than he imagined—that he was to her a crazed man like her father, controlled by anger and without the cheerfulness that could win her heart?

"Dear Beth," Judith admonished, "go with Mr. Harris and see what he is offering. All of our work here is finished. We have time. You have not been to the river today. You like it so well, and 'tis a fine day for a walk."

"I would be glad to accompany you to the river," John quickly offered, trying not to sound too eager. Inwardly he wanted to thank Mark's wife for the suggestion.

Beth hesitated. He waited for what seemed like a long time. Finally she nodded, much to his relief. John escorted her out into the bright sunshine. She kept her gaze averted, concentrating instead on her surroundings as if taking it all in, piece by piece. At the river there were children playing and a few women doing the wash. They both meandered farther upstream. No words came to his mind. Instead, they walked until they came to an area filled with blooming flowers. Here Beth stopped. A smile lit her face.

"How lovely," she cooed, picking a flower. "There are no such flowers like these in England. I wonder what they are."

"I'm not certain, madam." He picked one flower with a particularly large golden head, turned upward as if poised to drink of the sun's rays. "This looks much like a china cup in its saucer, ready for tea."

Beth laughed. The tension began to melt away. "It does indeed. Are there flowers like these at Hatorask?"

"Along the shores, the tall grasses sometimes put forth heads that look as if they could be flowers. But I've seen pointed plants that sometimes send up flowers in a straight stalk. The tips of the leaves are sharp and can cut like a knife."

She stood perfectly still, seeming to absorb every word he spoke. "A leaf of a plant as sharp as a knife?"

He nodded. "Look in the woods about you, and you will find other flowering trees as well."

Beth slowly sank into the patch of flowers. "Why does such a place like Hatorask intrigue you, Mr. Harris? 'Tis because of these things you've described?"

"Hatorask is unlike any place I have ever seen. The land by the ocean has its own way about it. And, I suppose, without any settlements, it seems very new, like the hand of God just created it. There are long stretches of untouched sands as far as the eye can see. Tall grasses. The never-ending sound of the ocean speaking. Even shells where one can hear the echo of the ocean."

Beth straightened. "How I would love to see and hear all this!"

John smiled, feeling as if he were beginning to draw her heart unto his. "There are islands as well, surrounded by waters. Small bits of land allow one to cross here and there by boat. You need a boat to see much of it. One could live on an island and feel separated from the world."

"I don't know if I would want to live like that," she said. "People need people. To be so isolated. . .where do you worship God? Or trade for supplies?"

"One can worship God in any place. Where two or more are gathered, He is there with them."

"I suppose." She plucked several more flowering teacups. "This will make a fine bouquet to give to Judith." She paused. "So what concerns you about the Indians, Mr. Harris?"

The suddenness of her question took him by surprise. "Please believe me when I say 'tis of no further concern, Miss Colman."

"There must be some reason why you have such strong feelings on the matter." She glanced at him out of the corner of her eye.

"I was hasty and judgmental, seeking only my needs and not the needs of others. I hope you will forgive me as your brother-in-law has done."

"Of course. I only thought. . ." She paused. "Sometimes 'tis good to speak of one's ills."

If only he could. But it would be too difficult. And he refused to shed tears before her, to show any sign of weakness when he must be strong and capable with the journey close at hand. "A friend I think of as a brother knows everything. I have confessed to him so I might find healing."

"I see. I only hope you realize that I, too, have been through much concerning my father. I can provide a listening ear whenever you wish."

"I will remember that, Beth. I mean, Miss Colman."

"You may call me Beth. At least 'tis better than Elizabeth. Imagine being named after the queen of England from long ago." She chuckled. "I do hope I don't carry the stigma of being unmarried, like our virgin queen."

John stared, unable to believe what he was hearing. After all that had occurred, he felt certain Beth would spurn him. Let him go. Have nothing more to do with an angry man such as himself. And here she was, plainly talking about marriage as if she were considering it.

"Not that I mean to hint—" she added hastily, her cheeks all aflame.

"Of course. Though I'm certain a woman of your virtue does consider such a union from time to time."

"And do you, Mr. Harris? Or do you seek only to explore and conquer a new land?"

He couldn't tell if she was exploring the new land of a relationship by way of these questions or simply looking for honest communication. "I open myself to whatever the Lord wills for my life. And it appears His will right now is to lead you and your family safely to Hatorask."

Beth nodded and gathered the flowers she had picked. "A wise answer," she mused. "We are two of a kind, don't you agree, Mr. Harris?"

"That remains to be seen, Miss Colman. I mean, Beth. But I would say we are indeed on a path of mutual understanding and maybe admiration, as well."

Her face grew even rosier. He escorted her back to the tavern, wishing her a good day before a sigh of blessed relief escaped. The meeting had gone far better than any dream he could have mustered. Just then, he opened his hand and saw the small cross he had whittled. And he had not even given her the gift he'd promised! John closed his hand over the precious item. But God had done so much more. He would save the cross for some time in the future, he decided. A time when it would mean the most to the both of them. Maybe even on the day he asked for her hand in marriage...as a symbol of an everlasting covenant. *May it be Your will, Lord, and in Your time.*

⤙⤚

On the day of their departure from Jamestown, John witnessed a new and vibrant Beth Colman standing by her family, ready to embark on this latest adventure. He took little notice of the Indians ready to serve as bearers for the company's belongings. He kept his sights trained on Beth, who appeared radiant in the morning light, wearing a slight smile on her lips.

"Are we ready to depart for Hatorask, Master Harris?" Mark inquired.

"Yes, my lord. 'Tis a fine day for travel. I have never seen the sky so blue...." *Or Beth looking so radiant.* He forced the thought away to concentrate on the tasks before him. He must give all his attention to the matter at hand, knowing there would be many quiet moments in which to reflect on the woman who had all but captured his heart.

Mark Reynolds knelt in the dirt, bowed his head, and offered up a prayer for their journey. John listened carefully to the man's humble prayer. At once, he sensed peace for the venture. "Guide us in Thy heavenly light, O Lord," Mark prayed. "Preserve us by Thy mighty hand. Keep us in Thy tender mercies, we pray. And reveal to us the mystery from the past ages through Thy wisdom, the mystery of our family, long since parted from us."

When the prayer had concluded, Mark slowly stood to his feet, a smile on his face. "We are ready."

Are you ready as well, John Harris? came a quiet voice within his spirit. John arranged the two sacks he had slung over each shoulder and felt for the snaphaunce pistol tucked in a leather strap about his waist. *Not by your might or your power, but only by His spirit, John Harris. Remember that, lest you forget and you find yourself on a journey of no return.*

Chapter 6

Slap! Her hand went for the whining mosquito that hovered over her arm, ready to embed itself in her flesh. Again she slapped at it, managing to crush the tiny menace beneath her fingers, finding a trickle of blood in its wake. *How dreadful,* Beth mourned, taking out a bit of cloth to wipe the dampness from her face. Never had she witnessed such warmth nor seen so many of these mosquitoes that bit her exposed flesh. She couldn't recall a day like this in England. Then again, it was rare she found herself in tall grasses, walking for any great distance. In England, only the cold walls of Briarwood surrounded her, the stillness broken by Father's moans for help. After slapping her arm when she again felt an annoying bite, she had to wonder if that time spent at Briarwood was any more dreadful than what she'd been experiencing here these last ten days.

"Try this salve, madam," John offered, holding out a small flask. "It will help keep them from biting."

"This is terrible," Beth complained, smearing the foul-smelling grease on her hands and arms. "Why is there such a plague here?"

" 'Tis very warm for this time of year," he admitted. "The sun has driven them out of the swamps. Usually there are no such swarms until later in May."

Beth watched another of the biting mosquitoes. It flew above her skin as if examining the strange oily substance she had smeared on before it decided to find a tasty morsel elsewhere. "I've never seen such land, either," she remarked, again patting her forehead with a handkerchief. "There is so much water. My feet are very wet. I don't think I've ever had wet feet like this. I'm afraid my shoes will never hold together." She gazed upward, allowing the breezes to sweep across her flushed face, providing a cool respite from the hot day. "I smell salt. Or fish, perhaps."

" 'Tis the swampland filled with water from the ocean. The land here is quite low. When the oceans rise in a storm, water flows upriver, bringing with it the creatures of the sea."

What a strange land this was, this Virginia, or now this province of Carolana, as John called it. Beth had already witnessed a few large flying seabirds that John pointed out. One had huge wings and a long, pointed beak. John said the beak was used to grab fish from the sea for the bird's dinner. Despite the swarms of mosquitoes, the heat, and the dampness, Beth had to admit she was learning something new each day, even if the circumstances were difficult. There was a certain joy to be found in a new and different place. The Lord God had made it all, both the good and the bad.

When he mentioned the ocean, she asked how far away it was.

"Well, if one goes east," he said, pointing, "one would see the beginnings of the ocean in a few hours."

"Then we must go at once!" Beth announced, lifting her skirts, ready to see the spectacle so described to her in the conversations of late. It would be grand to see the white sandy beaches and the ocean tides sweeping the shore. She could hardly wait.

John laughed. "We are not going that way, madam. Patience. There is plenty of time. When we reach Hatorask, there will be ocean waters as far as you can see. You will have no want of it. None at all." He paused. "So tell me about your home in England."

"Surely you remember our mother country."

"I lived by the sea. I never traveled to the interior regions. Only to London on occasion, to engage in business for my father. He was a fisherman by trade."

Beth turned, suddenly curious. It was the first time he had spoken about his family.

"Why do you look at me so?"

"I only thought perhaps you might be an orphan. I've never heard you talk about your family."

He shrugged. "They remain in England. I've not heard from them in a very long time." He paused as if ready to say something else, but instead said, "Tell me about your home. Where in England did you dwell?"

"In Cambridge, a small town with many fine dwellings and great men of wisdom, it seems. My father gained his title by birthright. Our manor was Briarwood. A fine home with many beautiful gardens. Mother loved her gardens, and I suppose I did as well."

"I saw your interest in the flowers by the river James where we spoke," he commented. "There are many flowers here in the land, as well as flowering trees. Many things exist here that one doesn't see in England. Animals also."

"Besides the seabirds with the long beaks?"

He chuckled. "In fact, there is a strange animal here that washes its food in the water. I saw it one evening by the river James."

Beth halted, even as the party consisting of her sister, brother-in-law, and the Indians disappeared through a bank of thick rushes. "An animal that cleans its food? I've never heard of such a thing."

"A furry little animal, about this big." John spanned the width with his hands. "It has thick fur, useful for many things." He then circled his eyes with his fingers.

Beth laughed at his antics. "Why do you do that?"

"Because the animal has large, black circles around its eyes."

"I only remember the black circle Father once had around his eye when he fell and hit his face," Beth recalled. "I don't think I've ever seen an animal like that."

"The heathen...that is, the Indians, call them *aroughcuns*. They are native to this land. Maybe we will see one if we come upon some fresh water at our camp. They like to roam about at night and sleep during the day."

She laughed. "I must say, all this conversation regarding some black-eyed animal has me wondering what other surprises lay ahead on this journey."

He winked. "There could be a great many. One never knows."

Beth tried to imagine such a creature, even as she gazed about to find that her brother-in-law and sister had vanished, along with the Indians. How she wanted to share with them this new discovery, like so many she was making in the heart of a new land. "I wonder where Judith and her husband are. I must tell them about this aroughcun." She hurried a few paces, calling for them. Only the sound of the wind met her ears. "Where could they be?"

John said nothing, his cheerful countenance suddenly replaced by narrow eyes and tightness around his mouth. Beth tried not to come to any conclusions, but the look he gave concerned her. They hurried through the reeds, even as John called loudly for Mark.

"I'm sure they are fine. . . ," Beth began. Instead she found herself trying to keep up with John, who began to run, his hands batting away the foliage. Something possessed his steps, an urgency that sent fear welling up within her. "Mr. Harris...John...please wait. I'm sure they haven't gone far. We were talking for a time. They must have gone on ahead."

He only looked wildly around. "I knew this would happen. I said as much. But your brother-in-law chose not to heed me."

Beth panted, even as she drew close to him. "W–what?" she inquired breathlessly, trying to wipe away the dampness collecting on her forehead before it stung her eyes with its salty touch.

"I knew trouble would arise with these heathen when our backs were turned. He would not listen. He is as obstinate as any I have ever met."

Beth stared. "I don't understand."

"They are evil! I warned Master Reynolds with every part of my being, but would he listen? No!"

She gasped. "John, don't say such things! Th–they are fine. I'm certain of it." But doubt began to creep up alongside the fear and made a combination that nearly paralyzed her. *Please help us, dear Lord!*

"Hurry, we waste time!" John urged, taking her by the hand. They traveled what seemed a very long time, though Beth didn't know how far. Her legs began to grow heavy. Her parched throat begged for a few droplets of water.

"They are deceptive, wily. We only stopped for a moment, but a moment is all they need." He swept his face with his hand. "Why did this have to happen, Lord?"

Suddenly they heard the sound of exclamation. Beth turned and found a small rise of land, and standing on it were Judith and Mark. They waved at them. Beth hurried forward with John close behind.

"Come see!" Judith exclaimed. "'Tis not much, I know, but we can see a little bit of the lay of the land."

Beth instead ran up and clung to her sister as if she would never let go. "We were so worried, Judith! We stopped to talk, and then I couldn't find you."

"There's no reason to fear, sister. The Indians communicated to us this lookout. I needed a bit of rest after the long walk. 'Tis quite warm today. And while we were here, they found us water to drink."

Beth couldn't believe how cheerful Judith was, even after what she had been through. Looking back at John, she saw the reddish hue of anger begin to seep across his face. He was staring at the Indians, who pointed to themselves and then to the white people in their presence.

"I will not be made a fool again," he snarled at them. "I know what you're planning. I have my eye on you, to be sure." He withdrew his pistol.

Both the Indians grew rigid. They made loud sounds, pointing to the weapon, and from what Beth could discern, uttered the words *fire stick*.

"Master Harris, what are you doing?" Mark exclaimed, holding out his hand. "Put that away."

"I told you they couldn't be trusted. You chose not to listen."

"They guided us to this place and then went to find us fresh water. There is no cause for this. They are only doing what I hired them to do. They mean us no harm."

"They are sneaky and deceptive. What will it take to convince you, my lord? You need to understand, once and for all, that they can't be trusted."

"Or is it you that can't be trusted with other living souls, John Harris? Let us be honest, for they have done nothing on this journey to betray your trust."

John whirled, his eyes widening, as if the words hurt him more than if Mark had struck his face. Beth closed her eyes, praying against another altercation between John and Mark. When she opened them, John had vanished. Her feet shifted, ready to follow him. Instead, she felt the firm hand of Mark on her arm. "Let him alone, Beth."

"I wish I knew what troubled him," Beth murmured with a sigh. "He refuses to say. Whatever it is runs deep, so deep no one can find it, maybe not even John himself."

"Only God can give him the strength to face it," Mark said. "We can't do it alone. And you mustn't think this is your quest to help him, Beth. You will only find yourself swept away by it. All you can do is pray for him."

How much she needed to pray, more than ever. She paused to consider the many prayers offered up while she cared for Father and the way her strength nearly gave out by tending to his needs night and day. Only when she spoke to a caring minister, who came one day to Briarwood, did she find her strength renewed. He told her, as Mark had done now, not to carry the burden of her father's illness. She must cast it upon the Lord and allow His strength to sustain her. After that, she felt the weight fall from her heavily laden shoulders and found the ability to face a new sunrise. And likewise, she would be able to face the sunrise of each new day here in this land, praying and hoping that the burden would soon be lifted from John. When that happened, perhaps they might embrace a future together, if God be willing.

Some time passed before John finally returned. He said nothing, not even acknowledging her, but pointed the way back to the original path and their journey southward to the land of Hatorask. Beth tried to quell the disappointment that rose up within. They had been having such a pleasant day, too, except for the biting mosquitoes and the warmth that even now renewed the dampness on the back of her neck. How she wished he would reveal more about this land, but in particular, more about himself. If nothing else, there was one thing she realized in light of all this. Somehow, the Indians had wounded his soul, and one day he would have to reconcile the cause of his pain.

When the sun began to dip low in the horizon, they stopped to make camp. As usual, John went seeking stout evergreen boughs with which to build a shelter for her and Judith. Beth did what she could with Judith to help prepare some kind of meal for them. The Indians had taught them how to bake corncakes on a stone in the fire. This and whatever meat the men were able to procure became their evening meal and their morning victual. Beth immediately set to work grinding corn kernels into meal while Judith fetched water. Beth had hardly worked with food back in England, as the servants did most of the cooking. She found the chore tiresome but worthwhile, especially the first time she made the corncakes. John had given her a smile, telling her how wonderful they were—much better than anything Mistress Worthington at the tavern could make. But now she didn't see him about, even as she began mixing the batter. She wished she could see the twinkle in his blue eyes and the smile that warmed her more than any blazing fire.

"It will be well with us," Judith tried to reassure her.

"I only wish it would be well with Mr. Harris," Beth murmured. "You don't think he will use his pistol against the Indians?"

"Oh, Beth, I pray not." She hesitated. "Have you talked to him about his anger?"

"I have asked, but he refuses to say. 'Tis painful for him. I wish he would talk about it. Maybe he believes we will think ill of him if he does. A matter of pride." Beth formed the cakes between her hands, putting them at once on the hot stone in the middle of the fire pit. She wiped away the dampness on her face. "Someone has to break through to his heart, or he will never be able to give his heart away to anyone."

Judith gave her a knowing nod. They finished their work in silence. When the cakes were done, the men returned empty-handed from their hunting venture. The cakes would be their meal. They ate quietly. The Indians sat off by themselves, saying little, though Beth could see how they stared at John with a certain trepidation outlined in their black eyes. *God, please bring Your peace to this place and to John's heart.*

Just then his voice broke the silence. "In two days we'll camp in sight of the ocean."

The announcement took them all by surprise. "I thought we still had quite a journey left," Mark said.

"We'll need another day on land, and then we'll need canoes for the crossing to Roanoke Island."

"Will there be canoes waiting for us?" Mark wondered.

"If there are none left from other explorers, we can make them," John told them confidently before taking another bite of the cake Beth had made.

Beth could not comprehend how one made a boat seaworthy enough to cross some wild ocean to another land. When he explained how the water in the sound was a mere third of a fathom deep and without waves, she rested a bit easier. At least they wouldn't be in some tiny little boat in a vast ocean, tossed here and there by the angry waves, perhaps even to be cast out to sea, forever lost in the powerful deep. The crossing he described seemed easily done.

"Surely the naturals know how to make boats, as well," Mark commented.

Beth wondered how John would react upon the mention of the Indians. He only shrugged. "I'm certain they do."

She breathed a bit easier. Perhaps God had heard her prayer and brought peace to their camp. *Oh, may it be!*

Later that evening, as the sun made its departure, the western skies turned a dazzling red. Beth gazed at it for a time, marveling at the beauty, until she felt a presence draw near. She knew without a word it was John. She could sense his strength and purpose, despite the trouble he held within.

"May I sit with you?"

She nodded, and he took a seat beside her.

"You must see the sunrise over the ocean," he said, acknowledging the pretty sight before them. " 'Tis a wonder to behold. A giant red ball of light slowly rising out of the ocean depths."

Suddenly the words rushed out of her in a tumult. "You wouldn't have used your pistol on the Indians, would you, John? Would you have killed them?"

He turned in a start. "Beth. . ."

She continued to stare as the reddish haze began to fade, replaced by the shadows of night and the twinkling of the stars in the sky. "You frightened everyone. Is this the way it must be? Is there no other way?"

Silence met her earnest questioning. Doubts once more assailed her concerning this man and the shadow of his past that seemed to follow his every move.

"There are always other ways," he finally conceded. "I did what I did only out of necessity. An act of readiness, I suppose."

"Readiness for what? Do you truly think the naturals wish us harm?"

"I don't know. I pray not. I am concerned about what lies ahead. That your brother-in-law's fascination with finding out the truth about your relatives may be clouding his judgment. You truly don't understand the dangers that exist here. You must be on your guard at all times, lest you be caught unaware." He sighed. "That's why I don't sleep much at night. I keep awake to watch the camp and you. You all are my responsibility. And I won't fail you, even if you don't understand or accept my actions."

"Then I guess we're truly blessed to have a man like you to protect us." She noticed the look of gratitude that filled his face.

"I'm very glad to hear you say that." He took her hand in his for a moment. "As I said in the tavern, I will do whatever I must to see that you're protected. With my life, if necessary. I give you my word."

She looked at his hand covering hers, a large hand, strong and able, with skin slightly weathered and tanned by the wind and sun. How could she doubt his sincerity? Even with the untold anger stowed away inside, he wished only to do good. And she would accept what he said and the hand that held hers, at least for now.

Chapter 7

Beth tried to keep her attention on her surroundings but couldn't help but be distracted by the stirring of the paddle and the one who commanded it with a firm grip. They sat facing each other in the canoe, John on one end, Judith on the other, while Beth occupied the center. She had thought of sitting in such a position as to keep her back to him as she had on previous crossings. Instead, this time when she came into the boat, she sat facing him. From that moment on, their eyes were locked in silent communion but for occasional glances at the scenery. She liked the way he commanded the paddle. His shirt billowed with the breezes off the bay, making the shirtsleeves appear like miniature sails. Back and forth his arms moved, drawing their canoe ever closer to the island chain he called Hatorask.

When they had first arrived at a place where they saw the coast of some distant land, John had let out a gleeful shout. It was unlike the other river crossings they had made where Beth thought the time had come for their arrival. From his reaction, Beth knew they had at last made it. He left them to explore the thick rushes by the water's edge, hoping to find some abandoned canoes. Again came his glee-filled shout. "God is with us," he declared. "There are several boats where others have left them. Praise be."

"Have many explored this region?" Mark inquired.

John nodded, describing how he once came as an explorer, too, not only to map the region, but for curiosity's sake. He admitted the draw of the famed lost colony also brought many others here, seeking their whereabouts. "You are not the first hoping to learn what happened to that colony," he said.

"Have you heard what others have found?" Mark asked.

"From what I've learned, the news is not good. Most believed they were massacred." John cast a glance toward their Indian companions, who were loading possessions into one of the canoes. "There are many unfriendly Indians in the region, particularly in the interior parts. But there were a few friendly souls among them. One, Manteo, befriended the colonists. He knew some English. In fact, I heard it said he even went to visit England."

Mark smiled. "Then there's hope."

John raised his eyebrow. "Hope, sir? We speak of a time sixty years past. People long since gone, if not killed, then dead from age or other circumstances, with their whereabouts unknown. It will be difficult if not impossible to find what you seek."

Mark appeared to pay John's words little mind. As Judith had so rightly observed, once his attention was engaged in a matter, he refused to be moved. Beth had to admire her brother-in-law's resolve in those instances. Up against such obstacles, most would grow weary and give up the quest. But Mark possessed a strength about him that Beth couldn't help but admire. How she prayed she would find a husband his equal, if not greater.

She now turned, watching John while he manned his post, even as his attention remained on the land mass that grew ever closer. Did he also have characteristics of strength and tenacity? He did traverse these places without fear. He had a determination back in Jamestown to come find others and seek reconciliation when things were amiss. These were all excellent qualities in a man. If only there were not the shadows of past events clouding it all.

"Are we soon upon Hatorask?" she inquired.

"This is all Hatorask. We go first to the island of Roanoke. 'Twas once called the city of Raleigh for the man who helped finance the colony. When I came here last, 'twas more a city of desolation."

"Are there any remains of the colony to be seen?" Judith asked.

"Only a little. Scavengers have devoured it. Not many clues linger."

Beth nearly chuckled. Such news would not dissuade Mark. He would inquire of God for clues and no doubt would find some. She sat up straighter as the vegetation became visible. Thick forests came into view but nothing of any settlements. No boats could be seen either but only the vast blue-gray waters before them. Just then, she caught sight of something darting in the water. The strange, large gray fish leaped into the air before burying itself once more in the ocean depths. Another followed suit. "Look at that! Up there!"

John turned. "Yes, I see them."

"What large fish!"

He laughed. "And strange fish they are, as well. They can jump quite far out of the water. And they blow water out of the tops of their heads."

Beth would have stood up were it not for John's hand on her arm, urging her to stay seated. The canoe pitched with her excitement. "Look! They seem to stare at us from out of the water, as if to inquire why we're here." She laughed in glee. John smiled, too, as if enjoying her discoveries. "I can't begin to think what else we might find in this place."

"One never knows," he admitted. "But I'm certain you will remember this time always."

Beth hoped to recall such things in her thoughts and her heart, even as the land suddenly came upon them. John guided the canoe to the sandy shore and promptly helped her and Judith to firm ground. "Welcome to Roanoke Island."

"So this is the place, my wife," Mark said expectantly. "The place where your grandparents once lived."

Beth gazed about at the trees swaying in the fine breeze. It seemed strange not to see a house or two. Everything appeared quiet and still but for the movement made by the play of wind upon the leaves. Following John, she brushed by rushes nearly as tall as she. Birds chirped from the trees. They had not gone far when Mark hailed a halt to the procession.

He knelt and picked up a hewn timber. "This was cut by an ax."

"We will find some remains of the colony," John admitted. "This may have been from a stockade they once built."

As they continued on, Mark found more evidence of habitation long since decayed by time and weather. More hewn timbers made by the tools of men. Beth was so intent on finding an artifact from long ago, she tripped over a rock and landed in some leaves. John was by her side at once, helping her to her feet. "Are you hurt?" he asked, picking out the leaves entangled in her hair.

"No. Thank you." She tried not to look at his face, even as steady warmth once more began to invade her cheeks. Peering instead at her feet, she then noticed the cause of her fall. It was not a rock but some round object, solid and black. "What could that be?"

Mark was at her side, picking up the heavy fragment. "This is made of iron," he said, his voice barely able to contain his excitement. He began searching the ground for more clues and soon found other pieces of shot and metal armor cast aside. "We must be in the vicinity of the original colony, Master Harris."

"It would seem so. But I'm afraid it will hold few clues. Many have come here but found nothing to tell them what happened to the colony." John took a seat on a fallen log and fumbled for his leather water bag. " 'Twas said the colonists had time to gather most of their belongings. One could say they didn't leave because of an attack but more out of a decision to abandon this place." He gazed at the land. "Maybe they had run out of food. Or winter was coming and they didn't want to be trapped here on some remote piece of land surrounded by water. They had time to gather their possessions and only left behind what they could not carry, like these metal objects."

"Where is Croatoan?" Mark asked. "I heard they had carved such a word on a tree before they left."

John pointed beyond the woods. "West from here, on the mainland. But little remains of the Indian villages there. Most of the Indians moved on to other places."

Mark sighed. "How I wonder where they went. If we knew, then maybe we would have some knowledge of the colonists' whereabouts."

"I think it would do us well to stay here for a little time," Judith said. "Maybe we'll find more clues, if the Indian porters could construct a shelter for us?"

"I will do that," John said hastily. In no time he began wielding an ax, cutting down pine boughs to construct a shelter. Beth watched silently as he took up the thick boughs and tied them together with the rope he had brought. He had seen to their safety, just as he said he would. He had led them here without difficulty. He was even constructing a shelter for them. And soon they would return to Jamestown, perhaps even to embrace a future that was shining brighter to Beth as the journey progressed.

"So when will we see the laughing gulls?" Beth asked him. "And the shells that talk?"

He looked over at her, wiping at his damp face that showed the beginnings of a bemused expression. "Perhaps we can take our leave for a bit with a canoe, and I can show you. 'Tis not far to cross over to another island there in the distance." He acknowledged the strip of land across the water. "There you will see everything I've described to you."

Beth hurried to inquire of Mark if she and John might take the canoe to the land and see the ocean, the seabirds, and the shells. Mark looked between her and John, his face puzzled. "I don't wish you to go unescorted, Beth. Surely we'll all venture there on the morrow."

"But 'tis only to the land there. You can see it from here. We won't be gone long."

"And it might be best to first scout the lay of the land, my lord," John added.

Looking back at Judith, who was busy arranging the shelter for the evening, he finally nodded. "I intend that you be only a scout," he said to John, "and to ensure my sister-in-law's safety and virtue in this venture."

"I give you my word as a Christian gentleman."

He nodded. "Very well."

Beth could hardly wait to begin the venture in the canoe. John picked up the paddle. "What else might we see there?" she inquired breathlessly, barely able to contain her excitement.

"Just remember what I told you," he said.

She closed her eyes to envision it. The endless stretch of sandy coast. Soaring birds like messengers sent from heaven. The talking shells that shared their secrets of the deep. When she opened her eyes, they had traveled quickly toward the new land. "We're like explorers, aren't we?" she said with a sigh. "Going to a land we have never seen. Or rather, one I have never seen."

He laughed. "Beth, you're becoming an explorer, sure and true. Though many would say exploration is not in keeping with a properly reared English lady."

"Many fine ladies did make the journey to Virginia and beyond," she said. "Perhaps I have a bit of my grandparents in me, after all." She didn't realize until then how much Briarwood had kept her imprisoned from life and unable to embrace all the world had to offer. When she stepped onto the land, alone in a vast area of reeds and sand, without a house or living soul to be found, she felt what her grandparents must have felt—a great awe.

"I claim this land for our Savior Christ," Beth said in glee. "Just as the minister of the gospel once did long ago at the founding of Jamestown." Suddenly she heard loud squawking and saw a flock of birds swoop down from above. They seemed to laugh in a way, as if they found her words humorous. "Do the birds mock us?"

"As the lone inhabitants, they only ask why we've come to their home." He looked with satisfaction before pointing southward. "Come. There's more to see."

Along the sandy ground they walked until she could hear a strange sound like a mingled roar that slowly grew as they approached. White breakers formed across the wind-driven water as far as the eye could see. It was the great ocean, the same ocean she had crossed not a few weeks ago. To the left and the right, she saw long stretches of sandy beach with gulls and other seabirds flying in midair.

"What a beautiful sight," she said with a sigh. "When I came here by ship, I only wanted to feel dry land. But now that I can see the ocean without fear, 'tis a grand sight, indeed. No wonder you like it so."

John nodded, sharing the view with her. "It draws me back time and time again. I think often of this place, like a dream that stays with me. My friend Samuel thinks 'tis a part of me and that I should settle here."

"But no one lives here!" she exclaimed. "No one at all. How can you think to settle here all alone?"

"How did other great civilizations come into being? Someone must place his feet on the ground, drive a stake into the land, and call it his own. Then he must take up timbers and build a home." He sighed. "But one person can't survive alone. Civilization can't be built unless there are heirs to possess it for the future. The Roanoke Colony came into being with the idea of establishing a settlement through families." He turned to look at her.

Beth shuffled her feet at the implication. Surely they could not be called a family. Judith and Mark were, yes. Maybe he was thinking that Mark and Judith should be the ones to establish a new settlement. He couldn't be thinking of them together as one, could he? This was not the time or place to consider such things, especially while she was engaged in this new land, the journey, and hoping to discover more about the man who led her here. Maybe one day, if God be willing.

Suddenly he stepped toward her. The wind whipped his hair about him. Again the sleeves of his shirt billowed. He looked perfectly handsome.

"Where are the shells that speak?" Beth inquired hastily, breaking free from the tender look he gave.

John stepped back and searched the surface of the sandy beach. For a time they said nothing, only picked up shells. Beth marveled at the different colors and shapes. She tried to keep her thoughts on her discoveries and not on the way he looked at her just a moment ago as though he might kiss her. What would

Mark and Judith say if such a thing occurred?

"I found a small one," John said, coming up behind her. She took the strange shell that looked like a little horn.

"Hold it up to your ear."

She did so and to her delight heard a dull roar, the same sound she'd heard when they first arrived at this place. "Why, it does sound just like the ocean! John, it's true." She was so excited over the discovery, she didn't see him step toward her again until his arms curled around her.

"John. . . ?" she whispered.

He bent his face to greet hers. His eyes softened. His lips found hers. To her surprise, she found herself responding to his kiss. She might have stayed in his embrace, enjoying his warmth and the feel of his lips on hers; but her senses were awakened to what had happened. She stepped out of his embrace. "Please take me back to my sister and brother-in-law. We have been here too long."

"There is no need to be angry, Beth."

She cradled the shell, refusing to meet his gaze. "Take me back. Please."

He said no more but helped her into the canoe. She didn't want to upset him but felt upset herself for having responded to the kiss the way she did. What would Mark and Judith think? If only she had not come to the island. . .but the lure of seeing the ocean and the sand proved too enticing. So, too, did the figure of John in his billowing shirt, with his look of affection that spoke to her heart unlike anything else.

The return journey was begun in silence. They stared at the scenery, all the while pondering what had passed between them. Every so often Beth could sense John searching her face for a reaction. At times, he would heave as if in distress. Finally he rested the paddle inside the canoe. Beth watched in alarm as it slowed to a drift upon the open waters. "W–what are you doing?" She tried to steady her voice. "I asked to be taken back."

"Not until we talk about what happened. I can see you're troubled, but I don't understand why."

Beth raised her head and crossed her arms before her. "My brother-in-law begged you to act as a gentleman and a guide, Mr. Harris. You gave him your word."

"I did act as a gentleman and a guide. But can I help it if I feel led to guide in matters of the heart as well?" He leaned closer. "And you can't pretend to be innocent in this. You enjoyed the kiss as much as I did. Can you deny it?"

Heat quickly entered her cheeks. "How dare you say such things!"

He rested against the bow of the canoe, his gaze unwavering. "Then why did you kiss me back? Surely you sense it, too, that we were meant for each other. The moment we saw each other, we were destined to be together."

"I don't know what you're talking about. But I ask that you return me at once to Roanoke Island. I'm certain my brother-in-law is worried. And I—I pray he doesn't make matters worse for you when he discovers how you betrayed his trust."

John continued to stare at her but with a bemused expression on his face. "Not that I have done any such a thing, but how will he know, pray tell?"

"If I'm asked, I won't deny it."

"There would be no reason for him to ask unless you wish to reveal it. Do what you feel you must when we return. I have done nothing wrong, and neither have you. In fact, it might be better that he knows where we both stand concerning each other." He picked up the paddle.

Beth gnawed on her bottom lip, feeling utter confusion. She did find herself very much attracted to this man, more so than she could have ever hoped or dreamed. How she'd longed for a man to notice her and to fall in love with her. But was that man supposed to be John Harris? The guide of their trip? The one with a strange past, who could vacillate from love and concern to anger and vengeance? And the one who even now looked at her with such tenderness, she could scarcely draw a breath?

The trip concluded in silence. Returning to the camp, Beth saw that Judith already had a cooking fire ablaze. The Indian porters had arrived with fish, lanced by the long spears they had made. "Did you see the ocean, Beth?" Judith asked.

Beth could feel John's presence behind her as if daring her to tell her sister what had transpired between them. "Yes. It—'twas lovely. We saw the laughing gulls." She hesitated. "And we. . .we. . ."

"What? Tell me everything."

"We. . .we found a shell that sounds just like the ocean."

Again she sensed it—John's silence that spoke louder than any words. *Are you going to tell them that I'm a betrayer of their trust? Or that you also shared in the kiss?* She choked down the words that began to rise in her throat even as Mark arrived.

"I'm glad you returned safely," he said with a smile. "Perhaps soon you can take me there, Master Harris. I'm very curious to see all of this Hatorask for myself."

"As you wish, my lord."

Judith and Mark both returned to the dinner at hand, even as Beth went to the water barrel to refresh herself.

"I knew you wouldn't say anything," John whispered huskily, his face lightening, even as he scooped up water to splash on his face.

She whirled. "Maybe not now, but I may need to. . . ."

He only smiled. "Even so, we are meant to be together. You know it as well as I. And to betray this would mean betraying yourself." He shook his hands dry and left in a flourish.

Beth returned to the water in the barrel, which rippled with her dusky and distressed image reflected on the glassy surface. *Dear Lord, what am I to believe? If this is all good and true, please show me before I forsake my heart for something that isn't meant to be!*

Chapter 8

John set about gathering more wood for the evening fire, though his thoughts were a jumble. He knew the encounter had startled Beth and perhaps even himself, but he couldn't help how he felt. And he was certain she felt the same way. Whether she denied it or not, she had responded to his kiss with equal fervor. Why she insisted, then, on toying with his emotions—even going so far as to threaten discussing the encounter with her brother-in-law—went beyond his sense of reasoning. He had expected demureness but instead found a woman of independence and strong will. Perhaps it came from the harsh life she'd endured in England, caring for her ailing father and running a large estate. He wasn't certain whether he would be able to bear up under such things, but he asked God for grace. Beth meant too much to him to let her go. And in time, with gentleness, she would embrace a sound future with him as her husband.

Besides, it might do us well if she acted upon her threat and told her brother-in-law about us, he mused, nearly chuckling aloud, even as he continued to gather wood for the evening fire. *Maybe the whole world should know, from the land to the sea. But now is not the right time, not with Beth feeling so uncertain.* Since the encounter at the sandy beach, she stayed a good distance away from him, though he could see her glancing in his direction every so often. When she did, a flush would tint her cheeks a delicate red. The reaction told him she must still be interested, that God was at work, and in due time their relationship would strengthen. In the meantime he would be patient.

John unloaded wood by the blazing fire, pushing it into a pile. Then he asked Mark if he required anything else of him.

"Yes, as a matter of fact, there is." Mark motioned for him to follow him to a place within the wooded glade, away from the camp. "Judith couldn't help but notice that something seems to be troubling Beth. Do you know what it could be?"

John found himself speechless at first. *Dare I tell him right now that we have fallen in love and we declared our love with a kiss?* He was uncertain how such news would be received. After all, this man had entrusted his sister-in-law to him and asked him to safeguard her virtue. He might face condemnation or worse. He decided to stay silent until he knew Beth's heart and matters were as clear between them as fresh water. "I'm certain the journey has been quite overwhelming for her," he finally said.

"She doesn't appear to be herself. I only wonder if perhaps something passed between you both on your journey to the other island."

Now it was John's turn to feel the warmth of a flush enter his cheeks. Mark knew everything. Beth must have acted on her threat and told him. And now he needed to heal the breach and swiftly.

He opened his mouth to speak when Mark said, "Did you have some manner of disagreement between yourselves, perhaps?"

John sighed so loudly that Mark raised an eyebrow. *No, she didn't tell him about our kiss.* "More a wonder, my lord, with all the coast has to offer," he said in haste. "The sand. The gulls and the shells. Other things. Perhaps it was too much for her."

Mark nodded. "Yes, she did tell us about the glorious things she had seen. Perhaps it's mere sorrow that she can't remain there. I must say, I find the description intriguing. I would like you to take me there early on the morrow so I can see this place for myself."

"Certainly. I would be honored. 'Tis a grand place, unspoiled and rich." *A place where love can take root and find a place to dwell,* he thought.

"We will all go there at sunup," he declared. "You and Beth can then show us what you have seen."

John nodded and returned to the fire where Beth was busy cooking. They came so close to each other, the sleeves of their garments brushed. Beth jerked back as though he had touched her with a thorny branch.

"Did you tell him?" she whispered fiercely. "I saw you both talking."

"We talked about many things."

She withdrew, her eyes large, her mouth falling open in astonishment. "How could you do such a thing? I'm now disgraced in his eyes."

"Calm yourself, madam. I only told him about the journey to the beach and the wonder of it. And he wants to see it. But pray tell, to what are you referring?"

"You know very well what I speak of. Why do you make light of it?"

"Believe me, I take this quite seriously. If you don't see it already, I'm in love with you. And I believe it might be mutual."

She gasped and returned to the cooking, even as Judith came forward, her face all smiles. "I heard the plan!" Judith called out. "So we will go see the ocean and all these wonders you speak of, Mr. Harris. How grand, indeed."

"Very grand," he agreed with a sideways glance to Beth, whose cheeks grew even rosier than the fairest rose in an English garden. When Judith disappeared, he turned back to see the water in the jug rippling in Beth's shaking hands.

"How can you do this to me?" Beth murmured, heaving the jug to the ground, even as water splashed a mottled print on her dress. "You know nothing of what I feel."

"If I'm so wrong, then you have nothing to fear. But you know I'm not.

I loved you the moment you stepped onto this land. This place has grown much more inviting by your charm."

"You speak senseless words."

"If they are senseless words, then I'm made senseless by your presence." He saw it then, a flicker of appreciation in her face, her eyes softening, her lips upturned—dare he think—into the semblance of a smile? Then a thought passed through her, and the frown returned.

"You mustn't say anything about what happened between us in that place when we return to the sands."

"I have no plans to do so, madam. But didn't you once threaten to tell everything anyway?" He couldn't help but smile, even as he could see her discomfort rise with each passing moment. "I guess there is no longer such a threat."

"I only said what I shall do should the need arise. Just be careful. Please."

John had never felt more hope than he did at that moment. *I know our destinies are linked, even as you sense it now, my dear Beth. Even if you can't speak of it, the time will come when you can. And when it is time, you will be my wife and we will make our home together by the ocean.*

∞

With Beth in his presence, John found it difficult to stay his thoughts on his duties as keeper of their canoe and guide to the far reaches. He rowed swiftly, noting the excitement on the faces of both Mark and Judith in the other canoe and then the trepidation that sent tense lines running across Beth's forehead. Despite the hat she wore, deep tones, painted by the wind and sun, replaced the paleness that once washed her cheeks. At times she complained to her sister about her complexion. He thought her fairer than any woman he had seen. Even now, he wanted to gaze longingly at her fine features, but she had turned aside. The large straw hat blocked his view of her. She kept one hand on her hat to keep the wind from stealing it away.

He made haste for the island, thinking how much this place had awakened his senses when he first arrived here several years ago and did so again when he brought Beth to its shores. The first time he came here it had been a simple exploratory trip to see all there was to see. He could still remember Robert's exclamations as he ran along the beach and then fell face first into a sandy bank, laughing all the while.

"I want to build my home here, John," Robert had told him.

"And a perfect place it would be, too," he had replied.

"There is not a soul to be found anywhere."

John glanced up, half expecting his brother to have uttered the comment. Instead he heard Mark shout and point out the vacant area devoid of people. Only the plants and animals lived there, placed by the hand of the Creator. John easily brought the canoe to rest at an embankment. Mark helped Judith out of their boat. Together they headed across the island toward the roar of the distant ocean. John waited as Beth slowly gathered herself, appearing as if she didn't want to leave the security of the canoe.

"You have nothing to fear, madam," he whispered to her. "Our secret is safe."

"I fear nothing," she retorted. But clearly she looked troubled at returning to the place where their love for each other had been kindled in a kiss. Why would she feel such discontent and not pure joy? Unless she truly didn't experience the same love he felt for her. He frowned, wishing he could read her thoughts. But they remained as private as the confines of her heart and indiscernible to his curious eye. Beth was leaving him more and more puzzled as time went by.

He followed her as she made her way to the beach where Mark and Judith stood looking at the ocean. "What a magnificent place," Mark acknowledged, "as if Almighty God had just spoken the word and formed it all. An unspoiled and rich land, indeed." He made haste down the shore, with the others struggling to keep up.

"I've often thought of settling here," John admitted. "Jamestown and the area around the river James are growing thick with colonists. But this land of Carolana has few to call its own. An unspoiled land, as you say, just waiting to be inhabited."

"I can see why such a place would be tempting," Judith added. "Don't you agree, Beth?"

John waited for her answer, only to see her nod. She was staring at the ocean. "Are you thinking of England?" he asked.

"I'm thinking of the people and places that do exist far away from here," Beth admitted. "The homes and the lands. If one were to set sail on a boat, they would come to such a land in due time. It seems hard to believe."

"Are you wishing you were there still?"

She turned then, the hat she wore casting a shadow across her face. "Now why would you think that, Mr. Harris?" She wandered off to join her sister.

John didn't know why. Maybe searching for evidence in her heart, just as the sisters now began searching the sand for shells.

Just then, John heard a shout of exclamation from Mark. He turned, his hand instinctively touching his pistol at his waist. Judith ran up to Mark, gripping his arm as he pointed in the far-off distance. John squinted to see several figures approaching, walking swiftly along the sandy shore. At first he thought they might be fellow explorers. As they drew closer, he could plainly see the shocks of dark hair flowing in the breeze, and the tawny-colored complexion inherent to the Indians of the land. His muscles tensed at the sight. His fingers closed around the snaphaunce pistol, slowly drawing it.

"Calm yourself, Mr. Harris," Mark said to him. "They have shown no aggression. Let's find out what they want."

John wanted to answer to the contrary but kept his emotions at bay. At the same time, Beth drew closer to him as if seeking his protection. "What could they want?" she asked, her voice fearful.

"Just stay by me."

"Welcome," a voice announced.

They all stared at each other in amazement at the greeting uttered in English. Upon closer inspection, John could see that these Indians were not of the sort he had seen at Jamestown. Their eyes lacked the fierce color like the black of night concealing some mischief. Maybe it was the sun reflecting in them. Even their skin lacked the deep earthy tones of the Indians in Jamestown.

"Thank you," Mark answered. "We are from a great white man's village up north called Jamestown. I am Mark Reynolds. This is my wife, Judith, my sister-in-law, Elizabeth, and our guide, John Harris."

"Welcome," the Indian repeated. "We good friends."

A strange statement to make, John thought. *How can we be friends when we have only just been introduced?* He fought to bury his misgivings even as they surfaced quicker than he could drive them back. He looked each of them over carefully while his fingers caressed the hilt of his pistol. *If they but flinch in the wrong direction, they will wish they hadn't.*

"How is it we're friends?" Mark asked.

"We good friends of the white man. He come much and we bring him to village." The Indian pointed down the coastline, far into the distance.

"You mean that other white men have come before us?" Mark asked. John detected the excitement escalating in the man's voice. Surely Mark couldn't mean that these Indians knew the colonists from long ago?

"Some stay. Some go."

"They must be from the village called Sandbanks," John said to Mark in a low, even voice.

"Are there white men now in your village of Sandbanks?" Mark asked the Indian.

"Some stay, some go," he repeated. "You welcome in village."

Mark turned, his eyes wide, his lips upturned into a smile. "Glory be! The Indian talks of white men visiting their village. Maybe they came long ago, such as those from the Roanoke Colony. This could be our answer, sent from heaven above."

"That can't be, my lord," John interjected. "It has been sixty years. Surely they speak of other explorers who have come here." Even as he said it, he knew Mark didn't believe him. He chose instead to cling to his stubborn faith without any evidence that his wife's relatives or the colony had found refuge with the Indians. *Refuge indeed with such people. As if that were ever possible!*

"We must find out," Mark announced. "We will go with them to their village."

John stared, unable to believe what he'd heard. "But you can't mean it. You know nothing about them or in what manner they speak. How can you blindly stumble into their village, not knowing what lies there?"

"Faith, Master Harris. A belief that God has guided our footsteps. He allowed you to guide us to the Roanoke Island and then to this place where we were fortunate enough to meet the Indians. We have no cause to think they wish us harm. And if they do know of other English colonists from long ago, then it is only right that we seek them out and inquire."

John looked to Beth for her opinion. She only stood passively by, watching the scene unfold before her. Perhaps he could at least convince Mark to allow him to safeguard the women, to take them back to Roanoke Island while Mark went seeking the information he wished. When he broached it, Judith shook her head, clinging to her husband's arm. "Where he goes, I go, too. 'Tis my relatives we seek, after all."

"Surely you are not going also," John asked Beth in a low voice.

"Why shouldn't I? I trust my sister's husband. He won't lead us astray. And I think there may be something important there for us to discover."

He fought to come up with a reasonable excuse. How he wished he could tell her that if anything happened to her, he would cease to live. That he could not trust the one he loved to a people he knew nothing about. "Don't do this. Let us return to Roanoke."

"Alone and unescorted? Really, Mr. Harris."

"I'm thinking of you, madam, whom I pledged to safeguard when I undertook this journey."

"Can you not let go of your suspicions of the naturals for a moment?"

"Suspicion is also a manner of wisdom. A moment is all it takes for something to go wrong. And it's unwise to stumble into an Indian village just because one of them speaks English. It could be a clever trap."

"Then you must come along and be our guard," she said with a teasing lilt to her voice.

He sighed. *They don't know nor do they understand. They follow blindly after their own ambitions without giving a thought as to what might lay hidden.*

John hated feeling this way. He hated not knowing the tactics of this adversary in the Carolana region. If these Indians were like the others, they had weapons of cunning and evil. The ability to draw out a helpless prey and then pounce when one least expected it. He glanced over at Beth, even as the ocean breeze took up her brown hair. The straw hat she had worn to protect her from the sun had fallen behind her neck, allowing her hair to dance upon the wind. How could he let her walk into that place and put her life in peril? If only she would listen.

For a long time they walked until the journey took them away from the sandy shores and into the woods. Mark engaged in conversation as much as he could with the Indians, inquiring again of the white men who had come and gone. The Indians only smiled and shook their heads. Either they could not answer him or they refused to answer.

"Be patient," Judith admonished her husband. "We'll soon discover all there is to know."

"But I'm hopeful," he admitted. "To think that God has guided our very footsteps. And we have no one to thank but Master Harris. If he hadn't led us to these shores, we would never have met them."

"Yes, thank you, Mr. Harris," Judith echoed.

John could hardly accept such appreciation with the ill will brewing inside him. Reluctantly following the Indians along a well-worn path and then to a bank by the sound waters where they boarded canoes, he grew more agitated. If only he could convince them all to turn back, to retreat to Roanoke Island before it was too late. At least for Beth's sake. Maybe, just maybe, he could attempt one last time to convince her.

He came alongside her, opening his mouth, ready to speak the words on his heart. Instead Beth purred, "Just think, another adventure about to happen. 'Tis good you are going, Mr. Harris, for adventure is a part of you. And I must admit, I'm quite eager to know if they have had any contact with other English."

"Even if I tell you a secret about these people that may cause you to reconsider?"

She glanced back. "What secret?"

"You may not wish to meet them once I tell you."

She frowned. "You're going to tell me they are violent. And they have shown nothing of violence."

"I only say it might do well to hide your eyes when we arrive," he told her.

"From what, pray tell?"

"The savages, that is, the Indians of this place are not known to keep proper dress. They wear little clothing. You will find it quite immoral to your eyes."

She frowned. "Mr. Harris, how can you say such things? You only want me to turn aside, to return with you instead to Roanoke."

"I speak the truth, to prepare you, if you would only listen."

Her cheeks warmed. "I refuse to concern myself with such things. I know this land and the people are very different from England. I've seen it already." She settled herself quickly into a canoe.

"But do you understand just how different? And not just the animals like the aroughcun I spoke about with its black eyes or the seabirds with their large beaks. There are also people here you have never seen, who do things you wouldn't think civilized people could do. Who act and dress in a way you may have never imagined."

She hesitated. In that moment, John saw a spark of hope. Then she raised her head and leveled her gaze at him. "I will look on them as God does, as His creation made in His image. It will help, don't you think?"

"Perhaps for a time," he managed to say before retreating to help paddle a canoe. There was little doubt that Beth's faith paralleled her brother-in-law's, with their determination equal. John once thought he had such faith, too. He had trusted God many times for the circumstances of his life. Sometimes it took faith just to rise and face a new dawn, especially in this land. Faith to keep going when everything looked bleak. But Mark had turned the idea of faith into some reckless need for knowledge, set with unrealistic goals that would only be met by sadness. Yet what could John do? There was nothing left to do. Beth's brown eyes glimmered with anticipation, her lips parted, appearing as eager as her sister and brother-in-law to see this village of Sandbanks and find out about the English that had come and gone. Much to his chagrin, they were all one in their quest. If they were insistent on following the Indians, he must go as well. But his hand would not be far from his pistol. He would be ready. For all they knew, it could turn out to be their saving grace.

Chapter 9

After many hours of travel by land and by water, the village of Sandbanks appeared before them. Crescent-shaped wooden homes, covered with bark, stood in a semicircle. Cooking fires burned before each of the homes, laying a thick blanket of smoke over the area. Indians began to emerge from dwellings or from the nearby brush where they tended to the duties of the day, as if the arrival of the party had sent out an alarm among them. Beth pointed at the little children who hovered near their mothers. John wondered if she would also acknowledge the lack of dress, especially among the women. But she gave no such sign of alarm, or if she felt any, kept it well hidden. In fact, her peace with the situation that would horrify any lady of England continued to amaze him.

"Welcome," exclaimed a rather tall Indian, no doubt one of the leaders of the village. "Where come you?"

"Virginia," Mark said. "We seek family of ours who were lost long ago."

The leader looked to several of his councilors. They muttered amongst themselves. "Who lost?" the leader asked.

"They came from a ship many years ago," Mark tried to explain. "On a ship that went through the Great Waters from their homeland far away. There were men, women, and children on board that ship."

The leader shook his head.

John wanted desperately to tell Mark that these Indians knew nothing, that the Roanoke Colony had long since vanished, the people's whereabouts known to God alone. Their quest for knowledge had been of no avail in his opinion, until he heard Beth encouraging Mark to continue his inquiry and not give up hope. He held back any attempt to intervene. There was Beth to consider, after all. These were her relatives they sought. She was emotionally bound to the quest. And, in turn, he must keep alive his own personal quest to make Beth his, no matter what else transpired on this journey.

They were led into one of the larger dwellings in the village, where the leaders fed them food as they sat upon woven mats. John stayed alert to everything around him, knowing he might be depended upon if trouble arose. Mark continued to parley with them through words and signs as if they were his friends. Even Beth and Judith appeared interested in everything the Indians had to say—speaking of the lands around them and the possibility of encountering

Englishmen from past ships. But try as he might to stay confident, John couldn't help envisioning some terrible scene—an ambush while they reclined in the council house, the Indians doing away with them, one by one, as they slept, or scheming some other fiendish plot.

"Wise One know things," the leader of the village finally admitted to Mark. "Wise One know English long ago."

Mark sat up on his knees, barely able to contain his excitement. "May I speak with this wise one? It is very important."

"He go to Great Spirit. Return when sun down."

John wondered if Mark could wait that long. John had eaten a bit of the fish given to them, but found he had no appetite. If only they could find out what they needed to know and be done with this village and the people.

When time had passed and John saw little sign of danger in their midst, he left the council house, hoping to find peace by the shores of the sound. The sun had begun to dip low, reflecting its orange tint upon the waters. He pondered the wisdom of ever having accepted this task of guiding the family to Hatorask. Though he loved the land, and yes, the woman who accompanied them on the journey, he wondered if it had been a wise decision. Someone like his friend Samuel, who also knew the lay of the land, could have easily led them here. But likely, if John had stayed in Jamestown, so, too, would the pain from the past. Nothing would have been reconciled, as Samuel wisely warned. He faced it when he first saw the Indian couriers, and now he relived it every moment he remained in this village. It was like some unseen spirit forcing him headlong into a battle for his soul. "But I don't want to confront this," he voiced aloud. "Not here. Not now. Not ever. Can't I be at peace?"

"John, what troubles you?"

He spun about as if an angel had sung the question from the heavens above. He had not even heard the faint footsteps of Beth, who had come up behind him. Had she witnessed everything, even the groaning of his heart?

"I—I only pray we might leave here soon," he said hastily. "We still have our camp at Roanoke Island and our possessions there, you know."

Beth shook her head. "I hardly think that is what ails you. You said something about being at peace."

His cheeks flamed. " 'Tis nothing."

"But something surely troubles you. What is it?"

Why does she ask me these things? Can't she see I have no will to speak about this? That I refuse to do so?

"Do you still think the Indians will harm us?"

"No. They seem of a different sort than those who live near Jamestown."

Beth stood beside him, sharing in the sunset that graced the landscape. "Then what? I only wish you would share your troubling thoughts with me."

"Beth, you have secrets in your heart, I'm sure. Things known only to God so that God, alone, can bear them. Maybe even deep things concerning your father, for instance, that no one else could ever understand. Will you trust that I, too, have things I believe only God can carry? That no one, especially someone like you, need be concerned by them?"

Beth stood still and silent as if considering it. "Yes, I do know that we all carry deep secrets within. But I know, too, that one day they need to be reconciled, lest they dig away at us and leave us in a grave." She turned to him. "And I truly believe those secrets have allowed your peace to escape, and you are in some dark grave. It may be why you're so angry."

"When I'm with you, I have more peace than I could ever want." He reached for her hand, but she kept it tucked away.

She chuckled uncomfortably. "You're quite mistaken if you think I'm of a peaceful sort. I've contended with more trouble that only God could know. And I've had my trials. But I also know I needed to confide in those closest to me. To allow others to help bear my burdens. Find someone to help bear your burden, John. And let it go."

Just then they heard Mark calling for them to come attend the meeting. The Indian called Wise One had returned from his time of meditation.

"Will you come?" she asked.

"Of course." If anything, he did wish to know if there existed some answer to the mystery of the long-lost colony. But he could not forget the words that echoed in his thoughts. *Find someone to help bear your burden, John. And let it go."*

∞

The name *Wise One* fit well the elder Indian seated before them. But there were other striking features about him. A face nearly white in color, if wrinkled with age. Hair a dark brown with eyes to match. If John were not mistaken, the Indian could have surely been a white man at one time, even sitting there clothed in apparel bedecked in beads and accoutrements of the village. When he began speaking, John's curiosity rose further. Mark and the women stirred, too, as if they had come to a similar conclusion.

"There are pictures of ships," Wise One said, "painted on lodgings long ago. Say ships from the Great Waters with white men. One call white men friends. Spoke kindly to them. Helped them when their leader went to Great Waters."

"The women here. . .it is their grandparents who were a part of that ship," Mark explained. "But they were lost like the rest. No one knows what happened."

"They say many left. Some here. Some far away."

Judith grabbed Beth's hand. "Some did come here! Oh Beth, did you hear what he said?"

"What of the name Colman?" Mark pressed. "Does that name sound familiar to you?

64

"A cold man?"

"No. Colman. Thomas and Susanna Colman. Have you ever heard of them?"

Wise One shook his head. "No cold man here. I speak stories told me. We all there is."

"But you look as if you may have English blood in you."

The Indian stared long and hard. John stirred in discomfort at the frown that suddenly erupted on the Indian's wizened face. He wondered what it meant. Perhaps the Indian knew of something in his past, if English blood had mingled with Indian, although Wise One said nothing of this.

"I Wise One of the Croatoan people."

"I'm sorry. I didn't mean to offend you. I only wanted to know if the English did live among you."

Wise One stood. "It is as I say." With that he left.

The air grew still and silent. John wondered once more if all this had been in vain. But after a moment of silence, Mark hailed it an achievement of the greatest importance. "Praise be. We know much."

"But our relatives could be anywhere," Judith said with a sigh.

"Perhaps. But we know now that many from the colony did survive. They were not massacred or left to die of disease. That some found refuge among the Indians. And for all you know, some of these Indians could be related to the white men."

Judith stared at him, aghast. "That can't be! My relatives are not Indians!"

"Not yours, but there may be others from the colony. You see with your eyes how Wise One appears. He must have English blood somewhere in his lineage, even if he denies it. Many do in this village. Even if some have left, there are others here that bear the characteristics."

"If only one of them knew the name of Colman," she mourned.

"But Wise One did hear of the English. Those that came in ships. The stories that have been passed down. So be of good cheer. Our journey has not been in vain." Mark paused, then added, "We'll stay a few days longer, learning all we can. And maybe Wise One will remember other things that could be of great importance to us."

Inwardly, John groaned. He didn't find this news cheerful in the least. A few more days in this village to him would feel like months—and more time for further contemplation while existing among those who kindled memories of a pain-filled past.

Despite Mark's wish to remain and the way the rest of the family knit themselves with the Indian village, John did his best to separate himself from it all. One of them needed to keep sense in all this. John put it upon himself to remain on alert, though it pained him to see the family move easily among the Indians. Mark went out with several of the villagers to try his hand at spearfishing. Beth decided to do some beadwork using the gut of animals as the thread, enjoying the older

Indian woman who taught her the skill. She laughed in glee as several children came up to her, tapping her on the back, then jumping away as she tried to catch them. *Soften your heart, John*, he admonished himself. *These Indians have shown no aggression whatsoever. They have only been hospitable and kind.* Yet he could not help sensing his own personal departure from it all as if he were separated by some wide void, unable to communicate or enjoy a different way of life.

When it came time for the evening meal, Mark proudly offered as the main course the fish he had lanced with a homemade spear. "I rather fancied it," he said with a grin. Everyone helped themselves to large portions of fish cooked over hot stones. No one seemed to notice that John, again, ate little.

"And I see you made yourself a necklace," Mark observed, nodding toward Beth.

She wore an innocent grin. "Isn't it lovely? I like this place very much. And I even had one of the women tell me about her belief in the Creator God. These people seem to have a bit of understanding of the Christian God. Someone must have told them."

"Surely it wasn't an explorer," Mark mused. His gaze locked with John's. "That is not to say an explorer cannot be a believer. But from what I've heard about them, they are more intent on finding treasure than spreading the gospel."

"I suppose treasure is in the eye of the beholder," John said. "Treasures don't have to come by way of possession but sometimes in some idle quest, as well."

Mark put down his corn bread. "I see. Surely you don't believe we are still on some 'idle quest,' as you put it. Our quest is being fulfilled by God."

"And how is that, my lord? You know little more than when you first arrived. You see an Indian that might bear resemblance to the English, who knows a few tales passed down from the ages, and you believe this is your answer?" John saw the looks radiating in his direction.

"I believe more hope has been found here than any witnessed since the colony disappeared. And I think when we return to Jamestown, we should send news of our discovery and bring hope to those who, like us, lost loved ones."

"But the colonists remain lost. You have found no trace of them still."

Mark said no more, but John could see his opinion had dampened the companionship of the meal and the joy from the meeting with Wise One.

Again he took time that evening to contemplate. There would be no Beth by his side this night as he gazed out over the waters. She had looked at him in dismay during the meal, as if his words had quenched the flame of hope within them all. Despite what they thought, he sought the truth. To him, enough was enough. His mission here had been completed. He had fulfilled his duties as guide and protector. They had seen to their quest, as futile as it had been. Now the time was drawing nigh for his personal quest to come forth. He would see it happen and then remove himself from this village and from the past as quickly as possible.

Chapter 10

Beth uttered a sigh of despair as she walked among the reeds, thinking of the last few days. If only there were a way to break through. If only she knew the secret to reaching a hard heart. Kindness had always seemed to work with her father, whose heart was as hard as any stone fit for a wall. Kindness and a merciful heart. Drawing near with an ear ready to listen. But none of those things seemed to break the hard heart of John Harris. He remained aloof, trapped in some foreign land of his own making. She had thought with the attraction between them that something would reach inside him, that the pain he kept buried would be brought forth.

She considered her own actions of late. Maybe if she hadn't reacted the way she did after the kiss they shared—playing with the emotion of it all, threatening to inform Mark of their encounter when she knew she would never do such a thing. John had seemed amused by the antics, but now she realized it had been wrong. She should be open with her feelings if she expected him to be open with his. She should have told him that she did enjoy his kiss and his companionship, that she was inquiring of God if they were meant to be together or if this was for a season and God had other plans for them to embrace. She contemplated sharing these thoughts, in the hope that he would respond favorably, but was uncertain how to go about it.

Instead, she returned to the village and immersed herself in making a string of beads. Soon a young Indian girl with a broken front tooth joined her and, at once, took it upon herself to show Beth how to string the beads in vivid color combinations. The girl did not speak English very well, so communication was a challenge. But between the hand symbols and single words, they were able to tell each other their names and share a little about their families. The young girl's name was translated to Rising Star, which Beth liked very much. Beth then pointed to Judith, who stood in the distance.

"My sister," she told Rising Star.

The girl called forth a chubby little Indian boy and said, "Sister." Beth nearly laughed until she realized Rising Star thought *sister* meant sibling. "You mean brother."

"Brother," the girl repeated and laughed.

Just then, Beth caught sight of John staring at her. At first he seemed irritated that she sat with Rising Star, making Indian beadwork. Then he offered the semblance of a crooked smile, which set her mind at ease. He shifted a sack of supplies over one shoulder as if he were ready to go somewhere. "Are you going fishing with the men this morning, Mr. Harris?" Beth called out.

"I'm going back to Roanoke Island to break camp. Your brother-in-law asked me to retrieve your belongings from there."

Beth considered accompanying him but knew Mark would never approve. And after what happened the last time they were together, she wasn't certain she should. But the lure of being with him was strong. And there were things hidden in the dark that needed to be brought to light. She glanced back at the young girl. "Maybe Rising Star and I could go with you, just to the coast. Maybe we could find some of those talking shells. 'Tis a pretty day."

John gaped for a moment then shook his head. "There's no need."

"Why? I think 'tis a fine idea, and I'm sure she would like it. Wait for me."

Beth stood to her feet, determined to seek out Rising Star's mother and see if the girl could accompany her. At least it would give her time to be with John Harris under the guise of going to see the ocean. When Beth communicated to the Indian woman of going with the white man to see the great ocean, the woman hesitated at first. "Rising Star like you, Beth Cold Woman. She like Great Waters. Yes, she go."

"Thank you!" Beth hurried to inform Judith that she was taking Rising Star on a journey in John's company.

When she returned, John had already begun heading for the trail that led back to the canoes. The canoes would take them through the sound waters and farther up the coast. At first he said nothing. Finally, when Rising Star was occupied, he turned to Beth. "Why are you really coming? 'Tis a long journey, as you well know."

She saw his gaze focus on Rising Star. "You aren't dismayed she is going. . . ?"

"No, of course not. I thought you would want to stay at the village. You seemed to have found a home there and many new friends."

Beth smiled as Rising Star raced along the path toward the canoes beached by the waters, laughing all the while. "Isn't she sweet? She's like having a younger sister. She sits by my side, helping me make the beaded necklaces. Isn't God good, John?"

John heaved the canoe into the water, then helped them each aboard. "Certainly He is good. Sometimes I don't understand everything He does. I know it must be for good and not for evil, and that all things work together for His purposes. I only wish it were not such a mystery."

Beth sucked in her breath. *Remember, Beth. Show kindness and mercy.* Maybe he would use this time to unfetter the burdens of his heart. Perhaps God had set apart this place and time for new things to emerge out of things that were old and no more. "Sometimes His ways are difficult to understand, I know. I guess that's what faith is all about. To believe and trust even when we don't understand.

To accept His will and know He wants what's best for us."

"Surely you found it difficult to accept that after what you went through in England with your father."

" 'Twas difficult," she admitted. "Many nights I cried myself to sleep. But then I would wake up to find the sun shining in my window and see that God had made all things new. A new day, indeed. And I had a father who needed me, even if he was not right in the mind."

John stared at the open waters before them, paddling fiercely. "Did the physicians ever find out what was wrong with him?"

"No. Of course, after all that was shared about Father's losing his parents with the colony and his desire to find them, I wondered if his ill mind came from that loss. 'Tis hard to know what things can cause us to slip away out of despair and questioning. When Judith told me about Father's longing to find his parents, I had no idea he thought that way. It lay buried in him for so long. I pray it didn't drive him mad."

They talked for a long time about their families and their lives in England. When they finally arrived at the part of the island not far from where Beth and John first shared in the kiss, Rising Star leaped out of the canoe and raced along to the great ocean. It wasn't long before she found a shell, the same kind Beth had used to listen to the ocean sounds. She helped the young girl hold it to her ear and then pointed to the ocean before them. "A talking shell," she explained. Beth again felt familiar warmth at those words. She recalled how her own encounter with the shell led to the kiss. When she found John looking at her, she could sense that he, too, was reflecting on that time. But now everything was different. Even though the time was but a short bit ago, it seemed like ages past.

"I must leave now for Roanoke Island," John said, gazing at her. "I won't be too far gone. You can see the island from here."

"I'm sure we will find plenty to do while you're away."

He paused, staring at her as if wishing he could give her a kiss good-bye. Again a tingle rose up within her at the mere thought. But, at the last moment, he turned away for the canoe and his own journey to the distant island.

While he was gone, Beth spent the time with Rising Star, helping her with English words to describe the scenery before them. "Creator God made them all," Beth told her. "The sky, the ocean, even you."

"Great Spirit?"

"The Creator God is a Great Spirit, but also the one true God. A God of love. And He sent His Son Jesus to die for us so that we can live with Him forever in His home in heaven."

"Me see Jesus," said Rising Star. "Me go to heaven with Beth Cold Man."

Beth wanted to embrace the young girl. How might one show Jesus to her? She gazed at the island in the distance where John had gone. How they did need to show Jesus to these people. How to forgive. How to love. How to be salt and light in everything. But how difficult it could be as well, not only to speak of her faith but to live it, too. She realized it more than ever, with everything that had happened in this journey. A journey that tested not only her body and spirit but her heart as well.

Beth sat down in the sand and began shaping it into mounds. Rising Star laughed at her antics. She pretended to fashion the corn cakes as she had done on so many occasions during the long trip. Watching Rising Star make her own set of sand cakes, she wondered about Josephine, the servant who had helped at Briarwood and who had been like a sister to her. Before they separated, Josephine told her she was going to London to try to find her family. Beth murmured a prayer for her friend, hoping she did have a joyful reunion with her loved ones.

Time passed quickly. Evening shadows began to fall. Beth grew concerned for the late hour and stood to her feet, shaking sand out of her skirts. Rising Star was content to gather a mound of tiny shells with which to make more necklaces when they arrived back at the village. Beth instead looked westward, toward Roanoke Island, wondering what could be keeping John. Visions assaulted her then—from his boat tipping over, spilling him into the waters, to some surprise attack that left him wounded and helpless on the island.

"Look, look, Beth Cold Man," Rising Star said, showing her the many shell fragments she had collected.

"They will make a beautiful necklace." Again Beth gazed toward Roanoke Island. The sun had already begun its journey to the distant horizon. It would be dark before they arrived back.

At last she spotted a small vessel on the shimmering waters and murmured a prayer of relief. "Where have you been?" she demanded when he paddled up.

John raised his eyebrow at her. "There was another exploration party on the island. I met two of the men there—Anderson and Edgar. They talked about their party. Even mentioned having a reverend with them—I suppose for their spiritual guidance."

"Have you ever seen them before?"

John shook his head. "Many are starting to come here, looking for new land in which to settle. And 'tis well I went today to the island, or all your possessions would have become their booty. I had to do some bargaining to get back what I could."

"Oh, no," Beth mourned. "I thought our Indian porters would still be there at the camp."

"There was no sign of them. They likely left when we didn't return. But all is well. I even brought back your cloak." He held it up, winking as he did. "But let us make haste. Come into the boat. We should be back to the village by nightfall if we leave now."

Beth called for Rising Star. Soon they were off with John, paddling southward toward Sandbanks. Beth said little but soon became keenly aware that he was looking at her. Finally she asked, "Is there something you wish?"

"Just my curiosity, madam. Perhaps my eyes were deceiving me, but could it be you were concerned for my welfare back on the shore?"

" 'Twas growing late, Mr. Harris, and we have a young one here that must be returned to the village. I'm certain her mother is very worried."

The paddle assaulted the water with each stroke. "Is that all?"

"I don't understand what you're hinting at."

"Perhaps I only imagined a fair and desperate woman by the shore then, anxious for my return."

"You do think highly of yourself, don't you?"

"Only if I believe a woman cares for me. Then perhaps my life holds value."

Beth shook her head and looked down to find Rising Star observing their exchange with interest. "He your man, Beth Cold Man?" she asked.

Beth couldn't believe what the young girl had said. She choked and began coughing.

"What did she say?" John asked. "I don't know if I heard her right."

"Nothing. Nothing at all."

"I think I heard her ask if I was your man. Providential words, don't you think?"

"Please. . .we mustn't speak of it."

He said no more, much to her relief. In fact, neither of them said anything while they made haste toward the Indian village. Arriving at the shore, they walked through the rushes with only the moon to light their way, until they saw golden flickers and smelled the acrid odor of cooking fires tainting the night air.

Rising Star bubbled over with news of her journey to her Indian family and friends, showing them her collection of shells. Beth recognized Judith, who came into the firelight with concern etched in lines running across her face. "Where have you been, Beth? 'Tis long past sundown!"

"John spent time on Roanoke Island with some other explorers who nearly made off with our possessions. But I'm glad I took Rising Star with me. I was able to share a little of God's holy Word with her. And Judith, she told me she wants to see Jesus."

"I'm glad, Beth. I only wish you didn't forget yourself on these trips you take with Master Harris. I must say, it seems a marriage covenant is on some distant horizon for you. 'Tis the only explanation for the things Mark and I have seen and why you spend so much time together. Though I do hope John Harris will do what is proper and speak to Mark about it. And that you both will consider yourselves and your need for wisdom and guidance."

Beth froze in her stance. How could it be that others knew of some untold future, yet she had no peace for a marital covenant, even if she did enjoy being with him? "There is nothing like that between us," she denied.

Judith laughed. "Come now. 'Tis not difficult to see when two people are falling in love. I'm one who knows. Mark and I courted after our fathers agreed, but we loved each other even before they gave their approval. We believed long ago we were meant to be together in God's holy name."

If only I knew, Beth thought. "But we are not the same people. Although Mr. Harris may believe what you say, I do not."

"Why?"

Beth had no answer. She hurried away, hoping to collect her thoughts and keep her own tide of emotions at bay before she felt herself swept away by it all. *Why don't I feel as everyone else does? Oh Lord, show me what I lack.*

The large bonfire the Indians kindled warmed the chilly evening. Beth sat close to it with Rising Star by her side, wearing the new shell necklace the girl had made. This night, Wise One entertained them all with stories of the past, even of the large ships that once brought people like herself, Judith, Mark, and John to their villages. He talked of Manteo, who had befriended the white men and who eventually went to the white man's land across the Great Waters. Beth noticed the smile painted on Mark's face as if he were enjoying every bit of the story. Though they didn't know if the blood of the past lingered in this tribe or else-where, they had a peace that some of the colony had indeed found refuge. And for that, there was joy that their journey had not been in vain.

She glanced around to find John in the background, whittling at a stick with a sharp knife. Curly bits of wood fell under the knife's blade. He seemed preoccupied, as he had since the day they arrived. No doubt he was still anxious to leave the village. He had never been content while they stayed among the Indians. If only she knew what caused it. Why he could not be that friendly soul she had witnessed at various times on the trip but instead must turn into a man of disdain when confronting those he disliked.

She saw him move off, a silent and dark shadow with just the faint glow of orange from the firelight reflecting his sturdy form. After a time Beth stood, wished everyone a good night, and began making her way toward one of the lodges she and Judith shared with several Indian women.

The sound of her name uttered from the darkness stopped her. She saw John emerge from the shadows. He tossed away the stick he had been whittling and came toward her. She remembered the words Judith had spoken—how plain it was to see that they had forged a bond. But had they really? Or was it all still some dream?

"I haven't spoken of this. . . ," he began. "I'm not sure how to tell you, actually."

She stood still and silent, uncertain what he was about to say.

"I enjoyed very much the time we have spent together."

She sensed the warmth enter her.

"It means a great deal to me to know you care," he went on.

"Of course I do. We all do. We have to stay together when we make a journey like this. And you are our guide, after all. How will we return to Jamestown without you?"

John looked upward into the evening sky, just as the canopy of darkness began to fill with stars, and a sliver of moon materialized to give a bit of light. She watched him, sensing that his pain ran deep, deeper than the skies that held those stars. From whence came such sorrow, no one knew but God alone. If only he would speak aloud his thoughts while she stood waiting and hoping for them to be revealed.

"I've been thinking...," he began.

Oh, can it be? Is he finally going to tell me what I have yearned to know about him? I knew some trouble lay hidden and unspoken. Dear Lord, may this be the time.

"We all have our quests on this journey. Your brother-in-law and sister have theirs. No doubt you have yours. And yes, I have mine. Would you like to know what it is?"

"Yes, I would," she said quickly. "I've been waiting so long for you to tell me. I know it's been hard these last few days, that you have held yourself back. But we needn't wait any longer. Let yourself go free in God's grace and tell me everything. 'Tis the right thing to do."

John's gaze immediately leveled with hers. He took a step back. "I—I didn't think you would want me to confess this to you...."

"How could you think that? Of course I do. I just didn't know how to draw it out. Maybe I was timid. I don't want you to think ill of me."

He began to laugh. "Why would I ever think that? This is like a dream that has finally come to a place where it can be embraced and without fear." He stepped forward, his arms extended as if ready to draw her in.

Beth shook her head, retreating from his invitation. "John, I don't understand."

"Of course you do. I know now that our hearts are truly one, that we both think and breathe the same thoughts about each other. So now I can ask you, dearest Beth, to become my wife."

Beth gasped. Her hand flew to her mouth. "J–John." She could barely utter his name, so shocked was she at his proposal.

"I already know the answer, praise be, just by what was spoken tonight. Forever and amen, you are mine." He again stepped forward, his arms reaching for her, attempting to pull her into his embrace.

"I have hinted at no such thing!" She stepped away, turning from his confused gaze. "You didn't hear what I said at all."

"I heard every word—how you've been waiting for this time as much as I. That I needn't hold myself back any longer. It was like the feel of the ocean breeze to hear you say these words."

"Please. . .I. . ." She paused. "I—I can't marry you."

His arms fell limp. "What?"

"I can't marry you. Not after what's passed between us, or rather, what has not passed between us."

"Then what was all that just a few moments ago? About releasing ourselves to each other? Allowing God's grace to overcome? You even said you were waiting for me to ask."

"I wait for you to tell me who you really are, John Harris. What burdens your soul? Oh, I've seen glimpses of your true self, yes. But I don't know you. The true man lies hidden behind some wall."

He whirled in a start, tossing his hands. "Beth, we have been over this so many times. Why must I confess everything of my soul before you will accept me? Is that to be the price for your hand?"

"Isn't truthfulness a worthy aim?"

He shook his head. "There are some things that I will not bare. . .not to you, not to anyone. You can't force my hand like this."

"Then I would say we both were mistaken in our judgment." She turned and made haste for the wooden lodging, refusing to look back.

Once inside, her hand touched her neck and the jewelry lovingly given to her by Rising Star. She felt no comfort in it. Despite what had happened between them, John filled a void in her heart. Without him, she was half-empty. But how could she have a marriage of dark secrets, where one couldn't trust the other? She took up the wool cloak he had brought from Roanoke Island. She pressed it close to her face, allowing her tears to dampen the garment. "Dearest Lord, what shall I do? Help me."

Chapter 11

Depression was quick to settle over him. How everything could rapidly fade into some deep, dark chasm of no return, John had no idea. His mind was a whirlwind after the confrontation with Beth. Her words left a thorn embedded in his heart. For so long he had nurtured a desire to be with her and, ultimately, make her his forever. Now that he was spurned by her, the pain was even worse than the grief he held for the past. Once more, he faced another loss. Another good-bye. He couldn't understand it nor could he accept it.

The more he pondered the evening's conversation, the more confused he became. Why must he confess everything in his life so that she would find him acceptable enough to marry? Didn't he provide for her every step of the way during this journey? Didn't he see to her safety, her comfort, even hailing the good graces of womanhood God had bestowed upon her? Why then did she seek to dangle the wounds of his past above his heart?

She doesn't know you, John Harris, he reasoned. *She even said so. Who you really are.* He paused to consider this. *Who am I? A weary guide? A sojourner looking for his homeland? A wandering soul in search of fulfillment? A man entangled in a web of the past and unable to break free?* He thought of his good friend Samuel, who often spoke of reconciling the past. Setting things in order. Finding the peace that eluded him. Now other things commanded his soul. He was a dark grave, as Beth once said. Only those looking from the outside in could see it.

Still he refused to reconcile it, to believe that Beth should accept his past. He had tolerated being in the Indian village for her sake alone. Now that she had refused to marry him, he saw no reason to remain in this place. He had done everything required of him as the role of a guide. He would leave forthwith and never look back.

John remained awake all night, even as the village slumbered. He watched the stars slowly drift in the night sky and the crescent moon rise and fall. To think of sleeping when everything in his life had no direction seemed absurd. He thought of Beth asleep with the other women. Maybe she felt at ease to sleep now that his claim to her had been dissolved. Or she rested knowing God held her life in His capable hands. But he could find no rest. He called upon God to help him in this hour, to make straight his path, to show him where he needed to go.

When the first birds began to sing and the village stirred to life at the rising dawn, John felt weary in mind and body. He watched through bleary eyes to see

Beth emerge from the lodge, stretching her arms above her head as if to embrace the skies above. It pained him to see her loveliness after a night spent wrestling with his feelings. She moved toward a large earthen jar to splash water on her face. Only when she straightened, shaking free her hands, did her gaze lock with his. He thought she would turn away, but she did not. She simply looked at him, as he did her.

To his surprise, she moved toward him. "Good morning, Mr. Harris. How do you fare?"

"A bit weary, madam," he admitted, looking at his hands resting limp on his legs. "I could not find rest last night."

"I must say, neither did I."

His gaze again met hers, and she peered at him intently. How he wanted to nurture a hope that all was not lost, despite their conversation last evening. But he didn't want to succumb to the memory again. He refused to allow his heart the burden of bearing it.

"I think this is for the best," she continued. "I know we did not depart in the best of spirits last evening. But it will serve us both in the end."

"The only end I hope to see is what I asked," he said. The comment he uttered surprised even himself. Determination must be making its last stand.

"I'm sorry," she said gently, "but my answer has to be no."

Just then, Rising Star came to bid her good morning and accompany her to the cooking area where several of the Indian women were already making up cornmeal cakes for the morning's fare. She heaved a sigh and turned away from him, never looking back.

His eyes began to burn. He sighed with lasting despair. *This is the end, John. The time has come to make peace with the decision and embrace whatever lies ahead.* But without Beth to fill his life, the future looked bleak.

Later that morning, while everyone was engaged in the day's work, John looked about for his satchel of belongings. He had nothing of value, he knew, but a few possessions he might need as well as his trusty pistol. He took some of the morning's corncakes for sustenance and filled a leather pouch with fresh water from the water pot. He wondered if Beth could see his actions, but she had disappeared, likely with Rising Star to see the cornfields. They had already offered their farewells anyway. It was indeed the end of all things, and he would accept it.

"Are you going somewhere, Master Harris?"

He heard a voice behind him and turned to see Mark Reynolds looking at him and his bulging bag.

"I know the village is preparing to go on an expedition," Mark continued. "I thought I might try my hand once more at spearfishing." He chuckled. "It may be of great use for me to practice."

"I'm leaving," John announced.

"Good. I'll see you at the boats then?"

He shook his head. "You will not see me again, my lord. And since I have guided you here safely, I ask for the payment promised me."

The smile on Mark's face disintegrated into a picture of confusion. "You mean to say you are leaving us? Why?"

"I have my reasons, my lord."

Suddenly, Mark motioned him to follow. John resisted the gesture at first. He didn't want the man talking him out of his decision. But he also needed the money promised him, especially now that he was starting anew. He followed until they came to the lodging, where Mark disappeared. He soon returned with a small leather bag.

"You are an excellent guide, Master Harris," Mark said, handing him the purse of money. "I wish you well on your journey. Where will you go? Back to Jamestown?"

He shook his head. "No. I'm not certain where the Almighty will lead me, but it will be in the direction I need to go." He tucked the purse inside his leather belt around his waist. "Thank you for your sentiment." He could see the way Mark perused him, as if seeking out the manner of his soul. How he wanted to thrust up a shield to keep everything from the man's observing eye.

"I do hope you will find someone to whom you may express what ails you, Master Harris. God gives us those with whom to confess and to pray. To uphold and to guide. To help make right whatever is wrong. He doesn't want man to be alone, as one of the islands we have seen, alone in some vast ocean of trouble. He gives us men to help in times of need. To hold us up as they did the arms of Moses when one is too weak to go on, and we are alone, contending with our adversities."

John said nothing.

"All of us have trials and temptations, you know. We can sympathize with them."

John gritted his teeth. "You have not had my trouble."

"No, I haven't. I'm the least to offer my feeble hand of assistance in times of need. But God is stronger. When one is sinking into the ocean depths and death draws nigh, sometimes the hand of God is the only source of rescue to be had. I read of explorers that drowned long ago while seeking this new land. One of them, Sir Humphrey Gilbert, was caught in a storm off Newfoundland that destroyed his vessel. And it was told that he said, 'I am nearer to God by sea than by land.' Even in death, he called out to the one Supreme Being to receive him. To know that his Lord was there, even in a sea of trouble when death came calling."

"I, too, called out to God when death came calling. I pleaded my case before His throne." John ventured to a fallen log and sat down with a thud. "He stayed silent to my confusion. To my question of why? Why did this happen?" Suddenly it tumbled out in a fury. "Why did my brother, Robert, have to die like he did? He was young and eager. Only sixteen. A bright young lad. Full of life for a new land. Full of adventure and a yearning to see and learn." The emotion welled up within. John could see that fateful day played out as if it were happening right before his eyes. He told Mark how he had gone off to follow what he thought was a deer in the wood back in Jamestown. And then he heard the terrifying scream. He raced back to find Indians scattering, some holding glistening tomahawks. And Robert was there on the ground, crying out for mercy when there was none to be had.

He shuddered, unable to bridle the tears that stung his eyes. "I came to him. He was trembling so badly. His blood was everywhere. He said, 'John, I'm afraid. I'm so afraid to die. Please, don't let me die.' I tried to talk to him, to help him, but his life slipped away. And he was gone. He was alive, breathing, whispering to me. And just like that, he was no more."

Mark said nothing, though John heard a swift sigh escape. He lifted his gaze to meet the man's before him. "So please don't fill me with tales of fortitude when death is at the door. My brother saw none of it with his dying breath. He saw only fear."

Mark paused. He then asked softly, "And what do you see, John Harris?"

John turned away to see several Indians in the distance among the lodgings of Sandbanks. He clenched his fist and gritted his teeth. He fingers felt for the pistol at his side. He knew what it was that rose up inside of him. Hatred. Rage. Vengeance. The need to spill blood. A life for a life. It flowed so strongly in him that he could barely hold himself back. If not for Mark's presence, he might have acted upon the temptation that wrestled with his soul.

"John, I could say much, but they would only be words in your ears. I can't offer any comfort for your heart. Only God can, and He must reveal His strength to you. But I do urge you to leave now, before it's too late. Find a haven. Allow God to heal you wherever you find rest."

John was surprised at the words Mark spoke. He thought for certain the man would try to keep him here. He would fill his mind with scripture he already knew—of allowing God to take vengeance, of casting his burdens upon Him— verses that would fall empty on a cold spirit like his. Maybe that's why John didn't want Beth to know. She would try to heal him, too, when he couldn't be healed. No mortal man could heal him.

He stood to his feet and shook the hand Mark offered. "Thank you."

"God be with you, John Harris. And look to Him who holds all of us in the palm of His hand."

∞

Try as she might, Beth could no longer stay apart from John without some manner of reconciliation between them. As time passed, her feelings for him only strengthened. He had been her protector, as he promised he would. He had shared about the land he loved. He had been there for her through everything. Was it fair that she kept him at bay because of some manner of trial in his life? That she could not show him mercy as the Lord would have her do? If only she could take back the words she had spoken. If she could have bridled her tongue and not pressed him as she did, driving him further away rather than closer to her. Often she thought of his proposal—how eager he was to have her in his life. And while she did once doubt her love for him, she knew now that she loved him and wanted him to be her husband.

She searched high and low for John that afternoon, hoping to steal him away and confess these thoughts that had been her constant companion. But strangely, he seemed absent from Sandbanks. Perhaps he had gone on another one of his expeditions, maybe even to Roanoke Island once again, though she felt certain she would have heard of such a trip.

At last she found Mark. He appeared melancholy and not his usual jovial self, staring outward as if deep in thought. For a time she thought he might be ill. "Dearest brother-in-law?" she asked gently so as not to startle him.

He stood at once to his feet. "Beth, I didn't hear you."

"What is it? Are you ill? Is it Judith?"

"No, I'm fine. But I fear one of us is gravely ill."

Beth clasped her neck in distress. "Oh, no! Is Judith sick? Oh please, may it not be the fever or the pox."

"No, she is fine. 'Tis not a plague of the body I fear, Beth, but an illness of the mind within John Harris."

Beth lowered her hand. "I don't understand. He is ill?" All at once she envisioned her father and his distresses of the mind.

" 'Tis not like what afflicted your father," Mark said as if he could understand her worry, "but something I fear will destroy Master Harris in the end unless the Almighty intervenes."

"Oh, no. I asked him if he could share his trouble. But he gave no sign at all. No eagerness. No will."

"Beth, John's younger brother was brutally murdered by Indians near Jamestown."

The statement he uttered was like a blow to her heart. She sank under the weight of it, not caring that her dress drowned in a sea of dirt below. She had known something happened between John and the Indians but never realized it could be something this tragic. "H—how did it happen?"

"He told me he had gone off to hunt a deer and heard the scream. When he returned he found his brother, the life draining from him, a cry of fear in his words. And 'tis that fear John cannot reconcile. That there was no peace in the death, but rather fear unlike any he had ever seen."

"How dreadful." Now she could clearly see why John refused to tell her. So terrible a circumstance would be hard to even utter, yet alone reconcile without the strength of God. "Oh, I want to comfort him in his time of need, Mark. Where might I find him?"

"He's gone."

"Gone!" She flew to her feet, gathering her dress about her. "No, he can't be gone! He can't!"

"There is nothing you can do but allow God to minister to his heart and give him peace."

"You mean leave him alone with such grief? Let him go mad? Or even die? No! You don't understand. I have seen how the afflictions of the mind can tear one apart. It can kill swifter than any sword. I can't let that happen to John."

Mark quickly grabbed her arm. "Beth, you don't know where he has fled. For all you know, he is on his way back to Jamestown. 'Tis better this way. He can make peace with himself and with God."

"He can't make peace. He's had all this time to make peace, even before we set foot in this land. And did he? No. We are the only ones who can help him." She lowered her head. "Perhaps we tried too hard. I fear it sent him away instead of drawing him near."

"All you can do now is pray. You can't find him here in this vast land. No one knows where he went. You must entrust him to the One who holds us all in the palm of His hand."

Beth shuffled off, her heart overwhelmed by sadness, the tears flowing free. *If only.* She heaved a sigh. Maybe if she had said yes to his proposal that night, he would have shared the heavy burden of his soul. Maybe it would have been different. Now he was gone, and there was nothing she could do about it. She entered a forest of trees and a place of solitude. Mustering the strength, the words soon poured out. "Help him, God. Oh, help him, God. Please spare his life! Don't let this grief consume him. And help him know, somehow, that I care more deeply than even I knew. That I do want to become his wife. Oh, God, help him know my heart, wherever he is."

Chapter 12

John didn't want to leave, but he had no choice. No strength. No will to remain, even if he did pause numerous times during his journey to gaze back down the sandy coastline to the village of Sandbanks where Beth remained. If he had the fortitude, he would sneak back that night and whisk her away from the place and the people who had bewitched her. He would take her to their own haven where they could bask in their love and forget about the past. But it was not to be. Her feet were firmly planted in the village, and his were directed by his circumstances. Neither would change.

He chose, then, to be a wanderer of both body and soul. A wanderer through the desert as Jesus had been. What he would find, he didn't know. Would the devil try to conquer him there as he had tried to do with the Lord and Savior? John prayed not. He murmured a prayer, even as the wind whipped sand into his eyes and snarled his hair. He coughed a bit, thinking of the scripture, how Jesus stole away into the desert for forty days with no means of sustenance. Maybe this was what he needed to do to be cleansed. To wander about without victuals or a place to go, wander until he could go no farther, when exhaustion would finally overtake him, and he would fall to the ground in complete surrender.

But try as he might, he could not get Beth out of his mind. He wanted to go back and tell her everything, that evil had taken away his flesh and blood. How he heard the cries of Robert in some nightmarish delirium and felt helpless to stop what happened to him. He knew Beth would reach out to him with compassion. Her arms would cradle him, her voice crooning as one might to a child, seeking to drive away the torment. But he could not revisit it all again, especially not with Beth. And because of this decision, she had refused him. There was only one thing left to do. Travel as far as he could away from the pain and seek out a new place and a new life.

Soon he came upon a place similar to where he and Beth had looked for the talking shells and marveled at the screeching gulls that flew in the skies. The birds were there to greet him, laughing all the while before settling down in the sand as if asking for his companionship. He could confide in a gull of his woes.

He sat down to watch the ocean roar and foam before him. Waves lapped the shore, coming closer and closer with each pass. The gulls toddled on their twin legs that appeared like fragile limbs, looking around, seeking a victual to share. "I have no food," he told the birds. "All that I had I left behind, except for a few things in this satchel."

He opened it then and took out some papers. On one parchment, angry words spoke of a debt he owed back in England. The purse of money from Mark would cover that. The second note was from his father. Why he kept it, he wasn't certain. Nor was he certain why he took it out now to read.

> *My son, I beg you to reconsider what you are doing. The land of Virginia holds nothing. Your place is here, in our family fishing business, to continue what we have labored so long to bring forth. And yet, you wish to leave without my blessing. But in the least, you will not take Robert with you. He is to remain here, under my guardianship. In that, there is no question.*

John's hand tightened around the paper. He had disobeyed Father's order and taken Robert anyway. His parents would never forgive him if they knew what happened. "No, they would not," he said as a lone gull continued to keep him company while the others flew off, calling to each other. "I can't imagine a worser fate than telling them what happened to Robert. Even though he was excited and begged me to take him, it was my decision to have him disobey Father and allow him to come with me." Perhaps the guilt was twofold. Maybe he was seeing more than he had realized. Not only the guilt for Robert's death, but also the guilt for having brought him here against his parents' wishes. Could God be trying to heal him, as Mark had said? Or simply allowing him to wallow in further guilt and confusion?

John stood to his feet, crumpled up his father's letter, and tossed it into the ocean. It played on the waves for a moment until the water consumed it. "In this I rid myself of the past," he said. "My father's directives. My love for Beth. I toss it all away."

Suddenly the gull took flight, screeching as if in a warning. John spun about to see several men, outfitted in heavy armor, approaching. Instinctively, he felt for his pistol. He soon recognized them as the same party he had met back on Roanoke Island when he'd fetched the family's possessions.

"Ah, the one who rescued a fine lady's attire before we could make sport of it," the first man said with a chuckle. "Remember me? Anderson is my name."

"Yes, of course," John said, shaking the man's hand. "John Harris."

"And I am Edgar." The second man grunted, forcing a thick metal helmet from his head. "A grand sight indeed, this ocean. And not a soul to be seen anywhere about. We have been exploring these parts for several days."

"There are no white men," John agreed, "but there is an Indian village down the coast."

"Indians!" Anderson bellowed. "I thought they had long since left this place."

"They are still living there in a village they call Sandbanks. About a half day's journey south of this location."

"Are they friend or foe?"

"Friend, from what I've seen. Several even seem to have white men's blood in them."

The two explorers looked at each other. "From where, pray tell?" Edgar inquired.

"It is only an observation, but the family I led here believe the white men's blood may come from the lost colony of Roanoke."

The men burst into laughter. "Rather, you mean they have the colony's blood on their hands," Anderson growled. He brought out a snaphaunce pistol similar to John's.

"They are not a violent sort. They welcomed us. But I could not stay there any longer." John bent his head to see a few crabs skittering along the sand.

"Why?"

John glanced up to find the two men staring at him, ever curious. For some reason, he had no trouble confiding in them his hatred of the Indians at Jamestown for what they had done to Robert and how he would have nothing further to do with them. "But the family I led here insisted on staying at the Indian village. And since I have done what was required of me, I left."

"Too bad about your brother, my friend. I hear you, I do. The Indians are but heathen murderers, that's what they are. They don't understand that this land has been given to the white men by Almighty God, and we are the masters." Anderson stomped his foot to emphasize the point.

"Enough of this. Come show us this land, Mr. Harris," Edgar urged. "Do you know it well?"

"I know it," John said, even as they began walking along the shore. He took them north rather than south toward Sandbanks, glad for the friendly banter that temporarily rid his mind of the past. They talked of exploration, of the high cost in making such journeys, of the rumors of copper and other fine metals to be found in the area called Carolana, all for the gathering. But when they talked of the Indians, John said little. He would rather avoid the subject, even as they pressed him for more information about the Jamestown Indians and what they had done. When, at their insistence, John finally told them the details, anger filled the men.

"I killed an Indian once myself," Anderson boasted. "His friends came looking for me. That's why I came here. They can't be trusted."

For some reason, John thought of the Indians of Sandbanks; the girl named Rising Star; Wise One with his brownish hair and eyes so similar to those of a white man; the ones who talked of the white men as though they were friends. While he wanted to bask in the animosity shared among his fellow explorers, he considered the good things, things above, things they had done and his Beth among them. Rising Star and Wise One were innocent. And he had to admit, the other Indians of Sandbanks were innocent, too. They had nothing to do with what occurred at Jamestown. Then why did he possess some great boulder of anger, ready to thrust it at them and crush them to pieces? He swallowed hard. As if he had not already allowed that boulder to fall, even upon the one he loved. And the truth be known, he'd been crushed along with her.

"You have deep thoughts there, friend," Edgar commented. "But tell us, is this a place where we can live?"

"I would like to settle here," John agreed. "But I don't want to settle alone."

"Nary a woman to be found in these parts," Anderson chided, "lest you fetch her from Jamestown fresh off the ships."

John nearly told them of Beth's existence but stopped himself. Be they explorers, he knew, too, they were men as well, and he didn't want them stumbling upon her. She was his. Or she used to be his. He paused then, even as the two men continued on their journey, oblivious to the fact that he no longer walked with them. What was he doing? How could he leave her? How could he abandon the woman God gave to him by allowing grief to control his life?

"Are you with us?" the men called out.

John looked at the men. He turned and stared southward to where Sandbanks existed. No, he couldn't leave, not with everything he believed and the emotions he still carried. He loved Beth. He felt certain she loved him, too, despite what had happened between them. The separation would go no further. He would return, and somehow, by the grace of God, he would make her his wife. He would see that patience became his overriding virtue. And if he needed to confide in her concerning his past, so be it.

John shook his head. "I have duties to attend."

They laughed and asked what duties could beset him in this place of sand and sun. But John said no more. He would venture back to the village and, along the way, think about what he would say when he saw her. He couldn't plead sickness of the mind or some numbing fear. He would say that love had returned instead. It could not be forced into submission, but rather it drove him to his knees. Love was able to conquer all, even the darkest and most depressing moments of life.

"Find us when you have come to your senses," Edgar said with a chuckle. "We will be going back to Roanoke Island and our party. Perhaps we will meet again as we explore more of this place."

John wished them well before turning southward, to the beckoning sounds of love on the wind and the roar of the ocean waves. He walked slowly, considering what was to come. Never in his life had he been put in such a place. If only he knew what to do when he arrived and how to confess the past.

Just then he heard Robert's pleading voice in his mind. It filled him, drowning the thoughts of Beth with the age-old grief once more. *John, I'm afraid. I'm so afraid to die. Please, don't let me die!* The ocean filled his mind, followed by a scream. It was the gulls again, but it could have been the Indians, screaming sounds of victory. He wavered and closed his eyes.

"Robert, I'm so sorry," he said aloud. "I'm sorry I took you here when Father told me not to. I'm sorry I wasn't there to help you when you needed me most. Forgive me." He sucked in the air. A bird suddenly landed at his feet. It wasn't a gull this time, either, but a different one. A dove.

His heart leaped. A dove of peace. Surely this was a sign from Almighty God. He sighed and closed his eyes, allowing the pain of the past to melt away. There must be more to all this than what he could see with his eyes. Things eternal. The peace that Robert felt at this moment, even if he felt fear before he left the world. Surely he was at peace in a place with no pain, home with his Savior. How then could he, John, be troubled in spirit?

John continued south toward Sandbanks, to the woman he should have never abandoned to this unpredictable place. His pace increased in his eagerness to see her again.

Suddenly he stopped short. Someone was approaching quickly, running toward him. He thought he saw what looked like a spear. He glanced wildly about and took cover behind some scrubby brush. He withdrew his pistol, checked the weapon, and waited. The figure stopped, breathing hard, glancing to the left and to the right. John could plainly see it was an Indian, with his sparse clothing and beadwork native to the Sandbanks village. In fact, the man himself looked vaguely familiar.

The Indian began to call out. John wondered what he was saying. He saw no one else besides the Indian. Surely it could not be an ambush. The man looked as if he had come alone. Slowly John came out from behind the brush.

The Indian paused. His eyes were large, the wind catching his long hair. He pointed wildly in the direction of Sandbanks and began speaking some frantic gibberish.

"I don't know what you're saying," John muttered, "but I don't intend to go anywhere with you." Then, to his surprise, the Indian came forward, waving his hand. Ignoring the pistol John held, he grabbed hold of John's arm. "What are you doing, you scoundrel! Let go of me." Even when he brandished the pistol, the Indian refused to waver.

Then he heard familiar words uttered from the Indian's lips. "Cold Man! Cold Man sick! Come. Come."

John froze. Cold man. Where had he heard that before? Colman! The Indians called Beth—Beth Cold Man. "Beth? Are you speaking of Beth? Where? Tell me where she is!"

"Yes, yes. Come." The Indian raced off, urging John to follow with words in his native tongue.

He had no idea what had happened and wished with all his might he could understand the Indian's mumblings. Even so, the words rushed out, short and raspy from the quick pace. "Is—is she hurt? Wh–where is she? What has happened?" The Indian said nothing more. John could not settle the rapid beat of his heart, both from the travel and the fear, which again reared its head to confront him. He tried to calm himself, thinking of the dove of peace at the water's edge. God desired peace to rule his heart and mind. To allow whatever happened to rest in His hands. But even as he considered these things, fear again wrestled with him, trying to prove the more powerful force. He fought to subdue it with everything in his being. John wiped the dampness that collected on his brow and drifted down his temples. He prayed like he'd never prayed before.

When they came upon the canoe the Indian had left, he entered and took up an oar along with the natural. He knew the canoe would bring them back swifter than walking. The Indian never stopped to draw a breath or drink from the leather water sack at his side. John found it difficult to keep up but did what he could, even as his throat became parched and his arms began to seize.

Finally, when they came to the bank, he expected to find Beth somewhere nearby. Instead, to his astonishment, the Indian left the boat and sat down on the ground.

"You can't sit!" John shouted. "To your feet, man! Show me Cold Man!"

The Indian only sat still and closed his eyes. Frantic, John searched the landscape, shielding his eyes from the intensity of the afternoon sun. How could the man stop here of all places? If what he said was true and Beth was in trouble, they had precious little time to waste. Pacing back and forth, John again shouted at the man. The Indian would not be moved. He only sat upon the ground as if in prayer. None of this made sense. But he refused to see some Indian cause another's death. He drew his pistol. "Take me to Cold Man now," he demanded.

The Indian ignored him.

John gritted his teeth. "Why do you do this? Don't you know a life hangs in the balance? Another life that I refuse to sacrifice to your confounded ways?"

Without a word, the Indian suddenly leaped to his feet and pointed. John whirled, dropping his gun when he saw several people in the distance. He moaned and raced over to find Mark there, along with several Indians. They stood hunched over a figure lying on the ground.

"Mark!"

The man looked up. His eyes were glazed, his face clearly broken by distress. "John."

"What happened?"

"It's a snakebite, John. Beth suffered a snakebite."

John looked down to find Beth with her face beginning to redden. He could see the poison already battling with her body. Then he saw deep gashes on her frail leg, the blood trickling down her pale skin. He whirled, watching an Indian clean the sharp blade of a knife. "What did that heathen do to her?" His hand brushed his side, and he realized his pistol was missing. He lunged forward with his fists clenched.

Mark held him back. "John, they helped her."

"They did no such thing. They. . .they cut her. . . ." *God, please, not again. I can't bear this. Not another life sacrificed to this place.* He struggled with his own pain even as Mark gently explained how the Indian had cut her leg to suck out the poison. His sight grew bleary, watching the Indians bind up her wounded leg. He fought to calm himself. The Indians did not seek death in this place. This was not Jamestown. This was Carolana where the Indians struggled to preserve the life of his beloved.

"Life and death in Creator God's hands," a voice pronounced. John looked over to find that Wise One had arrived from the village. "This yours," Wise One said, handing him the pistol. "My councilor find it."

John took it slowly. "So it was your councilor who came to find me at the beach. But ask him why he stopped when we were so close. He just sat down and would not move. I could have hurt him had I not seen you all here with Beth."

"You no understand. He pray to Creator God," Wise One said solemnly. "You need strength, man of fire, more than you know. You white men think you know everything. But Creator God know everything. You understand this, you do well."

John could not believe what he was hearing. He gazed at the pistol he held. He would just as soon cast it aside in light of the words Wise One had spoken, words that offered healing and hope. Instead he placed the pistol deep inside a bag of belongings, out of sight and away from his hand. God had sent His messenger in the form of this Indian to help when Beth and he needed it most. He now worked with the Indians to construct a litter to bear her up to the village. *Lord, I have made my peace with the past. Now please, I beg Thee, Almighty God, help my love get well.*

Chapter 13

She heard the voices all around and wondered where they came from. Perhaps they were angelic voices welcoming her into a heavenly realm. That was, until she felt intense pain. She cried out. *What is happening to me?* Voices of concern filled the air. Then came the touch of hands, first on her hand and then on her leg. She felt herself being moved, and suddenly the skies above moved as well. She was being taken somewhere, where she didn't know.

Oh, how she wanted to sleep. She was so tired. She didn't need to rest from fatigue, but something else, some weakness that gripped her body with tentacles that wouldn't let go. When she tried to speak, the words refused to come. Instead her face felt very hot. Her eyes burned. Her leg burned even worse. All she could do was pray. *Dearest Lord, I don't know what's wrong with me. I don't know what happened. Please help me. Oh God, what about John? Does John know? How I want him to know.* She felt the tears in her eyes. It was no use. John was gone. Gone like the flowers that fade after a brief time of blooming. Gone like her parents who were no more. Despite her effort, as weak as it was, she had driven him away when he needed her and she needed him. *Dear God, forgive me.*

❧

God, forgive me, John pleaded. How could he have let this happen? Again, he had turned away, and again, another one he loved was stricken. He tried to listen, even as Mark insisted this wasn't his fault. Beth wanted to go find him. It was her decision. But, he reasoned, she never would have left the safety of the village had he not walked away and left her. Despite Mark's words of comfort, this *was* his fault. He had not allowed Beth's concern to soften his heart. Now it was too late.

He glanced down at her still form, borne up by the litter they had constructed from a blanket and several stout poles. The Indians, led by Wise One, insisted on carrying the litter, even when he asked if he could help. Instead, he walked alongside Beth, praying for her all the while. When they paused to rest, he thought he saw a tear trickle down her face. He wanted to cry with her but held it back. She looked dreadful with her red face and damp brow. Like a brave warrior, she was fighting the poison within her. No pistol could fight such a battle. Only her will could do it.

"She is strong," Mark observed as John watched her face. "I don't believe this is her time to leave us."

"If anything happens to her, I refuse to live," John said quietly.

"Don't confess such things. We can do all things through our Savior Christ who strengthens us."

"But I can't do this. Not again. I will not lose another."

"John, you must realize this was her decision. If you could have seen her determination to find you, to risk whatever danger lay ahead. She blamed herself, as you now blame yourself. She believed she had driven you away. That mercy failed to reach you when you needed it. I daresay you both are more similar than either of you ever considered."

Mark chuckled then, a strange sound to be heard at this somber time. But the words ministered to John's confused and hurting heart. In them, he did find a reason to rejoice, that he had not been wrong when he sensed he and Beth were meant for each other, that his quest, his journey to love, had not been in vain. God, in His wisdom, had brought them together, and now He must restore her so their journey might be completed.

When they arrived at Sandbanks, it appeared the entire village came out to greet them. Immediately Beth was whisked away into one of the lodgings. A leather flap closed, sealing Beth from view, even as an old Indian woman wagged her finger and spoke harshly to John. He knew what she meant—that he was to remain outside while they tended to Beth. He maintained a vigil by the lodging, waiting for any news. Rising Star came by with another beaded necklace she had made, but even she was turned away by the old woman.

Now the young Indian girl came and sat down beside John. He didn't know what to say to her. But looking at her large black eyes that stared up at him, he could sense her worry. "She will soon be well," he told her.

"I pray," the young girl said. "I pray to Jesus."

John stared at her. "You know about Jesus? Who told you?"

"Beth Cold Man. Say He Great Spirit of love. Say He heal like Great Spirit."

"Yes," John said, recalling the scripture that teaches that by His stripes one finds healing. He confessed it aloud, even as Rising Star sat patiently beside him. He found a soothing presence in the young girl, who seemed to help him in his faith, especially when tested in these murky waters of anxiety.

When John saw the leather flap rise and Judith emerge from the tent, he immediately stood to his feet. "What do *you* want?" she asked, her gaze leveled at him, her face rigid as stone.

"Is there any news of Beth? I've heard nothing."

"Yes, there is news. For all we know, she could die. How could you do this to her?"

John stared. "Madam, I—I don't understand."

"This all happened because of you! Beth went after you because you left the village. Oh, why did you make her fall in love with you? You don't understand how sensitive she is. How she always wanted someone to love her. . .and now she could die because of it. If only you had left her alone and not wounded her heart." Judith bent her head, allowing her tears to flow unabated.

His throat closed over in a hard knot. He found the words difficult. "I—I'm sorry for all of this. Truly I am. I—I didn't know she would come after me. If I had known, I never would have. . ." He paused. "It doesn't matter. None of this can be changed now. The only thing that matters is that she gets well."

"If she dies, I will have no one left at all. No one, don't you understand? I will be alone." She hurried off, the sound of her weeping echoing in his ears.

John looked back at the lodging where Beth lay inside, battling for her life. How he wished it were he in there instead of her. He would gladly have taken the snakebite and more.

Finally, after another agonizing hour passed, he could stand it no more. He simply had to see her. He lifted the animal skin that covered the doorway. Inside it was dark. He could barely make out the figure lying still on a bed made of poles and skins. When the old woman noticed him, she tried to shoo him away.

"No. I will see Beth Cold Man."

Reluctantly the woman stepped aside and allowed him to enter. A strange poultice lay on Beth's stricken leg, which had swelled to twice its normal size. Her breathing was labored, her face red, her dry lips moving. He stared long and hard, maintaining his silence, though inwardly he groaned. *God, if only I had known. If only she had given me a glimpse of her true heart. I never would have left. I would have stayed forever and waited as long as need be.* He heaved a sigh, watching the old woman come and change the poultice. "What is that?" he asked, pointing to the strange bandage.

She muttered in some foreign tongue. Then suddenly he heard the answer spoken in English.

"Red elm."

John turned to see that Wise One had also entered the lodging to stand by his side.

"Will. . .will she live?" he asked.

He shook his head. "No one know. No one but Creator God."

He looked back at Beth's feeble form, once so vibrant and alive, now teetering on the precipice of life or death. "She must live."

"Not for us to say. Only Creator God know."

"I thought you would believe in many gods," John muttered. "All this talk of Creator God. Who told you about God?"

"A white man long ago. He came with book and taught many things. It has been passed down. Many in village believe in Creator God. He true God. One God."

"Three persons in the Father, the Son, and the Holy Spirit, but one God," John added.

Wise One nodded. "And see? She hears your voice."

John looked to find Beth stirring. He slowly approached. "Beth?"

She then appeared to drift off once more into a land of peace, away from the pain and misery of life.

"Patience," Wise One said.

Patience. How he needed that along with faith. He sighed and retreated from the lodge to find the daylight slowly melting away with the coming shadows of evening. If only a new dawn would arise. If only the night would stay away and instead the sunrise would come. But night would fall and, as Wise One said, he must patiently wait for a new day.

⚬⚬⚬

Bright sunlight assaulted her eyes from the open doorway. She was in her room of stone at Briarwood, waiting for Father to call for her and Josephine to come with the morning bread. She stirred and tried to raise herself. She felt the pain in her leg and opened her eyes. Above her, a face peered into her own. It was wrinkled and dark, with large dark eyes and a swath of black hair fastened behind at the nape of the neck. This woman wasn't Josephine but some strange woman who even now fumbled with something on Beth's leg. Beth wanted to scream but forced the reaction away.

Suddenly everything came back to her in a tumult. The conversation with John when he asked her to become his wife. The utter sadness when she learned he had left after she told him no. Her voice begging Mark to go with her as she went seeking John by the great ocean. Then the pain of something on her leg and her screams at seeing a snake with its fangs tightly embedded in her flesh. *I was bitten by a snake,* she told herself. *Oh dear God, help me! Will I die?*

She tried to raise her head, but it felt like a large stone. She looked around for a familiar face, especially for the one she had sought to find when the snake found her instead. *John, oh, John. Where are you?* Tears slid down her cheeks. *Even now, when I'm so ill, you won't come. Oh, why?* She closed her eyes, hoping to bury away the pain of the bite and the agony in her heart. She was too late. Too late for love. Too late for life. Too late for everything, it seemed. She wanted to have a good, long cry, but even that proved too tiring. Everything took effort, even trying to reason out what had happened to her. *If only John were here. If only he could know that I care. . .that I love him.*

Then, just like that, he was there. Tall, commanding, dressed in the billowing shirt she found so appealing. She wanted to weep for the sight of him. Was it really him or some feverish delirium? It must be the fever. He couldn't have known about the snakebite. He had left, perhaps to meet up with the other explorers, journeying far away from her and from the love they could have enjoyed together. She turned her face to the bark walls comprising the lodge, unwilling to witness such a vision that tore her heart into pieces.

91

Then she heard his deep but gentle voice. "Beth."

She forced her head to turn. It was so slow to obey. There stood her vision once more. And then it spoke again to her.

"I'm here," the deep voice said gently.

John? You can't be real. Oh, dear God, please don't punish me with the sight of him. It's too much to bear. But his large hand that rested on hers felt alive with the warmth of life's blood flowing through it.

"Beth, I'm here," he said once more. "It's me, John. I will never leave you again. I will be here to protect you. Always."

John, oh, John. It is you!

∞

When he came in to see her the following morning, she was sitting up on the bed of skins, her eyes bright and alert, and to his astonishment, a smile lighting her face. "You look much better."

"I feel better, thanks to Rising Star's grandmother who knows medicine." She scrutinized the poultice on her leg. "Though I must say this poultice smells terrible."

He looked at her for a time until he found her returning his gaze. He immediately set his sights elsewhere. For some reason, he found the words difficult. What could he say after all they had been through? He knew he could no longer bring up the idea of a marriage covenant. But he still remembered that she had sought him out, even after her answer had been no and he had left. Surely that meant something was still alive within her, some manner of care, some bit of love left over to embrace.

He sat down by her bed. All at once it came to him, the words to say through a symbol of a covenant between God and man. He brought out the wooden cross he had whittled long ago in Jamestown. "I made something for you." He held it before her eyes.

"Oh, John, it's beautiful."

His lips twisted into a lopsided smile at her eagerness and the way she spoke his name.

She examined it carefully. "I know how much you like to work with wood. I've seen you whittling. God has given you a gift."

"My father always wanted me to be a fisherman, but I must say that I do like to work with wood. I considered one day that I might apprentice with a furniture maker or another of that sort." He chuckled. "But what is a furniture maker to do in a place like this?"

"I thought you only liked to explore."

"I do, but I like to create, as well."

She smiled. "I can see how the two are linked. God's work is a heavenly creation in the way of the ocean, the talking shell, and the seabirds."

"He made them all for us to enjoy."

She held up the cross. "And so, too, you like to make things for others to enjoy. I think you should become a furniture maker, John. There must be someone in Jamestown who can teach you the art. When we return, perhaps. . ."

He shook his head. "I can't go back to Jamestown, Beth."

She set down the cross, her eyes widening at this news. "Please don't say you are leaving again!"

"No. I won't leave, as I promised. Whether I'm to remain in this area or even Roanoke Island, I'm not certain. But I know I must stay here."

"Even if I ask you to go?"

Her question cut him to the quick. "Beth. . . ," he began. He felt the draw upon his heart, even more so as the deep color of her eyes pleaded with him. "I've betrayed my heart to you, and so I will not speak of it again. I will look to God who holds my life in His hands, wherever that may be."

Beth laid the cross beside her on the bed of skins. "Thank you for the gift," she said softly. "I must rest now."

He stood to his feet, bidding her a gentle farewell before stepping out into the brightness of a new day. Yet he couldn't help thinking of her words that echoed in his thoughts. *Even if I ask you to go?* He considered, again, the idea of an apprenticeship in the skill of furniture making. But the lure of this land, the ocean, the sands, all beckoned strongly to him. It had never faded, even with the time he spent in Jamestown. He loved this land of Carolana. He admitted he loved it as much as he loved Beth. If only he could have both.

Chapter 14

Beth was thankful for the quick return of her strength. Now able to move about the village, she smiled at the Indians who came to greet her. Rising Star became her constant companion, often fetching what she needed and then remaining by her side. Through their encounters, Beth talked more to the young girl about the Savior and found a captive audience to anything she wished to share. But the time she spent with John brought her the most happiness. He seemed a different person, as if he had made peace with his past. Though she often wanted to talk about that time, she restrained herself. She felt certain John would speak of it when he desired.

"We go see shell that speaks?" Rising Star asked one day while sitting by Beth's side as she worked on weaving a basket. Since stricken by the viper's bite, Beth had taken to learning other crafts to pass the time. The thick rushes that grew by the ocean made perfect tender from which to construct baskets. Though at times her hands became raw from the strips, she enjoyed the work.

"Not today," Beth said. "I know I'm better, but I think I still need more time."

Rising Star gazed longingly at the small trail they used to make their way toward the great ocean. Beth smiled at her eagerness. "My shell no more," Rising Star mourned. "Give it to another. Want more."

"You should have kept it. But I promise, as soon as I'm better, we will ask Mr. Harris to come with us and look for other shells. He knows the perfect ones." She sighed, for the mere thought of such a journey made her insides tingle. Yes, he did know the perfect shells. The perfect scenery, by the ocean waves. And yes, the perfect way to kiss by the roar of the ocean, even if she had been blind to it all. She picked up another reed, ready to thread it through, when she heard the rumble of thunder—or rather, the steady hum of some deep voice greeting her.

"You seem better, madam."

She glanced up, blinking at the full sunshine in her face. She saw the outline of a tall figure standing above her and the ever-present shirt that reminded her of clouds drifting in the sky. "Quite. And I am a bit handier these days, as well." She picked up a basket for his inspection.

"Perfect." John stood unmoving and silent. His presence filled her with warmth.

"And what are you doing this day? Staying out of mischief, I hope?"

"Indeed. I daresay your brother-in-law will try to convince me to do some spearfishing."

"Good! I expect you will return with a bounty for our dinner."

Again he only stood as a tower, the sun outlining his solid form. "Beth...," he began.

She looked over at Rising Star beside her. "Rising Star, go see if there are more reeds. I only have a few left to work with." She held up the reeds she needed.

The girl nodded and pranced away. John chuckled, settling himself down beside her. "You can read my thoughts."

She laughed. "I could never do that, Mr. Harris. You're a man who buries thoughts deeper than anyone I have ever known—with the exception, perhaps, of my own father."

"I'm trying not to keep those thoughts hidden but to reveal them to those who care." He picked up a slim reed and ran his finger across it. "I haven't spoken of the past, but your brother-in-law told me you knew."

"Yes. I'm dreadfully sorry to hear about your brother. You can't possibly know my grief for you."

"I think I do know. Anyone who would come after me, taking such risks, and then suffering a snakebite for me knows well. And she has a merciful heart beyond what one could hope or think."

"I prayed for that," Beth said softly. "I prayed God would give me a merciful heart, that I would understand and not condemn. I wanted to be a part of your life, John. Not just in the corner of it, lingering there, but right in the middle. Only it seemed you didn't want me there to share in your sorrow."

"I know, and I was wrong. I didn't really know the treasure sitting right before my very eyes, of one who cared enough to share my pain. You've had pain in your life, as well. You can sympathize with sorrow. I don't know why I was blind to it."

"We're not without our own enemies of the soul," Beth said. "Even scripture speaks of the pain of this life. But we can lay it all to rest, knowing God is the great victor." She watched as he rested his hand on hers. She did not stir, even as he leaned over to greet her with a kiss. This kiss proved more wondrous than the first, sealing a future covenant between them. There was no mistaking it, no driving it away, but only an eagerness on her part to embrace it.

All at once, they were jarred apart by some commotion stirring within the camp. Several Indians raced by, shouting at each other, pointing to the trail that led toward the beach. "Something's happening," John murmured in concern, helping Beth to her feet.

Just then, Beth saw Wise One stride forward, his face a picture of concern, his fists clenched.

"Wise One, what has happened?"

"White men come to the village," he said. "They have taken one of our own!"

Beth and John exchanged incredulous looks. "Stay here, Beth," John told her. "I don't wish you in danger, and you're still weak." He soon disappeared among the Indians, whose voices rose in fear and uncertainty. Beth began to pace, unable to believe what was happening. She prayed the first prayer to come to her lips. "Oh merciful God, help us!"

∞

John didn't know what to make of Wise One's announcement but entered the lodging where he kept his bag of meager belongings. He retrieved his pistol and tucked it into the belt around his waist. He joined the throng making haste down the trail until he stopped where they had gathered. Before them stood several white men, two of whom he recognized. They were Anderson and Edgar. To his horror, Rising Star stood between them, trembling. Sunlight was reflected in the tears on her face.

"Surely one of you heathens here speaks English!" Anderson shouted to them all. "Meet our demands, and she goes free."

"What is it?" Wise One said.

"Ah, I knew it! See?" Anderson said, slapping his cohort on the shoulder. "One of them does know English. Well, you see, we like your land here. A fine place indeed for a new village, a white man's village. So we're commanding you to leave your village."

"No! We no leave. This our land."

Anderson chuckled. "You don't understand, do you, Chief? If you don't leave, then we're obliged to keep the heathen girl for ourselves. We could use a good cook in our camp."

"This our land," he repeated. "We no leave." He paused. "Offer much. Beads. Fish. Corn."

"Not interested."

Wise One raised his hands. "No leave land of our fathers."

"Then I guess you don't care if you ever see this young thing again." He shook Rising Star's arm. She seemed to faint in his presence. "Let's be off, then."

John pushed through the crowd of Indians. "Anderson, wait!" he shouted.

Anderson stepped back in surprise at the sight of him. "Well, if it isn't John Harris."

Edgar hooted in agreement. "Glad to see that you came here ahead of us. You never told us what a fine place this is. Plenty of good land and a village to establish our presence here, with the water to our back and the ocean before us. Everything we could want."

"Let the young girl go. You don't need her to get what you want."

Edgar and Anderson looked at each other in surprise. "What's this?" Anderson retorted. "Surely you of all people aren't defending the likes of these murdering heathen."

"They've done nothing to you. They are innocent. Let her go."

"Innocent? The Indians have done plenty to you, or did you forget already? Murdered your own flesh and blood, they did! How you watched him die before your eyes. And now you can stand there and defend the likes of them? Stand with us instead."

A tremor seized John. He wavered. If only they had not brought up the pain once more. *Robert.*

Just then he felt a brush of wind. Out of the corner of his eye he saw Beth venture forward to stand by his side. "Beth, no," he whispered fiercely. "Please go back."

"No. We stand together, John. You and I. I won't have them deceive you like this." She linked her arm through his.

He gently removed her arm. "Please, I don't wish you hurt. Please go back."

She stepped back but a few paces, remaining just behind him, in his shadow, rigid in faith, with the strength he desperately needed at this moment. "Don't let them do this to you, John," she said. "Remember. Please!"

"So, Harris, what say you?" Anderson shouted. "Are you going to stand with us in the memory of your fallen brother? Will you defend his honor? And what better way than to declare this place for the white man, eh?"

John looked over at the Indian tribe that had gathered. Their dark eyes focused on him. He could see Rising Star's mother there, the grief written on her face, her eyes pleading with him. Then, the face of Wise One, standing firm, his arms crossed before him, his feet planted as if refusing to be moved. Just beyond him stood Mark and Judith, with Mark gently shaking his head no, his hand extended as if begging John to relent.

"Yes," John agreed, redirecting to Anderson and Edgar. "If you will allow me to come parley with you about the matter and you set Rising Star free in the meantime."

"Surely, though we keep the heathen girl with us as our bargain until they leave. We think it only fair."

John hesitated. "I will speak to the village councilors." He then noticed Beth's startled expression.

"John, what are you doing?" she cried. "You can't let Rising Star go with them! Have you lost all reason?"

"Please have faith, Beth. And say no more."

He nodded toward Wise One, asking him to summon the elders for a meeting. They gathered in a group, even as John kept the corner of his eye trained on Edgar and Anderson with Rising Star between them.

"Why you do this?" Wise One said sternly to John. "Now must we withdraw as the price of my councilor's daughter? We no do this. There be war first."

"I will not let anything happen to Rising Star, as God is my witness. But if we raise a confrontation now, many will be hurt. Maybe even killed by their fire sticks. They are not easy men with whom to parley. They mean to take what they wish. But there are other ways. I will go with them and seek an agreement to the matter."

"They are here for evil. And they have the daughter of my councilor."

"I swear upon my life and upon the Word of Almighty God that she will be safe. Let me deal with these men, for they are explorers like me. And if I fail, you may do as you wish."

Wise One nodded. John returned to address Edgar and Anderson. "Come, let us talk. The Indians are considering your proposal. And in the meantime we can eat hearty and discuss the matter."

"We are not changing our minds, Harris," Anderson warned. "And the Indian girl stays with us."

John said nothing, only murmured a prayer for guidance, even as he glanced back to see Beth's worried expression. He did not know what he would say or do when they arrived at the explorers' camp. He could only pray to God for an answer that would win back not only Rising Star but also keep the village of Sandbanks.

They didn't have to travel far before John came upon the base camp of the explorers. The other men of the party who had gathered around a fire immediately came to their feet upon their arrival. They inquired about the native girl and what Anderson and Edgar were up to.

"She's our bargain, she is," Anderson commented, accepting the cup offered to him. "If the heathen don't leave their village, she's ours."

Just then, John saw a man step forward, dressed in dark clothing. "What is this?" the man demanded. "Who is this poor child?"

"We are only keeping her for safety, Reverend," Edgar said. "Till the Indians leave, that is."

"And why must they leave? Have you informed Captain Browning of your deeds this day?"

John's ears pricked at this information. Captain Browning. So the men did have a leader among them. "I would like to speak to the captain, if I may," he said.

"And you are. . . ?" the reverend inquired.

"John Harris. Fellow explorer. A friend of the Indians."

Edgar and Anderson scoffed at his words. "He don't need to be telling our business to the captain," they both said at once.

"Anything having to do with this mission is important," the reverend said. "Please, Master Harris, come this way."

John found himself scrutinized by every eye as he made his way past six other men to the rear of the encampment and a shelter erected in the distance. There he met the lanky Captain Browning with a large map spread out before him.

"Captain, may I present Master Harris," said the reverend.

"To what do I owe the pleasure of this meeting, Master Harris?"

" 'Tis a grave matter I seek, sir, having to do with two members of your party—Anderson and Edgar. They have taken a young Indian girl captive, demanding an exchange for Indian land. They claim to do your bidding. So I have come to negotiate a compromise, if you will."

Browning put down his quill. "You must be mistaken, Master Harris. I gave specific orders that the naturals be offered compensation for their land. We favor its location in the marshland, you see."

"Captain, if I may say, there are plenty of equally fine areas to establish your-selves. The Indians only inhabit a small part of the Hatorask region. Surely you can find another place just as suitable."

"Not from what my men have reported to me. How is it you know the land so well?"

"I have been here many times, Captain. In fact, I led a party here myself from Jamestown a fortnight ago. If you wish, I will help you find a better place."

"Captain, the Lord would have us do well among the naturals of the land," the reverend added. "Are we not here to keep the peace and not brandish the sword? Can we not do better here than at Jamestown?"

"I have no intention of bringing forth a conflict, Reverend Robins," the captain said. "We were only to bargain with the Indians."

"A conflict you will have, sir, if your men do not release the Indian girl whom they are using as part of that bargain," John said. "She is the daughter of one of the councilors, and the Indians mean to make war if necessary to gain her release."

The captain frowned. "I did not give orders for captives to be taken." He called to the sentry. "Have the Indian girl released at once to Master Harris's guardianship. And bring me the offenders that I may deal with them."

Edgar and Anderson were hurriedly brought to the captain's tent. "Sir, we thought you would agree to our plan," Edgar began when Browning confronted them. "You trusted the matter to us."

" 'Tis a plan wrought by fools," he snarled. "We are not here to take land by force. Others have done so and were massacred, as it was in Jamestown and beyond. Now it may yet bring an Indian war party upon us for your foolish act."

"There is no need to be concerned," John assured the captain. "The head councilor of the village, Wise One, only wishes to live in peace with the white men. His village even cared for stranded men long ago. We think perhaps they might have once given shelter to survivors of the lost colony."

"And you dared to incite a rebellion with these people?" the captain bellowed to the two cowering explorers. "You will be dealt with in the utmost severity. Sentry, keep watch on them." He then turned to John. "I beg forgiveness for this matter. And I would like it indeed if you might show us other areas that would do well for settlements."

"If I may say so, sir, why not here? You have the sound to your back and the ocean before you. The land is good. 'Tis no different than at Sandbanks, I can assure you."

The captain looked about, even as John exchanged a small smile with the reverend.

"Aye, as it is with most things in life that lie right before our eyes. I will consider it. But if not, I do ask for your help in seeking another place."

"Certainly. And if you wish, sir, you would be most welcome to come parley with Wise One of Sandbanks, in whom you will find a beneficial ally in this place."

"Thank you, Master Harris. Without your help, I daresay we might have only brought blood upon this land instead of new beginnings. And our very names would have been cursed for all time." The captain offered his hand, which John shook.

Outside the shelter, the reverend likewise shook his hand. "Praise be for miracles!" the reverend exclaimed. "If I may ask, I should like to visit this village of Sandbanks. My desire has always been to reach the lost with God's saving message. And here you have made the way for me, Master Harris."

" 'Tis not my doing, Reverend, but the hand of a merciful God." John sighed then, thanking God for His blessings, even as he saw a joyful Rising Star run to embrace him.

∞

Beth remained awake, refusing to allow sleep to claim her. She had heard only fragments of John's plan and wondered what would happen. She hugged her arms close to still her trembling, thinking of Rising Star and John among those hate-filled men. Ever since the confrontation, she prayed for them and for her own strength to bear up under it all. She prayed they would call on God to help, that somehow through this they would all grow in their faith. But at that moment, her faith rested in God and the man named John Harris, the one who once despised the Indians, the one who listened as the men taunted him about his fallen brother and then urged him to side with them. If only she had confidence in this night and in John's wisdom. Even if her confidence waned at times, she could trust in God and His power working through John. God would not abandon them in their hour of need.

Rising Star's mother came to her then, a sad figure in the darkness, with the flames of the fire illuminating her distressed face. The Indian woman drew close to Beth as if seeking shelter from uncertainty. She began to mumble words in her native tongue. A bit of English came out of the woman's anxiety. "What they do?" she asked.

"I don't know," Beth told her, "but I do know John will do everything he can to bring Rising Star home safely. He cares for her as I do." She knew this to be true. He had said from the beginning he would protect and defend. And she believed he had experienced a change of heart, that anger no longer ruled him. She squelched her rising tide of doubt by placing her trust in him, for the first time in her life.

For a good part of the night, Beth and the Indian woman kept vigil by the fire kindled between them. Soon Judith and Mark came to join them, searching the darkness as Beth did, with only the call of insects and the sound of their anxious breathing to break the stillness. They sat side by side, shivering from the steady breeze, waiting for what seemed like hours, each of them thinking and praying. Only when they saw the flicker of torchlight and the sound of voices did they spring to their feet and head down the trail to meet the returning party. It was John with Rising Star and a stranger wearing black.

Rising Star's mother took the young girl in her arms, weeping for joy. Beth shook her head in wonder, staring at the wide grin painted on John's face.

"I'd like you to meet Reverend Robins," John said, stepping aside. Beth welcomed the stranger accompanying them—a short man dressed in dark clothing.

"A pleasure, madam," he said with a smile.

"Thanks be to God and to the reverend here," John said. "God was with us. And, thanks be to God, the captain of the exploration party was a man of sound mind and godly character. He made amends for the foolish actions of his men. Now I only need go with them on the morn to find another good place, and the matter is settled. Lest they find the land they now dwell in to their choosing."

"Praise be!" the reverend added.

Beth could only marvel over what had happened. Joy filled her heart, even as she followed John to the water pot. There he dumped water on his head from a large shell. "Ah, that is good."

"I can't believe this," she murmured, watching the water trickle through his hair and down his face. " 'Tis a miracle, John."

"I must say I'm amazed as well. I thought for certain I might have walked into a trap. Or onto a path of no return. But when I met the reverend upon arriving at the camp, I knew God was with me. And speaking of the captain, he is not unlike me, a man who wishes to settle in peace and without the bloodshed we have seen in Jamestown."

"Oh, John! So the men relented their claim to the land?"

"I told them there was plenty of good ground for them to build a separate village elsewhere, that the white men and the Indians could live peaceably together. That we could live as brothers—and the reverend agreed."

"John, I don't know what to say." Beth stared at him for the longest time, seeing the goodness flowing from him like milk and honey. How she loved him with all her heart. At one time she thought that Judith had found the perfect man with his merciful heart and the righteousness of God permeating his being. But now she knew she was blessed beyond measure to have John Harris for her own. She sighed. If only she did have him. The covenant still needed to be revived. How or when, she did not know.

⨯⨯⨯

The next day was marked by thoughtfulness and contemplation. At high noon, the Indians put on a feast with much food and drink to celebrate the return of their beloved daughter, Rising Star. During it all, Beth saw John off by himself as he had done when they first arrived, whittling on a stick. Only this time he seemed content, with a smile on his face, as if he had found his own special place among it all.

Beth slowly approached him. When she did, he directed a smile toward her. "This is indeed a time to rejoice." He showed her another cross he had whittled. "I will give this to Rising Star as a token of remembrance." His smile faded away. "But it seems my lady has some other matter on her mind?"

"John, I'm sorry to say this. . . ," she began.

Immediately he stood upright as if ready to face yet another plague upon his being. "Beth? Is something wrong?"

"There is still a matter that must be dealt with," she said.

"What?"

"If you don't know by now, John Harris, then I think we still need a long talk between us."

He appeared confused. "I don't understand. Have we not spoken openly? I've kept nothing else in secret, if that is what you fear. I've tried to lay everything open to you."

"We have accomplished our quest in this journey. But now I wish to know of your own personal quest."

He chuckled, and his smile returned. "Ah. My own quest. Miss, you needn't concern yourself with it. I'm quite fulfilled. . . ."

Immediately she sensed sorrow at these words. She thought he would leap at the idea that she hinted at a marriage covenant. But had that all changed, too? Was it now lost forever?

". . .Or rather, I *will* be fulfilled if you were to remain by my side forever. And so I ask if—"

"Yes!" she interrupted with glee.

"But I haven't yet finished my question to you," he said, his voice expressionless but his eyes twinkling in merriment. The chuckle rising up within him played like music to Beth's ears.

"You have indeed, Mr. Harris, who is my personal guide in matters of the heart. And my answer to you is—yes, forevermore!"

Chapter 15

"Dearest Beth, you must hold still if you want me to put this on right," Judith said, rearranging the wreath of flowers in her hair.

Beth tried but couldn't help shuffling her feet in anticipation. She felt Judith's hands steady her, a broad smile filling her sister's face as she secured the wreath to Beth's head. For so long, Beth had dreamed of a day like today, when she would meet her love and accept his hand in marriage. And now it was about to happen, with the man she met here across a wide span of ocean, to the very place where he had been waiting. Even now, she could picture John waiting anxiously by the tribal fires, along with the reverend, who had been with the other explorers and who, since the incident with Rising Star, had taken up residence within the village of Sandbanks. She sighed, thinking how perfectly Almighty God had arranged everything. Only He could have done it. Only He could have known the secrets of the heart and brought her the perfect man to fulfill her deepest longing.

Beth whispered a prayer to calm herself. In the distance, she could see the villagers gathering to watch a white man's ceremonial marriage. No doubt they were curious. She was thankful Reverend Robins was here to conduct the ceremony. She could not help but giggle over it all.

"Why do you laugh, Beth?"

"Oh, Judith. . .to see how much God loves us all. And to think, even with the explorers who came seeking mischief, the Almighty used it to bring a man of God here to Sandbanks who can conduct our marriage."

"'Tis indeed a wonder," Judith agreed, stepping back to observe her. "And you, dear sister, will be a wonder to your husband-to-be."

Beth felt for the ring of flowers cradling her head and touched the necklace of shells about her neck, a gift from Rising Star. When they heard the beat of a drum, Beth came forward slowly toward the array of people, both white and Indian, assembled before God to witness a covenant of love. But at that moment, Beth's gaze turned away from all the well-wishers to center on the one she loved with all her heart. Their eyes met. Their gazes lingered. A small smile fell across John's lips. His face glowed in the sunlight. He wore the billowing white shirt she loved. When his hand grasped hers, she felt peace and joy in the same instance. Facing the reverend as one, they spoke their vows and were married before the eyes of Almighty God and the witnesses there gathered.

After the proclamation was given, cheers arose from the masses, led by Mark and Judith. They grew into a tumult that echoed throughout Sandbanks. Drums began to beat. Indian children danced in circles. Women laughed. Beth felt the embrace and tears of her sister, who gave her a kiss.

"I'm so happy for you," Judith whispered.

"I am, too," Beth admitted, with a sideways glance toward her new husband. John received handshakes from Mark and good wishes from Wise One and his councilors, who rewarded him with a pipe, feathers, and an earthen pot filled with seed corn.

"May Creator God shine upon you," Wise One said solemnly.

John bowed before the Indian, who seemed to have aged in the weeks they had been there. "Thank you. May His face shine on you and this village as well." John then took up Beth's hand as if to share in this hope with her. She welcomed his touch, especially when she began to think of their new life and all the challenges yet to face.

At that moment, Rising Star came up to greet them. At first Beth smiled until she noticed the girl's cheeks glistening in the sunlight. They were wet with tears. "I miss you, Beth Cold Man," she said. "I ask you not leave, but I know you do."

"Yes. But we will see each other again someday. God keep you in His tender care."

Rising Star dried the tears from her face and held up a shell. "Talking shell," she said proudly. "The one we see at water. I get another. So I give to Beth Cold Man to remember."

Beth couldn't help but laugh as she took the shell, thinking how much it had shown love to her—first by a man who used it to display the wonders of the sea, to the time when she showed the love of the Creator God to Rising Star. "John, look. It's our shell."

He took it and held it up to his ear. "It's playing the same music we once heard and kissed to, my dear."

She giggled before thanking Rising Star for the gift. The girl nodded, shyly backing away until she ran off to her mother's lodging. There were more gifts, earthenware, even a pair of leggings for each of them, and fine beadwork. Looking upon it all, Beth couldn't help but feel sadness. Soon they would leave this place, she felt certain. Perhaps to return to Jamestown and establish a fine plantation on the James River. But she wondered of her promise to Rising Star. Would she ever see the young girl again?

⋙

"You are very quiet," John observed. "Too much excitement for one day?"

Beth glanced over to see but a glimpse of John's face, the rest of him overshadowed by the night. He was propped up on one elbow, staring at her. How she did love him. It had been a sweet time together after the ceremony, with the Indians giving them their own lodging for the night. But once more she sensed a new part of her life waiting to be written. The next chapter that began with this marital covenant. As it happened once before in England upon the death of her father, she now wondered about the future. What should she do? Where would they call home?

" 'Twas a wonderful day," she said with a sigh, intertwining her fingers through his. "I only wonder about our future. Where we should go and make our home?"

"I'm quite certain I know," he said quietly.

She glanced over at him. Surely he couldn't know her thoughts, though she had heard from Judith how much she and Mark often came up with the same idea in the same instant. Not that she had any idea for the future. There were only four possibilities. Return to England from whence they came. Go back to Jamestown where they had first met. Find another place to dwell within Virginia or Carolana. Or stay here in the village. But none of them seemed right.

"You want to go back to England," he said solemnly.

She stared at him in surprise. "Why do you think I'd want to go back there?"

He shrugged, stroking the top of her hand with his thumb. "I remember how you were when we first met. Unsettled and unsure. You looked as if your heart remained in your homeland."

"Do you have people waiting for you there?"

He shrugged. "My parents. They would be sad for certain to know what happened to one of their sons."

"But what happened to Robert was not your fault."

He hesitated. "Yes, it was. My father told me not to take Robert. He went anyway."

"But did you steal Robert away out of disobedience to your father, John? Or did he come willingly?"

He twisted his lips. "Actually, Robert sneaked aboard the ship. But I didn't tell him to leave, either, when I found him. He begged me to take him."

"Then it was your brother's decision to go. And you did all you could for him. Cease blaming yourself for this. He is at rest."

John sighed. "And what about you? Are you at rest?"

Her head found a place of comfort on his shoulder. "If you mean at this moment, yes. And I have no desire to return to England. When I left Briarwood, I left it forever and took my heart with me."

His hand caressed her hair. "Then we can at least say that the New World is now our world. So where would you like me to build you a home?"

She opened her mouth to offer an opinion, only to quickly shut it. If only she could know his thoughts. Where he truly wanted to be. She thought long and hard. Then she saw it. His blue eyes sparkling at the mention of Hatorask. His gaze encompassing the vast ocean. His large hand scooping up the talking shell. His first kiss as the waves came forward to lap at their feet. It seemed so plain to her eye at that moment. "I think I know what to do," she began, "but we've only been married a day. I want this to be our decision, not one or the other."

"I agree. It needs to be from our hearts."

They remained quiet, each thinking and listening to a heart beating rapidly, accompanied by the sound of insects buzzing outside the dwelling.

Then it came at once like a chorus of hearts turned into one.

"Hatorask?" they both said.

Beth and John broke out into laugher before their arms found each other in a tender embrace.

"Hatorask it is," John said with glee.

Peace filled her heart. Yes. Hatorask, indeed.

⁂

"We shall miss you dreadfully," Judith said with a sigh as they gathered together for their final meal. Beth could hardly swallow down the morning's cornbread for the thought of leaving her sister. Mark and Judith would be returning north to Jamestown, while she and John would be drifting toward Roanoke Island in search of a place to build a home. "There is no one here, Beth. No other women. And no church."

"The reverend has said he wishes to remain in this area," John added. "We are already seeing people coming from the north. This is a wide-open land. It won't be long before there are settlements."

Beth could see the longing on Judith's face. She didn't know what to say. "Jamestown is but a few weeks' travel," she added with hope. "John knows the way. We will see each other again."

Judith barely touched her breakfast. The distress on her face was evident. Beth then realized what plagued her sister. They were all that was left out of the family. All they had was each other, and now they would be separated.

"I think 'tis best we get ready," Mark told Judith, gently ushering her to her feet. "We have found another Indian who can guide us back to Jamestown," he said to John.

"And what of your quest, sir?" John inquired.

"There are still questions left unanswered, Master Harris. Answers known only to God, I daresay. But I'm very much satisfied with the conclusion, that is, the new Indian friends we have made and the new brother-in-law I welcome."

John smiled, even as they both shared a hearty handshake.

Judith embraced Beth. "I shall miss you dreadfully, dear sister. A few weeks' journey seems so far away. But I know God has you in His tender care."

"Good-bye, Judith." With a sigh, Beth stepped back. Judith returned to her possessions, hardly giving her another glance, as if it proved too painful. Slowly

Beth made her way to where John had assembled their belongings, along with a few Indian porters who would help them bring their possessions to a canoe resting in the water.

"You don't regret your decision. . . ," he began in concern.

The distress must be evident on her face. She lowered her eyes and managed a smile. "Of course not. Judith is all the family I have left. But I know we can't be far apart with God watching over us both."

He nodded, though quietly observing the moroseness that plagued her. When they began the trip, Beth soon forgot about the emotional departure and concentrated instead on a new land. When they arrived at the place where they had first shared their kiss, she asked John to leave the canoe there. They approached the beach to find the waves rolling against the shore, bringing with them many shells that would whisper their welcome.

"This was an interesting journey here," she marveled. "And now we can claim this place for God and for the Harris name."

"The Harris name?" he wondered.

"Of course. A blessed name, and I am the most blessed woman."

He chuckled. "I'm glad you found joy in this journey. 'Twas difficult for me, I must say."

"But look what we found at the end. New discoveries. Friends. Healing in our times of greatest need. Love. More than anyone could ask or hope."

"Praise be to His name," he said softly, gathering her in his arms. "So are you ready to call this land of Hatorask ours?"

"Yes, dearest John. Let us begin."

Lauralee Bliss

Lauralee is a published author of over a dozen historical and contemporary novels and novellas. Lauralee enjoys writing books that provide readers with both an entertaining story and a lesson that ministers to the heart. Besides writing, Lauralee enjoys hiking in the great outdoors, traveling to do research on her upcoming novels, and gardening. She invites you to visit her Web site at: www.lauraleebliss.com.

CORDUROY ROAD
TO LOVE

by Lynn A. Coleman

Dedication

To my son, Tim, and his wife, Farrah—the newest member of the family.

Chapter 1

I da Mae, I can't believe you're renting the barn to a tinker. I daresay, isn't he a week late?"

"Minnie, I told you he's a tinsmith, not a tinker."

"Tinsmith, tinker—doesn't matter, he's a stranger. He's not one of us, Ida Mae, and you ought to know better. With the way your pa and ma... Well, mark my words, it ain't right, you letting a stranger move in so close to ya. Unless you're reconsidering Cyrus's offer."

Ida Mae loved her cousin, but sometimes the woman could really tangle her threads. "No, I'm not going to marry Cyrus Morgan. He's a kind man, but the Lord and I have an understanding."

Minnie's brown hair swayed back and forth as she shook her head. "Ain't no man going to fill that understandin', as you say. Only one that could is the good Lord Himself, and He chose not to marry when He was on this here earth. So I say you're aiming to be a spinster, in both meanings of the word."

Ida Mae often thought it odd that her profession was also the name for an old woman who never married. And it seemed odd that Minnie, who was nearly the same age as herself, would feel the need to inform her on the ways of man, courtship, and marriage. Ida Mae sat back down and started spinning the flax into threads. Tomorrow she'd have to get to work on the wool brought in by John Alexander Farres. Folks used John's middle name to help distinguish him from the various cousins in the area. Not that she should have a problem with that, since she answered to her first two names.

"I give up." Minnie stomped out the front door and headed across the street.

Ida Mae closed her eyes and prayed she hadn't offended her cousin again. Minnie and the rest of the family meant well, but it seemed ever since her parents died last year, everyone thought they had a right to tell her what to do. Ida Mae blew a strand of blond hair from her face. The order of flax needed to be spun before she could begin work on the woolen yarn for the Farreses. Mama used to weave the linen threads into fine cloth, but Ida Mae didn't have the same hand. The woven cloth was adequate and could be used for work clothing and such,

111

but it wasn't the kind of fabric that could grace the tables of elegant homes.

Cyrus had been mighty helpful after the fire that had killed her parents and destroyed their home last year. He had single-handedly performed most of the reconstruction. But she couldn't marry him. She didn't love him, not like the Bible talked about in the Song of Songs. *Cyrus is a good man but. . . I don't know, Lord, is there something wrong with me? Am I made like the apostle Paul and meant to be single all my life?*

A wagon full of wares pulled up outside the storefront that had been doubling as her living quarters for the past year.

A man with an odd-shaped hat jumped down and secured his horse. He marched up the steps right to her open front door. "Good day, would you be Miss McAuley?"

"Yes, sir."

He swooped off his odd cap, revealing a healthy crop of black hair, and bowed slightly. "Pleasure to make yer acquaintance, Miss. I'm Olin Orr. I believe you've been expecting me."

Ida Mae tightened her jaw to make certain she hadn't dropped it. No man had ever bowed to her before. Folks around these parts weren't lacking formal manners—they just didn't have much use for them. Not like Mr. Olin Orr from the big city of Philadelphia, Pennsylvania. His hair was a mixture of silk and dark walnut, and curls that a woman's fingers could have fun— Ida Mae quelled her foolish thoughts. "Yes, your post said you'd be arriving last week."

"Aye. I'm afraid I misspoke in my correspondence. The roads were far worse than I recalled them. I often had to make or repair some corduroy roads in order to pass with my wagon. Springtime brings many showers and the creeks are up."

"I see." She could well imagine how many trees he'd had to cut down to get over those muddy holes. But she wondered if he was the type of man to place the logs securely over the road for the next passerby. She glanced at his wagon in front of her shop; even riding over the felled logs, it must have been difficult because of the constant bumps, so like corduroy fabric. In fact, she should fell some trees on the road leading up to the family homestead, but she didn't see much point since she wasn't using it. "Let me show you the barn. I hope it is what you were expecting. I tried to be honest and fair with our dealings, Mr. Orr."

"Aye, more than fair, Miss McAuley."

Ida Mae nodded and headed out the front door. She locked it, then gestured to her right and walked north toward the end of the building. Mr. Orr followed close behind but left a distance of several feet between them until rounding the corner and stopping at the door to the smithy. Father's blacksmith shop was a stable that he had converted. It seemed the perfect place for a tinsmith. But she had hoped the man would want to blacksmith. Too many folks had high dreams of finding gold like the members of the Reed family had found on their property thirty years ago. The Reed farm was a gold mine now, and word around town was they were talking about digging tunnels to remove ore from the quartz rock below, unlike the way they had been mining. Gold had been found on various farms all over the area. The way folks were moving into the area, you'd think they were just fortune seekers.

"What brings you to Charlotte, Mr. Orr?" She slid the large board to the right to open the barn door.

"Work," he answered. That, she already knew. For a man who could toss out some fancy words, he sure seemed quiet when it came to details about his personal life.

Slivers of sunlight poured into the old shop. Ida Mae hadn't stepped foot in here since her father's death. A knot in her stomach threatened to squeeze the tears right out of her. She cleared her throat. "I'll let you have a look around. I'll meet you back in the store."

"Thank ye, Miss." He plopped that odd hat back on his head and stepped inside.

Ida Mae couldn't face the memories of her father and hustled back to her shop. Quickly setting her hands to the wheel and her foot to the pedal, she began spinning the flax once again.

∞

To do his tinwork, Olin didn't need the equipment that the blacksmith had used. But the additional income from making horseshoes and such was worth keeping the equipment in place. The shop had a year's worth of dust and grit all over the tables and equipment. His parents had written and told him of the tragedy that had befallen Thomas McAuley and his wife. It seemed odd that a man who worked with fire would die by it in his home. He'd heard of blacksmiths dying in accidents relating to their work—but that was between Mr. McAuley and his Maker.

Stepping back into the open doorway, he looked over the town. It had changed in the past seven years he'd been gone. Olin wondered how many would remember what happened before he left. He had been seventeen at the time and full of himself. *Should I have stayed away, Lord?*

Thankfully, Ida Mae didn't remember him. Not that she would, he supposed. She was two years younger. And by the time she was twelve she had stopped going to the church school to work full-time with her parents. They were an older couple. She was ten years younger than her brothers, who had all moved away with the promise of larger amounts of land in the frontier.

He would have gone west if his father hadn't intervened and set him up in the apprenticeship. He slapped the dust from his hat and gave the barn one final glance. Taking a determined step forward, he headed back into the store.

"Mr. Orr, is it satisfactory?"

"Aye, Miss. I'll bring in the twenty-five dollars after I visit with the bank tomorrow. Is it all right if I begin moving my belongings in now, or would you prefer I wait until a lease has been signed?"

"Beggin' your pardon, Mr. Orr. I'm afraid I should wait until the papers and money have been exchanged."

Olin nodded. He would have done the same if a stranger had asked him. "You're a fine businesswoman. I'll see ye on the morrow. God's blessing to you."

He strode up to the wagon and checked his horse before pushing on the extra thirty minutes to his parents' farm. He would have preferred to leave the wagon in the barn to lessen the horse's burden. On the other hand, he had a few gifts for his family stowed in the wagon. The animal needed a good grooming and a comfortable stall to sleep in. Ida Mae McAuley's barn had room for one horse. The loft would make a suitable place for him to live until his business was established enough to provide sufficient income to support himself. Mother would make sure he had enough to eat. He'd been sending money home for years, but he'd also had few expenses in Pennsylvania. The closer he came to the old farm, the more memories swarmed around like a stirred-up hornet's nest. He supposed it only seemed fitting since the area had a reputation of being a hornet's nest from the Revolutionary War.

One of the things that seemed different was passing slaves working on a large plantation just outside the city. Years ago that property had belonged to three different yeoman farmers, like his parents. Each had lots of five hundred acres, enough to make a profit, but not so much that a man would need to hire slaves.

"Olin!" His mother ran out the door with outstretched arms.

Joy erupted through his body. *Aye, it is good to be home.* He jumped down from the wagon and wrapped his mother in a bear hug. He'd missed this woman and, until this moment, hadn't realized just how much. It had been seven years. *Why didn't I come sooner?* "Mother, it's good to see ye."

She wiped her blue eyes with her apron. "Aye, it's good to see ye, son. I thought I'd never see ye again."

"I'm home, Mother. I plan on staying and living here the rest of my days."

"Well, God be praised! Then it was a good thing ye left for seven years. Now I shall see ye marry and give me lots of grandbabies."

Olin chuckled. "I had better find a wife first, Mum."

"Aye, or I would do a whole lot more than just pull your ear."

He rubbed his right ear, remembering all the times he'd been hauled off to the woodshed to be paddled by his father for misbehaving.

"Your father says you'll be living at Mr. McAuley's blacksmith shop. Ye need to stay here. I won't be having ye living in no barn. No son of mine—"

"Mother, please." He cut her off. "There's plenty of time to discuss this, but let me take care of my horse. He's worked hard."

"Aye. I'll be settin' a place for ye at dinner."

"Thank ye. It's good to be home."

Fresh tears spilled from his mother's eyes. He turned as his mother left. His own eyes moistened as he unfastened the carriage from his horse. He patted the brown stallion. "I bet that feels good, boy."

Carson neighed his approval.

Olin gave the familiar *cluck*, and the horse obeyed, following him to the barn. Fresh oats, water, and some overdue grooming set the beast up for the night. Finally, Olin pumped some water into the outdoor basin and cleaned off some of the caked-on road grime.

"Well, well, it's the devil himself!"

Olin spun around.

❦

"Ida Mae, Ida Mae!" Minnie came running into the shop, breathing hard. "You'll never believe this, but Mr. Orr is not a stranger. He's from around here."

Ida Mae glanced up from her spinning. *I already suspected that.* "Several Orr families live around here."

"Yes, but how many do you know are murderers?"

Murderer. Ida Mae stopped the wheel. "What are you sayin'?"

Minnie's brown eyes darted back and forth. "Rumor has it that Bobby Orr killed another miner seven years back."

"I can't be going on rumors. What are folks sayin'?"

"Well, you remember seven years back when there was some fighting going on at the Reeds' gold mine."

"There's always fights going on at the gold mines."

"Well, this one ended in a fella getting killed. A Bobby Orr was the one responsible for the man's death."

"Honestly, Minnie, I don't see what this has to do with our Mr. Orr."

"That's just it; he's the same man."

"His name is Olin. Folks must be mistaken."

Minnie tossed her head back and forth. "Nope, he's the one. I tell ya, he's the same man."

"How do you know?"

"Folks seen him, that's how. Not to mention, his own kin been tellin' folks he's comin' back, and they ain't none too happy about it neither. They say he's the devil himself. He has a temper that makes the devil run."

Ida Mae took in a deep breath and let it out slowly. She didn't care for gossip and knew Minnie could keep a person's ear full for years. *But is it true, Lord?* She had to admit, she was concerned.

"Ain't he planning on livin' in the shop? I don't mean to tell ya your business,

115

Ida Mae, but I wouldn't be sleepin' on the same property with no killer. No sirree!"

Fear spiraled down Ida Mae's spine like a thick wool thread spun on the spooler. She'd been putting off moving back into the farmhouse. Maybe it was time. "There must be some mistake; Mr. Orr is a perfect gentleman."

"Don't be fooled. Even the Good Book says the devil—he comes as an angel of light. I'm tellin' ya, nothin' good can come of this, Ida Mae. You best tell him to pack his bags and move on."

And wouldn't her father roll in his grave if he knew she'd treated someone so poorly, not knowing for certain if he was guilty? "If he's the one, why wasn't he arrested and hanged?"

Minnie marched back and forth with her hands on her hips. "That's the odd thing. No one seems to know. All folks can say is that he got away with murder and left. Maybe his daddy paid off the sheriff. 'Course, they never found any gold at the Orrs' farm. I don't know, Ida Mae, but it don't seem right."

"Minnie, thank you for telling me. I'll speak with Mr. Orr when it is appropriate and ask."

"I'm tellin' ya, mark my words, that man is trouble. Even his own kin ain't none too happy. This just ain't a good thing, Ida Mae."

You've already said that. "Thank you, again. Let me get back to work and finish up this order. I need to go out to the farmstead before dark."

A glint in Minnie's eyes made Ida Mae aware she'd said or done something that met with her cousin's approval. There seemed to be precious little that did since her folks died. Why Minnie had decided to become Ida Mae's self-appointed guardian, she would never know.

"I heard Cyrus was going out there this afternoon. He's planting for you."

Yes, I know that. "I might just run into him out there. What are you folks planting this year?"

"Cotton, beans, some corn. . . Same as usual. What are you an' Cyrus planting?"

Ida Mae didn't like hearing her and Cyrus's names wrapped together in the same sentence, knowing what Minnie and others thought. "Those, plus a few other vegetables. I'm hoping to do some more canning."

"How's your peach and pecan trees coming along?" Minnie asked, and the two of them talked for the next ten minutes about farming and marketing the farm's surplus.

If only the road to the north was in better shape, Ida Mae mused. Then she remembered Olin saying how he'd repaired quite a few places along the road. *A killer wouldn't do that, would he?*

After Minnie left, Ida Mae finished the flax order and rode her horse out to the family farmstead. The peach blossoms were in full bloom, lining the road to the house. The rebuilt two-story federalist-style house was freshly painted. Cyrus did fine work. How could she ever convince him she wasn't interested in marrying him? Perhaps she *should* marry him just to ease her conscience.

Ida Mae's thoughts wandered to her childhood days as she rode up the drive. Her parents' farm was smaller than most in the area, and her father had been content with small crops, especially when demand for his blacksmith talents became more lucrative than farming. When her older brothers were able to tend the land on their own, her father bought an old barn in Charlotte and transformed the north half into a smithy and the south end into a shop for his wife's spinning wheels and loom. Her parents hadn't anticipated that the boys would head west, leaving the farm available for Ida Mae's inheritance, either to sell or to work the land with her future husband. How quickly things had changed.

As she reached the end of the drive, Cyrus's rugged, six-foot frame slipped out of the barn. He was a good enough looking man, and he was kind. He'd make a good father, she tried to convince herself. He smiled and waved.

"How ya doin', Ida Mae? I didn't expect to see you out here tonight."

The barn door creaked open.

Rosey Turner peeked around the door, her hair all mussed.

"Cyrus?" Ida Mae pointed to Rosey.

Crimson filled Cyrus's cheeks. "Uh, Rosey came to lend me a hand tonight."

Chapter 2

"Percy Mandrake, what brings ye here on this fine day?"

Percy relaxed his accusatory stance and turned toward Olin's father. "Uncle Thomas. Good to see you."

Olin stretched his neck from side to side to release the tension that had filled him when Percy surprised him from behind. There never had been any love lost between him and his cousin. Each meeting tended to end in fisticuffs. Olin redirected his gaze to his father. It was good to see him. He had aged some in the last seven years but still retained his rugged stance and the square set to his shoulders.

"Aye, but we've not seen ye for pretty near a year. Is your mother all right?"

"She's fine." Percy turned toward Olin. "I heard Bobby was back in town and thought I'd pay him a visit."

"Well, that be mighty nice of ye. Your aunt has put on quite a spread. Would ye care to stay for dinner?"

Olin dried his hands on the towel kept by the pump.

"Don't mind if I do."

Give me grace, Lord. Olin placed the towel back over the pump handle. He thought about telling his cousin he went by his given name now, but what would be the use? To Percy and the rest of the clan he would always be Bobby.

"What are ye doin' these days?"

Percy narrowed his gaze and focused directly at Olin. "Been making an honest living."

Olin walked toward his father, directly past Percy. In the old days Olin would have taken Percy's words as a challenge. But today—and hopefully the rest of his days—he would continue to let negative comments pass.

"Doing what?" he asked Percy.

"Farmin'. Your mother says you're a tin man. Ain't got much use for them down in these parts. Them Yankees are cheats."

Olin had heard about the Yankee merchants who had come to the South, charging three to four times more for items than they were worth and hurting the poor area farmers. "I am a tinsmith. Came here to set up shop so folks can buy from a local."

"And I'm mighty pleased. Good to have ye home, son." His father enveloped him in a big bear hug.

"Good to be home, Pa."

Olin thought he heard Percy snicker behind him but didn't let that bother him, either. Nope. A lot of things in the past that would have given him cause to get angry just didn't seem important now.

"How was the trip? In your letters ye said you'd be home a week ago."

"The roads were in horrific shape. A lot of spring flooding. I had to spend quite a few hours repairing the stretches of corduroy roads. My wagon," Olin said as he pointed to an overburdened cart, "wouldn't make it without me fixing 'em."

His father whistled. "What's in there?"

"All my tools, plus a few things I brought from Pennsylvania to set up my living quarters."

"Your mother will persuade ye out of that."

"She'll try."

"Why would you want to live in town?" Percy looked downright confused.

"Been living on my own for a while now. If I live at the shop, I can work late hours if I have an order that needs fixing as soon as possible."

"Ain't no one in a rush around here." Percy stepped up to the two of them.

Olin suspected that Percy still lived at home and enjoyed having his mother do his laundry, clean his room, and make his meals every day. Personally, Olin liked being on his own and felt Percy—at twenty-five years of age—ought to. Then again, folks tended to live at home until they married, and even then they'd sometimes live in their parents' house until they could build their own home on the family property. Percy's father was one who kept a tight rein on his money and land, so it was quite possible his father wouldn't give him a piece of land to build on.

Olin's older brothers, John and Kyle, came in from the fields and joined them with warm welcomes and genuine love. Percy seemed to be the only curious feature in the small family gathering. Olin's sisters were married and living with their husbands. Janet lived in the area and had several children, including a set of twins. Olin's heart tightened. He hadn't even come home for his sisters' weddings.

They went into the house and sat down at the fancy, dressed table. Mother had even pulled out her Sunday china. He felt like the prodigal son home from his years of squandering. But he hadn't been squandering his inheritance; he'd been working hard at his trade and at controlling his anger. His mentor, William Farley, had been more than a mentor of tinsmithing. He'd helped Olin heal his heart and develop his relationship with his Savior.

Percy leaned over to Kyle and whispered, "Wanna run him out of town?"

⚈⚈⚈

Ida Mae glanced at Cyrus, then back to Rosey. *There is more going on here than Rosey just giving Cyrus a hand. Why would he ask to marry me if he was interested in*

Rosey? And why do I not feel offended that he might marry her? Ida Mae knew she didn't love Cyrus but. . .why wasn't she more upset?

"Cyrus, is the house habitable?"

"Yes, it's all set."

"Good, I'll be moving back in tomorrow."

"Tomorrow?" Cyrus and Rosey said in unison.

"Is there a problem?"

"No, it's just I've been talkin' to Rosey about renting the house and farming the place for you. I was meanin' to speak with you about it next week."

Rosey put her hands on her hips. "Cyrus, you said. . ."

Cyrus's cheeks flamed scarlet red. "Rosey, honey, I meant to speak with her. I just got busy, is all."

Ida Mae sighed. She didn't want to get in the middle of a lovers' spat. And at the moment she wasn't too pleased with herself for even considering the possibility of marrying Cyrus. "Let's go inside; I want to see the work you've done."

After a fifteen-minute tour of the house, they sat down at the kitchen table Cyrus must have built. There were only three chairs, but that worked fine.

"See, Ida Mae, I was planning on asking you if I could live in the house and do the farming on the land. I'll show a profit to you every year. Unless, of course, the good Lord brings about bad weather and insects."

Every farmer knew they were dependent on the weather, rainfall, and no swarming locusts to have a good crop.

"I'll even pay ya something to rent the house, if'n ya feel it's necessary. But if Rosey and I are going to be able to save for our own farm, it will take longer."

Rosey smacked Cyrus on the arm. "Tell her all of it."

"Me and Rosey got married this morning. Family don't know yet. We're planning on keepin' it a secret for a spell."

Ida Mae rubbed the back of her neck. "You're married?"

"Yup, got the paper right here."

"Pa will explode," Rosey interrupted, "since Cyrus don't own his own land and home yet."

All the pieces came together—why the secret, why the desire to rent her property. And it solved the uncomfortable problem she had with returning to her home where her parents had died. She hadn't expected much from the land this year, what with her brothers being unable to help and their parents' estate unfinished, not to mention the house needing to be rebuilt. But now. . .

"I'll have my father's attorney draw up a lease agreement for one year. I'll pay you a percentage of the profit from the harvest, if there is a profit. I won't charge for the house, but I'll expect you to finish the barn and do upkeep on the house. How's that?"

Cyrus's smile barely curved his lips. "Sounds right nice, thank you."

"Come to town tomorrow eve and I'll have the paperwork ready to sign."

His Adam's apple bouncing up and down in his throat, Cyrus swallowed hard. Rosey beamed.

"I best be going, seeing as it's your wedding night and all." Ida Mae pushed her chair from under the table and got up to leave. Minnie would not be happy with her staying in town.

"Cyrus, can I speak with you for a moment outside?"

"Be my pleasure, Ida Mae."

Her backbone twitched just hearing his words. Memories of his latest proposal—a mere month ago—flooded back into her mind, leaving her feeling rankled. The walk out to her horse helped soothe her nerves. "You've been planning this for a while, and you didn't speak with me."

"I'm sorry, Ida Mae, I meant to. I've been so busy getting the house ready, plowing the fields, and courtin' Rosey, I just ran out of time."

"It's not sound business, Cyrus." *Not to mention, the last time we spoke you proposed marriage to me. I hope Rosey knows what she's getting into.*

"You're right. You always did have a good eye for business. Take a look at the fields I've been plowing and planting."

Scanning the fields, Ida Mae saw little done. *Father would have had it all plowed and planted by now*, she thought wistfully. "Are you planning on planting all the fields?"

"No, I felt most of the land would prosper better with a year of rest. I'm going to bring the cows and horses out in the idle fields over the summer and allow them to do their job."

Resting the land was not an uncommon practice, and since she hadn't given him any orders, or even spoken with him about the farm, it seemed a reasonable plan. Something she realized she should have considered much sooner. But farming had been far from her mind, and living on the farm once the house was rebuilt, even farther. "That will be fine, Cyrus. I'll expect to see you tomorrow eve."

"Thank you, Ida Mae. And again, I'm sorry for not speakin' with ya sooner."

"I understand." Ida Mae climbed onto her horse and sat in the saddle sideways, already regretting having made such a hasty decision.

She waved him off and headed back toward town. It would be dark before she returned and she hadn't brought a lantern with her. *Lord, there's a part of me that isn't excited about renting the house and having Cyrus farm the land for me, but honestly, I can't do it. I wasn't planning on becoming a landlord. Give me grace and the knowledge to handle all this.*

Her mind wove back to her other tenant, the murderer, if Minnie was correct. Truth was, she trusted him more than she trusted Cyrus. *Dear God, please give me wisdom.*

Olin sat back in his chair. Percy left just before it was time to clear the table and do evening chores. The ring of Mother's finest silver on the china reminded him of many meals he'd eaten with his family over the years, so unlike the past seven years.

"It's good to have ye home, son. And don't ye worry none about Percy. Folks just need to gossip every now and again. Once you've been living here for a while, things will get better. Won't they, Kyle?"

Kyle forked the last potato chunk from his plate. "Yes, sir. And after ye were gone, folks were pretty divided about who started that fight. Everyone that was at the fight acknowledged it wasn't your fault."

Olin nodded.

"Bobby, why'd ye come back?" his oldest brother, John, asked.

"Mum wrote about the Yankee traders selling tinware in the area and how so many folks paid too much for them. I'm fairly good at the trade and thought folks would like to buy tin made from someone who grew up here."

John wiped his mouth with the linen napkin. He raised his right eyebrow and said, "I accept that. Welcome home, brother, and I'll do whatever I can to help ye and your business."

"Thank ye, I appreciate it. I know some folks, like Percy, won't be pleased with my returning. But Percy and I never did get along."

Kyle laughed. "Does a cow have spots? You two have fought since ye were in diapers."

"He started it."

Mother chimed in with her own riotous laughter. "The Lord be praised, I haven't heard that in years."

"Glad the boy can tickle ye, Mother." His father turned back toward Olin. "Bobby—"

"Olin, if ye don't mind, sir. I've not gone by Bobby since I left town."

"Olin it is, then. Why don't we start unpacking that wagon of yours?"

Olin pushed his chair back. "I have my things for tonight, 'tis all."

"Bobby?" His mother's voice quivered.

"Mother, I mean no disrespect, but it's good for me to establish my business, living at the shop. I promise I'll come home as often as possible." He flashed the smile that got him out of trouble more times than he could count. "My cookin' don't compare to yours."

"I wish ye would stay. It's safer," she mumbled.

Olin walked behind his mother and put his hands on her shoulders. "I'll be fine, Mum. The good Lord's taught me a few things about my anger. I haven't been in a fight since."

She nodded, but he could feel the tension in her body.

"Have ye met your pretty landlord?" Kyle smiled.

"Aye."

John got up from the table and picked up his plate and silverware. "Do ye remember Minnie Jacobs?"

Olin nodded. That gal didn't know how to keep her mouth still, from what he could remember of her.

"She's Ida Mae's cousin and, from what I hear, bends Ida Mae's ear quite often."

John's message was perfectly clear. Ida Mae no doubt knew all about him. If not before she rented the shop to him, certainly by the end of this day. "Thank ye."

"Come on, son. The sun be settin' soon."

"Yes, sir. Thanks for such a wonderful dinner, Mother." Olin bent down and gave her a kiss on the cheek. "It's good to be home."

She placed her wrinkled hand on his. Another twinge stabbed his heart. When had his mother aged so? With a brief squeeze, he extracted himself and went outside with his father to discuss the comments about his homecoming that had come up at the dinner table. Olin prayed he hadn't made a mistake coming back home.

Chapter 3

Ida Mae stretched, trying to wake up. She snuggled deeper under the covers. Work demanded her attention. She tossed off the covers, went to the washbasin, and scrubbed the sleepy sand from her eyes.

The clanging of the storefront doorbell her father made had her glance at the clock and groan. *Today's going to be a wonderful day,* she mumbled, leaving her living area and running toward the front of the shop.

Peeking through the heavy linen curtain, she saw Olin Orr smiling without a care in the world. How could he be a murder? Shouldn't murderers look...evil? Speaking through the closed door, she asked, "What can I do for you, Mr. Orr?"

"I have your rent."

"I'm sorry." Looking down at her nightclothes, she asked, "Can you bring it back in half an hour?"

"As ye wish. May I bring my wagon to the barn?"

"Yes." Minnie's haunting words came back. Ida Mae fired off a quick prayer. "I'll be ready in thirty minutes."

He nodded, and his vibrant black hair bounced. Ida Mae suppressed the vain desire to run her fingers through his wavy locks. Her tactile senses were excellent for a spinner. Touch was so important in producing fine thread and yarn. But how does one resist such an urge for propriety's sake? She shook off her foolish ramblings and ran back to her room to dress. She didn't have time for entertaining such fanciful thoughts. Two hours behind and an order due this evening. Ida Mae would have to push herself hard.

The bell over the entrance jangled not more than thirty seconds after she'd unlocked the door and opened for business. Ida Mae turned, expecting to see Olin. Instead, John Alexander Farres stood with his broad shoulders squared, wearing a trim, three-piece business suit. "Good morning, John Alexander."

"Morning, Ida Mae. I came to say I'll be pickin' up my order two days from now. I'm heading out of town on business and Mother said she could wait until my return."

"It will be ready."

John Alexander reached out and put his hand on her shoulder. "I know it will. Is it true that you married Cyrus yesterday?"

"No." Cyrus and Rosey had sworn her to secrecy. "How do you suppose that rumor started?"

124

John Alexander scratched his beard along his right jaw. "Half a dozen folks said they heard it from so-and-so, who supposedly heard it from Cyrus."

"I can't imagine who started the silly rumor, but I won't be marrying Cyrus."

A smile broadened on John Alexander's face. "Cyrus is a fine man, but I don't think he'd like having a wife who can handle financial matters as well as—if not better than—himself. I heard you rented out your father's blacksmith shop."

The delicate hairs on the back of her neck rose, sensing what? Fear? Concern that another would think her unable to discern good character in a person? "Yes."

"Heard he was a tin man from the north."

"From Pennsylvania."

"Not too fond of those Yankee traders. Took my uncle's winter cash one year, selling him a clock that didn't work and a bunch of tinware that fell apart the first time he poured something hot into the cup."

Did she dare tell him that he might be a local boy? "We shall have to see how good of a workman he is. He had high recommendations from those he worked with in Pennsylvania."

"I'll keep a watch out for you. I'll check on you when I come into town and see how you're faring."

"Thank you. It isn't necessary, but I appreciate your lookin' after me."

"Your pa wouldn't have it any other way."

John Alexander was ten years her senior. *He wouldn't make a bad husband*, she thought.

Sitting down at the spinning wheel, Ida Mae had just put her hand to the spindle when the bell over the door jangled again. This time it was Olin Orr. Not a glimpse of the smile she had seen thirty minutes prior remained. "Mr. Orr?"

"Here's your rent." He slapped the money down on the counter. "Do you have the papers for me to sign?"

Ida Mae got up, opened the locked cabinet door in her desk, and pulled out a rental agreement. "I've signed my name and dated it." She handed him the papers.

He read it over. "May I?"

He held his hand out for a pen. Ida Mae dipped the pen in the inkwell and handed it to him. He signed with a flare she hadn't seen in most men's handwriting.

"Thank you, Mr. Orr."

He nodded and left without saying another word. *What has him in knots?* she wondered.

"Most peculiar." Ida Mae went back to work.

She took a break at lunchtime and went to the lawyer's office to have the lease agreement for Cyrus drawn up. She wondered whether she should go back on her word and contact her brothers for their advice, but she'd already told Cyrus he could rent the property. In the end, she felt she'd spoken before prayer and proper consideration were given. Perhaps one day she'd learn to think before she spoke. On the other hand, it was only for one year and she didn't have time to seek out another tenant who would farm the land. She returned to the shop, picking up where she left off. Later that evening, Cyrus came in and she repeated the process of signing a lease with yet another tenant.

∞

Olin had been tempted not to sign the lease after seeing the man leave Ida Mae's shop moments before. It seemed strange the doors would still be locked at ten thirty, but seeing a man leave. . . Well, he'd seen those kinds of establishments up north. What bothered him most was that Ida Mae didn't seem to be that kind of a woman. And with her family farm, her spinster business, and now renting him the barn—how much money did she need?

Burning off steam, he worked through lunch. At two in the afternoon he finally sat down to eat, after retrieving a cool glass of water from the town water pump, twenty feet outside his business door.

"Bobby, is that you?"

Olin turned to a female voice he couldn't quite place.

"It is you. I heard the grapevine humming all day and just came to see for myself."

Olin smiled and opened his arms to embrace her. "It's good to see ye, Jane."

Jane gave him a hearty pat on the back. "I didn't believe it, but it is you. Heard you've gone Yankee on us."

A strangled chuckle escaped. "No, I just worked for them for a while. I learned a trade and thought I'd come home and put it to good use. Mother and Father wrote about how the tin men from the north were overpricing and selling less than good wares to area farmers, so I thought it would be good to have a local come work in the area."

She placed her hands on her hips. "Well, I'll be, you're so grown up. You became a man, huh?"

"I'd like to think so." Olin held back the memories of him and Jane and growing up together. Theirs had been a school-days romance. She had broken off their relationship, calling him immature. He reached for the nail barrel he'd been carrying from his wagon into the barn.

"Did you ever find your pot of gold?"

"In the Lord, yes. But no, I've given up on finding my fortunes in the gold mines."

She nodded and gave him an assessing glance from head to toe. "I believe you. Now, what's this I hear about you being a murderer? What really happened seven years ago?"

Olin set the small barrel down on the broad floorboards and offered it to

Jane to sit on. He briefly went over the fight at the mine and the decisions that followed.

"I'd say you've got some enemies out there. Folks have been talkin' up a blue streak about it since you rolled into town. My husband—do you remember Richard Johansen from over the hill?"

Olin shook his head no.

"Oh. Never mind. Richard says the sheriff will be wantin' to talk with you, just because everyone is talkin' about it."

"I suspect he's right. So, you're married? Any children?"

"Four."

Olin raised his eyebrows and whistled. She didn't look like she'd even had one child. She'd always been a slender woman. "Four," he repeated in awe.

Jane rattled on for ten minutes about her family and life in Charlotte. She also mentioned that his landlord had apparently married last night, which explained the man leaving her office earlier this morning.

After Jane left, Olin worked his frustration out by scrubbing and cleaning the barn. Hard physical labor had always helped to release some of his pent-up frustrations. He knew the Lord was allowing this test for many reasons, but the primary one was to test his resolve to handle his anger. He knew now that coming home meant dealing with some of the issues he'd abandoned by running off to Pennsylvania seven years ago.

Thankfully he had worked up quite a sweat by the time the local sheriff came knocking.

"John Thatcher," the sheriff said, introducing himself and extending his hand.

The man stood like a thick chestnut tree: rugged, sturdy, and full of authority. Olin took the proffered hand and gave it a firm shake. "Heard ye might be coming around."

He lifted the brim of his hat off his forehead. "Word travels fast. What do you have to say about the past?"

" 'Tis in the past. I was found not at fault, but I still blame myself. I'm not the same man I was seven years ago. I don't know how to explain it apart from saying having a man die by my hand isn't something I enjoy living with."

"What makes you think your temper won't get the best of ya now?"

"I haven't lifted my hands to fight in seven years."

Sheriff Thatcher gave a slow nod. "Do ya mind if I come callin' from time to time?"

"No, sir. I reckon that's all part of your job."

"Good to meet you, Mr. Orr." He stepped back toward the doorway. "Are you any good?" He pointed to the tinsmithing equipment.

"My master taught me well and he was pleased."

"Good. We need an honest tradesman in the area. Are you still looking for gold?"

Olin let out a nervous chuckle. "No, sir. I gave that up, too."

The sheriff gave a final nod and slipped out.

Later, as Olin prepared for bed, he prayed. *Father, thank You for the grace and the strength to deal with my past. I know I'm a lowly sinner and that You've forgiven me, but I don't feel worthy. Bringing up all this past history today simply confirms how unworthy I am of Your grace. Forgive me again, Lord, for doubting Your will to have me return home.*

The loud crash of glass shattering, followed by a scream, jolted him out of his prayer.

∞

Ida Mae's heart raced. Fear sliced through her as a rock flew through the glass window in the east wall of her room. She pulled the quilt from the bed and wrapped it around herself for extra protection. Pressed against the room's southeast corner, the window on her right and the door to her left, she hoped to remain out of the way if another rock should fly through the now broken window.

Moments ticked by, silent except for the thunder of her heartbeat. Finally, she slid down, sat on the floor, and cried. Sometimes life overwhelmed her. The lonely days since her parents' tragic deaths flooded her mind. Grief over the loss washed over her with an intensity she hadn't felt in months.

At some point she heard some rattling at the storefront's door. It was locked, but the door and the rest of the shop's west wall had windows. She huddled in closer to herself and stayed sequestered in the corner, hiding in the quilt. Shock had overtaken her senses.

"Miss McAuley, are ye all right?"

Ida Mae focused on the deer-like eyes. She closed her eyelids and opened them again and refocused. *Who?* She pulled the quilt closer.

"Shh, you're safe with me. What happened?"

Ida Mae just shook her head from side to side. Mr. Orr stood there holding a lantern over her.

"Let me help you up." He placed the lantern on the small table by the bed and lifted her as if she were nothing more than a feather. How heavy could tin be? He didn't appear to have huge muscles. He placed her on a chair and looked around the room.

"There's glass everywhere. Where's your broom?"

She pointed to the large closet that had been her parents' bedroom when they occasionally stayed in town.

He took two strides and crossed the room with ease. Admittedly her one-room living area was small—containing her bed and night table, chest of drawers, a couple chairs, and a small kitchen table near the cooking alcove—but to see him walk the width of the room in two steps... She wondered how long his legs were.

He went straight to work. Ida Mae sat there, numb, and watched. He was a handsome man, long legs and all. The heat of a flush brushed her cheeks. Ida Mae quelled her thoughts.

"What happened?" he repeated.

It finally dawned on her. "How'd you get in here?"

"I picked your lock. I heard the glass break so I was concerned that ye were injured, especially when ye didn't answer my knocking on your door. Who would throw a rock through your window? Where is your husband?"

"My husband?"

"Aye, shouldn't a newly married man be at his wife's side?"

"I'm not married." Then she remembered John Alexander and the news he'd heard. "It's a silly rumor with no bearing in fact."

"Oh, I assumed. . ." His words trailed off as he pushed the bits of broken glass into the dustpan.

Feeling more herself, Ida Mae jumped up from the chair. "Just what did you assume, Mr. Orr?"

"Forgive me. I assumed the man who left your establishment this morning was your husband."

"Man? What man?" Ida Mae replayed the day and realized what improper thoughts Mr. Orr had of her.

"Mr. Orr, you don't know me, so I'll forgive your rude insinuation. I am a woman of integrity. What you've entertained in your mind is simply unspeakable. The gentleman in question came in for business only." Ida Mae stammered. "Linen business. I am spinning for him."

"Forgive me." Olin Orr bowed. "It's been a rough day."

"Yes, it has, for both of us, I presume. Can I get you a cup of tea?"

"That would be wonderful, thank ye. I'll go to my shop and cut out a piece of wood to cover the broken window."

"Thank you."

"You're welcome. And please forgive my rude assumptions. If anyone should know better, it should be me."

Ida Mae stood there while he slipped out of the room and through the front door. The rumor that Olin Orr had killed a man was no longer rumor. The sheriff had come into the shop at closing and informed her it was the truth but that Olin had been found innocent, that it had been a death caused in defense of his own life. The sheriff's words had reassured her, but at the same time made her question Mr. Orr and his reasons for returning to a town where half of the people believed he'd killed a man in cold blood.

Ida Mae placed the half-full teapot on the stove. She covered her bed with the quilt, washed her hands and face, and placed a heavy housecoat over her

129

nightclothes. Married? How was it that everyone thought she'd married Cyrus yesterday? She had a good mind to go back out to the farm and tell him in no uncertain terms to tell everyone that he'd married Rosey. On the other hand, he'd been telling folks for a long time that he asked Ida Mae to marry him, so it was human nature to assume that she'd been the one. But how could anyone know Cyrus had married? It didn't make any sense at all.

Ida Mae sighed. It had been a very long day and looked like it would be an even longer night.

She heard the banging of a hammer on the window frame and saw a large board over the broken window. It didn't take Mr. Orr long to fix the damage.

Olin knocked and Ida Mae opened the door to let him in, then quickly relocked it.

"All fixed. If ye purchase the glass I'll put it in for you," he said as he followed her to the table.

"Thank you." She poured the hot water into the china teapot to let the tea steep.

"Who do ye think would throw a rock through the window?" he asked as he sat down at the small table. The kitchen alcove contained a small stove that doubled for heating in the winter, a sink, and a few cabinets. It was large enough for the small table and a couple of chairs. Not that she entertained often.

"I don't know. Just some wild children, I imagine. There was no noise, no shouting. Just a rock crashing through."

She placed a teacup and saucer in front of him and another at her seat.

"I reckon you've heard the rumors about me."

Ida Mae nodded.

"If you're not comfortable with my renting from ye..."

She raised her hand. "No, I'm fine with you renting the shop. Sheriff Thatcher explained it all."

"I see."

She sat down. He looked down at his lap. "Mr. Orr, you should know that my parents died last year. Many of my parents' friends have taken it upon themselves to oversee my life. The sheriff is one such friend."

"I understand. I don't mean to pry into your business, but why are folks saying ye married yesterday?"

"The man who asked me to marry him, several times over the last year, got married yesterday and folks are just assuming it was to me. I promised him I wouldn't tell anyone who he married, but it's been a difficult day. I've had people coming and going all day, wanting to congratulate me, wondering why I was still working today and not enjoying my new married life."

Olin chuckled. "I'd forgotten how small this town really is. Living in the city of Philadelphia took awhile to adjust to, but there are some advantages to living in a place so large ye only know a handful of people. Down here, just about everyone is related."

Ida Mae had to agree.

Olin downed his tea. "I shall call it a night, Miss McAuley, and thank ye for the tea."

"Thank you for boarding up the window."

He stood up. "Ye probably need to sweep the floors again. I didn't find the rock."

Ida Mae nodded and Mr. Olin Orr retreated.

She picked up the broom and swept the floor. She reached first under the small chest of drawers, then the bed, using the broom handle. She knocked the rock out from under the bed. Wrapped around it was a piece of paper tied on by a piece of twine. Untying the note, she read, "Get rid of your tenant or else."

Earlier fear returned and slid down her spine like the shuttle on the loom.

Chapter 4

Four days later, Olin still couldn't figure out why his landlord was avoiding him. Did it bother her that he'd come to her rescue? No doubt opening her locked door would give her an insecure feeling, but he had had little choice once he'd seen the broken window and heard the delicate cries. At least he felt that way at the time. Now he wasn't too sure. Mayhap he should have simply fixed the window and let her be.

Olin shook his head no. He knew better than that. He made his way down the road to his parents' house. He'd been invited to dinner, and his sister Janet and her family were going to be there, as well. Today had been different from the rest since his arrival. No one came to see if it really was him at the shop. Word must have gotten around enough so that people's curiosity had been settled.

He glanced at the peach trees laden with blossoms. After they ripened, the harvest would begin. He remembered the days he'd spent canning and preparing peaches with his mother. The entire family would get into the act. Among the gifts he'd brought for his mother had been two cases of canning jars and a new canning pot. He hoped a few of those filled jars would end up in his cabinet.

"Evenin', son." His father waved as Olin approached the main house. "How are ye doing?"

"Fine. The shop is all set up and I've even begun working on some pieces."

"Aye, 'tis good to keep a man busy."

"Aye. That it is, Pop. Looks like a good crop of peaches this year."

"Ye can thank your brother John for that. He's been pruning and keepin' those trees healthy for the past couple years."

John was a natural farmer and the oldest son. The farm would be his one day, as it should be. Kyle also had the ability and interest in farming, unlike Olin.

"Sheriff came by."

"My place, too."

"Seems like a good man."

"Aye. He actually talked with the owners of the mine before talking with me." Olin dismounted and tied the horse to the hitching post out front.

"Good. Percy hasn't been around."

"Good."

His father's bushy gray eyebrows rose on his forehead. "I imagine so. But the Good Book says to keep an eye on your enemies."

"Has Percy been in trouble since I left?" Olin hadn't been able to shake the feeling that Percy may have been responsible for the rock going through Ida Mae's window. After all, he did ask Kyle if he wanted to help run him out of town. *But why would he attack Ida Mae?*

"He's not a hard worker and hopes to get enough from his father's property so he doesn't have to work hard the rest of his life."

"If he doesn't work the land he won't get much from the property."

Kyle rounded the front porch, taking off a pair of work gloves. "Welcome home, little brother. How's the shop coming?"

"All set up, just waiting on orders to come in."

"Ye might be waiting for a spell. Percy's been telling folks you're just like those Yankee tin men."

"I suspected as much." He and Percy had always been like oil and water.

"Mother, on the other hand, has been bragging up a storm." Kyle rested his right foot on the second step.

Olin chuckled. "Mother would."

"It helps that you've sent her some of those tin cups and pans over the years. She can claim just how good your work is.

"Pop, there's a problem with the grain chute in the barn for feeding the hogs. I tried working on it but I think the pin is shot. I'll need to run to town and order a piece." Kyle turned toward Olin. "Ye know, it would be nice if ye knew how to work Mr. McAuley's blacksmithing tools. We really need a new blacksmith."

"I'm not that skilled in blacksmithing, but I know how to do some small things. What do you need?"

Kyle pulled the worn pin from his hip pocket. "This here pin should be this thick the entire shaft. See how thin it is here and how it's bent?"

"Yup."

"Well. . ." Kyle went on to explain how the pin worked.

"Can I see where it fits the chute?"

"Sure." Kyle, Olin, and their father went off to the barn.

Olin examined the mechanism. "If I made a couple adjustments here"— Olin pointed to the pin—"and opened it here to receive a cotter pin, it might put less strain on the shaft."

His father scratched his chin. "Make both, son. That way if your idea doesn't work we'll still have a working pin."

"Fair enough."

"I see what you're suggesting, Bobby. I think it might work." Kyle leaned away from the chute.

"Ye boys go on discussing this. I best get back to your mother if I want some supper tonight. She sent me out to fetch a bucket of water fifteen minutes ago."

Kyle and Olin glanced at one another and grinned. Olin resigned himself to the fact that to his family, he would always be Bobby.

After Father left the barn, Kyle leaned back. "Percy really is set to run ye out of town. What did ye do to the man?"

"Nothing."

"Come on, this is me you're talkin' to. What happened between the two of ye seven years ago?"

"Nothing to say, apart from me trying to defend him."

"What? Ye mean after all this time you're saying Percy is the reason ye were fighting with Gary Jones?"

Olin shrugged. He shouldn't have said that much after all this time. What did it really matter anyway?

"Little brother, ye better watch your back. I'm afraid Percy isn't going to stop."

Like Father, Olin knew Percy didn't have the ambition to continue bullying him. One day Percy would tire of his attempt to get him kicked out of town. Olin hoped. "I imagine he'll tire of this."

They left the barn upon hearing a wagon pulling up. Janet's rich, black curly hair, so like his own, glistened in the sunlight. Four children jumped out as her husband secured the wagon. Olin smiled. Janet rushed over and gave him the best hug of his life. "Hey, little brother, it's good to see ye."

He squeezed her slightly and whispered in her ear. "It's good to be home."

"It's about time. Come meet my husband and our children."

∞

Ida Mae finished the jobs lined up for the rest of the week a day early. Today she planned to spend some time cleaning her living area and baking for tomorrow's church picnic.

Olin had replaced the glass in the window, but she'd been avoiding him. He made her feel things a single woman shouldn't. He lived too close; and to build up a friendship would take time and lots of space. She didn't dare share these thoughts with anyone, especially Olin.

Cyrus had come by a couple days ago and apologized again for the misunderstanding about his hopes and plans to rent the farm. And told her he was just as concerned as her about the rumors spreading around town regarding their marriage. He hinted that Rosey's parents would have their marriage dissolved if they found out about it. For the moment, she snuck out on occasion to join her husband on the farm. Ida Mae didn't think this was a wise way to start a marriage.

He had also mentioned he was turning the back forty acres to help the soil for next year's planting. A part of her wanted to check on Cyrus's progress on the farm, yet another part of her didn't want to bother. Perhaps she should consider selling the land and purchasing a smaller cottage closer to town, as her brothers had suggested.

Minnie ran into the shop. "Ida Mae, you won't believe what I just heard."

"What's that?" Ida Mae looked over the next day's schedule.

"That Bobby Orr's cousin is trying to get him kicked out of town."

"What?"

"Percy says that Bobby has a horrible temper. He doesn't trust him and he's quite concerned about you. Percy says he has a mind to keep an eye on you just to make certain you're safe."

"You can tell Percy I'm just fine." Ida Mae slipped her hand into her pocket and fingered the crumpled note that had been tied to the rock. She'd read it a hundred times and prayed over it at least a thousand more. She didn't know if it referred to Cyrus Morgan or Olin Orr. In either event, she wouldn't give in to such tactics. After all, she had roots from the Hornet's Nest, as the British had referred to this part of the country during the Revolution.

"Why aren't you working today?"

"Finished all the jobs. I thought I'd give my room a good cleaning and prepare some food for tomorrow's church picnic." Ida Mae led Minnie to her private living area.

"Wonderful. Mother's packed a bunch of pickles and spring vegetables for the picnic. Father's donating a couple chickens."

Ida Mae had already heard someone was donating an entire hog. She imagined they had started to cook the pig in the pit. It would take close to twenty-four hours to roast. They walked into the small kitchen area, Minnie sat down, and Ida Mae went to the cupboard. "I think I'll make some biscuits."

"You do make a fluffy biscuit," Minnie said. "Why do you think Percy is trying to get Bobby to leave town? The way I heard it, the fight was self-defense."

How the gossips will change their thinking, she mused. "I don't know. I don't know Mr. Orr all that well. I think I've only seen him maybe thirty minutes since he moved in."

"As good a-lookin' as he is? Why, he could visit me as often as he'd like. Have you ever seen such unruly curls on a man?"

Ida Mae turned away from her cousin. "Can't say that I have."

"By the way, I heard someone broke one of your windows." Minnie put her feet up on the small footstool.

Four days. Minnie is slowing down. "Yes, I believe it might have been some boys."

"Who fixed it?"

Ida Mae grinned. She knew Minnie was fishing. "Mr. Orr. He heard the crash and came and lent me a hand."

"Guess it ain't all bad havin' a man livin' next door."

"No, it's not."

Minnie scanned the room. "Where's your ma's cranberry glass vase?"

Ida Mae turned and looked at the shelf where the vase usually sat. "I don't know."

❧

Olin came home in the dark. A single light burned in Ida Mae's room. He wondered about her and what her life must be like. He imagined it to be similar to his when he had lived in Pennsylvania with no family around. On the other hand, she did speak of her parents' friends keeping an eye out for her. And then there were her cousins in the area. She wasn't totally alone.

A shadowy figure slipped past the rear of her building.

"Whoa, boy."

His horse snorted.

Olin waited a moment, then proceeded to where the shadow had disappeared. A bright light burned in the window across the alley. If anyone had walked by, he or she would cast a shadow across Ida Mae's building. Olin waited a moment longer. After the rock incident, he wasn't going to take any chances.

A moment later, the back door to Ida Mae's opened halfway. "Hello?" Ida Mae called out.

"It's just me, Miss McAuley—Olin Orr."

"Mr. Orr?"

"Yes, I'm returning home from dinner with my family. Is everything all right?"

"Ah." She paused. "If it is only you, I guess so."

"Miss McAuley, has something happened?"

"No, I suppose not. It just felt like someone was—oh, never mind. I'm just being foolish."

Olin nudged his horse closer to the back doorway of Ida Mae's private quarters. "Are you certain you're safe? What happened?"

"Nothing. I guess it just seemed like someone was hovering around my back door."

"Give me your lantern." He hopped off his horse.

When she returned with a lantern, he reached out for it. Their fingers touched. Hers were warm, soft. His stomach did a flip. "Step back inside. I'll check the ground for any noticeable tracks."

"Thank you."

Olin searched the ground carefully. It was difficult to see, but everything appeared to be in order. None of the various-sized tracks seemed to indicate that anyone had been loitering there. He knocked on the door. "Miss McAuley, no one is around; you're safe."

She opened the door. "Thank you. I'm just being fearful."

"You have reason to be."

"Why? What are you not telling me?"

"I didn't mean to alarm you, Miss. I was referrin' to what my parents told me about the loss of your parents in the fire. Anyone in your circumstance would feel a wee bit alone and scared."

"Oh."

"Forgive me, but if ye are fearful of me renting from you, I'll find a new location."

"No, this has nothing to do with you."

"Very well." He bowed slightly and walked over to his horse. "I'll see you on the morrow."

They said their good-byes and he walked his horse around to the livery stable on the side of his portion of the building. After the animal was unpacked and ready for the night, Olin worked his way into his small room, a tool and storage area in the workshop he had converted to basic living quarters. It didn't compare to the lovely living area that Ida Mae had made for herself, but it was functional and served his purposes.

A gentle knock echoed through the room. "Hello!" he called out.

"Mr. Orr, may I come in?" Her voice sounded close yet muffled.

"Yes." He waited to see where Ida Mae was coming from. A noise came from the closet so he opened the door. A panel serving as a hidden door opened in the wall that joined their two parts of the building. There was no handle on his side.

"Please come in," he said, stepping back.

Ida Mae stepped through the closet and into the room. "I hope I didn't alarm you, Mr. Orr. My father built this passageway for my mother so she wouldn't have to go out around the building to speak with him. Given what happened. . ." Her voice trailed off.

"How can I help ye, Miss McAuley?"

"I've been less than honest with you, Mr. Orr." Ida Mae stepped up beside him. She pulled a wrinkled piece of paper from her pocket.

He took the worn paper and read, "Get rid of your tenant or else." "I'll leave in the morning. I'll stay with my parents until I find a new location for my shop."

"No. I don't like giving in to idle threats."

"Ye know my history. I can't put you at risk."

"Minnie says your cousin Percy is. . ."

"Trying to have me kicked out of town." He finished her sentence. "Aye, I know. Ye don't need this kind of trouble in your life. I'll leave immediately."

"I appreciate your concern for my well-being, but I'm not certain this note pertains to you. I rented my parents' farmhouse to Cyrus Morgan."

"The man everyone claims you married?"

"Yes." She let out a nervous giggle that played havoc with his senses. "He might be the person someone is trying to get rid of."

"For what possible reason?"

The knit of her eyebrows told him there was nothing in Cyrus Morgan's past that would cause such a warning. "Ida Mae, ye must realize"—he brushed his hair from his eyes—"they're after me. Perhaps it was wrong for me to return."

She looked pointedly at the curls brushing his shoulders. "You need a haircut?"

"I've been meaning to have it cut."

"Would you like me to?" she offered shyly. "My mother taught me how to cut my older brothers' hair."

"Aye," he whispered.

Chapter 5

Ida Mae savored every stroke of her fingers through Olin's hair. "Finished."

Olin opened his brown eyes wide. Wild energy targeted her. He hooded his eyes once again and reopened them slowly. The warm glow of a lightly creamed coffee came to mind.

Ida Mae swallowed, grateful they had cut his hair in the barn with the door wide open for anyone to see they were not acting improperly.

"Thank ye." He cleared his throat. "I'll move my personal items out tomorrow after church."

"Please don't." She bit her lower lip, not wanting to say another word.

"Ida Mae, ye must be protected. I don't know who sent this note, but I daresay it could be my cousin, or it could be someone else, someone more violent. It is not wise for me to live here and put ye in harm's way. Besides, my mum will be thrilled to have me living at home."

Ida Mae smiled. Parents could be like that.

"Thank ye for the haircut. I'll see ye in the morning. But before I go to bed I'll take one last look around the place. Don't forget to lock your doors."

She acknowledged his warning, slipped back into her own section of the building, and did as he instructed.

⁂

The next morning, Ida Mae readied for church and the picnic. Walking the length of the town to the church, she left her biscuits in the fellowship hall where the women would prepare for the dinner outside. The church seemed full this morning. Many came in anticipation of the meal, as usual. The message given by the preacher reminded her of the need to walk in faith.

"Good morning, Miss McAuley." Olin Orr came up beside her at the park and smiled.

Earlier she had tried to scan the congregation for him but couldn't see him through the sea of people. "Good morning, Mr. Orr."

"Bobby!" A woman a handful of years older than Ida Mae waved.

"There's my sister, Janet. She's been anxious to speak with me all week. Would ye care to join us?"

"Thank you, but. . ."

He reached out his hand. "My mum can't wait to thank ye for the haircut."

Ida Mae let her hand rest in his. It was a strong hand.

After several introductions Ida Mae settled on a blanket next to Olin's oldest brother, John. "Fine day," he said.

"Yes, it is. Perfect for a picnic."

"Aye. Are ye plannin' on enterin' any of the competitions?"

"No, I'm fond of just being a spectator."

Cyrus Morgan strolled by with his hands in his pockets. "Afternoon, Ida Mae. How are you?"

"Fine."

She could feel John's watchful gaze. She'd love to ask Cyrus how Rosey was, but that would clue in the entire town that Rosey and Cyrus had married. "How's the farm?"

"Good. I'm planting corn this week."

" 'Tis a bit late in the season to be plantin' corn," John offered as he reached for a fresh strawberry.

"I'm praying for a late winter."

"Cyrus just rented the farm from me. He hasn't had the normal time to plant as he just finished rebuilding the house." Ida Mae defended him but checked herself from going further. Cyrus could have planted the corn earlier, before completing the house, if he had bothered to speak to her about his plans.

Cyrus's glance flickered between her and John. John reached over and rested his hand on the blanket behind her, as if letting Cyrus know that the Orr family had taken her under its wings. Without a doubt, Olin must have shared with his brother the threatening note.

As Cyrus made his farewells, she turned to John and waited for Cyrus to leave them, and then spoke. "That wasn't necessary."

"Unfortunately, I believe it may be. Bobby told Kyle and me what's been going on at your home. And I've personally heard the rumor Cyrus has been spreading, claiming he married you."

"You heard him say that?"

"Not in so many words, but he strongly implied it. He's a lazy farmer. Ye should have asked Kyle or me to work your land. We would have brought ye in a profit."

Ida Mae smiled. "You probably would have. I was just so startled to hear his plans and meet his wife."

"So, he did marry?"

"Yes."

"Who?"

"He's asked to keep that private. He's hoping to tell her parents after the harvest."

"I don't like it."

"I'm not fond of it, either. But I wasn't doing anything with the land. He's certainly turning the soil over."

John snickered. "Ain't no use in doing that more than a time or two in the late winter, early spring."

"No, I suppose it isn't. But he's been good to me, and he rebuilt the house."

"Aye, I'll give the man that."

Olin returned with two cups of iced tea. "Would ye like one, John?"

"Nope. It's my turn to enter the sack race."

John left and Olin took his brother's place on the blanket beside her. "You told your family?" she whispered.

"Just John and Kyle. I wanted them to understand why I was moving back home. Mother and Father are just happy to have me back. But I wanted my brothers to know I wasn't after their inheritance."

"Do your brothers believe you about what happened years ago?"

"Aye, even though they know my anger. I have a good family."

"You are blessed."

"Uncle Bobby," one of the twins squealed, running up to him with open arms and strawberry juice running down her chin.

Ida Mae's heart clenched. She missed her brothers. She missed her family. It was like Olin said last night—she was alone, so very alone.

∞

Olin watched Ida Mae closely throughout the day. His family took turns speaking with her one at a time. She blended well with them. As the day wore on, she relaxed perceptibly. He couldn't have asked for a better opportunity than what the picnic had produced. Between him and his brothers they each took a stroll down to her shop and inspected the outside for any possible trouble. Ida Mae didn't know it, but they were going to be watching her closely over the next few days.

He finally met Cyrus Morgan. John had pointed him out during the picnic. A young woman with strawberry blond hair kept a watchful eye on Cyrus all day. Olin speculated she was Cyrus's secret wife.

By evening the picnic broke up. He escorted Ida Mae back to her shop. He took advantage of the fact that he, too, had to go that way to pack his wagon and move back home. "Wonderful day, wasn't it?"

"I had a great time. You have a nice family."

"Aye, but they can run all over you if you're not careful."

Ida Mae giggled. "Your nieces and nephews are precious."

"Aye, even if they do stain my best dress shirt with strawberry juice."

"I can get that out."

"Thank ye for offering, but Mum will be able to."

"I reckon that she's done it a time or two. She loves her grandchildren."

He smiled. "Mum loves all her children. She's always been full of love. I didn't appreciate it in my youth. I felt suffocated. There's no reason I should have had such a temper and an anger streak meaner than any mountain lion. I'm not sure where that came from. My father never showed any signs of a temper, and neither do my brothers. I used to wonder if I was an orphan left on their doorstep, until I noticed the strong family resemblance between me and my mum's father."

"You're a handsome man." A deep crimson blush covered Ida Mae's cheeks.

Olin's chest puffed out slightly. "I thank ye for sayin' so. You're a mighty fine lass yourself."

"Forgive me, we shouldn't. . . ."

Olin wrapped his arm around her shoulders, then quickly removed it.

Ida Mae looked down at her feet.

"I didn't mean that the way it sounded, Ida Mae. I just moved back to town. I don't own anything and. . ."

She lifted her head and gazed into his eyes. "You're right. I'm just getting my parents' estate settled now. My brothers and I are finally at a place where we can decide who gets what."

"Ye know, a man would be foolish not to marry a lass such as yourself. With all your land and properties, ye would make him rather well-off."

Ida Mae stopped.

Olin noticed she no longer followed and stopped a couple paces ahead of her. Her eyes widened and she lifted her right eyebrow.

"What, what's the matter?"

"Forgive me, I've got to go." She marched toward her building.

Olin watched and waited until she slipped safely through the doorway.

❧

Ida Mae tossed and turned all night. Olin's words swirled around in her mind like the spool of thread on her spinning wheel. Why hadn't she thought of that before? If she were to marry, the law stated that the man would assume the rights to oversee all of her properties. New doubts about Cyrus surfaced, not to mention Olin and his family. John had made it perfectly clear that he and Kyle would inherit their father's farm, not Olin.

Could he have thrown the rock through the window? He was outside her back door at the time she thought she had heard something.

After hours of remembering her moments with Olin, she no longer felt that way. She was glad he was moving to his parents' house. Her heart would be safer now. *Dear Lord, give me strength.*

The next morning she spent hours searching the shop for her favorite shears.

"Good morning, Ida Mae. How are you today?"

"Fine, and yourself, Mrs. Connors?"

"God's been blessing my boy. The corn is sprouting and nearly a foot tall already. The cotton is coming in, as well."

John's words about Cyrus planting late in the season came back. "What can I help you with, Mrs. Connors?"

"I wondered if you could spin this." She lifted a cloth covering a basket full of fur. Ida Mae lifted a few strands of the soft hairs. It would take some work but she could probably do it. "I reckon I can."

Mrs. Connors' smile went from ear to ear. "Thank you. Will it cost much?"

"It will take some time. I'll try to give you a good price."

"Thank you. I want to knit a lap blanket with it, help remind my boy of his favorite rabbit."

Ida Mae wouldn't question the woman's reasons for asking her to spin rabbit fur. Income was income. "How soon do you need this?"

"Next week should give me plenty of time."

After the woman left, Ida Mae gave in to her senses and chuckled all the way to the spinning wheel. The fur was soft and it would make a fine yarn, perhaps too fine. The question was: Would the fur bind with the other hairs to make a strong enough yarn for knitting? "Wouldn't it have been easier to tan the hide with the fur on?" she mused.

"Tan whose hide?" Olin asked as he closed the door.

What happened to her bell? Ida Mae looked up to where the bell once hung over the door. "I can't believe it."

"What?" Olin spun around, looking behind him.

"My bell is missing."

Olin looked up at the hook that once held the bell. "I'll fix ye up with another. Is anything else missing?"

"I couldn't find my shears this morning, and Minnie noticed my mother's cranberry glass vase missing the other day."

"Ida Mae, is there someplace safer where ye could live?"

"No, there's only here and the farm, and I don't want to live at the farm with Cyrus and. . ." She cut off her words before she broke confidence with Cyrus.

"My guess is Rosey Turner," Olin supplied.

"You didn't hear it from me."

"No, but I watched folks at the picnic, and she was the only one who couldn't keep her eyes off of Cyrus."

Ida Mae smiled. "Well, that's good for young love, right?"

"Right." He stepped farther into the shop. "With your indulgence, Ida Mae, I'll be workin' late this evening. Will that be a problem?"

"No. As I said before, you could have stayed here."

"I still think it best. I hope that whoever sent ye that note saw me pack my wagon and move back to my house. I've been asking around for a new place to rent. Unfortunately, several folks have come needing some help with basic blacksmithing. I don't know much about that skill, but I picked up a few things along the years. I can make a set of shoes fit the horse, and a few other simple things, like nails and such."

"A town always needs a good blacksmith. I'm glad you can help folks out."

"Ye should place an advertisement for a blacksmith. I really work better with tin."

Ida Mae clutched the counter to steady herself. How could she be taken in by the stranger's charms so quickly? Cutting his hair had unraveled her sensibilities.

∞

Olin wanted to stay the night and watch over Ida Mae's place. Instead, he had arranged for Kyle to keep watch in the shadows. The only way for Olin's plan to work would be if he truly went back to his parents' house tonight and tomorrow night. How long he would be followed, *if* he would be followed, he didn't know.

He bade Ida Mae good-bye and couldn't help noticing the tension that grew in her as he left her shop. *Father, protect her,* he prayed as he saddled his horse for home.

He returned home and, with a great deal of self-control, managed not to wear a hole in the parlor's braided rug.

Kyle came home close to midnight.

"Anything?"

"Not even a stray rat. Are ye sure there's a problem?" Kyle flopped down in the chair by the large window in the living room.

"The bell over her door went missing today. Now why would someone take that bell unless they were plannin' on sneakin' into the place?"

"Don't know, little brother, but ye got your hands full with this one. John will be out there tomorrow night, but you'll have to be there the night after that."

"I know." Olin walked over to his brother and placed a hand on his shoulder. "Thank ye for your help."

"Is there a wedding in the near future?"

Olin huffed. "She'd make a fine wife one day, I think."

Remembering her touch, his gut felt like a piece of tin under the hammer, being shaped into something new. The tender touch of her fingers reminded him of a gentle summer rain.

"I need to call it a night, little brother. Perhaps we could spend the night in your shop rather than come back so late."

"Not for a few days. If there is someone watching her, I don't want him to know that we're watching for him."

"I hope ye are wrong."

"I do, too."

After saying good night to his brother, Olin returned to his childhood bedroom. At one time he had shared this room with Kyle. He now had one of their sisters' rooms. Olin wondered when Kyle would find a wife and move on to his own section of the farm. John, as the oldest brother, would inherit the main house. But there was the old log cabin in the side acres of the property. Perhaps Kyle planned to move in there one day.

Olin stretched and slipped under the covers. Tonight he would trust the Lord to keep Ida Mae safe.

∞

A week later he found himself crawling into bed after still seeing no sign of someone watching Ida Mae's. Perhaps he'd been wrong to assume. And she hadn't said anything about any other objects being missing. He made a crude bell out of the iron her father had in his shop. Someday he hoped to find the original bell, or replace it with a shiny brass bell.

The next morning while Olin was at work, Ida Mae walked into the shop from the street entrance. "Olin?"

He looked up.

"We need to talk."

Chapter 6

Ida Mae knit her fingers together to keep them from shaking.

"What can I do for ye?" Olin set aside what appeared to be a large pair of shears.

"I saw you last night."

"Pardon?"

Ida Mae squared her shoulders and grasped her hips. The familiar scent of a recent open coal fire filled her nostrils. Memories of her father and the hours she'd spent with him in here aroused a tingling sensation that traipsed down her spine. She fought the memory and recaptured her resolve to address this man. "I saw you hiding around the corner of the building behind mine last night. What's going on?"

He picked up a metal rod and rolled it in his stained fingers. His focus remained on his hands as seconds chipped away at her unyielding stare, then he captured her gaze with his deep brown eyes. "My brothers and I have been keepin' watch every night since I moved out, to be certain that ye were safe."

How could she tell him she was grateful but at the same time resented the overprotectiveness? Nothing had happened in days. Seven days, to be precise. The same amount of time since Olin no longer lived there. Which gave credence to the possibility that the note was about Olin and not Cyrus. "Olin, I appreciate the concern but..."

He closed the distance between them. "Ida Mae, I think all this trouble is because of me. The least I can do is watch over you."

"Won't they see you in the shadows like I did?"

Olin reached out toward her, then quickly pulled back his hand. Ida Mae didn't know whether to be pleased or disappointed. One thing was certain, since Olin Orr had arrived, her life had not been the same. She couldn't even think straight.

"Aye, it is possible. I shall be more careful."

"No. I don't want you out there. Whoever is out there isn't causing any further problems. Stay home, Olin."

He cocked his head to the right and raised his left eyebrow.

"I'm fine." She shifted her weight to her right hip. "I have a gun for protection and I know how to use it."

"Ida Mae..." He inched forward.

She stepped back. He stopped his approach, tossing the small rod down on the bench where he'd been working. "As ye desire, miss." He took off his apron and hung it from a wooden peg. "Till the morrow, then."

Ida Mae clenched her jaw to keep from saying she wanted him to watch out for her. She wanted him to stay overnight in his shop. She felt safer knowing he was there. Instead, she gave in to Minnie's insistence that things would be better when Olin moved his shop.

The walls of the tiny room seemed to move in around her. Ida Mae scurried out of Olin's shop through the hidden doorway.

∞

Leaning farther into the shadows, he watched as Olin Orr left his shop. "Where is she?"

Olin left with his horse. He'd stopped following him the third night. The first night, he followed Olin back to his family farm. The second night he followed him to the edge of it; the third night to the edge of town, where he watched Olin go down the outbound road toward his house.

"Did he hurt her?" Sweat filled his palms. He rubbed them on his trousers. He eased his head out slowly for a better view. A quick glance told him no one would see him. With his hands in his pockets, he walked down the street as if he hadn't a care in the world.

He snatched a look at the lock on the blacksmith's shop door. If she was in there, she was locked in. He walked three more blocks, then one block south. The back of Ida Mae's building loomed in the distance. Ida Mae popped out the back door of her shop, on the side of the building.

He scratched his chin and waved as he walked past on the opposite side of the road. *She'll be mine soon.*

He smiled and tipped his hat.

∞

Olin raced back to the farm. John and Kyle were nowhere to be found. "Where are they?"

"Your brothers have an engagement at the Bowers'." His mother stepped into the parlor with a fresh vase of flowers.

"Oh."

Olin paced back and forth.

"What is it, dear?"

Olin stopped a couple feet from his mother. "Nothing really. I'm just concerned for Ida Mae. She's asked me not to keep watch over her."

His mother sat down in her sitting chair. "Aye, I can see her asking that."

"Why? Doesn't she know how dangerous it could be?"

"Perhaps ye aren't thinkin' with your head, son. Ye fancy the lass, yes?"

"Aye." Olin sat down in his father's chair. "But I can't entertain such foolish thoughts at this time in my life. I have nothing to offer a wife."

"The heart pays no never mind to such things. Yer father and I had nothin' when we married."

Olin nodded. He knew the stories.

"Bobby, if the good Lord wants ye to be together, He'll work it out. Seems to me, you're afraid to trust the Lord for Ida Mae's protection."

"It's not that." Olin paused. Did he trust the Lord?

"Son, ye always had a strong streak in ye to plow ahead and do what ye thought was best. Like deciding that because ye were the third son ye would have the smallest share of the land and moved on to make your way in this world without the help of your parents."

Olin took in a deep sigh.

"I say this not to remind ye of what happened but why it happened. In your father's will ye will inherit ten acres. It's been that way since the day ye were born. It's plenty of land for a man to provide for himself and a family if ye were to accept it. But ye told your father over and over again to give the land to Kyle. And while Kyle is planting those ten acres along with the other fifty he's to inherit, the land is not his. Ye could speak to your father and ask him for your inheritance if ye wish to marry one day."

Olin fought down the old argument that he didn't deserve the land after what he'd done to shame his family. Should he accept the gift? Should he pursue a relationship with Ida Mae?

"Have ye told Ida Mae how ye feel?"

"No. I don't know how I feel. I'm attracted to her, but she's always pulling away from me."

"Well, dear"—his mother slapped the arms of her chair and lifted herself out of it—"dinner is on the stove and your father shall return quickly. I don't see what all the fuss is about if ye haven't spoken your intentions."

"She's in danger, Mum."

"Aye, but what kind?"

His mother left him in the room to ponder her last comment. As Olin rolled it around, he had to wonder, was she really in danger or was it all about him? He had moved out and, with some luck, he'd find a new place to rent soon and would be permanently removed from Ida Mae's life. Whoever sent the warning wasn't out to hurt her, but rather to force him to leave the area. Perhaps if he showed Ida Mae a little interest the individual would let her be.

∽∾

Ida Mae stretched her back as she got up and walked around the shop. Sitting on the stool hour after hour had a certain disadvantage. She glanced up at the clock as the brass hammer struck three times. She twisted her body to the left, then the right, and caught a glimpse through the curtained window of the bright sunny day. With a roll of her shoulders, she decided to call it a day. Grabbing her bonnet from the peg by the door, she ventured out of the shop and walked down the street toward the center of town. A small fountain stood in the center of the marketplace. Ida Mae went over and sat on the outer wall with the fountain cascading behind her. People traveled quickly from place to place. Women held bundles and packages while the men loaded freight on their wagons. A lively melody streamed out of the pub. Everyone seemed to have a place to go, a place of belonging.

Chester Adams passed by with a brief wave and a smile.

Regan O'Malley swung a basket full of vegetables in perfect rhythm with her stride.

Then her eyes caught on Cyrus Morgan. She was too far away to hear the words exchanged between him and Mr. McGillis, the merchant of the Grain and Feed store, but Cyrus's rigid posture left little doubt that it was an unpleasant conversation. Cyrus boarded his wagon and slapped the reins. His horses—*correction, my father's horses*—whinnied and rushed the wagon down the street.

Mr. McGillis scanned the area. Seeing her, he marched over to the fountain. "Ida Mae!" He rubbed the dirt and sweat from his hands on a rag. "Cyrus Morgan says you're paying for all his orders. Is that true?"

"All?"

"Yes. I understand he's working on your farm, and there are expenses toward rebuilding the house, but a plow is an expensive item. I told him I had to check with you first. I'd say he didn't like that much."

I could see that. Ida Mae held back, then asked, "What kind of a plow does he say I need?"

"Another one like your father ordered a couple years back. It didn't make sense to me. He also ordered a bunch of hoes and rakes."

"Did he order any seed?"

"No, and that's the oddest part. If a man is going to be planting fields, he should have done it sooner, but he also needs to buy seed."

"Mr. McGillis, I appreciate your concern for my interest. I agree we don't need another plow. I'll speak to Cyrus about it. I would, however, like to order some seed. Corn and cotton is out of season for planting now. What do you recommend?"

"You could get some beans and other summer vegetables started now. Some winter squash might be good, as well."

"Thank you. I'll ride out to the farm this evening and look into Cyrus's plans."

"Very well. Thank you, Ida Mae."

"Thank you. Father would be so happy to see how his longtime friends continue to watch out for me."

" 'Tis an honor, lass." With a tip of his hat, Mr. McGillis headed back to his shop.

Ida Mae nibbled her lower lip for a moment as she pondered this new information. She had to confront Cyrus Morgan and find out what was going on. John Orr had been right. Cyrus should have planted long ago. And what had happened to her father's plow?

She scurried back to her shop, changed into her riding dress, and grabbed her horse from the stable. The entire trip she prayed for wisdom. She wasn't surprised to find Cyrus sitting on the front porch with his feet up on the rail. Rosey brought him a tall glass of tea.

"Welcome, Ida Mae." Cyrus came to his feet. Rosey gave a slight smile. Cyrus beamed. "What brings you out here?"

"I just spoke with Mr. McGillis." Ida Mae decided to hit him hard and watch his reactions.

"Ah, I've been meaning to tell you about the plow."

"What about it?"

"I hit some bad patches of rock. Tore the plow right up. Without your father, there's no one else to fix it, so I was trying to order you a new plow."

Her father had worked this land for many years. There was no deep patch of rocks that she could recall. All that had been turned up years ago went to build the fireplaces, walkways, and root cellars. "Where'd ya hit rock?"

"Uh, over by the river."

"Why were you trying to plow over there?"

"Ida Mae, if you don't think my decisions are right, go and hire yourself another farmer." Cyrus stomped his foot.

Rosey's eyes widened but she didn't speak.

"Cyrus, I simply asked why."

"Ain't no need to explain to a woman. You ain't got no business sense at all."

"Cyrus, I happen to own this land, and you won't be speaking to me in such a manner."

Cyrus dropped his chin to his chest for a moment, then eased it up slowly. "You're right. I apologize. I don't fancy folks calling me a liar, and I'm still steamed at Mr. McGillis."

"Apology accepted. I can't afford a new plow this year. Perhaps when the harvest comes in. The expenses to rebuild were much higher than I anticipated. I've been going over the books and I'm just about ready to settle my parents' estate with my brothers."

"I'm sorry. I'll be more careful with the expenses. I built ya a fine house, though."

"Yes, you've done a wonderful job, thank you."

"Maybe I'm a better carpenter than a farmer."

Rosey coughed. "I think you did a mighty fine job on the house. I don't smell a bit of smoke in it except around the fireplaces where that would be natural."

"Thank ya, darlin'." Cyrus spun around after giving his wife a quick wink. "I'm sorry, Ida Mae. Is there anything I can do to make it up?"

Buy a new plow from your own money, she wanted to say, but she held her tongue. "No, I guess not. But I'll be renting the farm to someone else after the harvest."

"I could leave now." Cyrus's voice sounded strained.

"No, you and Rosey need a place. Do her parents know yet?"

"Not until the harvest."

Right. Cyrus's charms no longer worked. Ida Mae now knew he'd been taking advantage of her, and she was too smart a businesswoman to let him continue. She mounted her horse once again. "I'll be approving any order with Mr. McGillis before he fills it. Like I said, I have to be careful with my expenses for a while."

"I understand."

From her horse, she saw a small patch of summer vegetables growing. Cyrus couldn't have planted those. "Garden looks nice, Rosey."

"Thank you."

"She's a right fine catch." Cyrus wrapped his arm around his wife and pulled her closer to him.

Ida Mae's trip back to the town seemed longer than usual. Cyrus Morgan hadn't planted a thing. And what was he doing using the plow by the river? Something wasn't adding up. She'd be rid of him by fall. She prayed the Lord would have him understand it wasn't personal, just wise business.

Or was it?

Chapter 7

Unable to sleep, Olin tossed back his bedcovers and dressed. In the wee hours of the morning he rode back to town. A faint scent of smoke crossed his nostrils, intensifying as he got closer. He pushed the horse faster. Outside Ida Mae's private quarters a cast-iron barrel containing burning debris had fallen on the ground and rolled very close to the steps leading to the door. Olin hustled to the town well and pumped out a bucket of water. In a matter of minutes the fire was out.

Ida Mae opened the door a crack. "What's going on?"

"It's me, Olin, Ida Mae. I found this trash bucket on fire and was putting out the flames. Go back to bed. Everything is all right."

"Olin," she whispered, "I told you—"

"Shh," he said. "I'll speak with ye later."

She slammed the door. His back muscles tightened. Olin worked them until they relaxed. The fire appeared to be the result of someone carelessly knocking over the incinerator, rekindling the flames.

Olin search the ground for any sign of an animal, or a human animal, knocking over the barrel. Seeing no evidence, he breathed a sigh of temporary relief. He walked over to Ida Mae's door and tapped it twice. "Ida Mae, it is me."

"Olin, I told you—" She opened the door. He stepped across the threshold but stood in the doorway.

"I couldn't sleep so I rode into town to check on you."

"Olin, you have to stop. I'm fine."

"Are ye, lass?"

"Y–yes," she stammered.

He reached over and held her by the elbows. "Ida Mae, I am concerned for you."

"Olin, how can I trust you? Every time something happens, you're there, lurking in the shadows. Minnie says. . ." Her lips went silent.

Olin dropped his hands to his side. "Ye don't trust me?" He took a tentative step back.

"Olin," she whispered, "I don't know what to think."

He saw tears filling her eyes. "Ida Mae, I care about you. I would never hurt ye."

"I know, but Minnie—"

"Is a gossip," he finished for her. "I'm sorry, but she's been that way ever since she was a wee one."

"True."

"Minnie doesn't know who to believe or trust. Have I ever done anything to ye? Have I ever snuck into your home without an invitation? Well, except for the time when I picked the lock because of the broken window."

Ida Mae sniffled.

"My sweet bonnie lass. . ." He reached out and wiped the tear from her cheeks. "The good Lord as my witness, I would never hurt ye."

"I want to believe you." She sneezed into her handkerchief.

"Pray, and trust the Lord. I think the fire was an accident. Have ye had any other problems?"

"No. Well, yes, some." She explained what happened with Cyrus as they stepped outside and sat down on the back steps. She also mentioned the loss of a few other small items.

"No further threats?"

"No." She wrung her hands in her lap.

"What are ye not telling me, Ida Mae?"

"Minnie says you may have taken liberties with the sister of the man you killed."

The heat of anger pumped through his veins. He silently counted to ten and fired off a quick prayer. "Ida Mae, Gary Jones didn't have a sister."

"Ah, so it's another misspoken piece of information."

"Aye, I'm afraid so. I swear, Ida Mae, I've never been less than a gentleman when in the presence of a woman."

She paused for a moment. "I believe you."

"Thank ye."

"Olin, I misplaced my mother's silver hairbrush earlier this week. Minnie said you probably took it to melt it down to cover a piece of tin."

"Of course I didn't, but ye are free to check my shop and my home if ye so desire."

"I don't believe it. I mean I'm trying not to believe all the things said about you. But sometimes it is just so hard."

"What have others said, if ye don't mind me askin'?"

"One of my customers has heard the same rumors Minnie has reported to me. Another suggested that John Thatcher doesn't trust you, that's why he's kept watch on your place."

"The sheriff?"

⚭

"Yes." Ida Mae held her sides. It was so easy to talk with Olin, and in his presence she believed him. How could she not be strong when Minnie reported all sorts

153

of untruths to her? And why would Minnie care?

"I wasn't aware of his watching my shop. He's come in a time or two, but he came in regarding my work."

"What is the sheriff ordering?"

"Ah, lass, I'm afraid I can't tell ye. It's a confidential matter."

"Confidential tinsmith?"

Olin chuckled. "I was as shocked at the time the sheriff spoke with me, as anyone would be. But it is confidential."

Calm continued to sweep over her as she sat next to him. Inhaling deeply, her nostrils filled with the scent she'd come to know as Olin's. The hint of wood smoke, not coal, reminded her as to why they were here sitting on the back steps outside her room instead of inside. "Are you sure the fire was an accident?"

"Appears to be. But, Ida Mae, my concerns are increasing. Ye need to be safe. Why don't ye come stay at my parents' until we know who's behind all this."

"No." Ida Mae closed her eyes. Fire had caused her parents' deaths. Fear wove around her heart like a coarse thread. "Not yet. If you think the fire was an accident, then there isn't anything more to be concerned about."

"Aye, there is. Ye mentioned your mother's hairbrush. It appears to me someone is watching you, sneaking into your home, and stealing personal items. What if ye walk into your private quarters and startle the thief?"

"Olin, I've given this a lot of thought. It seems to be the actions of a child."

"Mayhap, but I believe caution is in order."

"Olin, I can't live in fear. It's taken me the better part of the year since my parents' deaths to even venture out in public settings. For the first few months after they died, depression ruled my days, then it switched to fear that I would die a horrible death, as well. Cyrus started rebuilding my parents' house right after the fire. He'd work evenings and weekends. You know that is what truly puzzles me about him. He worked in earnest to fix up the house, but his farming skills are—well, let's just say most ten-year-olds could do better."

Olin rested his arm around her shoulders.

"All of that is to say, I can't go back to living in fear. I have to face this, catch whoever it is in the act. If I go to your parents' house, I'll never find out who is doing all this."

"Have you told John Thatcher?"

"No. Well, I mentioned the bell missing from my shop door."

"Good, he needs to be aware."

She sensed Olin would be talking with the sheriff to apprise him of all the recent events.

"I should go back to bed."

"Aye." Olin stood up and brushed the backside of his pants. "I'll see ye in the morning."

"Sleep in your shop. Don't go home."

"Aye, it would be easier. And no one should be watching the shops now."

"Good night, Olin." She stood up and made her way to the top step, then turned back to look at him. "You're a good man, Olin."

In the shadowy light she could see his face brighten. *A very good man.*

"By the good Lord's grace; but ye are a fine lass." He opened the door for her, then slipped off into the darkness. Her heart plummeted. In spite of what Minnie had said, she felt safe with Olin. And her growing attraction deepened. It was no longer just his fine looks but him, his character, the way he treated her. Perhaps spending time at his parents' home would allow her to really get to know this mysterious man that trouble seemed to follow. *Perhaps.* She closed the door and secured it, grateful for the bolt lock her father put in so many years earlier.

∞

Olin woke to a thundering crash. He bolted up from his cot and tried to get his bearings. "Who's there?"

Seeing nothing, he slipped on his boots and worked his way to the front of the smithy. Opening the barn door allowed full light to flow into the area. Seeing nothing out of place, he ran around the corner of the building to Ida Mae's front door.

The iron handle wouldn't move. "Locked." He rattled the door in its hinges. "Ida Mae!"

The sign in the window said Closed. He didn't like it. He ran back to his shop and picked up the tools he needed to force entry. That's when he spotted the window. How had he missed it? Framed by shattered glass, Ida Mae stood looking out toward him. "Let me in, lass."

She stood for a moment looking past him, then shook her head slightly and walked toward the door.

He slipped through and had her in his arms before she'd fully opened the door. "Are ye all right?"

The blue in her eyes darkened. She said nothing. He held her closer and whispered in her ear. "You're safe now."

He swept her up into his arms and carried her over to the area where the rock had been tossed. This rock was much larger than the one before. Carrying her to the back room, he gently set her on the chair. "I'll be right back."

She nodded, but not a word came from her lips.

He pulled himself away and went to the rock. A note was wrapped around this one, as well. He untied it and read the ugly message. A horrible word he couldn't even repeat blazed across the crumpled paper. Olin shoved it in his pocket and went back to Ida Mae.

He pulled out a carpetbag from her closet and shoved a dress, a couple of blouses, and a skirt into it. Then he went to her chest of drawers and pulled out some unmentionables, not bothering to ask if they were what she needed or not. "Come on. You're going to my parents' house. It isn't safe for you to be here alone and it isn't proper for me to stay to protect ye."

She seemed to be in shock. "Ida Mae?"

She closed her eyes, then opened them slowly. The deep blue of her eyes focused on him. "For a couple days, just until the window is fixed."

No way would he allow her to return until they caught who was behind all this.

They rode together on his horse. He wrapped his arms around her. Several people stared as they made their way out of town. He knew the tongues would be wagging after this, but what choice did he have? Whoever was after her had been there last night. He'd seen Olin come out of the building and assumed. . . Well, he wouldn't let his mind go to what the viper of a man had thought.

She didn't speak the entire trip to his parents' house. After a brief recap of the night's and morning's events, he left Ida Mae in his parents' able care. His father, Olin knew, would keep his rifle handy.

❧

Olin waited most of the day at the sheriff's office. Several townspeople had come in to report the broken window at Ida Mae's shop. Some of them looked at Olin as if he stank. But Olin kept his mouth shut tight and answered questions only if they spoke to him. Fortunately, no one asked him anything more than if he was here to report the broken window. Which he was.

The door slammed open and Percy barged through. He stopped short upon seeing Olin. "Where is she?"

Olin stood up and squared his shoulders. "Safe."

"Why don't you go back north? You're not wanted here."

Olin sat back down.

"Minnie says it's all your fault. The broken window was meant for you."

Olin bit down harder. He knew the truth, and he wasn't about to give Percy any information that might go back to Minnie.

"What? Someone cut your tongue out?"

Olin narrowed his gaze and seared it into Percy as if it were red-hot metal ready to be molded and shaped.

"Ah, you were never anything but a yellow belly." Percy stomped out of the sheriff's office.

Olin closed his eyes and prayed for the Lord to remove his anger. He was certain his cousin had come once again to try to persuade the sheriff to run him out of town.

Finally, by mid-afternoon the sheriff strolled in. "Sheriff," Olin greeted with a nod as he stood.

"Mr. Orr, I heard we have a problem."

"Ye might say that."

"Folks say you hustled Ida Mae out of town, that she was screaming and hollering the entire time."

Olin snickered. "She didn't say a word. She's at my parents' farm. Safe."

John Thatcher removed his hat and nodded.

"Good, now tell me, what happened?"

Olin went over the entire history, starting with the first window and message. "Today, this was the message." Olin pulled the crumpled paper from his pocket and handed it over to the sheriff.

"I see. Have you had improper relations with Ida Mae?"

"No." Olin defended Ida Mae's honor perhaps a bit too loudly. "Don't ye see? The person who did this must have set the fire last night. They must've seen me leaving after having been inside for so long."

John Thatcher scratched the day-old growth on his chin. "This whole affair might cause Mr. Bechtler some concern about you making the mold for his gold coin mint."

"Aye, it wouldn't be much of a secret if the thief found the plates before I'm done with them."

"How long can Ida Mae stay at your folks' home?"

"As long as needed."

"That should work fine. You are aware the gossip will spread quickly that you've taken Ida Mae off. If she doesn't return to work tomorrow, they may start suspecting you."

"I'm aware. Please, go to my parents' farm and see that she's all right. She's in shock, but I expect her to be doing better now. Mum has a way with calming a person."

"That she does. I'll swing over to your farmstead and have a long talk with Ida Mae."

"Sheriff. . ." Olin looked down at his dusty boots. "She doesn't know about today's note."

"I'll be sensitive. But she's a grown woman and has a right to know."

"Aye. Who would say such horrible things about Ida Mae?"

A slow smile creased the leathered cheeks of John Thatcher. "You fancy her, don't you?"

"Aye. When all is settled I shall tell her of my feelings."

John slipped his hat back on his head. "I reckon she probably already knows."

Chapter 8

Would you wash those spinach leaves, Ida Mae?"

"Yes, ma'am." Ida Mae went to the kitchen pump, pumped out a small amount of water, soaked the bright green leaves in the bucket, and shook out a handful. Preparing a meal for a small army hadn't been a part of her life for many years. She enjoyed it and she missed it.

"Bobby says ye be a fine spinster. How's your weavin'?"

"Fair. Mother was the best."

"Aye, that she was. Did ye know that my clansmen brought the flax to this country a hundred years ago?"

"No."

"Well, it be a fact, darlin'. Me maiden name is Steele. In 1718 Thomas Steele sailed from Ireland with a group of others to the New World, seekin' a place they could worship God and make an honest wage. The governor told them to head north. The French and Indian War was heating up at the time and the governor thought sending me clan out there would make a great first line of defense. What the governor didn't know was that the reverend was an old classmate with someone in the French army. I used to know who, but I don't keep these things straight."

Ida Mae watched the delightful woman work as she talked, quickly preparing the dough for the bread. Her own family lines came to America later but had moved away from the clans. She had many ancestors who were not Scots-Irish, unlike the Orr family.

"The Frenchman told his Indian friends to leave this group of people alone and they were never attacked during the war."

Ida Mae giggled. "I reckon the governor wasn't pleased."

"I always pictured him just standing there scratching his wig, trying to figure out what these Presbyterians did to keep the Indians away. The Puritans considered our people a rowdy sort. In the end, it was that ship of people who brought the potato and linen flax to the New World. Many say that without us the War of Independence would not have been fought."

"How do you know so much about your family?"

"Me mum and pa passed it down. There's another story about the Great Wagon Road, but we'll save it for another time."

Ida Mae wanted to hear it now. It had been so long since she'd been around a real family. Her stomach flipped. Memories resurfaced. Ida Mae dipped her hand back in the bucket and shook out some more of the leafy greens. The Orr farm was already producing peas, beans, spinach, and radishes. Cyrus hadn't even started to plant the seed yet. What had she gotten herself into letting him rent the farm and house?

"Ida Mae, I told ye that story about my family because we come from good stock. Ye can trust Bobby—Olin," she amended.

Bobby, she mused. He didn't seem like a Bobby to her. Olin fit him better.

Mrs. Orr went on and on about her family's history. While the facts were interesting, the information wasn't enough to keep Ida Mae's mind from drifting back to seeing that rock come through the front window. If she had taken one more step she would have been hurt, if not killed. Who was so angry with her for letting Olin rent her father's shop? It didn't make sense.

"Ida Mae?"

"Sorry, my mind drifted."

"That's all right, dear. I can rattle on a bit about family history. It goes back hundreds of years. . . ."

Hundreds. Ida Mae raised the corners of her lips and hoped the smile appeared genuine.

Mrs. Orr giggled. "I won't be putting ye through all that. I'm just trying to distract ye from dwellin' on your shop. Which I be doin' rather poorly."

"I'm sorry. I don't understand why someone would be attacking me in such a way."

"Rumors. And mind ye, these are just rumors. Word was that someone deliberately attempted to start a fight with Bobby all those years ago. His father and I decided we needed to remove him from the area and arranged the apprenticeship. I reckon we figured enough time had passed and no one would hold a grudge for seven years. Mayhap we be wrong. I'm so sorry."

"But that's what is odd. Why haven't they attacked Olin's shop? Why mine? If someone were truly out to ruin Olin, wouldn't they send rocks through his windows?"

Mrs. Orr raised her right eyebrow.

"There aren't any glass windows in his shop, but still."

"Ye might be right. But why would anyone want to hurt a bonnie lass such as yourself?"

"I don't know. I wish I did, but nothing has made sense since Olin came to town."

"Then marry my boy and be done with it."

"Pardon?"

∞

"Afternoon, Sheriff, what can I do for you?" Olin put the hammer down and walked over to meet the sheriff.

"I had a visit from one of Ida Mae's neighbors. They say they saw you out last night behind Ida Mae's and setting the fire."

"What?"

Sheriff Thatcher held up his hands. "Hold on. That's what they said. I pushed them further and they admitted that they didn't see you start the fire. They just assumed that Ida Mae caught you and you put it out."

The vein on Olin's right temple started to pulse.

"Seems to me someone is anxious to get you out of town, or at least far away from Ida Mae."

Olin crossed his arms and leaned back on the beam holding the corner of the loft. "I feared that be the case. I'll move my business out today."

"Lawrence McGillis at the Grain and Feed store says he has a back room where you can set up shop. The only problem is it isn't within eyeshot to watch over Ida Mae's. My wife won't appreciate it, but I'll spend the next couple of nights here in the loft. I should be able to sneak in early enough so no one will know I'm inside."

"There's a secret passageway between her private quarters and my shop. I don't know how to get into her place from here, if there is a way, but on her side it's a door in the back of the closet."

"Show me."

Olin pointed out the opening and together they went around to the front and then inside Ida Mae's shop. Olin leaned over and pulled out two thin rods, one with a small hook on the end. He inserted them into the keyhole and jiggled them into place, then opened the door.

"How many folks know you can open a lock like that?"

"Ida Mae does. Apart from her, I don't think there's anyone else."

"Let's keep it that way, or you'll be blamed for every crime in the area."

"Yes, sir." Olin slipped his tools into his pocket. They went past the counter in her shop and entered Ida Mae's private quarters. The sheriff scanned the orderly room. He appeared quite at ease being in someone else's home when it was vacant. Olin felt as uncomfortable as a man sitting in church with wet clothes. It didn't seem right for him to be standing in the room without her. In the full light of day he saw that she'd taken the small area and made it quite warm and welcoming.

"Where's the secret doorway?"

"Over here." Olin pointed to the door in the back of the large storage closet against the wall of the smithy.

The sheriff examined both sides of the entryway. "While I'm keeping watch I'll want this doorway open. But if I don't catch who's behind all this red-handed I'll want you to nail your closet door shut in these corners. If the thief has been using this passage to sneak out through the barn, maybe we can trap him in your closet."

"I don't want Ida Mae in any danger."

"Nor do I. The best thing to do is to keep things as normal as possible. What concerns me is the note on the rock this morning. By now the entire town knows you brought Ida Mae to your family farm. Let's keep it that way. Tomorrow, bring her back and I'll watch over her all night. Those two nights should give me a chance to catch this guy. If he is simply taking things out of her place, then he'll want to come in while Ida Mae isn't home and while the building is vacant. I'll be there ready and waiting. If, however, they are after her, they'll wait until tomorrow night when she appears to be vulnerable."

"I don't like it. What if something happens to her?"

"You'll have to trust me. Don't try takin' the law into your own hands again, son. You know what happened the last time."

Olin's stomach soured. "Fine."

"Olin." The sheriff placed his hand on Olin's shoulder. "Trust me."

"What if nothing happens in the next two days?"

"We'll decide what to do then, agreed?"

"Agreed."

They left Ida Mae's shop. Olin checked the boards he'd put up to cover the broken window. All was secure. Back in the smithy he packed up his tools, then went over to the Grain and Feed shop to speak with Mr. McGillis. They agreed on a fair price, and the rest of the day Olin spent moving and setting up his shop in the new location. He drew up a note telling folks where to find him. Anything to put Ida Mae in a safe position.

"So, you're leaving town?" Percy stood in the doorway with a smug grin.

⁂

"Ida Mae, sit, please." Mrs. Orr rubbed her hands on the skirt of her apron.

Ida Mae sat down at the small kitchen table. "Mrs. Orr, Olin and I aren't—"

"Ye have eyes for one another. Anyone can see."

Ida Mae cast her eyes toward her apron.

"Darlin', ye and Bobby—Olin—snatch glances at one another all the time. If ye love him. . ."

"We haven't spoken of such matters."

"Ah, me boy is takin' his sweet time. I thought with him having his brothers out all night, watchin' over your place, that ye and he were closer."

"No, ma'am."

"Do ye love him?"

Ida Mae's fingers started to shake. She laced them around the hem of her apron. "I'm attracted to him, but love? It is too soon to tell."

"Aye, I understand. Ye love him, but ye don't know it yet. That's fine. What

161

I was thinkin', and mayhap it be an old woman's need for more grandchildren, is ye and Olin could marry and perhaps this would stop the person."

"I can't marry Olin."

The screen door to the kitchen slapped shut.

"Mum, what are ye suggesting?"

Mrs. Orr's face turned a brilliant shade of crimson. "Foolish thoughts, an old woman's foolish thoughts. Forgive me, son. Forgive me, Ida Mae."

"Forgiven." Ida Mae grasped the hem of the apron so tightly her fingers started to numb.

Mrs. Orr scurried out of the kitchen. Olin sat down beside Ida Mae. "I'm sorry."

"Olin, she was just probing."

"Aye. I daresay something she is quite proficient at. I had a talk with Sheriff Thatcher. He's going to stay in my shop overnight and hope to catch whoever is slipping in and removing items from your shop and personal quarters." He went on to explain in greater detail about moving his business and the two-day plan to watch the place. He concluded with, "Percy came to see me as I was getting ready to close up the shop."

"Oh?"

"He heard I was leaving town."

Ida Mae shook her head. "The gossip in this town can be incredible."

"Yes, and today a couple of your neighbors came to the sheriff to report that I had attempted to start a fire last night."

A wave of doubt instantly rose and fell in her stomach.

"Ida Mae, the sheriff questioned them thoroughly and found they never saw me start the fire. They just saw me when I ordered you back into the building and put out the fire."

"What did the note say?"

"Ye don't want to know."

"Olin, tell me."

Olin jumped up and walked away from her. "No. It was rude and something a fine lass should not see."

"Olin." She stood up. "I will not have you treat me as a child. Give me that note."

Olin came behind her and wrapped his arms around her. His lips were mere inches from her ears. Gooseflesh rose down her neck to her arms. "Ida Mae," he whispered, "please trust me."

She twisted in his arms and faced him. "I do trust you. Please trust me. I can handle it."

He released her and stepped back. Looking down, he swept the floor with his right boot. "It was a single word meaning a lady of ill repute."

Ida Mae's nerves kicked in once again and her stomach twisted like a lemon being wrung out of all its flavor. Taking in a deep breath, she let it out slowly. "More than one saw us last night."

"Aye, I'm afraid so. Ye and the good Lord know nothing inappropriate happened between us last night, but someone doesn't see it that way."

"Did Percy mention that?"

"No. He only knew I was moving out of the shop. He didn't even know I was moving into McGillis's Grain and Feed store."

Ida Mae paced. "Then Percy didn't throw the rock."

"No, I suppose not."

"Olin, I believe someone is out to get me. It isn't you they are after."

"Perhaps, but I believe there is more than one person behind all this. It is obvious someone didn't want me renting your father's shop. Hopefully, my move will stop that issue. Are ye up for staying in your place tomorrow night with the sheriff hiding in my shop?"

"No. . . Yes. . . I suppose I have to be. I want this to end and I want it to end now."

"Do ye know ye are beautiful when ye are determined?"

His smile melted away her anger over the situation.

"You're incorrigible."

"Aye, but that's why ye love me." He winked.

Heat blazed across her checks and down her neck. "I care, Olin. I don't know if I love."

He closed the distance between them. The touch of his fingers brushing the stray strands of hair from her face excited and calmed her all at the same time. "I care, too."

She closed her eyes, willing him to come closer and kiss her.

"May I?" he whispered.

Chapter 9

B obby. . ." His mother's voice skidded to a halt.

Olin's heart thumped. Ida Mae buried her face in his chest. The raw emotions mixed with the memory of her lips doubled his determination to help this woman.

"I'm sorry," his mother mumbled. She silently slipped out of the room.

Olin pulled back from Ida Mae. He gave her a wink, then called out to his mother. "Mum!"

She reentered the room. "Ye know I'm not sorry. Here ye be claimin' ye ain't in love, and what do I find? Ye young'uns best learn what love is."

Ida Mae pulled his shirt around the edges of her face.

His love for her deepened a hundredfold. "Hey, sweetheart." He nudged her chin with his forefinger. "Mum won't bite."

"Aye, I might take ye over my knee, but I won't bite ye."

Ida Mae moaned.

It took all of Olin's strength not to laugh at her embarrassment.

"Your father was on my heels. Ye best come apart or you'll be even more embarrassed."

Ida Mae released his shirt and stepped back, turning away from him, away from his mother.

"Mum, would ye excuse us for a moment?"

He took Ida Mae's hand and tugged. She resisted for a moment, then followed him out the back door. He led her to the shade tree and the swing his father had built years ago. "I'm sorry to have embarrassed you, but I'm not sorry for kissing you."

Her eyes glistened. "It was wrong."

"Why?" He sat down on the swing and patted the seat for her to join him. She continued to stand.

"Because it isn't proper. You and I haven't courted."

"Ida Mae, I'd ask yer father for your hand in marriage, but he's not here. This has to be your decision."

"Marriage? It was just a kiss."

"Was it?" He couldn't argue with her. It was simply a kiss. But the moment their lips met he knew beyond any human reason this woman was made for him, that God designed them to be together one day. She had to feel it, too.

"There's too much going on right now for me to know whether I love you or not. My emotions have gone from one extreme to another. How can I know what I'm feeling is real and not the result of all the turmoil I felt before we kissed?"

"Sweetheart, please sit with me. I promise not to kiss you unless ye ask." He wiggled his eyebrows.

Ida Mae let out a strangled laugh and joined him.

He wrapped his arm around her but didn't draw her close.

"We can hold off on marriage for a while."

"You're worse than your mother."

"Aye, I suppose I am. Before I kissed you I knew I cared for ye deeply. But when we kissed my love for you grew."

Ida Mae sighed. "I can't trust my emotions. Look what happened after the fire and my foolish trust in Cyrus. I don't know what that man is doing on my farm, but he isn't farming. I think he's found a free place to live and I let him."

What does this have to do with the kiss? "Did ye kiss Cyrus?"

"No. I mean I trusted him because of how he helped me after the fire. He took care of so many things. But he wasn't the man I thought him to be. I reckon I shouldn't have let him farm the land when I caught him and Rosey out at the farmhouse, but it made sense at the time."

"Cyrus isn't a farmer. Neither am I for that matter. But he did do an excellent job rebuilding the house, didn't he?"

"Yes."

"Don't doubt yourself, then. Ye did what was right with what facts ye knew. We now know he can't farm, so you will not let him live there again after the harvest."

"True."

"Ida Mae, I see in ye an incredible woman. Yes, I want to protect you. But ye have done well to settle your parents' accounts and work out a plan with your brothers for the family assets. You are a smart woman. Not to mention a wonderful spinster."

"Don't remind me."

"Pardon?"

"Never mind. Just my foolish ramblings about the two meanings of the word."

Spinster? Ah, one who spins and an old single lass. "I can change one of those meanings for you."

She slapped him on the knee.

"Tell me this, at least. Are ye at peace with me beside you?"

She glanced down at her hands. Her soft, delicate hands. Olin swallowed a desire to kiss each and every one of her fingers.

"Yes," she whispered.

Olin's heart soared.

The sound of a horse approaching caused him to remove his arm from around her shoulders.

∞

Ida Mae was more confused now than she was on her arrival earlier that morning. Olin had no idea how much she enjoyed and longed for another kiss from him. Even if it was just an emotional response to the shocking events of the day.

"Ida Mae?" The deep voice of her uncle, Minnie's father, echoed between the house and the barn. "Where are you?"

Olin jumped up from the swing and held out his hand to assist her. She took it but let go as soon as she was on her feet. There was no question what her uncle was here for or who told her uncle where she was. "Uncle Ty, I'm out back."

The man stood about six feet tall. "Your cousin told me I'd find you here. Come on. You're coming home with me."

"I'm fine, Uncle Ty. Have you met Olin Orr?"

"Hello, sir." Olin extended his hand.

"I ain't met him, nor do I have a mind to. You're coming home with me right now. I ain't having the whole town shaking their tongues about our family and how my niece is a lady of ill repute."

Olin's shoulders squared as he stepped in front of the man. "Ye will not speak of Ida Mae that way. Nor shall ye speak to her in that manner."

Ida Mae placed her hand on Olin's forearm. "It's all right. I'll go with him."

"Ye will not. I won't have ye subjected to such evil thoughts."

Uncle Ty paled. "What gives you the right, son?"

"I love her. And if ye did, ye wouldn't have spoke such to her."

Kyle, John, and Olin's father came out of the barn and stood beside her and Olin.

"Uncle Ty, I've done nothing wrong. Olin simply offered a place for me to stay while my window is repaired."

"And his mother and I would nay allow any improprieties in our house."

"I'll go if you insist. But at least here I have my own room and my own bed. I'm not partial to sleeping with Minnie. The girl tosses and turns all night."

Uncle Ty relaxed. "You weren't taken against your will?"

"No, sir. Olin's a perfect gentleman."

Mrs. Orr joined them, rubbing her hands on her apron. "Can I get ye a glass of iced tea?"

"That would be mighty neighborly of you. I guess I let my emotions run away with me."

Olin's father walked up to him. "I have a couple daughters of my own. I understand. Come in the house and let's set a spell."

Kyle and John went back to the barn. Olin, his parents, Uncle Ty, and Ida

Mae sat down in the front sitting room. "Mighty fine house you have."

"Thank ye. The good Lord's blessed us."

Uncle Ty's house was a rugged log cabin with small rooms. They finished off the dirt floors a few years back. He was a hard worker, and over the years Minnie spent more money than they could afford. Thankfully, they sent her to work at the local bakery a few years back and it had been a huge help.

"Ida Mae, Minnie's been tellin' us all kinds of things. Has someone been stealing from you?"

"Yes."

"And there have been broken windows?"

"Yes."

"What about this fire? Minnie said Olin's been rumored to have started it."

Mr. Orr cleared his throat.

"Forgive me; she said it was a rumor."

Olin spoke up. "Most of what Minnie has shared with you is true. For some reason folks are trying to bring up the past and make me leave town. You may speak with the sheriff and confirm his re-investigation into Gary Jones's death. I admit he died at my hands while we were involved in childish fisticuffs, but it was accidental."

Ty turned to address Ida Mae. "I'm still concerned about folks thinking you are not behaving as a lady should."

"I can't do anything about gossip, and I certainly can't do anything about Minnie. She means well, but she'll listen to anything and assume it is so. As I said outside, I'll stay with you for the night if you insist, but I'd prefer to stay out here, if you don't mind. I'm returning to my home tomorrow."

"Well, I don't know. Your aunt will have my hide if I don't bring ya. But I can see that these folks will watch over you. Why don't you stay in your shop tonight, Olin?"

"I moved my shop to McGillis's Grain and Feed. There isn't room for a cot in there."

Not to mention the sheriff will be sleeping in his old shop tonight. Ida Mae smiled. "Uncle Ty, I am fine and I am safe."

"Very well. But I want you to let us know the next time."

There hadn't been time. "Sure. I'm sorry to have put you through so much worry."

Olin stood first. "Mr. Jacobs, who told Minnie that the town was gossiping about Ida Mae being a woman of ill repute?"

"I don't know. She said someone saw you entering Ida Mae's late last night."

Olin glanced over at Ida Mae.

"That was in the middle of the night."

"You mean it's true?" Ty's hands clutched the arms of his chair until his knuckles turned white.

∞

Olin had taken just about enough from Ida Mae's *caring* family. "Sir, I told ye once, ye will not speak thus to Ida Mae. I shall not warn ye a second time."

"Uncle Ty, relax, please. There was a fire outside my house. Olin put it out. We were talking in the entryway. Nothing happened."

"I ain't about to put up with the likes of you speakin' to me in such tones. Ida Mae, come with me now. Pack your bags and come."

Ida Mae stood up.

"No, she's not leaving. She's safe here and she'll stay here."

"Olin Robert Orr, sit down." His father stood with his hands on his hips and pointed toward Uncle Ty's chair.

"Mr. Jacobs, have ye ever known Ida Mae to be anything less than honorable?"

"No."

"Ye should be trustin' your niece, not the gossip of others."

Olin fought the desire to escort the man from his home. He was looking after the well-being of Ida Mae, even if it was misguided.

"On my word of honor, Mr. Jacobs, we did nothing inappropriate last night or any other time."

The sheriff and Olin had decided to keep the message from the rock hidden in hopes of exposing the person who had written it. But it appeared the individual had already started informing others. Olin wanted to be on the streets, watching Ida Mae's. He wanted to catch this man in the act. No, he *needed* to catch this man. *Ida Mae should not live in fear or humiliation because of her relationship with me, Lord.*

"I'm sorry I spoke poorly of Ida Mae. I do apologize. I've been up all night, helping birth a calf. But it ain't right for Ida Mae to stay here when folks are suspectin' the worst. I think she should stay with us."

"I'll come." Ida Mae stood. "I'll get my carpetbag."

"Are ye sure?"

"Yes, Olin, thank you. It's for the best."

"As ye wish. I'll lend you my horse." Olin walked out to the barn.

"What's happenin'?" John and Kyle jumped on him when he entered the barn.

"She's going home with her uncle."

"I don't like it," Kyle said, twisting the rope in his hand.

"Neither do I, but it is her family and it is her choice."

"Aye, 'tis true. What should we do about the recent rock?"

"Let me give Ida Mae my horse. I'll come back and tell ye the plans."

Olin walked the horse over to the front door. He'd left it saddled when he returned from town; he'd been waiting to discuss his returning tonight to watch the street when he was pleasantly interrupted. Olin thought back on their kiss. Warmth and a huge sense of protectiveness came over him.

Ida Mae and her uncle exited the house. "Are ye sure?" he asked again, praying she'd change her mind.

"Yes."

His heart sank.

"I love ye," he whispered as he helped her mount the horse.

Ida Mae's smile sent his heart thumping again. "I'll see you in the morning, Olin."

"Aye."

"Come on, girl, the sun will be setting soon." Ty Jacobs clicked his tongue and his horse trotted forward.

Ida Mae followed.

Olin watched as they made their way down the long dirt road. She turned back and waved just before the bend. *Please, Lord, keep her safe.*

Olin ran back to the barn. "Saddle up the horses, boys. We have a long night ahead of us."

Chapter 10

"Minnie, please stop. What is it with you?"

"Me? You're the one that won't listen to common sense. The man is dangerous, I tell you."

Ida Mae's patience was wearing thin. She would much rather be savoring the memory of Olin's kiss than arguing with her cousin that she didn't know what she was talking about. "Minnie, I don't know why you believe Percy Mandrake anyway. The man is not the most God-fearing man in the county."

"But he's fine-lookin'."

"If you say so." Olin's deep brown eyes and wonderfully curly black hair flooded back in her mind.

"See, ya know what I mean. Percy also knows how to treat a woman."

Ida Mae's smile slipped. "Minnie, I don't know Percy, but he's never struck me as being completely honest." *And how does one trust a male gossip? Not that I trust a female one, either.*

"He says Bobby has always been a problem."

"Maybe for him. Olin says ever since they were children Percy and he never got along. They've been oil and water forever."

"See, you have to agree with me. Percy is telling the truth."

"No, I don't have to agree with you. Percy is not telling the entire truth. How'd he know that Olin came into my house last night? It was the middle of the night. No one should have been out there walking the streets."

"So, why was Bobby?"

"He couldn't sleep and came by to check on me because of all the problems I've been having."

"Neighbors said he started the fire."

"And the sheriff got the truth out of them that they didn't really see him start the fire. And why does Percy want Olin out of town so badly?" Ida Mae pressed. "After all these years, why does he care? It seems to me he goes out of his way to interfere with Olin's life, and Olin hasn't done anything to Percy."

Minnie curled her knees up to her chest. "You trust Olin that much?"

"Yes. Do you trust Percy that much?" Ida Mae sat down on the bed beside her cousin and faced her.

Minnie hung her head. "No, I suppose I don't."

"Ah, so who do you think might be right in this case, Olin or Percy?"

Minnie shot her chin upward. "I'd hate to admit it, but probably Olin."

Ida Mae smiled. "Thank you. That's what I wanted to hear. Now, let's get to sleep so I can go to work having rested a little bit."

They shifted and slipped under the covers. "Ida Mae?"

"Hmm."

"Cyrus is still telling folks you and he are married."

"What?" Ida Mae shot back upright. "He's married; I'm not."

"He's married?"

Ida Mae closed her eyes and sighed. "Yes, but promise me you won't tell a single soul. I mean it, Minnie, not one person."

"Who to, if it ain't you?"

"I can't say. I promised I wouldn't. They haven't told her parents yet."

"Oh, brother. If I marry I won't be staying in my parents' house and pretending I'm not."

"Nor would I."

Ida Mae lay back down and slipped the covers over herself once again.

"Ida Mae?"

"Hmm." *Please, God, let her sleep. My nerves are shot. I need some peace.*

"Do you think you'll get married?"

"I hope to."

"I'm worried. We're getting too old. Men like the younger women."

"Minnie, trust the Lord."

"I suppose."

Ida Mae thought of a hundred things to say to her cousin about trusting the Lord and not throwing herself at men as she had in the past. Minnie rolled to her side. Ida Mae rolled to her other side and faced the dark wall. Choosing to think on better things, she allowed her mind to go back to the kitchen at the Orrs' farm. Olin's warm embrace, their tender kiss and his mother's. . . Ida Mae giggled.

"What?" Minnie whispered.

∞

Olin sequestered himself behind the houses of the nosy neighbors who had reported him to the sheriff. They had a fair view of Ida Mae's shop. In the dark, it didn't make sense that they could have made out that it was him who put out the fire. He didn't know these people. They were new in town, at least within the past seven years. Charlotte was growing. No one could know everyone any longer.

A man walked past Ida Mae's building. It was late enough that most folks were home in bed. Olin whistled the night owl's birdsong to alert his brothers that someone was walking past.

The man continued to walk at a slow but even pace.

Olin sat for another hour until a dim light appeared in Ida Mae's room. He eased out of his cramped space and stretched his muscles. Should he go in?

171

He signaled Kyle with the screech owl's birdsong, which would keep John perched with a perfect shot of the back door if someone should come out.

Kyle jogged quietly among the shadows.

"Look." Olin pointed.

"Someone's in there."

"Aye, it could be the sheriff. Should I go in?"

"No, little brother, ye stay here. I'll take a wide circle around the block and sneak up to the blacksmith shop and tell the sheriff."

"Tap the door three times lightly. If he doesn't answer, barge in."

Kyle nodded and slipped back into the shadows.

Olin moved to a location closer to the back door but lay down under some overgrown bushes, praying that he wouldn't disturb any snakes or other creeping animals.

Ten minutes later a man yelled in front of the shop. Olin bolted, immediately joined by John.

∞

Exhausted, Ida Mae prayed she could get some rest in her own bed. She didn't have any clients coming in this morning, so she decided to close the shop for the morning and take advantage of her own bed. Whomever Minnie married would have to snore louder than her or else be deaf, because he wouldn't get a wink of sleep otherwise. She felt some relief that her family believed her about Olin. Granted, the Jacobses were hesitant, but they did trust her. It had been a good decision to go home with Uncle Ty. She would have preferred to stay at Olin's, but her family needed to know Olin was not the man the rumors made him out to be. What still bothered her was Percy Mandrake. Why did he hold so much disdain for Olin?

"Ida Mae! Ida Mae!" Mrs. Waters ran up to her as she exited the stable. "Did you hear what happened last night?"

Dread spiraled down her spine. Olin said the sheriff was going to spend the night in the shop. "No, what happened?"

"In the middle of the night a man fell and broke his leg right in front of your shop. Can you imagine?"

"No, who?"

"Sheriff found him in the wee hours. What was the man doing out at that hour, I ask you? Up to no good, I tell you."

"He was in front of my shop?"

"Actually, by the town well, but that's just about in front of your shop. You didn't have a gentleman caller again last night, did you?"

Ida Mae held down her temper. "No. I didn't have one any other night, either, contrary to gossip."

"Where were you last night?"

"I spent the night at my uncle Ty's house with my cousin Minnie, if you must know."

"Oh, I heard you were out at the Orrs' farm."

"I visited Mrs. Orr during the day. Mr. Orr insisted I stay away from my shop while he cleaned up the damage and the sheriff investigated. Then I ate dinner and spent the night with Minnie."

"Oh. I knew you were a good girl."

"Mrs. Waters, who's been spreading ugly words about me?"

"I don't know, dear. No one seems to have seen anything, just hearsay, which is why I came to you directly."

Ida Mae smiled. "Please inform your friends I was safe with my family last night."

"I'll be happy to spread the word."

"Thank you."

Mrs. Waters left before Ida Mae remembered that she hadn't heard who got hurt in front of her shop. She unlocked the front door and went inside. Olin had cleaned up the broken glass. The window was covered by wood. It wasn't pretty but it was functional.

In her room, she flopped down on her bed.

The hammering of someone knocking and calling her name woke her up. She glanced at the clock. *Oh my.* Rattled, she jumped up and ran to the door.

"Olin, what's the matter?"

"Are you all right?"

"Yes, what's wrong?"

"Nothing now. I was worried when you didn't answer the door and I saw my horse in the stable."

"Come, come inside."

"Do you think it is wise?"

"Come, I need to speak with you privately."

Olin looked over his shoulder and walked into the shop, leaving the door open to the street.

"Olin, my reputation is already ruined."

"Not beyond repair. Besides, I'd want to sweep you in my arms and kiss you, if it were allowed."

Heat flickered across her cheeks. "And I you. Do you know what happened last night?"

"Yes, my brothers and I," he said, dropping his voice to a whisper, "came out after a couple hours' sleep to check on the shop and the sheriff. Someone came inside. There was a low light moving in your room."

"Did you catch him?"

"No. Kyle got knocked from behind and twisted his ankle. The yell sent

John and me to his side, as well as Sheriff Thatcher."

"Oh dear. Is he all right?"

"Doc says he'll be fine in a week or more, just has to keep off his leg for a while."

Ida Mae stepped toward him. Olin stepped back. "Please stay there, Ida Mae. I want to hold ye so bad I ache.

"The sheriff has a plan," he continued. "As you recall, the sheriff wants ye to stay here tonight, but he'll be here, as well. He's ordered the locks changed on your door, and that will be taken care of later today. Whoever it is has a key—or knows how to pick a lock like me. Either way, the sheriff will be staying with you, as will his wife. He wants everyone to know he's looking after you. He's hoping that will be enough to scare this man off."

"I'm scared, Olin."

⮾

Olin couldn't take it any longer. He closed the door with the heel of his boot and wrapped her in his arms. "I know, sweetheart, but it will be all right. We figure whoever it is, is coming late at night. That gives me time to go home and sneak back into town unnoticed. I'll be in the shop tonight, too, but we don't want anyone knowing that."

She trembled in his arms.

"This will be over soon, Ida Mae. It has to be."

He didn't have the heart to tell her they now suspected more than one person. Whoever was inside couldn't have knocked Kyle down.

"Ida Mae?" Minnie rushed through the door. "What are you doing? Get your hands off of her this minute." Minnie swatted Olin with her purse.

Olin blocked her blows with his arm.

"Minnie, stop." Ida Mae wiped the tears from her eyes. "Olin was just giving me some comfort."

"I bet."

"I'll be back, Ida Mae. Good day, Miss Jacobs."

Olin heard Minnie rush up to Ida Mae, asking her what happened.

The rest of the day went well. He worked on the few orders he had and on Mr. Bechtler's request. He'd formed other molds before, but this one would be the first he'd ever made for a gold coin. And it was still a secret. He tapped the mold into a piece of tin. He still had work to do, but it was coming. He flattened the impression in the tin so no one would know what he had been working on. His privacy in this small shop was limited. Carrying Mr. Bechtler's design back and forth with him each night gave him some security that it would not fall into the wrong hands.

Each evening nothing happened. The sheriff felt fairly confident Ida Mae was now safe.

Five days later everything seemed back to normal, except for Olin's growing attraction to Ida Mae. They were deliberately meeting one another in public places, being kind and cordial with one another, denying their true feelings, and otherwise keeping their distance. If Ida Mae was as half torn up about it as he was, she was hurting, too. He'd sent his mother in to invite her to dinner so they could have some alone time. John met them at the end of the day and escorted them back to the farm.

"Ye are causing a heap of trouble, little brother."

"Thanks for coming out, John."

"Ye are welcome. How are ye, Ida Mae?"

"Fine. The gossip is winding down about me so the shop is starting to pick up a bit."

"I'm glad to hear it."

As they left the outskirts of town John pulled his horse away from them. "How are ye really?" Olin asked.

"Better. I'm sleeping again."

"Good."

"How are you?"

"About ready to climb the walls if I can't be with you real soon. I miss ye so much."

Ida Mae giggled. "I miss you, too. How can that be?"

"Ah, me sweetheart, 'tis love." He wiggled his eyebrows for her.

"How's Kyle?"

"Grumpier than a bear woken from his winter slumber. But he's walking around a bit. Thankfully, the work is lighter around the farm right now.

"Have you heard anything from Cyrus? How the farm is doing?"

"No, and I'm not asking, either. Every time I go to deal with him the situation looks bleaker. I reckon this will not be an income-producing year. Any profits will go to my brothers."

"I thought the will was settled."

"It is, and the property is mine. But I want to give them a share of the profits for the next five years if I keep the farm. If not, I'll sell and divide the monies between us."

"You don't have to according to the will, right?"

"True, but I want to."

Olin smiled. This was the woman he loved. "I love your generous heart, Ida Mae."

When they arrived at the farm, Olin helped Ida Mae off the horse. She went inside while he and John put the horses in the barn.

"Is she spending the night?" John asked.

"I'd feel better if she did. But I don't think it would be wise for her reputation."

"Aye, ye are probably correct. Can ye give me a hand after dinner? It won't take but a half hour. It needs two sets of strong hands, and Dad's been workin' hard, covering for Kyle's share."

"Be happy to."

"Oh, bring a rifle with you tonight. I saw bear tracks today."

With all the things Olin had to worry about he didn't want to add one more. He knew it seemed that the danger was past for Ida Mae, but something he couldn't quite figure out was still nagging him about the night Kyle got hurt.

A shiver sliced down his spine. If a man would hurt Kyle for no reason, what would he do to Ida Mae?

Chapter 11

Ida Mae's heart warmed at Olin's touch as he wrapped his fingers around hers. "Come with me."

She couldn't remember a more pleasant evening. For the past thirty minutes she'd sat and read while Mrs. Orr played her piano and Mr. Orr read a book. Olin had been gone for nearly a half hour. She'd forgotten what it was like to be a part of a real family, and she ached to have it once again.

"Olin, I don't want to leave."

Olin wrapped his arms around her. "I'm just taking ye to the backyard to sit on the swing. The stars are beautiful tonight."

"I don't want to go home tonight. Can I stay in the spare room?"

"Ye need to go home, and soon. John and Father will be riding with us tonight. We're not takin' any chances."

"Then we should leave now. I don't want to keep your family up late."

"We can have a few minutes," he whispered. "Alone."

Gooseflesh tingled all over. "Kiss me, before I faint."

Olin chuckled. "Remember, I said I wouldn't kiss ye until ye asked. Thankfully, ye finally asked."

He captured her lips with a hunger that met her own. It had been nearly a full week since their first kiss and, oh, did she love kissing this man. She threaded her fingers through his silky hair. "I've missed you."

"I've missed ye as well. Will ye marry me now?"

"Olin, we can't."

"Why not?"

Why not? she wondered. "Because we have so much to learn about each other first."

"We can learn it married."

"Olin, you're impossible."

"I believe ye said incorrigible before."

She wrapped him in her arms and held on to him. She didn't want to leave. She didn't want to return to a life alone in her shop. She wanted what he had, wanted what his family had. "Where would we live?"

"Is that a yes?"

"No, it's a curious question. My room isn't big enough for two."

"My room isn't big enough for two here." He stepped away from her. "Before all these strange events I was determined to have a certain income, and a house, before I asked a woman to marry me. Now, all I can think about is you, and being by your side without fear of shaming ye."

"Olin, I do love you. But the time isn't right for us to marry."

"Aye, ye speak the truth, lass. But mark my words, we will marry."

"Aye," she agreed, mimicking his brogue.

Olin roared. "I love ye more than words can say, Ida Mae. Come, let's sit for a spell before we have to bring you home."

Ida Mae snuggled beside him on the swing. They rocked back and forth without saying a word and just relaxed in each other's arms. The stars sparkled against the black velvet sky. The fresh smell of cut grass seemed richer, more vibrant. Life felt better in Olin's arms. *Yes, I will marry you, Olin Robert Orr.*

"Olin, Ida Mae, it's time to be goin'!" Mrs. Orr called out.

They rode with lanterns burning, giving them a clearer path in the dark. Olin knew the roads well enough that lanterns weren't necessary, but for safety they felt it best to use them.

Olin walked Ida Mae to her door. His heart jumped in his chest when he saw it. He pulled Ida Mae back to the horses. "John, get the sheriff."

"What's wrong?"

"I'm not sure, but there is blood all over the front door. Let's not stir up attention. Move the animals to Ida Mae's father's shop and stable."

"I should check my place." Ida Mae took a step forward.

"No, honey, please. Stay with my father. I'll check everything out."

"All right."

After he had his father and Ida Mae settled in the blacksmith shop, he slipped into Ida Mae's shop through the secret door, still open as the sheriff had requested. As his eyes adjusted to the light of the lantern, he saw that nothing appeared out of place.

There was a knock at the door.

"Evenin', Sheriff."

"What happened here?"

"I don't know. There's blood all over the front door."

"Chicken or pig, I suspect. Is there a note?"

"Not that I've spotted so far. Father and Ida Mae are in her father's shop. I came in through the secret passageway."

The sheriff slipped his hat up his forehead. "I guess this isn't over."

"No, and I don't want Ida Mae staying here. It isn't safe."

"What do you suggest?"

"I don't know. I could bring her back home tonight."

"Someone must have known you were taking her home tonight. Doesn't this fellow usually come later in the evening?"

"Change of pattern?"

"More than likely. Let me look over the shop and Ida Mae's room. I'll meet you in McAuley's blacksmith shop."

"Yes, sir." Olin couldn't wait to be with Ida Mae.

"When the sheriff comes we're going to pack up some clothes and bring ye to our house."

"What was in there, son?"

"Nothing, all looks normal to me. But the sheriff knows what to look for."

"Aye, he's a good man. Ida Mae, ye are welcome to our home for as long as ye wish."

Olin winked. Ida Mae smiled.

The sheriff slipped through the secret doorway. "Hello, Miss McAuley. How are you?"

"Terrified."

"You should be. I don't know what's going on, but I think you'll be safer at the Orrs' farm." The sheriff started looking around to see if anything had been disturbed in the smithy.

He opened a cabinet door toward the front of the smithy that was slightly ajar and Olin blinked. "Where did that come from?"

"Ida Mae, please come here," Sheriff Thatcher ordered. "Are these the items that were missing from your room and shop?"

Even Olin recognized some of the items from the descriptions Ida Mae had given him before.

"Yes. Olin, why are they here?"

"I didn't put them here."

"Shh, relax, everyone. I believe someone is trying to have Olin blamed for all the missing items. Let's leave them here for now. Whoever stole the items wants them to be discovered. If Olin had taken these, he wouldn't have left them where customers could see them when he opened the cupboard. What concerns me is that the intruder now has a new key or has learned to pick locks like Olin."

"You can pick a lock?" John questioned.

Olin nodded.

"If I'd known that I'd have had ye open a trunk I lost the key to two years ago," John chuckled.

"Olin, take Ida Mae home. Tonight I'll need one of you to stay up all night or to work in shifts, but I want someone to watch over your home just in case. The blood on the front door is a more desperate warning."

"Sheriff, me boys and I will take care of Ida Mae and our own. Ye can count on us."

"Thank you, Mr. Orr." The sheriff extended his hand. "I'll ride out in the morning and tell you what I find."

Olin escorted Ida Mae to her horse. She was shaking now. The shock was setting in. "I'll ride Ida Mae with me. We'll leave her horse here. She's too shaky to ride alone in the dark."

Ida Mae nodded.

They removed her horse's gear and set him up with some fresh oats and water.

The sheriff stepped back through the secret door. John slipped out of the shop first, then Olin and Ida Mae, followed by his father. They kept the lanterns off until they reached the end of town.

"We forgot to pack her clothes."

"Your mother will fix her up, son. Let's get home. It's too late to stay out here."

Olin couldn't agree more.

John lifted his rifle.

☙❧

Ida Mae buried her head in Olin's back. *Blood! Blood on my door! Why, Lord?* Ida Mae prayed for understanding. What had she done to make someone so upset with her? Or was it that someone was so upset with Olin that they would go to such extreme lengths to have him blamed for all the weird happenings at her shop? It didn't make sense. Nothing made sense, except for her oneness with Olin. He'd been right; they should marry. They were meant for one another. He completed her in so many ways. All the unanswered questions in her life seemed to be answered, or at least calmed, by his presence. Yes, she loved Olin Orr, and she would be honored to be his wife. But would life allow it?

She held him tighter. He patted her hands. "It'll be all right, Ida Mae. With God's grace we'll get through this. I love ye, sweetheart."

By the time they arrived at the house and got Ida Mae set up in the spare room, everyone was exhausted. Kyle said he'd take the first watch. Olin would get up in two hours and watch until five. Then John would get up and watch for a half hour until Mr. Orr would get up, then John would get the morning chores under way. Ida Mae didn't think she could sleep, but the moment her head hit the feather pillow she was dreaming of living the rest of her life in Olin's arms.

☙❧

When the cock crowed for the third time, Ida Mae pushed herself out of bed. The smell of frying bacon drew her to the kitchen. Due to the lateness of the hour the night before, she'd received only sleeping garments from Mrs. Orr. As quickly as possible, she dressed in her own clothes before entering the kitchen for breakfast.

"Good morning, Ida Mae. Would you like some coffee or tea?"

"Coffee, if you don't mind."

"Coffee it is." Mrs. Orr poured her a cup and set it down on the small kitchen table.

"Is there anything I can do to help?"

Mrs. Orr smiled. "No, thank you. I've been in a rhythm for years."

"I understand." Ida Mae sipped the rich brew. Coffee would help dissolve the cobwebs in her brain.

"We're having eggs, bacon, grits, and blueberries this morning. Is that all right with ye?"

"I haven't eaten a full breakfast like that in over a year."

"And I daresay it shows. Ye are nothing but skin and bones."

"I've always been on the slight side. But I haven't eaten as well since my parents died. It's hard to cook for one."

"Aye, I can imagine. Ye will fill your belly this mornin'." She went back to frying up the bacon on the woodstove. "I tend to use the summer kitchen outside during these warm months, but I didn't want to have ye leavin' the house this mornin' in case anyone is watching."

"I appreciate that."

"Aye. A dip in the stream might be in order today. I could use a good scrubbin'. How about you?"

"Yes, I could use one as well."

"I'll find ye some clean clothes after breakfast. We'll have Mr. Orr join us for the bath."

Ida Mae nearly dropped her cup of coffee.

"Forgive me. He'll join us with his shotgun and keep watch over the swimming hole. He won't be bathing with us."

Ida Mae's cheeks flamed. Of course, Mrs. Orr was thinking of their safety.

The men came in from the morning chores, and breakfast was consumed faster than Mrs. Orr could cook it. "I've been thinkin'," Kyle said, breaking off another piece of bread to scoop up his eggs. "Since ye and Ida Mae will be gettin' married, why don't ye do it now?"

Ida Mae choked on her eggs.

Mrs. Orr slapped her back.

Mr. Orr coughed.

"What?" John shook his head.

Olin slipped down in his chair.

John reached across the table and grabbed the platter of bacon. "Kyle, you don't just get married to keep a woman safe."

"I know that. But I heard them talking about it last night."

All eyes turned to Olin and then back to Ida Mae.

Olin was at least as red as she was.

"Son?"

Olin cleared his throat and pulled at his open collar.

Ida Mae giggled. She couldn't stop it, try as she might. It didn't take long for Mrs. Orr to join her, then Mr. Orr, John, and Kyle. Olin was the last to laugh. "Aye, Ida Mae and I are talking 'bout getting married," he admitted amid the laughter.

"Congratulations, little brother." John slapped him on the back. "I can't believe ye will make it to the altar before me."

Olin grinned.

"And welcome to the family, Ida Mae."

"It's about time I had another lady around." Mrs. Orr got up and kissed her on the cheek. "Ye be makin' a good choice, son."

"Back to my question, so why don't ye?"

The front door knocker resounded through the room. "That must be Sheriff Thatcher." Olin excused himself and went to the front door.

Should we marry now?

Chapter 12

Good morning, Sheriff. What did ye find?"

"I'm concerned, Olin. Can we talk outside for a minute?"

"Sure." Olin shut the door behind him. "What's the matter?"

"I truly fear someone is trying to set you up, but I fear it is something far worse than stealing trinket items from Ida Mae. It doesn't add up that someone would be so upset with Ida Mae. She's done nothing wrong to anyone, intentionally or otherwise."

"I agree. And the town has been full of gossip regarding my return. I should have stayed in the north."

"Perhaps, but if we are dealing with someone so evil he would frame another man for acts of self-defense done in years past, I'm glad to know it now rather than later when it might be too late."

Olin didn't know if he agreed with that thought or not. He loved Ida Mae and wouldn't want to be the cause of all this bad will toward her, and yet he was. How could he possibly ask her to marry him with that kind of a stigma over them the rest of their lives? It just wouldn't be fair. "I can leave town in a couple days."

John Thatcher scratched his unshaved chin. "No, that's not what I had in mind. When I got up this morning the town was buzzing that someone killed Ida Mae and carried her body off. Apparently, three horsemen were seen leaving the town last night and one looked to be carrying a body."

"I think we should include Ida Mae in this discussion."

"We will in just a moment. What I want to suggest is a bit unorthodox, but I believe it might bring our enemy out of hiding. I'm suggesting we go along with the rumors."

"Pardon?" Olin rubbed the wax from his ears. The sheriff couldn't possibly have said what he thought he said.

"What I'm suggesting is we let folks believe she is dead."

Olin shook his head from side to side. "Ida Mae has to hear this."

Olin ushered the sheriff into the dining area where his mother quickly put a place setting in front of him. The sheriff explained to all of them what he had just explained to Olin. The room was silent.

Ida Mae opened her mouth, then closed it. Then opened it again. "Are you suggesting I pretend to be dead?"

"Yes. I can even go as far as putting out an arrest warrant for Olin."

"Thanks," Olin snickered. "I wouldn't want it in the records that I was accused of killing my wife."

"Your wife? When did you two get hitched?"

Ida Mae blushed for the second time this morning. Olin loved the playful shade of pink on her cheeks.

"We're going to get married. I'm thinking in the future."

"O–oh," Sheriff Thatcher stuttered. "Congratulations."

Olin's father got up. "I don't fancy lying to folks, but I'll mislead some to keep this young woman safe." He lifted his plate from the table. "Unfortunately, I have a farm to run and livestock to take care of. Olin, fill me in on what you decide before you go to work this morning."

"Yes, sir."

Kyle and John got up from the table and took their plates to the kitchen.

"Ida Mae, what do you think?" The sheriff forked some eggs and lifted them to his mouth. Olin had lost his appetite.

"I'll go missing for a while. If you think that will help."

"I can't promise it will, but I'm praying. Plus, you'll be safer if no one knows where you are. Even me."

"Olin?"

"Yes, Mum?"

"Ye say you've asked Ida Mae to marry ye?"

"Yes, ma'am."

"Ida Mae, ye say ye love my son?"

"Yes, ma'am."

His mother nodded slowly. "Sheriff, ye can finish your meal. But we'll take it from here. Don't be surprised if ye hear rumors that Bobby, pardon me, Olin, has captured and run off with Ida Mae."

Sheriff Thatcher lifted up his hands. "Don't tell me any more."

⬿⬾

A few hours later, Ida Mae was washing in the river beside her future mother-in-law. How life could turn around in a few short minutes could be an understatement for the past several weeks. Mrs. Orr sent Olin to town to sneak in and fetch some of Ida Mae's clothes. They were going to go on the run, but not until the middle of the night. John had been sent over to the next county to bring a minister home to marry Ida Mae and Olin. Tonight she'd be a bride, a bride on the run. It wasn't exactly the way she'd pictured entering into a marriage.

Kyle had been sent to the old farmhouse on the property to clean up the place for their wedding night. It all seemed too controlled and out of her control. *I can't do this, Lord.*

"Are ye all right, dear?"

184

"Nervous."

"All women, and men for that matter, are nervous on their wedding day."

"This isn't the kind of wedding I dreamed about."

"No, I daresay it wouldn't be. But it will keep ye safe."

I suppose.

"Ye do love him, don't ye?"

"Yes but. . ."

"Ah, it is still too new."

"Yes."

"Answer me this: When ye kiss him, do ye feel one with him?"

"Yes."

"Then ye are meant to be together. The Lord will bless ye even if ye don't marry in a church."

"I know but. . ."

"Ye don't have to marry him. It was only a suggestion."

And a reasonable one, given all that is going on. It would be safer for us to hide as a married couple than to be alone together day and night and not be married. "It's a good plan."

Ida Mae lathered her hair. Mrs. Orr had brought her special lavender-scented soap down to the river for them to bathe with. Mr. Orr kept his back to them but kept a watchful eye around the farm.

Lord, bless this family for all they are sacrificing for me. They don't know me and yet they've taken me in as one of their own even before they knew Olin and I wanted to marry. Bless them, Lord.

Ida Mae rinsed her hair.

"Come on, dear. We've got a lot to do."

And for the rest of the day Ida Mae found herself packing and repacking. At one point she and Olin were going to take his wagon. Then it was decided that it would be too easy to track, so they would go on horseback. A pack mule was discussed, but no one had one or knew of one they could obtain without raising suspicions.

Finally, the dinner hour had arrived and Olin came home. She did love him, but she still had huge doubts about their getting married in such a manner and so soon. John returned with a preacher a few minutes later. Kyle came in needing a bath and left as soon as he grabbed some soap and a towel.

Mrs. Orr somehow managed to prepare a huge feast for their dinner. Olin sat down at the table beside Ida Mae. He reached over and held her hand. Just touching him calmed her nerves, but was it enough?

"How is it in town?" Mr. Orr asked after saying the blessing.

Dishes passed from one to the next. Ida Mae did her best to keep up.

"Buzzing about what happened at the spinner's shop."

It was painfully obvious Olin didn't want to discuss details in front of the parson.

"I see."

"What happened in Charlotte?" Parson White asked.

"There was blood all over the door of the spinner's shop."

"That is rather strange news. I can see why everyone is talking. Is the spinster all right?"

"Yes, I am." Ida Mae spoke up. "We're not sure what happened." Olin narrowed his gaze, scrutinizing her. Ida Mae straightened in her chair.

"Do they suspect Indians?" the parson asked.

"No. But no one is quite sure who did this, or why." Olin squeezed her hand.

"We must pray for your safety. Are you certain you want to marry at this time?"

Olin didn't like marrying Ida Mae under these circumstances, nor did he like hearing the rash talk all over town. Many had given him a harsh stare today. And he still wasn't settled on running off to the mountains to hide from whoever was after Ida Mae. Keeping her here on the farm seemed more prudent. But Sheriff Thatcher had a point that they could be putting his family in danger if he kept her here.

The one positive in all of this was marrying Ida Mae. It was rather soon, but he'd seen and heard many a story where a young couple married quickly and were still happily married many years later. He caressed the top of her hand with his thumb.

"Ye best stop holdin' hands and eat," Mum instructed with a tease to her voice.

Ida Mae released his hand the moment Mum spoke and picked up her fork. He did the same.

Ida Mae's hand shook.

Father, give her strength, Olin silently prayed for her.

They made it through dinner, but Ida Mae had hardly eaten anything. She just swirled her food around her plate. Olin couldn't blame her, but he began to worry. Something was wrong.

"Shall we?" Father stood up from the table.

Mother led them all to the front parlor. The parson opened his black Bible and the pages crinkled as he turned them.

Olin took Ida Mae's hand and walked up to the parson.

"We are gathered tonight to join this man and this woman in holy matrimony. It's an honorable estate, not to be taken lightly, but reverently. . ."

Ida Mae's entire body trembled.

"What's wrong, child?" the parson asked. "Are you being forced to marry this man?"

"No."

"Are you prepared to marry him?"

She implored him with her gaze. Her brilliant blue eyes filled with tears.

"Sweetheart?" Olin reached up and caressed her face.

"I can't; I'm sorry." Ida Mae ran from the room and up the stairs.

Olin found himself a twister of emotions. He respected her if she wasn't sure, but he also felt the sting of rejection. "Forgive us, Parson White." Olin reached into his pocket. "Here's a little something for your troubles."

"Shall I stay for a bit in case the young lady changes her mind? On the other hand, the business with her front door sounds very compelling for her to want to wait."

"Let me talk with her," Mum offered and scurried off.

Olin felt helpless and dejected. For too long he'd been fighting the emotions of all the people who found fault with his return to the area. Mayhap it was best he and Ida Mae not marry. He would only ruin her and her reputation.

"Excuse me," Olin said, extricating himself from the room and going out to the barn. He kicked a clump of hay and fought the desire to punch the wall with his fist. He'd done that when he was younger and trying to control his temper. In the end, he had broken his hand.

"Wanna talk?" John asked, leaning against the door frame.

"Nothing to say. She's not ready."

"Aye, that is likely the case. But ye are takin' it rather hard if ye understand that."

Olin sighed. "She's probably right. I would only ruin her life."

"Bobby, sit down, please." John came beside him and sat down on the bale of hay. "When ye came home I didn't know you. But I watched, and ye are a good and honorable man. Pa is real proud of ye. Mum is, too, but ye know Mum—she's proud of us no matter what. And Ida Mae adores you. I know, I've watched her and you when ye were together."

"The feeling is mutual."

"Aye, I seen that, too. A man never looked more smitten than ye."

"What do we do about the plan?"

"I still agree you need to take her into hiding. How many are accusing you of harming Ida Mae?"

"No one said anything directly to me, but I'm certain the sheriff got an ear full."

"Don't be too sure. I've been giving this a lot of thought. Percy has been on a rampage since you returned. He has no interest in Ida Mae, but he does want to see ye fall for whatever reason."

"True."

"And, I'm not certain but I think I saw one of Ida Mae's customers sneaking behind her building one night while I was watching. I forget his name, but he still lives with his mother."

Olin crossed his arms. "So do we."

"Aye, but I think this man has eyes for Ida Mae."

"But to go to that extreme—pouring chicken blood on her door—it still doesn't make sense."

"They figured out what kind of animal blood?"

"Aye, Sheriff Thatcher had the butcher check it out."

"That would narrow it down some. Whoever it is has to have access to a fair amount of chickens."

"Sheriff's been checking with all the farms to see if anyone is missing any or has quite a few draining."

"He seems like a smart man. I think ye still need to take Ida Mae out of here. I know ye won't be married, and it could have a negative effect on her reputation, but I'd rather that than her not being alive."

"True. I just don't want to push her too hard."

John let out a nervous chuckle. "Let's see, ye asked the woman to marry ye after ye kissed her for the first time, and yet ye don't want to push. I've been waiting on a gal for a year now and I'm just about ready to ask her out."

"Really? Who is she?"

"I'm not telling unless she says yes." John smiled. "Some women take time. Ida Mae trusts ye, let her move at her own pace."

"Thank ye. I appreciate the advice."

"Welcome. Should I go in and tell the parson he can go home?"

"Yes, unless Ida Mae changed her mind."

"All right. Have a few words with the Lord and come and join the family. Oh, and I saw that restraint ye showed not punching that post. I'd say you've learned to control your temper."

Have I?

Chapter 13

"I da Mae, may I come in?"

She sniffled and walked over to the door. Taking in a deep breath, she eased it open.

"What's the matter, dear?"

"I can't go through with it. I love him, but it's too soon. My life has been turned upside down and I don't know what to do."

"Ah, 'tis my fault for sure. Let me call down and tell the parson he can leave. Then we can have some girl talk." Mrs. Orr left.

Ida Mae didn't know if she was up to girl talk at the moment. Fear that someone was after her had spun around her heart so tight she could hardly breathe.

She scanned her packed carpetbag. Tonight could have been her wedding night. Why couldn't she go through with it? *Why? Why? Why? Lord. I don't understand. I love him but...*

"Please forgive me, Ida Mae, I meant no harm tryin' to push ye and Olin Robert to marry."

"It's not your fault. I should have spoken earlier."

Mrs. Orr settled down on the bed beside her. "It will be all right, dear. The good Lord will see ye through. And I do believe ye will be my daughter one day."

"Why would you want me with all the trouble I've caused this family?"

"Nonsense. 'Tis not ye that has caused the problems. It is a sinner and his sin, not you."

Ida Mae closed her eyes. She tried once again to figure out who would want to harm her.

"Ida Mae, ye are always welcome in our home."

"Thank you."

"I'll give ye some time alone." Mrs. Orr leaned into her and hugged her. "Forgive me, child. I didn't mean to add to your confusion."

"You are forgiven." Ida Mae squeezed her future mother-in-law, hoping she still would be.

When Olin's mother left the room she closed the door behind her. Ida Mae collapsed onto her pillow. Gentle tears flowed from her eyes. She shouldn't marry Olin this way. Not under such trying circumstances. If she'd gone through with the marriage tonight she would never feel confident in her own love for Olin.

She needed more time. They needed more time.

Ida Mae wiped the tears from her eyes. She still needed to go into hiding, which would have been simpler if she had married Olin.

A purple glow from the setting sun filled the room. Rays of peace calmed her. She could face Olin's family even in her shame, and together they would need to amend their plans. She could go into hiding herself. She knew enough to survive for a few days. But, admittedly, she didn't know how to track or hide her own tracks. She was a farm girl who had worked in town for years. She knew her way around a spinning wheel, but she'd simply be spinning air, wandering alone in the foothills, and be an easy target if someone should try to come after her.

Composing herself, Ida Mae grabbed her carpetbag and went downstairs. Mr. Orr was reading, Olin was pacing with his back to her, and Mrs. Orr was washing dishes in the kitchen. "Olin?"

"Ida Mae." He scooped her in his arms. "Are ye all right?"

"I'm sorry."

"I understand. We'll get married sometime in the future. I can wait."

"You're not mad?"

"No, we were bending the metal before it reached its pliable point."

"I do love you." She rested her head on his shoulder. His hands caressed her hair.

"And I, ye. Come, we must decide what to do next."

"Yes. I can hide in the forest for a day or two. But I don't know how to hide my tracks. I can try—"

"I think it best if I'm with ye."

"I agree." Mr. Orr closed his book and leaned forward.

Mrs. Orr came in drying her hands on a dish towel. "So do I."

Kyle burst through the front door. "Olin, Ida Mae, the town is sending out a search party. They're organizing without the sheriff. We need to hide ye fast."

"The root cellar," Mrs. Orr offered.

"They'll search there, Mother. Can ye make it to the cabin on foot?"

"I believe so." Olin held Ida Mae's hand, then bent down and fetched a handful of ash. "Do ye trust me?"

∞

Olin held the cold ash in his hand. He hated to do it, but if the townsfolk were close on Kyle's heels there was little choice.

Her eyes widened when she saw the ash. She nodded.

"I'm sorry." He dumped the ash in her hair and streaked her face, then did the same to his face and hands.

"Come on. John, meet me an hour before dawn at the old parson's-nose tree and bring our bags."

His mother wrapped them in a hug. "Be off with the good Lord's blessing."

"And to think I bathed for this."

Olin laughed. He placed a bedroll and small pack over his shoulder that he had prepared earlier. "It will protect us from the full moon."

"And will I have a chance to bathe tomorrow?"

"Aye, if we are successful tonight. Come, we mustn't wait a moment longer."

Olin tugged and Ida Mae kept his pace. They ran through the back field, using the house and the barn as a cover. The wide-open field offered little protection. Olin ran toward the tree line as fast as he felt she could run. Once they hit the tree line he stopped behind a tree.

"Are we going to the cabin?"

"Not tonight. I don't know who is heading up the search party, but ye can be certain Percy is with 'em, and if he is, he knows about the old cottage. Unfortunately Kyle cleaned it up for us today so it will appear that we have stayed or are staying there. Or at least me, if they think I killed ye."

"Killed me? Why would they think that?"

"The blood. It doesn't matter that the sheriff found it to be chicken blood, not in the minds of these men. Truth is of little importance once a man makes up his mind that he is right."

Olin felt the worst decision he'd made was to come back home. And yet, having met Ida Mae and wanting to spend the rest of his life with her was a direct response to that decision. Was it wrong? Did the Lord want him here for this time and this place?

"I'm sorry, Olin."

"What for?"

She snickered. "For so many things, really. For the wedding that didn't happen, for the trouble with the shop, and for you being blamed for all of this. It's like you said before, it doesn't make sense. I can't understand why someone would want me dead or out of the way. Even to tell me to get rid of you as a tenant does not explain the chicken blood. You had moved out. The entire town knew that."

"Ah, but remember the gossip says that I ruined ye the other night. Perhaps ye have a man who fancies himself as yours. Do ye?"

"No." She cupped her face with her hands. "Only you," she muttered.

The distant sound of horses arriving at his parents' house jolted Olin back to the moment. "Come, I know a small spot where we can hide."

Olin pushed the thick brush away with his hands and held it back until Ida Mae passed. He eased the branches back as easily as possible, trying not to disturb or break any of them. He then fluffed the underbrush behind her to keep it from appearing disturbed.

Slowly they worked their way back into the woods. He followed as many deer paths as possible. An hour later they were at the mouth of a shallow cave he had played in as a boy. He had no memory of Percy ever coming to this place, but his brothers knew where it was. And Percy, being a cousin, would probably have an idea. "Come in here."

"It doesn't look inviting."

Olin eyed the small cave. "Would ye like me to go in first?"

"Uh, does a tin man have tin?"

Olin smiled. "Not at the moment." He slipped into the dark cavern. It seemed much smaller than he remembered. He sniffed the air. It appeared stale but dry, which would make it a much more comfortable night. He lowered the bedroll and removed his flint and steel. Feeling his way along the floor, he found the old campfire site and prayed that the small pile of kindling he'd always kept there as a child remained. Thankfully, it was, and extremely dry. It lit instantly as he started a small fire. He laid out the bedroll.

"Wow, I thought you said this was small."

"It is, but it's big enough to give us some protection from the night. Ida Mae, sit here. I'll be back as soon as I can. Let the fire burn out. There isn't enough wood to keep it going. I'll go gather some wood. We should be safe here for the night."

"All right."

Olin kissed her stained lips. "I'll try to be back soon. But if I'm not back by morning, go to my parents' house. Do you think you can find it?"

"No." Her voice trembled.

"It won't matter, ye'll be safe with me."

"Where's the parson's-nose tree? And why'd you name it that?"

"The parson's nose is just another name for the tail on a plucked turkey. When ye see the tree stump, you'll understand."

∞

The fatty end of the turkey's tail had been a favorite of her father's. "Do you have to leave?"

"I wanted to get some wood for a fire."

"I'm not cold." *Terrified, but not cold.*

"Yet," he added.

She reached out and held his hand, caressing it with her thumb. "Please, don't leave me alone."

"Sweetheart, I shall return."

"Do we really need a fire tonight?"

He sat down beside her. "I suppose not. Ye might get cold later."

I'm being foolish. "Olin, I'm afraid."

He wrapped his arm around her. "Ye will be safe with me."

"How can you know that? There are no guarantees in this world. Father and Mother. . ." She let her words trail off. He still had both his parents. He didn't know what it was like to lose someone so close. The past twelve months had been an agony she prayed she would never go through again. And yet the idea that someone would be after her— She felt like Job.

Olin held her tighter. "Tell me, what happened?"

"There ain't much to tell. I had to work late the night they died, so they returned home and I planned on sleeping at the shop. A fire caught in the kitchen and quickly consumed the house. The sheriff found my parents' remains in the kitchen." She paused. Olin waited while she collected her thoughts, then continued. "As best as the sheriff could tell, they were trying to put out the fire and were overtaken by the smoke."

"Did they cook often inside the house in the summer?"

"No, Mother rarely cooked more than once or twice a week at home. Since we spent so much time at the shops, she tended to cook meals there. On the weekends we'd cook the roasts or chickens. Then she'd make meals from the leftovers. We smoked a lot of our meat, so we had cured ham and bacon whenever we needed it."

That was one of the pieces of the puzzle that had made little sense to her. Why were they in the kitchen and why was Mother cooking?

"And the sheriff concluded it was an accident?"

"Yes." Ida Mae wrung the hem of her dress. "My birthday was a few days away. The sheriff thought she might have been making me a cake or something."

"Your mum made cakes in the summer for ye?"

Ida Mae giggled. She saw the same glee in his eyes that children showed in the past when her mother made a special birthday cake in the heat of the summer. Mother had said it didn't make the kitchen all that much hotter. But it had. And she loved that about her mother and father, and how they loved indulging their little girl. "I was spoiled."

"Aye, that may be an understatement. Mum uses the outdoor kitchen in the summer, but apart from bread making, she seldom fires up the oven hot enough to make baked goods, certainly not sweets."

"I was blessed."

"Ye still are, Ida Mae. Ye have all the memories, all that love, and ye are a special person. What about your brothers?"

"Randall's love is the city life and the sea. He's working in Savannah for one of the cotton shippers. His family is quite content there. Last I heard he was considering buying a plantation. But I know Randall—he'll hire someone to run it. He never liked getting his fingernails dirty. Bryan enjoyed working the land but he wanted to raise cattle, so he moved farther west to Kentucky to purchase a larger lot of land. Father sold half the farmland and gave Bryan the money for his future. He also gave a smaller share to Randall. Randall and I own the greater share in the farm. But Randall isn't interested in farming or concerned with whether I make a profit from the land. He's more concerned with his own job and how well it supports his family."

"As ye know, I, bein' the third son, inherit only a few acres of my father's property. I wanted him to give it to my brothers but Father wouldn't hear of it. So, someplace on my parents' farm I have ten acres."

Rolling her shoulders, she leaned back in a more relaxed position. "Do you know the law regarding women and their land?"

"No, not really. Why do you ask?"

"I once feared you might be after my property."

He leaned back and rested on his elbows. "What's this law say?"

"When a woman who owns property marries, the husband takes responsibility for taking care of the financial matters. He can't sell the property without her blessing, but he can do everything else. And with regard to the farm, he would have complete control over the running of it."

"Interesting."

Chapter 14

Olin slipped out from Ida Mae's embrace. The gentle purr signaled that he hadn't woken her. Outside, the sky was still black. He slipped through the bushes and found the deer path toward parson's-nose. John would be late doing his chores today, but not too late. By the time he reached the strangely shaped tree trunk, a small ribbon of deep blue showed on the eastern horizon.

"Mornin'," John said and wiped off the backside of his trousers. "How'd ye make out last night?"

"Fine. We spent the night in the old cave on the northeast corner."

John nodded. "Smaller, ain't it?"

"Aye."

John walked over to his horse and removed Ida Mae's carpetbag, a bedroll, and a sack. "Mum packed up some food."

"Tell her thank you. What happened last night?"

"Not too much. Most folks know us and respect us. Percy led the team. He went through the house like a wild man. Ye never did finish that fight."

"No, I never understood what it was all about. He just didn't see eye-to-eye with me since I was eight years old."

"This ain't an eight-year-old's revenge. What happened back at the mines?"

"That's what is really odd. I was actually trying to defend him when Gary Jones went after me."

"Ye were fightin' for Percy?"

"Aye. Silly, ain't it?"

John shook his head. "Keep her safe. Percy is out to destroy ye or worse. I reckon it might have to do with all the untruths he's said regarding you and the fight with Gary Jones. The cabin isn't safe with Percy leading them."

"You're right. I'll plan on heading toward the next county."

"Very well. Kyle said he'd catch up with you in two days. I'll tell him to meet ye at Paw Creek."

Paw Creek was a good location. A place where, even if followed, he would appear to be going into town on business. "Tell him I'll see him there around noon."

Leather creaked as John hoisted himself up on the saddle. "Be careful, little brother. I don't like the anger I saw last night. I understand some think ye killed her and that enraged them. But when Mum and Pop said she was fine last night when she came to dinner, there were a few who believed them."

"Percy wouldn't."

"Aye, but he wasn't so bold as that. He still has to remain respectful to his uncle and aunt."

"That might not last for long."

"Aye. Keep a watchful eye. Percy might drop everything if he believes ye have moved back to Pennsylvania."

"Mayhap I should." It didn't seem fair that a man couldn't return home. But if he had stayed in Pennsylvania none of this would have happened. Olin said his good-byes to his brother, picked up his and Ida Mae's belongings, and headed back to the cave.

Orange streams of light covered the trees with a crimson layer floating above. Another hot day, he mused. Another day he wasn't married. His shoulders slumped. Why had he come home?

⤫

The crack of a twig jolted Ida Mae awake. *Is someone out there?* Olin was gone. Clamping her jaw tight, she inched toward the opening. *Who is out there? Or better yet, what is out there?*

She scraped her knee on a jagged edge of rock. Keeping low, she closed the distance between herself and the opening. The dull light of dawn did little for her visibility. She craned her neck to the side and listened. Nothing! Fear swept through her. If everything were fine there would be noise of some sort. The insects alone should be chirping away. *Shouldn't they?*

Could they have been tracked to the cave?

Ida Mae squeezed her eyes closed and prayed. *Father, help Olin and me. Help us to uncover all that has been happening in town. Reveal it to us and keep us safe. Please, Lord.*

Another twig snapped. Ida Mae willed herself closer to the ground.

"Ida Mae," Olin whispered.

Joy surged through her.

"Olin?"

"Aye, come on out. It is safe."

She ventured through the small opening and blinked. Olin stood there with his ash-stained face. "You're quite a sight."

Olin chuckled. "Ye have seen better days yourself. Come, there's a small stream where we can clean up. It has a very small swimming hole, which was fine when we were kids, but as adults I'm not sure we'll be able to submerge."

Anything was better than the ash and dirt caked on her skin. She felt like she'd rolled in mud. Of course, she probably had, sleeping in the cave. "Did you bring soap?"

"Afraid not, unless Mother packed something in the bedroll. Let me pack up our belongings and we'll get on our way." Olin slipped into the cave.

Ida Mae scanned the area. She could see the lush farmlands, small creek, and the edge of the forest. It truly was a beautiful sight.

"Shall we?" Olin pointed with her carpetbag toward the foothills of the Smoky Mountains.

Ida Mae worked her way over a small path left behind from deer and other wild animals. She didn't want to think about the other kinds of animals. She was grateful they had survived one night without noticing any unusual activities, animal or human. With each step toward the creek she realized her life was slipping away. She was on the run, hiding from some unknown stranger.

Should I stay with him? And yet the very thought of leaving him made her cringe. Would it be wiser to stay with Uncle Ty and Minnie? No, she couldn't put them at risk. Uncle Ty barely made ends meet; he didn't need anyone endangering his family or destroying his property.

Peace filled her soul when she was in Olin's arms. But that thought brought a fresh wave of heat to her cheeks. She had spent the night in Olin's arms. She should have married him. What would Minnie say? What would everyone say?

Ida Mae shook off the annoying what-ifs and continued down the path. Truth was, he was an honorable man, and they had relied on one another to keep warm in the chilly night air.

"Down here," Olin directed.

He led her around a bend to where a small, clear pool of water shimmered in the sunlight. She bent down for a drink. Her reflection in the water looked like a sickly old woman. "Ugh."

"It's not that bad." Olin bent down and unrolled the pack from his mother. "Mum sent a bar of soap." He smiled and held it up in the air.

Ida Mae jumped up to capture the sweet-smelling ball of lavender soap. She missed and jumped again. The grin on Olin's teasing face brought out the memories of her older brothers always teasing her. She faked a jump and waited for his reaction. When he swung his arm up, she tackled him. He landed on the ground with a thud. She pressed her knee into his chest and captured the soap. "Don't ever get between a woman and a bath again."

His brown eyes were as wide as saucers filled with deep rich coffee. "No, ma'am."

She offered a hand to aid him in getting up. "You do know I have two older brothers and, being the only girl in the family, I suppose I wrestled with them a bit more than if I'd had a sister."

Olin brushed off his pants. "Ye are a wonder. Ye can slip behind those rocks and make yourself ready for the bath. I'll wait around the bend. Call me when you are finished."

Her respect for Olin grew. Again, he proved himself a gentleman and not the killer his cousin Percy claimed.

After she was bathed, and while Olin was taking his turn, she noticed something on the ridge. It appeared to be a wooden chute for gold mining. Gold mines had sprung up all over the county after gold was discovered on the Reed farm some twenty miles away. She hadn't heard of anyone striking it rich in the Charlotte area. But some farmers had found small nuggets on their land. Enough, sometimes, to help them purchase a few things they might not have without the precious ore.

"I feel better. How about you?" Olin walked up, shaking the excess water from his hair with his fingers.

Suppressing the desire to run her fingers through his silky strands, she answered, "Much."

"Ida Mae, we have a problem."

"What?"

∞

Olin sat down on the rock beside her. "Ye are so beautiful."

"How is that a problem?"

How could a man convey the intensity of his desire without speaking such? *A gentleman shouldn't,* he reminded himself. He wrapped an arm around her and pulled her closer into his embrace. He brushed away a few strands of her golden hair, then captured her sweet lips. She resisted for a moment, then allowed their kiss to deepen. It took all of his strength to pull back first, closing his eyes and asking the Lord for strength. "Ida Mae. . ." His voice was huskier than he'd hoped. He cleared his throat and proceeded. "I will not dishonor thee. . . ." He let his words trail off. Her brilliant blue eyes sparkled with understanding. She turned her head.

"I should have married you."

Olin's chest swelled with—what? Pride? Desire? Or was it confidence? Yes, confidence that their love was real. Young, but very real. "Ye weren't ready."

She turned to him and placed a finger to his lips. He kissed the tip of her finger. The fresh scent of lavender mixed with her unique scent gave him renewed determination to protect this woman.

"What did John say about the visitors last night?" she asked.

"Wasn't much to say. Percy's behind it. They searched the house, found evidence that you'd been there. My parents didn't deny it. They told them the truth that ye came for dinner. They said they simply didn't know where ye were now. John also said that because my parents saw you alive and in good health several of the men didn't want to continue the search.

"Kyle gave them the impression that we might be visiting with the parson."

"If I had married you they could have honestly said we were married and having some time to ourselves for a few days."

"Sweetheart, don't fret. There will be plenty of time for marryin'. Kyle will say he's going into town in a couple days, but he'll actually be meeting us at Paw Creek at noon."

"Where do we go from here?"

To the parson, he wanted to say. "How about west and towards Kings Mountain?"

"Walkin'?"

"I could return home and pick up my horse and wagon. But I don't want to leave ye here alone in the woods."

"I can shoot."

Olin smiled and wiggled his eyebrows. "Aye, but I don't want it to be me when I return." He'd never met a woman like this one. She excited him on so many levels. She wasn't ruled by fear, and yet she had let her vulnerability show to him on more than one occasion. *Lord, please help me protect her.*

"We don't have to run. I could bring ye back to town and let the rumors die down."

"No, the sheriff wants us to hide. Someone is trying to get to me. Even if it is simply to discredit me, someone is out there. And I don't like the thought that Percy is taking advantage of it to do some damage to you as well. We have to fight this, and I think giving the sheriff a few days to sort it out is the best way."

"Mayhap." Olin sighed. Did she have to be so logical?

"There is one problem that I see from our going on the road. Will that secret matter you can't discuss with me be a problem?"

"Possibly. But it is in the Lord's hands."

"What if I go back to town without you? Then perhaps folks will think we aren't together. I can slip out in the night and return to your parents' farm."

"No, I cannot allow ye to be out on the streets by yourself. Ye must trust me."

"Olin, it isn't a matter of trust. It is a matter of deceit. Can we fool people long enough to give us an edge and a way to get to safety?"

She had a point, but everything within him shouted no. "No, ye are safe with me."

Chapter 15

W here are ye going?"

"Back to your house. I'm not walking to the mountains."

Olin hustled up beside her. "And what makes ye think it is safe there?"

It's probably not. She didn't want to spend weeks on the road, in hiding, living off the land, even though she'd agreed with the sheriff the night before. Was it only last night? "Olin, I can't do this. My sensibilities are screaming this is wrong. I should stand and fight."

"Aye, and how long has your family lived in the area? Ye have a bit of the Hornet's Nest blood running through them veins."

"I reckon." Everyone knew how their ancestors had fought and held off the British during the Revolution. It was a matter of history and pride that kept the community together. Which made this misunderstanding with Olin such a puzzle. Why would the townspeople hold it against him and not believe her that he wasn't a threat?

She sat down on a fallen log along their path. Olin followed. "What's wrong?"

"If I say it doesn't make sense one more time I think I'll scream, but I have no other explanation for all of these bizarre occurrences. Why would someone steal items from my room and hide them in yours?"

"To make ye suspicious of me."

"Yes, but why?" She turned to him and reached for his hand. "Olin, I can't believe this is all about you and your past. As we said before, and the sheriff agreed, there is someone out to get me. But why?"

"Is your business a competition for another in the area?"

"No, and neither is yours." *So what are they after?* Ida Mae wondered. It couldn't be her wealth. There wasn't any. But some men would like the farm. "Olin, are you interested in me because of my inheritance?"

He opened his mouth in quick defense but closed it before saying a word. His eyes explored her own. A strong sense of honesty and love poured over her ruffled senses. "As we talked about before, a man could profit from your farm and the properties in town, but I am not that man. I never liked to farm...which bode well with my being the third son. Father has given me ten acres of land to build a house on. I do not need your farm."

A smile escaped. She knew it, but it was nice to hear it in his reassuring words once again. "But another man might."

"Perhaps. But ye professed your love to me." He wrapped her in a protective hug. "And I'm inclined to hold ye to it."

She fiddled with a loose thread on her skirt, rolling it to a ball. She silently counted to ten, willing herself not to respond to his touch. A part of her wanted to slip away and dissolve into his arms, to put an end to all the foolish thoughts that had been plaguing her since he moved into town. Another part of her wanted to stand and fight these attacks. To simply give in to Olin's protective love wouldn't accomplish a resolution to the problem. It would only forestall it.

He massaged her shoulder.

Then again, it would be so nice not to think about everything. She leaned into his chest and closed her eyes. She wasn't giving in to her emotions, she told herself, just taking a respite from circumstances.

"Father," he quietly prayed, "give us wisdom and strength. Help us find our way through this problem. Reveal to us how to expose our enemies. Guard our hearts, refine us as Ye would refine gold and silver. Thy Word says, 'The fining pot is for silver, and the furnace for gold; but the Lord trieth the hearts.' Help us to be worthy of this test."

Only a man who works with metal would equate the heart and metal, she mused. "Amen."

A surge of confidence welled up inside. "Olin, bring me home."

"But. . ."

She placed a finger to his lips. "Trust me on this. I need to return to my home, my business. I'm confident of that after your prayer."

"As ye wish. Come. . ."

They walked an hour in silence until they reached his parents' home. With each step closer, Ida Mae grew in her confidence that this is what she should do, for now. A time might come for her to go into hiding again, but for now she felt she needed to be in town, protecting her own property.

⚭

"Good morning, Mrs. Baxter, how can I help you?"

The older woman hoisted a fleece of wool onto the counter. "Been saving this for a while. I hoped to get around to it but I simply couldn't find the time. Ain't no sense letting it gather dust. What's it going to cost me?"

Ida Mae scanned the fleece. The sheep had been sheared properly. "It's not sorted."

"Nah, ain't seen much use for sorting. Them discolored parts can be sorted when you're spinning it, can't it?"

"Yes, I can sort it." *But I should charge you for sorting.* "When do you need it done by?"

"No real rush. As I said, it's been gathering dust."

Ida Mae rubbed her hand over the wool. It needed a good cleaning. "Ain't seen nothin' like it, I tell ya."

Realizing she had missed something in the conversation, Ida Mae tried to recall Mrs. Baxter's words. Nothing came to mind. "Pardon?"

"Sheriff said it was chicken blood on your door the other day. I ain't seen nothing like that before. No good will come of it."

"Yes, very unusual." She'd been fielding questions from her customers for hours. If nothing else, the incident certainly brought in more work. "Three dollars."

"How about two?"

Ida Mae held back a chuckle. "Three. The fleece needs scoring and sorting before I can even begin to work it."

Mrs. Baxter's jowls wagged. "Oh, all right. I knew I shouldn't have left it for so long."

In reality, you should be paying me five dollars. "I'll try to have this done by the end of next week."

"That'll be just fine. Can you use some summer squash? My cupboards are overflowing."

"I'd love some." Ida Mae missed fresh vegetables.

"Bless your heart, dear." Mrs. Baxter leaned over the counter and whispered, "Have you been treated properly?"

"Yes." Again, a question that had been asked so often she'd given up being angered over it. Folks meant well, they just didn't realize the effect the question had. "I had a pleasant visit with my family and with the Orrs."

"I heard—"

"Olin Orr is a fine and decent man, in much the same way as his father and brothers. I don't understand what his cousin has against him."

The methodical nod of Mrs. Baxter's head showed she comprehended the true source of Olin's problems. "I've seen Mr. Orr's work; it's mighty fine."

A smile creased Ida Mae's cheeks. "He made me this candlestick holder."

The older woman picked it up and examined the intricate design Olin had laid out in the thin metal. The tiny tin roses at the base made the piece quite ornate. "Very nice. I might just order myself a pair."

Perhaps the blood on the doorway would be a boon to both our businesses, Ida Mae mused. "Do you want me to save the discolored wool?"

"Ain't got much use for it."

The bell over the door rang as another customer entered the shop.

"Gracious, look at the time. I must be running. I'll be in the end of next week to pick up the wool yarn." Mrs. Baxter hustled out the door with a quick greeting to Elsa Perkins.

"How can I help you, Elsa?"

"Mother's wondering if you'll have time to spin this." Elsa plopped a bundle of cotton on the counter. It was too early in the season for cotton.

"I can. What does she want?"

"Thread to sew rugs with and other thick materials."

Ida Mae scribbled a note and attached it to the bundle. "How soon would she like it?"

"Right away. Are you staying in town or going off visiting again?"

"I should be here for a while."

Elsa leaned over the counter. "Are you married?"

The sting of heat flashed across her cheeks. "No."

"I heard you had a—"

"Friend who put out a fire, nothing happened. I don't know what people are claiming they saw, but we simply spoke for a few minutes in my hallway."

"Ma said you wouldn't behave that way. I kinda figured, but it's hard when you are alone and kissin' a boy."

Ida Mae's heart went out to the young woman. "Remember, if he's a man worth marrying he'll behave proper."

"That's what I keep telling Michael." Tears trailed down Elsa's cheeks.

Ida Mae ran around the counter and swept Elsa up in her arms. "Shh, now it will be all right. Have you?"

She shook her head no.

Relief washed over Ida Mae. "Good. You tell Michael you can't see him any longer. He'll be apologizing to you right quick if he can get past your father. I suspect if you tell your parents you don't want to see Michael for a while, they'll let him know in no uncertain terms he's not welcome in your home. If he truly loves you, he'll come back and he'll be apologizing to you and your parents and be asking for your hand in marriage as a young man should. If not, he's not worth losing sleep over."

"But don't you love Olin? He's not a perfect man."

Ida Mae chuckled. "No man is a perfect man, but Olin isn't the man others say he is. I have yet to meet more of a gentleman in all of the county."

"Really? But they say—"

"Elsa, I know what they say. You can't go by what others say. You have to judge people on their actions. Olin has never put me in the same situation Michael has put you. Who do you say is more honorable?"

Elsa took in a deep breath and released it slowly. "Mr. Orr."

"Remember, a man is only as good as his words and actions. I'd say Michael has some improving to do."

"Do you really know what folks are saying about you?"

"Yes. Thankfully, I have enough people who know me and believe my word."

"Including the sheriff. He's real upset about what happened the other night.

Why do you think someone poured chicken blood on your door?"

To implicate Olin.

❧

"How much is this?" A constant stream of women had been in his shop all day. Eyeing him and sizing him up, no doubt.

At this very moment he'd prefer to be alone with Ida Mae in the woods, or stuck on the farm, anywhere away from these busybodies. Not one item had been purchased, but if there were a way to count fingerprints he'd have the most in a day to be certain. "Fifty cents."

"What's wrong with it? The tin man last summer tried to sell me a candlestick holder that looked very similar for two dollars."

"It's a fair price. I made the items here so I can pass on the savings to you." *And keep ye from getting overcharged by the Yankee traders.*

"Heard you married Ida Mae McAuley. Is that true? Ain't no ring on your finger. Not that a man has to wear a ring, but my Tyrone, God bless him, always wore his wedding ring."

"No, ma'am, we are not." He'd known gossip would spread like wildfire, but he didn't anticipate it would remain, burning like coals in a firepot. For the past two days he'd been answering similar questions.

"She's a fine girl."

"Aye, that she is. Can I help you with anything else?"

The gray wisps in the woman's dark hair had him guessing her age to be around forty. The wrinkles on her hands added a few more years. Mayhap forty-five. Her features were somewhat familiar. Olin examined her a bit more closely. *Who is she?*

She picked up a snuffer and twirled it in her fingers, then placed it back on the table. "Are you truly an honorable man?"

"Pardon?"

"I've heard tales that make a person question your intent with my niece."

Olin relaxed. Seeing no one else in the shop, he closed the door and offered the customer a seat. "Mrs. Jacobs?"

"Yes."

"For you I will answer whatever ye ask. To strangers, I shall not."

Mrs. Jacobs' hands shook. "Forgive me for being direct, and I know you spoke with my husband, but for the sake of my dear departed sister's only daughter, I feel I must ask."

"I do love your niece and I hope to marry her one day. Only God knows that I've been a gentleman. There have been too many moments when we have not been in the companionship of others to vouch for my conduct. Ye may ask Ida Mae. I know the rumors circulating about the events that transpired seven years ago. Sheriff. . ."

She waved him to silence. "I am not concerned about the past, only the present. Am I correct in understanding that you spent a night alone together?"

Olin pulled at his collar. "Aye, that is the truth."

"Do you see my concern?"

"Aye, but we were trying to keep Ida Mae safe. The sheriff felt it best that Ida Mae go into hiding."

"Then why are you here now? No one has been caught."

"Ida Mae thought it best that we return. She did not want to live on the run." He still hadn't settled whether he agreed with her or not. Danger still lurked out there and he, for one, wouldn't rest until the person was apprehended.

She thought for a moment, then nodded before she spoke. "Yes, she can be that way. She's like my sister in that regard." Olin shifted as his guest scanned the room. "Do you make enough to support a wife?"

"Not at present." The words slipped out before he had a chance to think.

"Then why ask Ida Mae to marry you?"

"Because I love her and I have a savings to live on while I develop my business here."

"I see." Mrs. Jacobs narrowed her gaze. "And business is developing?"

Olin pulled at his collar once again.

"Are you planning on living off of Ida Mae's inheritance?"

"No, ma'am."

The steady drum of knocking on the closed front door made Olin grateful for the distraction. "Pardon me."

He opened the door to see Sheriff Thatcher with his arms across his chest. "Why do you keep doing this?" the sheriff asked Olin.

Chapter 16

The bolt clanged in the lock and relief washed over Ida Mae. Two days of nonstop customers and busybodies. The customers were all too curious and asking far too many questions for Ida Mae's liking. She leaned against the closed door and sighed. Her gaze settled on the various materials needing to be spun that were piled in a corner. The sight of it caused her back to spasm. She flipped the sign telling customers she was now closed, then pushed off the door to go to work. The constant stream of customers hadn't allowed her much time to actually spin.

She scanned the various bundles. "Where to begin?"

"With the easiest first," Minnie spouted as she came from the back room.

"How did you get. . ."

She held up a key. "You gave it to me."

Under duress. "I forgot."

"What happened here?" Minnie looked over the various piles.

"Everyone who was in the least bit curious has come by."

Minnie giggled. "Well, you won't worry about what to eat this winter. Not that you ever had to. But I'm tellin' ya, Cyrus ain't no farmer. Pa went by the place the other day and said it was a mess."

"Olin and his brothers have said the same. I know I won't be leasing the land to him next year. But I've since given up hope of seeing any profit for this year." Ida Mae sat down at the flax wheel.

"How can I help?"

"Start carding the wool or clean the cotton. Either one would be a tremendous help."

Minnie sat down at the counter and opened the cotton bundle from Mrs. Perkins. "Mother's in town. She might come over when she's done her shoppin'."

"Your mother hardly ever comes to town. What brought her in this time?" Ida Mae lifted some of the stringy flax fibers and rubbed them through her fingers.

"You. She's speaking with Mr. Orr right now."

"What?" The fine fibers fell to the floor.

"Don't go fussin'. She's just makin' sure Father was right about Mr. Orr."

When will this family let me make my own choices? She wanted to scream but bit her tongue to keep from exploding.

"She'll find him charmin'."

Ida Mae chuckled.

"Oh, hush now. You were right; I was wrong."

Which explained Minnie's offer to help. Her cousin could leap into anything once she had a mind to. "What about Percy?"

"What about him?"

"Weren't you and he—"

"He hasn't been around since I told him I didn't think Bobby—Olin," she corrected, "was the man he's made him out to be. I thought. . ." Her words trailed off.

Ida Mae knew what she thought. Minnie had hoped for a relationship with Percy, that he might be the man to spend the rest of her life with. "I'm sorry."

"Don't be. If he truly is that vengeful he'd make a horrible husband. Ain't gonna live like that. A man who can't forgive and move on with life. . ." Minnie shook her head. "A woman would be hard pressed to enjoy marriage with a man like that."

"Has he ever said what it was Olin did that got Percy so upset with him?"

"No."

Ida Mae wished something would come out. It didn't make sense that a cousin would hold a grudge for so long. Not when blood is thicker than water, as the saying was among the various Scots-Irish clans. Granted, Percy's father wasn't Scots-Irish, but his mother was. Ida Mae's own family tree descended from the same heritage. But her family had come to America several generations before Olin's father's, and they had long since lost their accent. Olin's accent woke something inside her. "Minnie, what if—"

"Open up, Ida Mae!" Sheriff Thatcher bellowed.

⚭

Olin's heart thumped in his chest when he saw the precious blond-haired, blue-eyed maiden he'd lost his heart to. Her eyes were as big as the end of a hammer.

"Sheriff, Olin." She stepped aside to let them in.

"Miss Minnie." The sheriff lifted his hat slightly and nodded. "Your mother waits in her carriage at Mr. Orr's tin shop."

Ida Mae hugged her cousin. "Thanks."

"I'll return before we leave for home," Minnie asserted, then marched out the front door.

Olin held back a laugh, thankful he wasn't called to be Minnie Jacobs's spouse. He worked his way around the sheriff and sidled up beside Ida Mae, capturing her in a protective embrace. "The sheriff has some interesting news."

"Miss McAuley, are you aware that Percy Mandrake has been arrested?"

Ida Mae relaxed in Olin's arms. He gave her a gentle squeeze, encouraged that his cousin no longer posed a threat to him or, more importantly, to Ida Mae. "Why?"

"Drunk and disorderly."

"He claims he was responsible for putting the chicken blood on the entrance," Olin supplied. She needed to know that the threat was gone.

"Did he admit to anything else?"

"No, ma'am, only the blood."

"Why?"

"He didn't say. He succumbed to the liquor and fell asleep."

"Does this mean I'm safe?"

"I'd wager to say it is a safe bet. Percy's been after Olin since he came back to town. He even came to my office to report Olin's past crimes."

"So all of this was about you and not me?"

Olin turned and faced her. "This is where the sheriff and I disagree. The notes were personal to you. Sheriff feels—"

"I can speak for myself," Sheriff Thatcher chided Olin. "The first note said to get rid of your tenant, that would be Olin, and we know how Percy felt about him. The second note revealed someone had been watching your place in the middle of the night. Again, it was an indirect reference to Olin."

"But what about the stolen items?"

"They were hidden in Olin's area of the shop."

Olin had to admit it made sense, but something in the pit of his gut told him there was something else going on here. Someone else was still after Ida Mae, but he couldn't understand who or why.

"So, I am safe." Ida Mae breathed a sigh of relief.

Olin's spine stiffened. A tiny muscle in his jaw started to twitch.

"Thank you, Sheriff Thatcher, for all your hard work on my behalf."

"Just doin' my job, Ida Mae. Olin, don't forget that special project. The customer is hoping to get a look at the design next week."

"Tell him it will be ready."

Ida Mae furrowed her brows. Olin reached for his collar and pulled. How long could he keep this a secret? If she were his wife, it wouldn't be a problem. His mind spun off in various directions. It's not that he didn't want to share the information with Ida Mae. Actually, he was longing to tell her. But the reality was, if he didn't keep the secret it would affect Mr. Bechtler and his plans to make the first gold coin in the area. A mint near the mines seemed like a brilliant plan. Currently, the gold was shipped up to Washington to be minted there. As much as he wanted to tell Ida Mae, he couldn't.

"Sheriff Thatcher"—Ida Mae turned her attention from Olin back to the sheriff—"am I really safe now?"

"It appears that way. I'd like you to continue to be cautious. Also, be aware that everyone in town is watching you now."

And me. Olin's mind drifted back over his day and the many curiosity seekers. "We'll be careful."

The sheriff paused for a moment, then gave a lift of his hat and departed.

"How was your day?" Olin asked before stepping aside and giving Ida Mae some room.

"Busy. And yours? I heard my aunt came by to see you."

Olin smiled. "She needed her heart settled—like your uncle."

"Do you think Percy was our problem?"

"If the sheriff believes that to be the case, I guess I do, too, although I'm still uncomfortable. Mayhap it could be we've lived in fear for so long our minds need time to adjust."

"Will you be moving back into the shop?"

I'd love to. "No. For now I believe I should stay where I am. Are ye hungry?"

"Starving."

"Mum came into town to invite you to dinner."

"Olin, tell your mother thank you, but I have to spend most of the night working. I need to get caught up on this rash of orders. I know most of them are from folks who didn't really need the work done, but some are legitimate requests. All these little orders will stop me from completing the bigger orders."

"Aye, I understand. I'll be working late tonight as well." He didn't want to tell her the gossip was so bad that when he closed his shop door with Ida Mae's aunt inside someone had gone running to the sheriff to report his illicit behavior. "I miss you."

She turned in his embrace and nuzzled her head under his chin. "I've missed you, too."

He kissed the top of her head. "I better go back to my shop or my parents will wonder what happened to me."

She stepped out of his embrace, and the cool wind of separation washed over him. He wanted her in his arms. Olin dropped them to his sides. *I can't give in to my emotions. Not now.*

"I'll see you tomorrow." The gentle whoosh of her skirt followed her back to the spinning wheel.

Olin stepped out the front door. "Don't forget to lock it." The bright setting sun caused him to blink. Could their troubles be truly over? Was Percy responsible for everything? And why the blood?

∞

Ida Mae worked until midnight. She finished a large order and several of the smaller ones. Tomorrow she'd work on John Alexander's newest order. He had pressed to have this one filled as soon as possible. She supposed it had something to do with the amount of people who had come through her door the previous two days.

Before bed she swept the floors and checked the locks. A twinge of hunger rumbled in her stomach, reminding her she hadn't eaten since breakfast. In the back room she cut a slice of bread, sliced a tomato, and sprinkled it with basil, salt, and pepper. She then peeled the layer of wax off a small ball of cheese she had made last week.

A flash of a memory of being in Olin's arms wiggled past her tired senses. *Lord, how can I love him so much having known him for so little time? Do I truly love him or am I caught up in the emotions and fear because of the events that have happened?*

Memories of the day's conversations swam through her mind as she sat down to eat her makeshift dinner. It bothered her that so many people had come just to satisfy their curiosity. And yet it was typical for the area. Many genuinely cared what happened to her, others were just busybodies trying to get the next tidbit they could share with someone else.

Ida Mae bit into the soft ball of cheese, a delicacy her mother had taught her to make. It melted well and was great for heating over a slice of toast. She'd love an open toasted cheese sandwich with tomato and basil right now, but her meal, such as it was, would have to do.

Closing her eyes, Ida Mae sat and enjoyed the peaceful night sounds. A distant owl hooted. Night insects hummed, building in intensity as the rest of the world's silence deepened. "If only life could remain this calm."

Taking in a deep sigh, she quickly finished her meal, cleaned up, and went to bed. Morning would be sneaking up on her if she didn't get to sleep soon. As she snuggled into her pillow, thoughts of Olin and being in his arms drifted back. "Lord, I should have married him. But—I'm doing it again, always questioning, never going with my first instinct. Why? Why can't I just make a decision and stick with it? Why do I flounder so?

"On the other hand, Father isn't around to give his blessing to Olin. I haven't known him all that long, and is physical attraction enough? How can a girl court when her parents are gone? How does one know if she is making the right choice?

"Then again, others seem to marry quickly and enjoy a happy marriage. Is a long courtship necessary to know if this person is to be your spouse?"

Ida Mae tossed and turned for thirty minutes, pondering these questions before falling asleep. She awoke the next morning with the same questions buzzing around in her head.

She dressed and made a large breakfast for herself, one that would hold a farmer all day if necessary, and she expected to have a similar day today as she had the day before. After breakfast she cleaned up and went out the back door to throw the dirty water away.

Fear spiraled down her legs like the wool circling the large spinner's wheel, tying her in place.

Chapter 17

Olin dug his spurs into the horse's side to catch up to the swarm of people huddled around Ida Mae's back door. He'd hoped to have a few minutes alone with her before they started their day. He jumped off the horse. Worming his way through the crowd, he called out, "Ida Mae?"

She stood there frozen, with tears running down her cheeks. He came up beside her. "Ida Mae."

"Get your hands off of her."

"Pardon?" Olin turned to see a man holding a knife.

"You heard me. Miss McAuley didn't have any problems until you moved into town."

"Stop!" Ida Mae cried and reached out toward Olin. "Cyrus, Olin is my friend."

"Ida Mae, you've gotta see that he's the cause of all your problems."

"No. He isn't. You're the one who scared me this morning."

A surge of anger pulsed through Olin. He opened and closed his fists. He had little patience for Cyrus Morgan, who had a wife but let rumors continue that Ida Mae was his wife. A man who claimed to be a farmer but turned her farm into a dirt farm where even weeds wouldn't grow. What was he doing with an unsheathed knife? "Folks, you can go about your business. I'll—good morning, Sheriff."

Sheriff Thatcher made his way to the center of the crowd. "What seems to be the problem?"

"Cyrus Morgan startled me this morning. He came to deliver a ham but all I saw was his large knife when I opened the door."

"I see." The sheriff turned toward Cyrus. "Is this true?"

"Yes, sir." Cyrus lifted the smallest smoked ham Olin had ever seen. He truly was a miserable farmer. "I came to deliver this from the farm."

"Mr. Orr, what brings you here this morning?"

"I came to check on Miss McAuley before opening my shop."

The sheriff nodded, then turned back to the crowd. "Y'all can go on now. I've got the matter in hand." Then he turned toward Ida Mae. "Are you all right?"

She nodded.

"Mr. Morgan, why don't you give me the ham? Mr. Orr, why don't you head on to your place of business?"

Olin stared in disbelief. Did the sheriff now consider him a suspect? Sheriff Thatcher winked.

Olin fought the desire to stay planted and ask a million questions. Instead, he abided with the sheriff's wishes and mounted his horse. He could hear Cyrus do the same behind him. He didn't want to leave Ida Mae, but he saw something in the sheriff's eyes, something akin to a gentle sternness that said, "Let me do my job."

Olin would let him for the time being. But the first opportunity he had he'd be at Ida Mae's door. He didn't like the look of Cyrus's knife, and could well imagine the fear it had caused her. "Lord, please keep her safe."

Olin arrived at his shop, dismounted, and readied his horse for the stable. *I should go back.* He tossed the saddle on the rail of the stall. *But the sheriff said to come here. Why?* He reached for the oats and filled the bin. "This is nonsense. I should be with her. I should be protecting her."

He grabbed the water bucket to top off the trough. After a couple of stiff cranks, the pump poured water into the bucket. "But Percy is locked up, isn't he? So where is the threat?"

∞

Ida Mae held on to the banister just a few minutes longer, hoping that her legs were no longer rubber. "What's the matter, Sheriff?"

"You tell me. I come into work this morning and there's a crowd gathering at your home. Doesn't make a man content with all that's been happening."

"It's as I said, I saw the knife and couldn't move. I'm afraid I can't tell you who gathered or when they gathered. It's all a blank to me. The only thing I remember is Olin calling my name."

"I see. Did Cyrus actually come to bring you a ham?"

"Apparently. It's my portion of the pig he slaughtered last week."

"Wasn't very big."

"No, I can see that." Ida Mae released the railing. "Would you like to come inside?"

"No, I think we've given the neighbors quite enough to talk about today." *Absolutely.* "I'm fine, Sheriff."

Sheriff Thatcher nodded with the tip of his hat. "I'll be off. I'll come around and check on you at noon."

"Thank you."

Ida Mae went into her room and collapsed on her bed. How could she have overreacted so? She'd seen large knives many times. Just about every man carried one in some form or fashion. But still, it was odd to see such a huge knife to simply cut the string he was using to hold the ham up on a nail.

Why would the sheriff send Olin away? "Time to face the day."

Several hours later, Olin returned. Together they discussed her tired nerves and his desire to take her away from all of this. Her love for Olin deepened as she watched him be more concerned about her and her interests than his own.

The next few days passed without incident. Even the constant stream of customers had slowed down to an occasional one or two a day. All caught up on her work, Ida Mae made a picnic lunch to bring to Olin. Today they would finally have some time alone, she hoped. They'd had dinner with his parents one night, but Kyle had escorted her back to the town. Time alone was at an all-time premium. If it wasn't the sheriff constantly separating them for some unknown reason, it was his family. *Do they not want me to marry Olin?* Ida Mae's step faltered at the thought.

She had sent a note to Olin earlier in the day to let him know her intentions. The door to his shop was closed. *Odd.*

Olin leaned against the stable doorway. "Hello."

She turned to the left. "Hello" His handsome face glowed. Ida Mae's heart clenched. She did love this man. A few days of calm allowed her to trust her instincts and not question whether she loved him only because he'd come to her rescue on more than one occasion.

∞

Ida Mae quickened her pace and came up beside him. "I've been looking forward to this for days."

Olin chuckled. "You only sent me an invitation this morning. Where are we going?"

"There's a spot on the river at my farm." *That's quite romantic*, she didn't add.

His smile slipped. "Honey, I can't be gone that long. I have orders to finish."

Ida Mae took a moment to inhale deeply and exhale slowly. She suspected that might be the case but had hoped he could simply close his doors the way she had. "I understand. But a girl can hope."

"Why don't we plan on going there after church on Sunday?"

"There's another church picnic."

"Ah, all right. How about—"

"Let's just go to the edge of town on the green overlooking the northeast corner," she suggested.

"Fine, you ride. I'll escort ye."

Ida Mae mounted and sat sidesaddle. "Olin, are your parents not—"

"No. They had Kyle bring ye to town for your honor. They felt ye have had enough trouble, so if someone other than me escorted ye home, they thought it wouldn't produce as much gossip."

"Probably so. But I prefer your company."

"And I prefer yours. Ye are the sweetest joy in my life."

They traveled a few blocks to the edge of the town and sat down on the green knoll overlooking the Wingate plantation. Slaves worked in the distant fields. It seemed odd to see so many. Most, if not all, of the yeoman farmers didn't own slaves. Olin reclined and leaned on his elbow. " 'Tis a fine day, lass."

"Yes."

"Now that we be alone, tell me what happened the other day with Cyrus."

"It's as he said, he came to deliver the ham and I froze at seeing that huge knife when I opened the door. I'm certain it was an overreaction due to the events that have transpired."

"Aye, ye are probably right. That was a right small ham."

Ida Mae giggled. "Tender, though. But yes, I think he killed one of the young ones. Perhaps they were low on food."

"Honey, ye should consider hiring Kyle to look after your farm."

"Trust me, I have been. I've written to my brothers and warned them that we'll receive little, if any, income this year. I've heard back from Bryan and he said not to fret over it. All indications are he'll be having a bumper crop this year. He also suggested that I sell the property and come live with him and his wife."

Olin stiffened.

It pleased Ida Mae to see that reaction in him. He truly did care about her.

"Selling your farm is an answer, but it's good land and should make ye a profit if it is farmed well."

She couldn't agree with him more. But she didn't want to spend the entire hour speaking about such matters. "Olin, I've missed you."

He sat up and slid closer. "Aye."

"Why did the sheriff tell you to leave the other day?" Sheriff Thatcher hadn't said a word about it to her, and she knew it had to do with appearances. But really, it was daylight, and they were in public. Who should be concerned about her and Olin speaking with one another?

"I'm not certain. Mayhap he suspects someone else besides Percy."

"Do you think I'm still in danger?"

"I don't know. But nothing has happened since Percy was arrested."

"True." Ida Mae pondered her own fears and concerns. "I haven't seen any sign of anyone breaking in or attempting to. There have been no notes—"

Olin jumped up. "That's what has been bothering me about this. I hadn't been able to put my finger on it, but that's it." Olin paced back and forth on the knoll.

"Finger on what?"

"The notes. Percy couldn't have written those. He might have had someone help him, but he didn't stay in school past third grade. He's been working on the farm all his life. He doesn't read well. And he certainly can't construct the penmanship we saw on those notes."

Prickly brushes of gooseflesh rose on her body. Someone was still out there who wanted to do harm to her. "Then who?"

"I don't know. But I'll not have ye spend another night in that building."

"But—"

Olin laid a finger to her lips. "I think we should put ye in hiding for a day or two and see what happens. The old cottage on my parents' place is clean and ready. I'll sneak out there tonight and bring food and supplies."

"No. I can't go on the run again."

"But ye must. Don't ye see, we have to bring whoever is after ye out of the woodwork. I won't go with ye. I'll come to work and pretend to be shocked and see what interest that brings."

"But the sheriff. . ."

"Will question me as long as the day has light, plus some, I'm afraid. I'll be his prime suspect."

"Shouldn't we tell him?"

"Mayhap, but let's pray about this. I don't want us running off without the Lord's blessing."

Ida Mae didn't want that, either. She didn't want to be running off, period. She certainly didn't want to go in hiding in a cottage with no one around, alone, and without visitors, without Olin. Her body ached to be held in his arms.

∞

Olin silently prayed he was doing what the Lord would have him do. Something about Cyrus Morgan still bothered him. And he still didn't have a clear picture as to why the sheriff would have him leave Ida Mae's side after a horrific experience. He didn't want to believe the sheriff was aware or possibly involved with the strange events. It couldn't be that, he argued with himself for the twentieth time since the incident. After having some measure of peace about hiding Ida Mae in the cabin, he left her on the knoll. She rode off to his house, never returning to her business.

He went back to work as if nothing had happened. It wasn't long before Sheriff Thatcher came knocking at his door. "Olin."

"Sheriff."

"Where is she?"

Who? he wanted to ask but decided not to bait the sheriff. "In hiding."

"What's happened?"

"Nothing."

The sheriff rubbed the back of his neck. "Then why? And I want more than a single word or two response, understand?"

"Percy couldn't have written those notes. His skills are limited in those areas. He only finished third grade. After that he worked on the farm."

"I thought education was a major part of your kin's heritage."

215

"Aye, but Percy's father is not Scots-Irish. He doesn't see education to be as important as his mother's family does."

The sheriff leaned back on the edge of the counter. "Then you went back to my original plan to hide her to flush out the culprits."

"More or less. This time I'm not hiding. This should rattle whoever is after her. If I'm in the dark as to where she is, then he truly will be."

"You'll be watched."

"I suspect so. I'll join her in a few days if nothing develops." Olin reached for his tin snips and cut the edge off the piece he had been working on when the sheriff came in.

"You two have kept my hands full the past few months."

"Aye, I'm truly sorry for that. But I think this goes beyond Percy and his hatred toward me."

"I believe you are probably right. I've heard some rumblings lately that suggest someone might be trying to persuade Ida Mae to marry him so he can have her property."

"Who?"

Sheriff guffawed. "Half the folks say it's you."

Olin dropped the snips.

"Hang on, son. I didn't say I believed them. I believe there is some truth in this rumor, along with others. Ida Mae in hiding might just bring some to the surface. You have to trust me. I can't tell you who I suspect because of that temper of yours."

"What temper? I haven't done—"

"*That* temper. You control it, yes, but it still flares. I saw it the other morning, too. Can you trust me?"

"Do you trust me?" Olin wasn't sure he wanted to hear the answer.

"Yes."

Olin's shoulders relaxed. "All right, I'll trust ye."

"Good. When you see Ida Mae, pass on a message to her. Let her know I'm aware and am still investigating."

"Yes, sir."

Olin watched the sheriff leave and went back to work. The minutes ticked by at the speed of a snail crossing the street. He couldn't go to her tonight. He'd have to send John or Kyle to go to town and then sneak around to the cottage. Whoever the sheriff was after would certainly be watching. He fought the desire to go to Ida Mae's side. He wanted to protect her but his best protection was to stay away. *Lord, help her understand.*

Chapter 18

For two days Ida Mae prayed, read, and reread the scriptures, partly out of boredom, but also because she was searching for answers. Not that anyone could ever truly understand the ways of God. Perhaps she should sell the property and move in with her brother Bryan and his wife. If it weren't for the properties she owned in town, the little income she made from spinning would not support her.

And where was Olin, and how did he fit in this conflict? Every time they tried to spend a moment with one another something came up. It reminded her of the corduroy roads in the area—up, down, up, down, bumpy at best.

The passage from Proverbs that she and Olin had shared the first time she went on the run repeatedly came back to mind. But after two days with no human contact, Ida Mae felt like screaming. She settled for a cool bath in the creek, the same stream she had bathed in the day she was supposed to marry Olin. That day seemed like an eternity ago.

She wouldn't stay here much longer. Instead, she figured, she should travel to her brother's home in Kentucky and visit with them for the winter if nothing changed. Dressed and ready to take her bath, she slipped out of the cabin and headed for the stream. She figured it would take a forty-five-minute walk, if she had her bearings straight. Generally, she was pretty good with directions, but her current ability to concentrate was sorely diminished.

A horse and rider approached, and it was too late to hide. Ida Mae continued her walk, then noticed it was Olin's mother.

"Ida Mae!" Mrs. Orr called out. "How are ye?"

Relieved. "Fine, I was going to take a bath."

"Let me join you."

Company sounded good. Mrs. Orr slipped off her horse and walked beside her. "How are ye really?"

"Bored."

Mrs. Orr chuckled. "Aye, I would be, too. Can I bring ye some more books?"

Ida Mae nodded. She always loved to read, although at this moment in time she wished for something else. "Do you have a spinning wheel?"

"Aye. Would ye like some cotton to spin? I finished the wool."

"That would be wonderful." *Anything would be wonderful, even weaving.*

Ida Mae mentally ducked as she imagined her mother listening from heaven at that thought.

"Do ye need more food?"

"Not yet."

"I don't understand why ye can't stay in the big house with us. Olin says ye need to be in hidin', and I suppose he knows, but it seems silly. We don't get many visitors here."

"That would be nice." As bored as she was, it was more comfortable than having to be social, especially in her dark moods of regret and wondering why things had gone so wrong in her life since her parents died.

"I came to tell ye that Percy is out of jail. The judge told him to pay restitution for the damages and he was free to go."

"Percy knows about the cabin."

"Aye."

"Am I safe?"

Mrs. Orr grabbed her hand and squeezed it. "I don't know, lass."

∞

Olin walked into the sheriff's office as ordered. "Sheriff."

"Mr. Orr, take a seat. I'll be right with you."

Amos Bentley stood a few feet from the sheriff. "I'm tellin' ya, Sheriff, it's those miners. I'm losing livestock left and right. Ain't like they can't afford to pay for their food."

"I'll look into it."

Amos nodded. "I'll check in next week."

"You do that, Amos. Have a good day." The sheriff stepped toward his desk, sat down, and wrote a note. Then he raised his head to focus on Olin. "We've got a problem."

"What?"

"Someone broke into Ida Mae's room. They tore it apart and. . ." The sheriff seemed to be collecting his thoughts. "And left evidence that she struggled and was possibly killed."

"What? Who?"

"I don't know. She's safe, right?"

"Aye. I've watched from a distance, but I can tell she's still at the cabin."

"Good. 'Cause there are more problems."

Olin braced himself.

"I hate to do this, son, but it appears you were the one to kidnap her."

"Pardon?" Olin held on to the arms of the oak chair so tightly his hands started to shake.

"Exactly. You're being framed for Ida Mae's murder."

"By whom?"

"If I knew that we wouldn't be having this conversation."

"What do we do now?"

"We wait. It's early and most folks aren't aware yet that something has happened. As you know, news travels fast in these parts and I expect to find folks in an uproar. Would you mind spending the day behind bars?"

"That doesn't make sense."

"I know. But I suspect you'll be framed for some other crime that I can't disprove and you'll end up behind bars anyway. If you are already in jail that won't be possible."

"But. . ." Olin clamped his mouth shut. Anything he said right now was being weighed. There seemed to be some level of doubt in the sheriff's eyes. *At the moment he seems to believe me.*

"Olin. . ." The sheriff's words trailed off as the door banged open.

Cyrus Morgan bustled in with the weight of a sledgehammer. "Sheriff, I. . ." He paused and focused on Olin, then narrowed his gaze. "Ida Mae is missing."

"I'm aware of that."

Cyrus finally broke his gaze and looked at the sheriff. "What are you doing about it?"

"I'm looking into the matter. She might be visiting—"

"Her room has been ransacked."

The sheriff leaned back. "And you know this how?"

Cyrus stammered. "A—a friend told me."

"Care to name names?"

Cyrus stepped back. "Rosey Turner."

Rosey Morgan, your wife, Olin wanted to blurt out.

"And how did Rosey hear this?"

Cyrus stretched his neck to the side. "I don't know. She just told me and I came running over here. Ida Mae and Rosey's family are good friends. As you know, I rebuilt her house and am running her farm this year."

"Yes." The sheriff relaxed his posture. "I appreciate your concerns, Mr. Morgan. But, as you see, I already knew and am investigating it fully."

Cyrus's gaze shifted back to Olin, then to Sheriff Thatcher. "Let me know if you find out anything. Ida Mae and I were close." He pulled a paper from his pocket and handed it to the sheriff. "Real close. And if you ask me, I think Mr. Orr has some questions to answer. She probably refused his advances—"

"Mr. Orr, sit down!" the sheriff bellowed as Olin shot to his feet. "And why was this a secret?" The sheriff held up the piece of paper.

What could be on it? Olin tried to get a glance but couldn't. It looked to be a parchment of some sort, fairly new but very wrinkled.

"Ida Mae asked me to keep our marriage a secret."

"Marriage?" Olin squeaked as he dropped back into his chair.

"Yes, she and I married a few months back." Cyrus grinned.

How can that be? Olin gripped the arms of the chair. *Father, give me grace and strength.*

"Cyrus, this does put an interesting spin on my investigation. If this paper is real—and I will be checking into its validity—then I will need to check Ida Mae's farmhouse to see that she's not at home with you."

"Of course she's not at home. Why would I come here to you if she were at home?"

"I don't know. Why would you keep the marriage a secret?"

Olin found his voice. "I heard rumors that Cyrus married Ida Mae several months back."

Cyrus grinned. "I got drunk one night and let it slip out. But ever since I've kept my mouth shut. Ida Mae wanted to keep it a secret—something to do with the settlement of her parents' estate. I told her I didn't care about the inheritance. She had to work things out with her brothers, though. They wanted to sell the properties, but Ida Mae and I wanted to keep the farm."

"I see." The sheriff shifted back in his seat and scanned the document in front of him. "Who's the judge?"

"Judge Weaver from Montgomery County."

The sheriff simply nodded.

"Ida Mae felt it would help keep our secret longer. Ya know how folks can be around here."

Olin didn't know what to believe. How could she have married this man? It didn't fit. *And why would she proclaim her love for me and attempt to marry me but not go through with it?* Dread washed over him. Is this why she couldn't, because she was already married to Cyrus? Olin's anger shifted from Cyrus to Ida Mae.

"Pardon me. You two obviously have a lot to discuss. I hope ye find your wife, Mr. Morgan." Olin slipped out of the sheriff's office. The bright sun caused him to close his eyes. *How could I have been such a fool?*

⚭

"Ida Mae, are ye through, lass?" Mrs. Orr called out from behind the bush.

Leaning her head back under the cool water, Ida Mae rinsed her hair again. "I'll be right there." Summer bathing in the river was such a delight. It was far less work, and the gentle roll of a stream seemed to relax one's muscles, rather than having to fill your own tub and drain it after you were cleaned.

On shore, Ida Mae dried herself off.

"Are ye decent?"

"More or less." She wouldn't want to be caught in her underclothing with anyone else but felt comfortable enough with Mrs. Orr.

"Would ye like me to brush out your hair?"

Memories of childhood flooded back in her mind, of sitting in front of her mother and father and having them brush her golden strands. "That would be wonderful, thank you."

"You're welcome. Here, sit down on this rock.

"I haven't been able to do this for years. I'd come down to the river with the girls and we'd bathe and brush one another's hair. It was a grand time. It's much more peaceful this morning than the last time ye and I were down here."

The wedding day. Her stomach flipped, then flopped like a spindle too heavy with thread. "I think I should have gone through with the wedding." Ida Mae felt the heat rise in her cheeks.

Mrs. Orr's hands stilled. "Don't regret saying no, child. If ye weren't ready it is not a good thing to start a marriage with doubt."

"I know, but it might have made life simpler. You wouldn't believe the people who have come to me because of the gossip they've heard. If I had run off and married Olin, then no one would say anything."

"Oh, I think they'd be inclined to still say a few words. But ye are probably right that they would have had less to say."

"Can I ask you something?" Ida Mae spun around and faced Mrs. Orr.

"I'd be honored."

How could she word this? "Do you think it is wise for me to go into hiding? I mean, shouldn't I be facing my problems and not running away from them?"

Mrs. Orr took a moment, then sat down beside Ida Mae. "From what Olin Robert has told me, ye are hiding because for some unknown reason someone may want to hurt you."

"That's one rumor. The other is that someone is out to discredit Olin. Percy, for example."

"Aye, Percy has never been a content man. He's always wanted more out of life than what he was willing to work for. And he has a mean streak that runs deep in his heart, though one rarely sees it. Generally, Percy is a good and kind man. But with Olin—well, those two never saw eye-to-eye on anything."

"But why would Percy want Olin out of the area?"

"Probably because he fears that folks would learn that Bobby was protecting him from Gary Jones."

What? "I thought it was just the two of them that got into a fight. How was Percy involved?"

"From what I can piece together, and mind ye, my boy won't tell me straight what happened that day, Percy must have done something or owed Jones some money, and he was wanting restitution. Olin tried to distract him so that he wouldn't take his rage out on Percy. Angry words built to fisticuffs. There were a few of the older men on the crew who told Mr. Orr and myself bits and pieces of what happened. Over time, Percy seems to have forgotten that he was the true cause for the fight. Truth is, Olin won't speak of the matter. He feels so guilty for killing a man, and he's taken full responsibility for the incident. As well he should. No matter what Percy may or may not have done, it was Olin who fought the man and it was his fist that actually killed him. He's always had a temper, and it got the best of him that day."

Ida Mae started to shake. If she married Olin would he get so angry with her that he might. . .

"Now, child, I can see it in your eyes ye are afraid of him. I'm so sorry. What ye may not know is that when we sent him to Pennsylvania he was mentored by a man who had a similar problem with his temper. Oh, he never killed a man, but he came close. Anyway, his mentor showed him how to curb his anger, give it over to the Lord, and remain in control. I truly believe Olin has changed. Look at all that has happened to you. Olin Robert has not lifted an angry hand to anyone and he's remained calm. Oh, I've seen the anger spark for a moment or two, but he's controlling it. 'Tis a sweet answer to prayer."

Ida Mae relaxed. She'd seen it, too. "So you think Percy is out to discredit Olin because he fears Olin will tell everyone what really happened?"

"Aye, and I believe money was involved, too, but I haven't been able to figure if that is the case or not."

Olin, we need to talk. There can't be any secrets between us.

Chapter 19

Olin hustled from the sheriff's office to Ida Mae's. Instantly his nostrils filled with the coppery scent of blood. Her bedding was pulled in different directions, giving the appearance of a struggle. A dark brown trail of blood angled off the bottom sheet. Fear washed over him. Had Ida Mae returned from the cottage? Had something happened to her?

He bolted from her room and ran to the stable where he kept his horse. Saddled, he hopped on and headed home. A chill ran down his spine. *What if someone is watching?* He pulled the reins. The horse halted.

He sat there for ten minutes, not sure what to do next. He should check on Ida Mae, but then again, the sheriff said there had been evidence suggesting he might have been the one who broke into Ida Mae's. He thought back on the scene in her room. Had it been staged? Had someone come in and planned that chaos?

If they had, they would have been watching him. And probably had been for the past two days since Ida Mae went into hiding. *No, I can't check on her. Mayhap after nightfall.*

He urged the horse forward and continued toward the house. He could send someone to check on Ida Mae. He would still need to talk with her, but it was imperative that he know for certain that she was still in the cottage and safe.

Married? How could that be? She didn't speak favorably of Cyrus and planned not to let him farm the land next year. If he were her husband, could she do that? Wouldn't she try to help him learn how to farm? *She can't be married, Lord, she just can't be. She's not the kind to be double minded.*

His mind whirled with questions. The Ida Mae he knew would never attach herself to someone like Cyrus Morgan. But how much did he know about her, really? Memories flooded his thoughts of their few intimate times alone, of the kisses they shared.

"Lord, please help me understand. Am I a fool?"

There was something about Cyrus he never cared for. Was it that he saw a hidden relationship between him and Ida Mae? She had said he had asked her to marry him on more than one occasion. Had it gone further? Was she really married? But if they were, why wasn't Cyrus helping her run from her troubles, putting her in hiding?

The weight in his chest plummeted to his gut. "Lord, give me strength."

∞

Under the cloak of darkness, Olin headed out to the cottage. He'd been relieved to hear from his mother that Ida Mae was well. He didn't tell his family about Ida Mae's marriage to Cyrus Morgan. He wanted to hear from her first. He'd been in an awful mood since coming home. He spent the day cleaning the stalls, chopping wood, anything to keep his body busy and wear off some of the tension and anger he felt.

He'd know in a few short minutes her side of the story.

A dim light burned in the window.

"Ida Mae!" he called before he got off his horse. "It's Olin."

The front door creaked open. "Has something happened?"

That's an understatement. Calm down, calm down. Let her explain what happened. "Yes. Someone broke into your room and made it look like there was a struggle and left some blood behind."

Ida Mae wobbled.

Olin reached her in a couple quick steps. "Can I come in?"

She nodded.

Lord, give me the grace. Help me give her reasonable doubt.

They sat down. Her hands trembled in her lap.

Silently, he let out a long, deep breath. "Ida Mae, there isn't an easy way to address this. Cyrus Morgan heard of the break-in and gave the sheriff. . ." He paused and rubbed the back of his neck. *She couldn't have, could she?* "He gave the sheriff his marriage license."

She lifted her head and knitted her eyebrows. "He finally told folks?"

"Aye."

Ida Mae sighed. "Good. I didn't want to keep that secret any longer."

"So it's true?"

"Yes."

Olin jumped up from his seat and began to pace. *How could she have fooled me so?* The drumming of his pulse echoed in his ears. "Why?"

"Why what?"

"Why did ye marry him?"

"Marry him? What are you talking about, Olin?"

∞

Ida Mae couldn't understand the mood Olin was in. If the floor were flint and he were steel, the cottage would have exploded by now. "Olin, talk to me. What are you talking about? I didn't marry anyone."

"Cyrus says ye and he were married in Montgomery County several months back."

"He said what? He married Rosey Turner, not me." So Cyrus was behind

224

all the rumors. "Why would he say such a thing?"

"Ye swear ye aren't married to Cyrus?"

"Olin, how could you think such a thing? I nearly married you a few weeks ago. Would I do that if I were married to another man?"

Olin collapsed in the seat. Ida Mae went on her knees in front of him. Reaching for his hands, she held them. *He has to know the truth.* "I love you, Olin. I never loved or ever had a desire to marry Cyrus. Oh, I gave it a fleeting thought once, but it did not stay with me for more than a few hours. Of course, that's when I found out he married Rosey Turner."

He rubbed the top of her hands with his thumbs. "He has a certificate, Ida Mae. Sheriff read it."

"And it has my name on it?"

"Apparently. Thatcher didn't let me see it."

"I don't understand how he could have gotten my signature. It has to be a forgery."

"The sheriff's trying to verify your signature. I hadn't thought of that."

Doubt filled her. If Olin truly loved her, would he have believed the words of Cyrus Morgan? "You don't believe me, do you?"

"I'm trying. I can't understand how he'd have a marriage certificate with your name on it, if you weren't there. It looked like a legal document to me."

"Legal document?" Ida Mae's mind flickered back to the time when Cyrus came in to sign paperwork for the rental agreement to the farm. Her eyes widened. "Oh no."

"What?"

"I signed papers for our rental agreement, just as you and I did. Do you suppose he slipped another paper in there and had me sign it? That can't be legal, can it? I can't be married to him, can I? And what would Rosey say? She told me they had gotten married."

Ida Mae released his hands, got up, and started to pace, just as he had done a few moments before.

"There be more."

She froze mid-stride. Icicles crystallized down her spine. *What else could go wrong, Lord?*

"The sheriff said there was evidence that made me look like the intruder."

Ida Mae relaxed. "At least he knew where I was and that you didn't have anything to do with it."

"Aye, that be a blessin'," he acknowledged. "Ida Mae, I hate to say this, but do you think Cyrus could be the one who's been causing the problems?"

She shook her head no, then realized everything started when she discovered he had married Rosey. Of course, that was nearly the same day Olin moved into town. "Is he behind it all, or did Percy have a part to play in that?" She sat back down. Now was the time for them to get to the bottom of all their problems, and this included Olin's past. "Your mother told me that Percy had something to do with you getting in that fight years ago."

"Don't—" A knock at the door stopped their conversation.

Chapter 20

Olin didn't know whether or not to be grateful for the interruption. The story of the past was long dead and buried and he wanted to keep it that way. What he didn't expect to see on the other side of the door was Sheriff Thatcher. "Evenin', Olin."

"Evenin'. What brought ye out here this time of night?"

Ida Mae came up and stood behind him, slipping her hand into his.

"I'm just returning from Montgomery County. The justice of the peace there has a record of Cyrus Morgan marrying Ida Mae on June third of this year."

"It can't be. I never married him, I swear."

The sheriff tipped back his hat. "That's what I expected you to say. So I asked the JP to come by my office tomorrow morning around ten a.m. I'd like you, Ida Mae, to arrive ten minutes later. Cyrus will be there already. My goal is to catch Cyrus in his lie."

"Cyrus is behind all of this?"

"Not all of it. As best I can figure, there were one or two incidents when Percy was involved. I'll deal with him later. What concerns me now is Cyrus, and I'm afraid his plans for Ida Mae may not be healthy."

Olin's back went ramrod straight. Ida Mae's fingernails cut into his wrist. Olin relaxed. She was of prime importance, keeping her safe and free from the claws of someone like Cyrus Morgan. "We'll be there."

The sheriff shook his head no. "Not you, Olin. Ida Mae. You're goin' to hafta trust me to take care of this. Olin, you can't be leanin' on the ways of the past to take care of things."

Olin swallowed hard. His stomach tightened into a ball. "Can I be close by?"

"Yes, so long as Cyrus doesn't catch sight of you with Ida Mae." The sheriff turned to the rocking chair. "May I?"

"Yes. Please." Ida Mae stumbled as she stepped toward the sofa.

Olin reached out to steady her. "Ida Mae seems to think she might know how her signature could have appeared on that marriage certificate, if it is her signature."

"I'd like to hear it." The sheriff leaned back.

Ida Mae went on to explain how she had been signing several papers one day for the agreement with Cyrus to lease her parents' farm. "I don't recall signing

227

anything but the lease, but I suppose it's possible. . . ."

"Am I correct in understanding that Cyrus told you he and Rosey had married?"

"Yes, sir."

Olin wrapped a protective arm around Ida Mae. This poor woman had been put in an elaborate trap. For what? Her property? "Sheriff, what made ye suspicious of Cyrus? I mean, that marriage certificate had me baffled."

"I'd been leaning that way for a while now. When he produced the certificate I was perplexed, but I knew about Rosey. As much as Cyrus is trying to hide it, he hasn't done a very good job. And then there's the gold mining he's been doing—"

"Gold mining?" Olin and Ida Mae asked in unison.

"I believe he found a nugget when he was working on rebuilding your farmhouse. I believe he thinks the farm has a rich supply. He just hasn't found it."

"Father and his friends churned that field over real well when gold was found on John Reed's farm back before I was born. The gold he found must have been the one small nugget Father kept as a reminder of how foolish a man could be if his heart isn't in the right place. It must have melted in the fire and hardened again."

"Possibly, but the reports I heard was he found the gold before your parents died. I have reason to believe Cyrus might have been responsible for the fire in your parents' house."

Olin held Ida Mae closer as her body shook.

"Are ye certain?" Olin wished the sheriff had never mentioned this tidbit if he had no facts to back it up.

"I'm sorry, Ida Mae. I don't mean no disrespect, but I'm very concerned about Cyrus being a real threat to more people in this community. I intend to look further into whether he's behind the fire, but for now, we need to clear your name and the fact that you are not married to the man. The false claim is enough to get him behind bars if you press charges. I'm hoping you will, miss."

Ida Mae sniffled her agreement. "Yes."

"Good. Now this is the hard part."

Can the situation get any harder than this? Olin wondered. He rubbed Ida Mae's upper arm and kissed her soft hair. "I love you," he whispered.

"Ida Mae, I want you to come with me and stay with my wife and me this evening."

"Why?" Olin squeaked.

"Precaution. I believe she's safe here, but let's not take any chances. Cyrus might be in a dangerous place, but at the moment he believes he has the upper hand. Let's keep it that way."

"All right." Ida Mae got up from the sofa. A cold chill swept over Olin's right arm and right side of his body. He prayed the only prayer he could for Ida Mae these days. *Dear God, please keep her safe.*

✤

Unable to contemplate the depth of Cyrus Morgan's greed, Ida Mae went over every detail the sheriff had told her. She even made him rehearse it again before she went to bed. Why would God allow the sins of a greedy man to take the lives of her parents? *Why, Lord?* she cried out in her morning prayers. She'd spent the night in a numb state, thinking and rethinking over the past couple years, ever since Cyrus Morgan entered her and her parents' lives.

The scripture reference that kept coming back to mind was the one Olin and she had shared about being tested and refined in the Refiner's fire. She could understand how a metal worker would cling to that verse, yet now the same verse was wrapping itself as a golden ring around her heart, sometimes a wee bit too tightly, or so it seemed.

Would God allow the deaths of her parents in order to teach her more about her own relationship with God? Ida Mae shook. Oh, sure, she knew and understood there was sin in this world, and sin caused death, but for the first time she was seeing how much she'd been holding on to "Why me, Lord?" regarding the tragic events in her life instead of asking "How can I grow from this?"

Look at how much you've grown, she told herself, *how many precious gifts the Lord has given you since your parents died. You're a thriving businesswoman graced with a man who is not intimidated by your career or income.* It was remarkably true. Olin found her to be a woman he could call a companion. That wasn't to say she wouldn't mind being a helpmate to him and helping his business grow. The idea of simply taking care of a house and raising babies sounded mighty pleasing at the moment.

"Ida Mae!" Mrs. Thatcher called from behind the closed door. "It's just about time, dear."

"Thank you, I'll be out shortly."

Ida Mae stayed on her knees. "Father, please reveal to all the sins of Cyrus. Please release me from any legal obligations with him. And please don't allow it to be so that I'm his wife. Please, Lord, not that."

Taking in a deep pull of air, she lifted herself off the floor.

The door opened with a creak. Mrs. Thatcher smiled when Ida Mae entered the kitchen. "I made you a cup of tea and there's a leftover biscuit from breakfast. There's honey in the pot. Help yourself."

Ida Mae sat down, scraping the chair along the floor. "I'm sorry."

"Don't pay that no never mind. You just relax. John told me about what's been happening to you." Mrs. Thatcher wiped her hands on a towel and sat down across the table from her with a bowl of peaches and a small knife. "Today I'm making preserves. Yesterday I canned three dozen jars of peaches. By the time I'm done with this I won't want to see a peach again."

Ida Mae remembered life on the farm as a constant cycle of canning and harvesting food for the winter. "Are you drying any of the peaches?"

"Yes. I have a bushel out back, drying as we speak. John loves them in his porridge. I'm praying we don't get rain."

Finishing up her biscuit, Ida Mae wiped her hands on the linen napkin, then replaced it in her lap.

"I'll be happy to walk you over to John's office. He suggested you wear a scarf over your bonnet."

Fear wiggled around her neck muscles. Was her life really in danger? *Lord, keep me safe.*

⬡

Olin sat in the saloon across the street from the sheriff's office. He had a perfect view. Cyrus Morgan had entered and five minutes later another man entered. More than likely, the justice of the peace. They hadn't been in there for more than five minutes when he spotted Rosey trying to peek into the jail. *What is she doing?*

Probably the same as me—watching, wondering, and waiting to see what final outcome the day will bring. Does she know? Is she a part of this? Truthfully, he hoped that Rosey was an innocent victim. If Cyrus had succeeded in this charade, Rosey might have been in grave danger, whether she was a part of it or not.

Two women approached the sheriff's office. A slit of a smile lifted his lips. He'd know that woman anywhere. How could every ounce of her be permanently attached to his brain in a few short months? "Lord, protect her," Olin mumbled into his sarsaparilla.

⬡

Ida Mae kept her head bowed as she walked into Sheriff Thatcher's office. The three men sat around the sheriff's desk. "Yes, it was a fine day," Cyrus crooned.

"May I help you, Miss?" Sheriff Thatcher called out to her.

Ida Mae lifted her head and removed her bonnet and scarf.

"Ida Mae," Cyrus squeaked. He seemed to visibly pale in front of her.

"Elmer, is this the woman you married Cyrus to?"

"Can't say I've seen her before."

"Married me?" Ida Mae objected. "What are you talking about? I didn't marry Cyrus. Rosey Turner did. What's going on?" She looked at the sheriff, then turned to Cyrus. She placed her hands on her hips. "Cyrus?"

He pulled at his collar and squirmed in his chair.

"The gal I married Cyrus to has strawberry blond hair, kinda curly."

That fit Rosey's description. She narrowed her gaze on Cyrus once again.

Cyrus gathered his thoughts. "Ida Mae, please tell me you can remember our wedding day."

"Cyrus, we're not married, never have been and never will be. Where's Rosey?"

"How should I know? Honey, please sit and tell me where you've been. What happened? Did you fall off your horse?"

Cyrus's attempt to play the part of a doting husband failed miserably in Ida Mae's assessment. "Stop lying, Cyrus. Whatever your purpose, it is over. I've been safe with the Orrs. The sheriff has known how to find me all along. We hoped whoever was behind all my misfortune would show his hand in my absence. And I must say, you've done that. But what I don't understand is why. Why would you do this?" She wanted to scream, *Why did you kill my parents?* but it was too soon for such an accusation. The sheriff had more investigating to do. Everything she'd ever believed about Cyrus had changed forever.

"Is this your signature, Miss McAuley?"

The sheriff handed the document over to her. It felt foreign in her hands. She glanced down at the signature, then held the paper up to the light. Something didn't look right. "It looks very similar to my signature, but it doesn't flow the way I flow my letters together. Almost, but not quite." She'd been fully expecting to see her signature after the discussion she and Olin had back at the cottage. "Cyrus, why are you doing this?"

The door slammed against the wall. Rosey stood there with her hands on her hips. "You told the sheriff you married Ida Mae? You lyin'. . . Father was right. I shouldn't have married you."

"Rosey, hush."

"I will not hush!"

"That's the woman," the justice of the peace pointed out.

"Cyrus, you're under arrest."

Chapter 21

Rumors and innuendos do not make it fact." The sheriff's words played through her mind over and over again. It had been three weeks since Cyrus was arrested, and still Ida Mae had more questions than answers.

Olin had moved his shop back into her father's smithy. Their marriage was pending, awaiting the outcome of the trial. There should be no question, but Cyrus was still standing by his statement that he had married Ida Mae. Olin and Ida Mae's relationship was blossoming even under the pressure. Ida Mae couldn't wait until the circuit judge would ride into town and hear their case. But until the sheriff had more proof that Cyrus set the fire to Ida Mae's parents' house, nothing further could be done on that charge.

Ida Mae prayed everyone would know what really happened once and for all. It had been hard enough knowing her parents had died in an accident. To think of them having been murdered bothered her in a way she'd never experienced before. In spite of, or perhaps because of, everything that had happened, her faith had grown tremendously over the summer.

"Good evening, Ida Mae." Olin stepped up beside her and gently squeezed her hand. She'd been waiting for him on the small front porch of the shop. She and Olin had set a couple of chairs out there so they could spend time with one another in public and yet have some privacy. "I missed ye."

"How was your meeting?"

"Good. I got the job."

"What job?" She knew full well which job. The one he couldn't speak to her about.

Olin captured her in his arms and whispered in her ear. The gentle heat of his breath caused her to melt like butter on a hot biscuit. "I've been commissioned to design the plates for the first gold coins to be printed in Charlotte."

"Really? That's wonderful." She hugged him tighter. She knew he was an artist and did the finest tinwork she'd ever seen. Even the jeweler chose to sell some of Olin's products in his store. But to be granted such a secretive task. . . "How'd this happen?"

"Come sit down. Believe it or not, we have Cyrus and Percy to thank for this opportunity."

"What?" How could that be—she cut her thoughts off. One thing she'd learned over the past few months is that God works wonders out of the ashes of grief.

Olin sat down on one of the sitting chairs. Ida Mae sat down beside him. "If Percy hadn't complained to the sheriff about me, he wouldn't have taken the time to speak with me. Then when the unusual events began to happen around you, the sheriff again found me to be a trustworthy man. He recommended me to Mr. Bechtler, who was looking for a craftsman to design his gold dollar."

"Olin, I'm so proud of you." She reached out and held his hand.

"Thank ye. It means the world to me that you're pleased. My work with Mr. Bechtler should produce further sales of my tinware. Hopefully by next spring we can get married and I'll be able to provide for you."

"I received a letter today letting me know that my brothers will be coming to town in a few weeks. If they agree, I've decided to sell the land. I don't think I can step back into that house knowing what I know now about Cyrus."

Olin got up and knelt in front of her. "Honey, I know this has been a hard decision. Do ye think we should go to the house first and see if it's still what ye want to do?"

"The house isn't the same, not after the fire. I'll miss the memories, but it's practical to sell the house and farm. You and I don't need it."

Olin smiled. "I'll see if Kyle will give me a hand building our house this winter so it will be ready for our wedding. Ye are still going to marry me?"

"Do you want to move into my parents' house?" she asked pensively.

"Honey, it can wait. We can wait. Ye and I have had a bumpy road to our love. I believe the extra time before marriage will be a blessing to us, a chance to really learn about one another."

But I want to marry you now. "Perhaps I should keep the house. We could marry sooner."

"Ida Mae, I'd marry ye today if we were settled on this legal proclamation, but I see this as another time of refinement. The time of waiting for the Refiner's gold to cool and harden, to become a permanent bar of precious metal. I can't wait to be able to purchase gold rings to wear on our fingers."

Lord, I love this man. He knows You so well. He teaches me daily to go deeper in my relationship with You. "Are you sure you want to wait?"

Olin chuckled and stood up. He stepped to the window and placed his hands on the sill. "Aye, I'm sure. The Lord has a design for our marriage. It's our choice to take the time and build a solid foundation."

And he couldn't be more right, Lord. "If that's what you want, I'm happy to go along with it. I love you, Olin, and I want to be your wife."

Between the beat of her heart and her last word, Olin closed the distance between them and held her close. "I love ye, Ida Mae, and I would be honored to be your husband."

Epilogue

Ida Mae couldn't believe her wedding day had finally arrived. Her mind flickered over the past two years. The judge found Cyrus to be a fraud, and eventually the sheriff found the proof that Cyrus was responsible for her parents' deaths. It had been hard to believe that Cyrus's original plan was simply to marry Ida Mae and gain control of the farm. He had found a few small nuggets of gold on the farm before the fire. According to the facts, Ida Mae's father refused to force Ida Mae to marry Cyrus and told him the choice would be Ida Mae's. In a rage, he killed her father, and when her mother came to see what the matter was, he killed her, too. The fire was to cover the fact that they had been murdered. When her brothers arrived last fall, they decided to sell the property to Kyle Orr. They waived the first year's payment because the land was in such sad shape from all of Cyrus's gold mining attempts. Cyrus was hanged for the murder of her parents.

Mr. Bechtler's son, August, and nephew, Christopher, were opening their private mint and assay office. The miners were delighted. Olin's design for the coin had been acceptable, and he and Kyle finally finished the house.

"Ida Mae, are you ready?" Minnie ran into the room off the foyer where the minister liked to keep brides waiting until the time of the service. "Oh my, you're beautiful, Ida Mae. You did a real fine job on your dress."

"Thank you." She had opted for a fine silk she had bartered from Mrs. Farres six months ago.

"I still can't believe you're marryin' Olin. He's too perfect."

Ida Mae guffawed.

"What?"

"You. The first time you heard about him, you—"

"Don't you go fussin' about what I said then. I was hoodwinked. Percy is a real. . ."

Ida Mae's thoughts drifted back to the conversation she and Olin finally had about what happened on that fateful day when he had killed a man. Percy feared Olin would reveal that Percy himself had set up the fight in order to intimidate Gary Jones into releasing him from a gambling debt. It was Percy who had kept the rumors of Olin's guilt alive for so long, trying to avoid the inevitable embarrassment, not to mention the gambling debt. Once the truth came out, Olin had persuaded Percy to make restitution to the widows' fund at church. But the truth hadn't changed the past. Olin had been wrong and had lost control of his temper, costing a man his life. Today Percy would be sitting in a pew with the rest of the family. Ida Mae didn't anticipate them ever being close, but she didn't foresee any further trouble, either.

"Anyway," Minnie fussed, "I'm so glad you finally came to your senses and are marryin' this man."

Ida Mae smiled. If Minnie only knew how close she'd come a year ago. Then it would have been for all the wrong reasons. Today she stood in confidence of her love and Olin's love for her.

Uncle Ty knocked on the door. "Are ya ready, Ida Mae? It's time." He had agreed to give her away on behalf of their family. Her brothers couldn't attend, as it was harvest time.

"I'm ready." Ida Mae stepped out of the room as the piano played.

∞

Olin stood at the front of the church, his palms sweating. He wiped them on his trousers once again. One of the first gold coins struck from the Bechtlers' mint had been given to him as a wedding present. Olin knew they'd never spend it. It would be an honored and treasured gift, and he knew Ida Mae would feel the same.

A little over a year ago, he'd come to town sure of himself and confident it was time to come home. But just like the corduroy roads he had to mend along the great wagon road to get here from Pennsylvania, so was the relationship between him and Ida Mae. She was a beauty too lovely to be his. A gift from God he didn't deserve. Refined gold and as pure as silver. *Lord, help me remain worthy of her love.*

The notes on the piano began to ring out. Olin turned toward the doors at the back of the church. In walked his nephew with pillow in hand. He prayed the thread his sister sewed the rings on with was strong enough to hold the rings and yet loose enough for him and Ida Mae to pull them off at the right time in the ceremony. Then the twins marched down in their precious flower girl outfits, tossing petals on the floor. Olin couldn't wait to have children with Ida Mae.

Then she appeared. His mouth went dry. His mind swam through the past sixteen months. It seemed like he'd always known her and yet, he really hadn't. The gentle sway of her hips as she came closer made him stiffen his knees so they wouldn't buckle.

She stood beside him. "Ye are beautiful," he whispered.

"Ye ain't so bad yourself," she replied with a wink.

Olin smiled. *Thank Ye, Lord.*

LYNN A. COLEMAN

Lynn is an award-winning, best-selling author of Key West and other books. She is also co-founder of American Christian Fiction Writers Inc., and served as the group's first president for two years and spent two years on the Advisory Board. She makes her home in Keystone Heights, Florida, where her husband of 35 years serves as pastor of Friendship Bible Church. Together they are blessed with three children and eight grandchildren. She loves hearing from her readers. Visit her Web site at: www.lynncoleman.com.

THE MUSIC OF HOME

by Tamela Hancock Murray

Dedication

With love to my North Carolina cousin, Gayla McGee Briggs.
Her light shines for Christ at all times.

Chapter 1

North Carolina, 1934

Singing a mountain ballad, Drusie Fields looked upon the audience at the church social. The meeting hall was filled with people who had known her since she was born. Drusie's friends and family encouraged her love for singing, applauding every time she performed. She played the banjo and sang, recognizing sweetness in her voice.

Drusie wore her favorite Sunday dress, sewn from red and white polka-dotted flour-sack material and fashioned from a store-bought pattern. In such splendor, Drusie felt she could hold her own with any other girl in the room. She surveyed the crowd and noticed most of the women were dressed in clothing they had sewn themselves, although a few wore outfits ordered from the Wish Book.

Only two of the men stood out to her eyes: Pa, who whistled and clapped, and the love of her life, Gladdie Gordon. She didn't have to search long for Gladdie. His manly face, so easy on the eyes, caught her attention. She smiled at him, noticing his dark hair shining in the dim lights. Applauding for all he was worth, he mouthed the title of a well-loved mountain song.

As usual, he had chosen one of her favorites, "This Is Like Heaven to Me." Drusie smiled and nodded. "This next number is dedicated to Gladdie Gordon. I think y'all are familiar with the tune."

On her banjo, Drusie strummed the first notes of the song he requested, and the rest of the band joined her. Approving claps resonated throughout the small wooden structure that served as a church, meeting hall, and schoolhouse for their Appalachian community.

Drusie hit the high notes with ease. Hearing her sister Clara join her in harmony pleased Drusie. Everybody said they looked perfect together on stage, with Drusie's dark locks and pale complexion complementing Clara's lighter hair and sharp features. Drusie sang as though she were performing for Gladdie and Gladdie alone. She couldn't help it. She loved him.

The song ended, and Uncle Martin shouted above roaring applause, "Sing it one more time, Drusie!"

"Again?" she teased. "Why, you're like to wear me plumb out tonight!" Despite her protests, she felt flattered and had every intention of singing for the crowd as long as they asked.

Drusie noticed Aunt Irma and recalled her recent comment that Drusie looked just like her mother. Ma didn't have a streak of gray in her black hair nor a wrinkle on her petite face. Pa said her eyes were still as blue as the day they were married.

Not that Ma did so bad for herself when she married Pa. Years of working hard as a lumberjack hadn't broken his spirit. Both of her parents were wiry and had passed on that build to Drusie and her five sisters. Pa always said he never stood a chance of getting a word in edgewise with all those womenfolk around, but she could tell by the twinkle in his eyes that he liked it that way.

Old Mr. Harper called out, reminding her she remained onstage. "How about singin' 'Amazing Grace'?"

Drusie gave her audience a good-natured nod. Clara nodded in turn, and the band played the chorus before the sisters sang the first verse. The room fell silent as they listened to the hymn of gratitude and repentance.

Drusie figured that would be the last song of the night, but the crowd wanted more. Tired but elated, Drusie was glad when Silas stepped up and played "Flop-Eared Mule," showing off for all he was worth. The crowd clapped in time.

She made her way toward Gladdie, feeling safe in his nearness. He'd shined up his hair with tonic and shaved closely. His arresting features caught the eyes of more than one girl even though everyone in these parts had known him forever. But everyone there also knew that he was hers, and she stood by him, her erect posture demonstrating pride.

He gave her a sideways grin. "You gonna take back to the stage after Silas finishes showin' off?"

"Again? Why, I'm about played out."

"You'll never play out, Drusie. That sweet voice can go on and on. Especially when you're singin' for the Lord."

She drew closer to him and looked him full in the face. "I love singin' for Him, darlin'."

He gave her a kiss on the cheek. "I love you mightily, Drusie Fields. Your devotion to God is one of the reasons I've loved you since we was nothin' but kids."

She smiled shyly. Looking up, Drusie noticed Edna Sue glancing Gladdie's way. She resisted the temptation to narrow her eyes at the girl who wanted to be her rival. From the corner of her eye, Drusie noticed that Gladdie took his glance away from Edna Sue's as soon as their gazes met. "She's a bold one." Drusie swallowed.

"Too bold for me," Gladdie said. "You know you're the only one I have eyes for, Drusie. I wish we could get married today." He took her by the arm. "Come on. Let's us go for a walk in the moonlight."

She peered around the room. "Will anybody miss us?"

"I won't keep you too long."

She acquiesced, glad to be away from the covetous eyes of the other girls. As soon as she and Gladdie left through the side door, Drusie noticed the chill of autumn air. Scents of leftover ham and sugary desserts from the potluck dinner still hung in the hall but faded as they walked away.

Drusie shivered. "Wish I'd've thought to bring my shawl."

Without hesitation, Gladdie whipped off his suit coat and placed it around her shoulders. The warmth of his body and manly scents of laundry soap and shaving tonic clung to the garment, making Drusie feel cozy and secure as they walked along the narrow moonlit path. It wound through a stand of pines, crossed an open meadow, and eventually led to the old Norman place. Abandoned years ago, the house was reputed to be haunted. For as long as Drusie could remember, local boys tested their bravery in exploring the rickety old abode. But on this night, Drusie and Gladdie wouldn't be walking far enough to test their courage.

"I didn't mean for you to give up your coat for me," she objected with a shy smile.

"Sure you did," he teased. "Naw, I'd've given it up for you anyhow."

Feeling guilty, she glanced back at the meeting hall and slowed her pace. "Maybe we should go back inside, lest you catch your death of cold."

"I'm too strong for that." He flexed a bicep.

She giggled and punched his arm too lightly to kill a fly. "Muscles won't help you none against a cold, silly."

"Oh yeah? Then what will?"

"Come to think of it, I don't reckon I rightly know. But Sarah May's studyin' to be a nurse, so maybe I can find out from her." Drusie shook her head. "She's the smart one out of all of us Fields sisters. I cain't imagine doin' somethin' that hard all my life. Havin' to know all about them medical potions and stuff."

"Aw, you're plenty smart. Smart enough for me. Smarter than I need in a wife." He placed a protective arm around her shoulders.

"Stop it, now." She smiled in spite of herself.

"You know, I've almost got enough money saved up to buy that little weddin' band with orange blossoms in Mr. Goode's store."

She gasped. "You do?" Drusie didn't bother to conceal her happiness. Gladdie knew her heart. The ring itself didn't matter. What it symbolized—their forever love—did.

"I sure enough do. Only, I'd better save up right quick like."

"Why?" she managed, even though she was almost scared to ask such a thing.

"Didn't you know? Mr. Goode's been feelin' right poorly lately, and he wants to go live with his daughter in Raleigh."

"Raleigh! A big city like that? Imagine!" Then a thought occurred to her. "But what will we do around here without his store?"

"We won't have to find out if I can help it."

Drusie didn't need to ask him what he meant. Gladdie came from a farming family, a hardscrabble life as far as he was concerned. Gladdie wanted a different way of life for himself and his future wife. A life that was a little easier than coaxing crops from the land. "So you're still of a mind to buy the store."

"More mind than money, sad enough. I was hopin' Mr. Goode could hold off lettin' go of the store for a couple more years. That would've given me longer to save up enough cash to make a down payment, anyway."

"Do you reckon there's anybody else wantin' to buy the store?"

"I reckon not, leastways nobody from around here. Well, except for the Moores. They'd love to own the only dry goods store in Sunshine Holler. If they bought Mr. Goode's place, they'd stamp out the competition."

"If you got ahold of the store, you'd be competition, sure enough. You're good with cipherin' and details. I know you can keep up with the stock, and I don't doubt you could remember to the penny who owes the store how much money."

Gladdie's chest puffed ever so slightly. "I sure could. Pa says I've got a head for that sorta thing."

"That's right. You can do anything, Gladdie." Drusie wasn't flattering her future husband. Her faith in him was sincere.

"Pa says I got the raw talent, but I got to give Mr. Goode credit. I've learned a lot from him by clerkin' at the store." He stopped under a large sycamore tree whose trunk had been carved with many initials over the years. Not so long ago, Gladdie had carved his and Drusie's in a heart. He shuffled his foot in the dirt. "I reckon I'm a silly dreamer. Who'd ever think a boy only a few years outta high school could own his own business, just like that?" He clapped once, punctuating his remark.

"If anybody can, you can." Drusie sighed. "I just wish I had enough money saved up to help you buy the store."

"I know." He leaned against the trunk, and his voice became dreamy. "Then we could get married in a hurry and I could build you a house of your very own."

"I'd like that. But it would still take awhile for us to get settled even then."

"I reckon so." He studied her, love shining in his eyes. Taking her by the hand, he led her farther down the path. "I wish I could buy you the world. Like pretty dresses. You're so sweet, you deserve fine clothes. And I'd love to afford a diamond ring for you, even bigger than the one that lady was wearin' in that picture show we went to see in town last month."

Drusie remembered. In anticipation of celebrating her twentieth birthday, Gladdie had saved up enough money for gas to drive them into town in the Gordons' Model T and pay the nickel admission apiece for them to see the show. Drusie had heard there were talking pictures showing in big cities, but the one they saw was a silent. She couldn't imagine people talking on film. What was wrong with silent pictures?

Drusie thought back to the picture they saw. She enjoyed the complicated story of how a rich man fell in love with a poor woman. After many setbacks and tribulations, the man's family accepted the woman and they lived happily ever after. The woman started out wearing rags that looked worse than a dress Drusie would cut up to make smaller clothes for her nieces. By the time the picture ended, the heroine was wearing fur coats, silk dresses, and big diamond rings. She recalled how the jewels sparkled under the light. Imagine!

"Wouldn't you like to have some pretty clothes and things rich folk have?" Gladdie queried.

She shrugged. "I figure if the good Lord planned for me to live like a rich city woman, He woulda plunked me right in Raleigh. Not here in Sunshine Holler."

They had reached the edge of the meadow. Gladdie turned them around so they could start walking back to church. "Not everybody stays put, though. Remember my cousin Archie?"

She remembered a red-haired youth who'd gone off to make his dreams come true. "The music producer?"

"That's him. Archie ain't got a bad life. He managed to get his education, get outta this here holler, and go on to make good in the city. I wish I had his courage. I reckon that's what I really mean. I wish I was like him in a lot of ways."

"I don't see a thing in the world wrong with admirin' somebody, especially somebody who shares your blood. Why don't you put that admiration to good use? Try developin' courage on your own, and you'll be more like Archie."

"That's a grand idea, Drusie."

"I don't know much about that, but I try to encourage you."

"And everybody else. I think they named this holler after you—Sunshine— because that's what you are."

∞

A few days later, Gladdie knocked on the door of the modest frame house where Drusie lived with her parents and Clara, the only other sister remaining at home. Upon hearing his summoning knock, Drusie set down her basket of clean socks and went to the door.

"Come on in, Gladdie. I was just about to start in on mendin', but that can wait." Drusie was more than happy to have an excuse to delay the hated chore. Her sister Clara didn't mind repairing little rips and holes in clothes so much, but she was already occupied helping Ma with sweeping and scrubbing the kitchen floor, a task Drusie detested even more than darning. To Drusie's way of thinking, the floor needed scrubbing entirely too often. Ma took pride in the house that Pa and his brothers had built years ago, and she insisted that they keep it spotless.

"I know how much you love mendin'," Gladdie teased. "Once we're married, I'll try to be real careful not to get holes in my clothes."

Drusie grinned and peered at the sun, which had begun its descent. "I don't think I'm the only one skippin' out on chores. Ain't it about time for you to milk the cows?" Her glance swept his form. "You sure are dressed for it, in them dungarees."

He laughed. "Sorry. I didn't have time to put on nothin' better. Ma said I could run over here for a minute or two, but not to leave my brothers with all the work. I've got to get right on back as soon as I share my news."

"If your ma let you get away from your chores, whatever you have to say must be important." She tilted her head toward two rockers on the porch. "We'd best sit outside. Ma and Clara are scrubbin', and that means we cain't let in any dirt for a few days."

Gladdie nodded. A gentleman as always, he waited for her to choose a cane-bottomed rocker before he took the one beside it.

"So your news is right important?" Drusie asked.

"It is." Gladdie's eyes were wide, and his tone of voice conveyed his excitement. "Archie's comin' for a visit. We got a letter from him today."

"Your cousin Archie?"

"I don't know no other Archie."

"I suppose not." A feeling of anticipation tugged at her stomach. "Wonder what brings him here. Did he say?"

"Just for a visit. Since I've always been fond of Archie, I was hopin' maybe you could set aside Wednesday afternoon to come over. Plan on stayin' until suppertime, if it's okay with your ma."

"I'm sure that'll be just fine with Ma. I'll make sure to get ahead on my chores before then." She stared at the dirt road winding past the house and breathed in a whiff of clear mountain air tinged with the musky odor of autumn. "I wonder if he'll even remember me. It's been so long since he took off for the city."

"Oh, I'm sure he'll remember you. But you've gotten real grownified since he left. And we weren't engaged back then."

Drusie couldn't help but notice the pride that colored his voice. "I'll be on my best behavior, then. I don't want to disappoint you."

"You never disappoint me." He rose from his seat. "I have to admit, I do want to show you off."

"You do?"

He nodded. "Bring your banjo. I want him to hear how good we can sing and play around these here parts. He's been in the city so long he's probably forgot."

"I don't know. My puny doin's won't sound like nothin' in comparison to a big act in the city."

He drew closer and put his arm around her. "Don't play for him, then. Play for me."

She smiled, lingering in the warmth of his presence. "For you, Gladdie, I'll do anything."

She didn't tell Gladdie at that moment, but a thought had just popped into her mind. A thought he would like very much.

Chapter 2

On the day of Archie's visit, Drusie and Gladdie sat on the Gordons' porch in rockers. Swaying back and forth, Drusie imagined they looked more like a couple of old folks with too much time on their hands than the young people they were. But she felt grateful for the chance to sit in silence with the one she loved. Drusie had been nervous earlier, but the interlude offered a chance to calm down before Archie Gordon arrived.

Unwilling to let Gladdie know how nervous she felt, Drusie concentrated on the rhythm of swaying. Ever since she'd known the Gordons, these rockers had sat in exactly the same spot on their front porch. They never had been painted, so the bare wood was smooth with wear. Sheltered as they were by the porch overhang, the rockers still displayed the burden of being outdoors since Mr. Gordon made them years ago. Nail heads showed themselves where the arm handles met railings. Every once in a while she rubbed the smooth metal. The presence of the rockers made Drusie feel secure. As long as they remained, so did the Gordons, and the community Drusie called home.

The Gordon house, like the Fields home, offered a pleasing view of the valley. Cool autumn weather had turned the leaves a variety of hues. Drusie enjoyed seeing bright red, shimmering yellow, blazing orange, and deep green leaves.

"Archie sure picked a pretty day to drive up here." With the back of his head resting against his chair, Gladdie looked with a lazy expression toward the valley. He inhaled an exaggerated breath, a sure sign he wanted to enjoy a good dose of crisp mountain air.

"He sure enough did." Without intention, Drusie followed his example. The air refreshed her, and the ordinary topic of the weather put her at ease. "Hope he enjoys the drive. Leaves sure are pretty."

"Sure are." Gladdie peered at the midday sun. "He left Raleigh yesterday. He's supposed to be here soon."

The fact of Archie's imminent arrival struck her. Drusie tapped on the arm of her chair and rocked faster. "It's gettin' late. You reckon he's had trouble?"

"I don't hardly know." Gladdie shrugged. "But if he ain't had trouble, he'll be here soon, just like he promised. He said noon, so I doubt it'll be much after that. Businessmen pride themselves on being prompt, you know."

Almost as soon as the words were out of his mouth, they saw a cloud of dust kick up on the road. A large automobile roared down the drive to the Gordon house.

"What in the world is that?" Drusie leaned forward in her seat.

"You mean, what kind of automobile is he drivin'?"

"Uh-huh. I ain't never seen one that fancy."

"It's an Auburn. You ain't never seen one of them before?" Gladdie teased.

She eyed the Gordons' aged Model T Ford parked in the side yard. The paint had chipped, but the tires were sturdy. Many of their neighbors didn't have transportation anywhere near that good. "I have a feelin' you ain't never seen an Auburn, either. If Archie hadn't written you about his fancy automobile, you wouldn't be able to tell what you were lookin' at. Now you just try to tell me I'm wrong."

Gladdie's ma rushed through the front door, a spoon coated in ham hock grease in hand, wearing her perennial apron and polka-dotted dress. "What's all that ruckus?" She looked to Archie's automobile and answered her own question. "Oh! He's here! And what an automobile that is!"

Gladdie peered at the vehicle. "I admit, I ain't never seen no automobile so light colored before. Kind of reminds me of the ivory pipe Uncle Ned used to have. Remember that, Ma?"

"I sure do. Sent from some friend workin' in Africa. Naruby or some place like that."

"I don't think that's a practical color for a car, considerin' all the dust on the roads," Drusie observed, then regretted speaking aloud. "I'm sorry. Didn't mean no harm. Just blurted without thinkin'."

"You didn't say nothin' I warn't thinkin'," Gladdie consoled her. "But Archie never was known to be practical. Reckon that's why he's so successful in the music business."

Drusie hadn't seen an automobile that wasn't painted black, either. "It may not be practical, but it's right pretty."

"Sure is," Gladdie agreed.

"Sure is," Mrs. Gordon opined.

Archie pulled up to the house and came to a stop so fast that Drusie was afraid its driver might fly right out of the seat, but he remained steady. She figured the beast of a machine was too weighty to flip over no matter if it got up to fifty miles an hour. "I don't reckon he had time to look at the pretty trees what with drivin' like that and all."

Gladdie agreed. "Maybe not. I imagine he's got more important things on his mind."

Archie cut off the engine, then waved at them as he got out of his car. Gladdie and Drusie stood, watching Archie approach. Though nowhere near as handsome as Gladdie, Drusie guessed that his swagger attracted the womenfolk.

Suddenly Drusie felt self-conscious. She smoothed the skirt of her dress, a cotton affair she had sewn herself from patterned flour sacks. She had to wait two months to use up all the flour, but pretty red flowers on a white background had been worth the test of endurance. As soon as the next batch of flour was done, she could sew a shirt for Pa from the striped material of the sack they were using now. Ma had just gotten some white cotton cloth and a good supply of chintz at bulk discount from Mr. Goode's store and had fashioned herself a new Sunday dress, Pa a shirt, Clara a blouse, and Drusie a skirt. At the rate they were going, the whole Fields family would soon be the best dressed at church.

She looked at Archie. When he laid his gaze upon her, his expression brightened. She was glad she had chosen to wear the flowered Sunday dress. She wanted to look her best so Archie would think his cousin's fiancée was a lady.

She tried not to study Archie too hard, lest he think she was being a flirt. She hadn't seen him in a long time—not since he went to Raleigh four years ago to make good in the city. He had changed from the acne-faced teenager she remembered. The trademark red hair remained, but the acne was gone and the face and physique had matured from a boy's to a man's. He was wearing a suit in a cut she'd never seen. The coat had buttons on both sides and came in at the waist. Perhaps that was the style in the city. A fine suit like that certainly set him apart from her friends and neighbors. He'd stick out like a sore thumb even in church. She wondered if men dressed like that in the city all the time. If so, they must be mighty uncomfortable wearing ties and starched shirts like they were always going to worship service.

"Hey, Gladdie! I'd recognize you anywhere." Archie tipped his hat at his aunt and greeted her, as well.

Gladdie approached Archie, and the two men met midway in the front yard. Drusie watched them embrace. She could see even from the distance that they shared a genuine fondness.

"That's a mighty fine automobile you got there!" she heard Gladdie say.

"A new Auburn Phaeton. Eight cylinder."

"She's a beaut." Although Drusie had never known Gladdie to covet anything, the admiration in his eyes for the automobile was obvious.

"She sure is a great little tin can." Archie gazed at the automobile like a miser would look at hoarded gold.

Mrs. Gordon shook her head. "Men and their machines."

Drusie giggled. The sound apparently attracted Archie's attention, because he looked up at her. "Butter and egg fly! What a tomato!" Ignoring Gladdie, Archie headed toward the house. "Is this Drusie Fields?"

Drusie had never been described in terms of an edible item before, but she assumed from Archie's animated expression that the words were complimentary. "It's me." She didn't make a move to go closer, feeling that to do so would be too forward.

He let out a low whistle, which at once made her feel complimented and strangely shy. "You grew up to be a dish. I'm not surprised. Your mama was always pretty. And what about Clara? Is she a looker, too?"

"We look right much alike for sisters, I reckon," Drusie acknowledged. "I think she's prettier than me."

"Then she must be a hot mama."

"Hold your horses, Archie." Gladdie's voice indicated his displeasure. "The Fields girls are respectable, not some floozies you might meet in the city."

"I know it, cuz." Archie tipped his hat. "Didn't mean to offend, Drusie. Or you, either, Aunt Penny. Although I hope you don't mind my saying that you are as beautiful as ever."

Mrs. Gordon swept her glance upon her apron and back to Archie. "Oh, you hush now! I've got to go finish up lunch." She went back into the house, not bothering to catch the screen door like she usually did. Even over the loud *bang* it made as it shut, Drusie heard Mrs. Gordon's giggles.

Drusie felt more shocked than flattered by Archie's bold words directed her way and a bit embarrassed that Mrs. Gordon acted like a schoolgirl, but she decided to be gracious for Gladdie's sake. "With smooth talk like that, Archie, you must be sellin' records left and right."

Archie laughed and leaned against one of the poles—which weren't anything nearly so grand that they could be called columns—that held up the porch covering. "I only speak the truth," Archie observed, still studying her. "Gladdie here tells me you take the roof off the house with your singing."

Drusie wasn't sure how to respond. "I reckon I do sing right loud."

Archie chuckled. "That's not what I mean. I mean, you're quite the canary, according to Gladdie. And from what I remember, you liked to perform. Is that still so?"

"Well, some people tell me I'm right good at singing, but of course, your ma is supposed to tell you that, I reckon." Now that Archie was asking about her singing, Drusie felt even more anxious. She wished she hadn't shown her unease by punctuating every thought with an expression of uncertainty.

"Your ma, huh?" Archie looked at Gladdie. "You say everybody likes her, not just her ma?"

"That's right," Gladdie said. "She's just bein' modest. I wouldn't have it any other way."

"That's just grand. So are you going to perform for me?" Archie asked.

"Perform? I—uh, sure." Drusie's anxiety turned to an excitement she tried not to display. Her plans were falling into place with no effort on her part. First, Gladdie had asked her to bring her banjo, which was no surprise since she was often called upon to entertain company. Archie, visiting from out of town as he was, would be no exception. But Archie wasn't just any company. He was a record producer—owned a recording studio, even. He was the big boss at his business. What he said went. At least that's what Gladdie told her. If she could impress

Archie, then maybe she could cut a record and sell enough copies that Gladdie could buy Mr. Goode's store. After that, she'd retire and they could live happily ever after.

"Sure," Gladdie piped up, interrupting Drusie's daydream. "Drusie will play the banjo for you. She'll even sing whatever song you request. If she knows it, that is. And she knows plenty of songs."

Archie took a seat in a rocker and rubbed his chin. "Hows about I let you pick whatever you want? Maybe a hymn and a traditional mountain tune."

"I have to say, you don't waste no time," Drusie said, hoping to stall him. She wanted to play for Archie, but she hadn't thought he'd go in for the kill before they could sit a spell.

Archie looked at his watch. "I don't have time to waste. Time is money."

Drusie wasn't sure his philosophy was the best way to go about living, but to be agreeable, she nodded.

Gladdie handed her the banjo, and she sat back in the rocker. After thinking a moment, she selected her favorite tune, one that she knew would show off her voice. She looked back and forth at both men. Pride made Gladdie's eyes glow.

Mrs. Gordon came back out on the porch and joined them long enough to hear the songs. She clapped and smiled after the performance of the first tune and asked for another.

As she complied, Drusie tried not to linger long on Archie's face, but she could see interest and contemplation when she met his eyes. At one point when she caught Archie's glance, she almost forgot the familiar words to her song. From the intensity in his gray eyes, she could see that how well she performed was important.

When she was finished singing, everyone applauded.

Archie grinned. "Gladdie didn't exaggerate. You're very good."

"Thank you."

"Yep, Drusie does me proud every time. Sing him another song, sweetheart," Gladdie prodded.

"Another song? Don't you reckon he's right tired of hearin' me?"

"Not yet," Archie said. "I want you to show me you can perform on short notice anytime. Try 'Down in the Willow Garden.'"

So this was truly an audition! She tamped down her nervousness and concentrated on the words to the song. The old tune told about a man who killed the one he loved with a saber. Its melody sounded sweet to the ears. One had to listen closely to realize the brutality of the act described.

"Very poignant," Archie said after the last note. "How about one more?"

Drusie wasn't sure what he meant by "poignant," but she took it as a compliment and then launched into "Who's That Knocking at My Door?" After she was through, the air fell silent.

"You have quite a repertoire."

Drusie wished he wouldn't keep using such strange words, even though he smiled as he said them.

Archie stood, exuding confidence. "I think the music industry is ready for her. Lots of acts are making good with the music of home, the music we grew up with."

"Our mountain music sure is special," Mrs. Gordon agreed. "Nothin' like them city folks hear in them fancy opera houses they go to, I imagine."

"Nothing like it. And I think that's why that music sells so well. But I must say, the audience for our type of music isn't really highbrow people in New York and places like that. The people who buy our music are good, hardworking country folk," Archie explained. "The music that I record at my studio reaches a large audience, and many of them are willing to buy a record or two."

"That's all fine and good, but I don't see what any of this has to do with Drusie," Gladdie said.

"You don't?" Archie poked Gladdie. "This won't be a trip for biscuits, will it?"

"Biscuits?" Mrs. Gordon asked. "I thought you liked biscuits. Matter of fact, I made a batch up just for you."

"Oh, I like your biscuits, Aunt Penny. I just mean, I don't want to waste my time." Archie looked at Drusie. "So what do you think?"

Unwilling to appear foolish and vain, Drusie decided she'd better get Archie to spell out his intentions for business, if he had any. "Think about what?"

"Leaving this place for something better."

"Leavin'?" Gladdie let go of Drusie's hand. "I don't much like that idea."

Drusie wasn't sure what to say. She had hoped Archie would like her singing, but at that moment, she realized she hadn't thought through everything his good opinion might mean. If he wanted her to perform for a crowd, he'd want her to leave home. Suddenly she wasn't so sure. She wasn't so sure about anything. "Why, I—I don't know."

Drusie observed her surroundings. Lush foliage was everywhere, along with birds that woke her in the morning with their singing and deer that would sometimes peer at her when she was in the yard. The majesty of Grandfather Mountain never failed to inspire. She took in a breath that was a little deeper than usual, enjoying the fresh air. "There's a lot to love about this place."

"True. But there's a big world out there, and I think they're ready for you." Archie studied her. "And they'd be willing to pay money to see a pretty canary like you sing. Wouldn't you like to have a few of the finer things in life?" He cut his glance to his automobile.

Drusie shrugged. "I wouldn't mind buying Ma some things for the house, and maybe a new truck for Pa, but I don't need nothin' for myself. The good Lord provides us with all we need. But I do have a dream. I mean, Gladdie does."

"You mean, the store?" Gladdie asked.

"That's exactly what I mean," Drusie answered.

"And?" Archie let the word hang in the air.

Drusie ignored the nervous knot in her stomach. "Gladdie has his eye on a store he'd like to buy."

"Goode's Mercantile," Gladdie elaborated. "You must have passed it on your way here. It's just up the road a piece. But I don't know what that has to do with anything."

"You'll see." Drusie reached for Gladdie's hand and held it.

"Sure, I remember the store," Archie answered. "The old man's been here as long as I can recall. He and the Moore family have always tried to outdo each other. Sure you want to take over and get in the middle of all that rivalry, Gladdie?"

"Well, Mr. Goode's ready to retire now, and this may be the only chance I get to own the store. I'm sure, with the Lord's help, I can handle whatever competition anybody else in these here parts has to offer." Gladdie tightened his lips.

"That's the way I like to hear you talk." Drusie patted his shoulder and turned her face to Archie. "The Lord ain't shown Gladdie and me a way to the money yet. We want to get married, and I sure would like to help him find that money."

Archie rubbed his hands together. "Then what better way to make some bacon than singing? You've got the talent."

"I do?" Drusie could hardly believe the conversation but decided if she really wanted to sing, she had better show some confidence. "I do!"

"You hit the nail on the head!" Archie's voice filled with cockiness. "Hows about you going with me to Raleigh? I have a recording studio, but you knew that, didn't you, doll? You can cut a record and we can sell it all over the country."

The idea, which seemed so enticing while still elusive, left her feeling unnerved now that the reality was closer. "But—nobody knows me."

"They don't know you now, but they'll know you by the time I'm done. We're going to tour, you and me. And the band, of course. We'll go all over hill country and the piedmont. Lynchburg, Roanoke, Greensboro, Charlotte, to name a few. You'll get to sing your little heart out, with professionals backing you up. Once they hear you, people everywhere will be clamoring to buy your records. I just know it."

"All that way?" She had just steeled herself for the idea of going to Raleigh. Now he was suggesting even more places. Fear struck Drusie. "Now hold on just a minute. I didn't think nothin' about goin' all over the countryside."

"How else will people get to know you?"

"I—I don't rightly know." Drusie felt dizzy. Recording? Touring? Singing in front of strangers every night? Such ideas overwhelmed her.

"You don't sound too excited."

"I'm not sure I am too excited about bein' involved in all that commotion," Drusie admitted.

Archie cast Gladdie a look. "You don't mind her going, do you? Sounds like she has plans for the money she'd make—plans that involve you." Archie punched Gladdie in the forearm. "Say, you sly dog, you didn't put her up to this, did you?"

"Why, no." Gladdie rubbed the spot where Archie's fist had made contact. "This is all her idea. She didn't say nothin' to me about it." The look Gladdie cast Drusie revealed that his feelings were hurt a mite.

"I'm sorry," Drusie apologized. "I didn't mean to keep secrets. I didn't wanna say nothin' because I didn't know for sure your cousin would like my singin'. Especially not so much that he'd make such big suggestions."

Archie chuckled. "I didn't think you were smart enough to put her up to anything."

"Hey, now!" Gladdie protested.

"I was just funning you, Gladdie. You've got one sharp dame here, and I think she'll go places if you don't hold her back. Man alive, by the time I'm finished with her, you won't just own a two-bit store out here in the middle of nowhere. You might just own a chain of stores!"

Uncertainty covered Gladdie's expression. "I just wanted her to impress you with her singin'. I had no idea things would go this far."

Archie cleared his throat. "I think it's time for me to let the two of you go it alone for a while." He rose from his seat. "Aunt Penny, have you got a glass of city juice—I mean, water?"

"Sure. And if you ask real nice, I might be able to come up with something better than that for supper. I bought two bottles of sodie pop from Mr. Goode's store, just for you. You still like sodie pop, don't ya?"

"I certainly do. Sounds good, Aunt Penny." Archie winked at Drusie. "Now you and Gladdie talk. I'll be inside if you need me."

As soon as Archie had cleared the door, Drusie took Gladdie by the hand. "I cain't believe it! I cain't believe Archie likes my singin' this much!"

"I—I'm happy and all, but I didn't think he'd make an offer to take you off to record your music. I might have known he'd only come all this way if he thought he could do some business."

"Oh, don't be so hard on your cousin. He's a busy man."

"Yeah." Gladdie didn't sound happy.

Drusie wished he were in a better mood, but she knew she had to speak up now if she had a chance of making a record. "I know it's hard, but don't you see? If I sing for this record, I might make enough money for us to get married and buy the store."

"I know. You planned this, didn't you?" His voice held no reprimand or accusation.

"I reckon I have to admit I did, after I realized he was visitin'. I thought, why not take a chance? I knew if the Lord didn't want this to happen for me, it wouldn't. But Archie hadn't been here five minutes before he asked me to sing. That's got to be a sign, doesn't it?"

"I don't know. I admit, I bragged on you mightily. Should have known better than to brag to a record producer."

"That's just it. Archie is the only person who can help us get the store. I don't want to be no big celebrity like the women in the Carter family. I just want to sing long enough for us to save up and buy the store."

"Really?"

"You know me. Archie's talk about riches don't matter to me none. Once we buy that store, all I want is to entertain my family and be Mrs. Gladdie Gordon."

"And you will be. I promise. I'm more proud of you than ever. And that you would do this for me, for us. . . I—I don't know what to say."

"Don't say nothin'. Just let me go."

"So your ma and pa don't mind?"

"Ma and Pa?" Her chest tightened. She hadn't thought they might disapprove, but they might. They never had much use for any type of show business. "I'm an adult and I can do what I want."

"Maybe in the legal sense, but not in your heart. And as long as we're not married yet, I want you to get their permission."

Drusie wanted to argue, but when Gladdie got that determined set of his jaw, there was no way he'd change his mind. They'd have to ask her parents. She could only hope they wouldn't put up too much of a fuss. If they did, Drusie saw no way for Gladdie's dream to come true.

Chapter 3

Drusie wanted some time to discuss her future with Gladdie, but Archie didn't leave them on the Gordons' porch long. When he returned, he had taken off his suit coat yet still maintained his swagger and confidence. "So have you two decided to take the road to fame and fortune and let Drusie come along with me?"

"Not yet," Gladdie said. "But I have to admit, I'm warmin' up to the idea of Drusie singin' for the public. Her talent shouldn't be kept a secret forever."

"That's the spirit." Archie looked at Drusie coolly. "So when are we leaving? Tomorrow?"

"Not so fast," Gladdie said. "We have to be sure this plan is okay with Drusie's ma and pa."

"Is she that young?" Archie studied Drusie, wide-eyed.

"No," Gladdie insisted. "Have you been away from home that long? People around here still respect their parents."

"Yeah." Sadness penetrated Archie's handsome face. Drusie remembered that Archie had lost his parents young, thanks to the influenza epidemic.

"I'm sorry," Gladdie blurted, obviously remembering Archie's loss. "I didn't mean to bring up bad memories. I know you'd respect your ma and pa if they was still around."

"Yeah." Archie cleared his throat. "Your ma said I could stay here as long as I want. Might as well. But I've got to have an answer early tomorrow."

"Will do. Maybe even sooner than that." Gladdie's cheerful assurance lifted the pall in the air.

"I think I'll go get me some more of that city juice." Archie disappeared into the house.

As soon as his cousin was out of sight, Gladdie took Drusie's hand. "Are you ready to ask your pa?"

"I don't know. I hadn't given it much thought before you mentioned he might not approve. Truth be told, I reckon I hadn't given any thought to what would happen if Archie actually liked my singin'. I warn't at all sure he'd want to cut a record with me. It was a dream. . .until now."

Gladdie squeezed her hand. "And you're scared."

"A little."

"I am, too, but not about you bein' famous or travelin' with Archie. I just hate that you won't be around no more."

"Oh, Gladdie, I'll come back sooner than you can say 'boo.' And I wouldn't go with Archie, 'ceptin' he's your cousin and all."

"That's right. Your pa don't got nothin' to worry about, and neither do you. If you go with Archie, everything will be right and proper. You can trust Archie on that. I've talked to him a lot about his business, and I know he keeps his singers protected. And if anything was to happen to you, well, he'll answer to me." Gladdie puffed out his chest, and Drusie knew he meant his threat.

His bravado shored up Drusie's private concern. "All righty, then. Let's go ask Pa what he thinks."

Gladdie turned to the front door and shouted to Mrs. Gordon inside that they were leaving. Her muffled response assured them she understood.

Since their houses were within walking distance of one another, Gladdie didn't bother to fire up the Model T. Instead, they ambled along a dusty cow path that meandered along the hillside from homestead to homestead. Since they didn't speak, only an occasional rustle of leaves from a little animal or the chirping of a bird made them aware they weren't alone.

Drusie took in the stillness. All too soon, she'd be in the city, far away from her beloved mountains. A city park wouldn't have such dramatic woods as those in a hollow that dropped off to one side of the path. In the deepest, shadiest parts of the forest, she could happily get lost in God's creation.

"What are you thinkin'?" Gladdie's gentle voice broke the silence.

"Not much. Just thinkin' about the forest. And fairy tales."

He chuckled. "Fairy tales? Are you already imaginin' you're Cinderella and your dreams will all come true?"

"I was thinkin' about Little Red Ridin' Hood and the forest. I'm already Cinderella, because I've met my Prince Charmin'."

Gladdie stopped and turned so they faced one another. He took both of her hands in his. They were hot, but she didn't mind. She just wanted to look into his deep brown eyes.

"I know you're my princess," he told her. "Always have been. Just wish I had a castle instead of a little home in the mountains to offer you."

"A little home in the mountains is all I want, as long as you're there."

"I cain't wait to marry you." He gave her a gentle kiss on the lips that grew in passion, expressing his love for her. Strong arms held her closely.

Returning his embrace, she marveled at how soft his lips felt, yet so manly. Tingles went through her body, and she pulled back from his embrace. "Come on. Let's go."

"You seem mighty anxious to talk to your pa all of a sudden." His voice sounded husky.

"Anxious, yes. But not to talk to Pa." She broke away from his spell and took a fast pace toward home.

Soon they were in sight of the house Pa and his brothers had built back at the turn of the century. The log house had aged well. Drusie imagined the homestead being there long after she had passed on to glory.

She almost wished Pa wouldn't be home, but no doubt he would just be finishing up lunch.

As soon as they stepped into the kitchen, Pa eyed her from his position at the head of the table, where he sat in the only chair that had arms. "Where you been, girl?"

Drusie eyed Ma, who was stoking the fire. The tantalizing scents of vegetable stew and biscuit dough filled the kitchen. Maybe such good food would help ease Pa's reaction to their news.

Ma eyed Pa. "Don'tcha remember, Zeke? Gladdie's cousin came in today. Drusie went to his house to visit and play the banjo."

"Where's your banjo?" Pa asked.

"Still at Gladdie's house. I plan to go back and fetch it later."

"I see." Pa looked at Gladdie, his rugged face expressing warmth for his future son-in-law. "How is Archie, anyhow?"

"He's doin' better'n ever. Wearin' a fancy city-slicker suit and everything," Gladdie answered.

"I see." The older man crossed arms that were muscular from years of work. "Now if I recollect right, ain't he the one that run off to Raleigh to be in the music business?"

"Sure is," Gladdie confirmed. "Owns his own record company and everything."

Pa let out a whistle. "Well, that's mighty fine. So are you stayin' a spell, or are you back off to do some more visitin'?"

"I cain't stay too long. I have to help Pa with the animals pretty soon." Gladdie's flat tone indicated this was far from his favorite chore.

"That's right. We shouldn't tarry long." Drusie wanted to sit, but she noticed that Ma was tidying up the kitchen and decided to help. Besides, wiping down the table would help her work off some nervous energy.

Gladdie took in a breath and looked Pa in the eye. "Drusie and I have some news."

"Is that so?" Pa smiled. "You two gettin' hitched?"

Gladdie leaned back with such force that Drusie thought he might knock over his seat. "Oh, it's not that, sir. But I want to get married as soon as we can. Real bad."

Drusie quickly agreed. "And so do I."

"But Drusie has somethin' else to do first," Gladdie elaborated.

"Somethin' else to do?" Ma intervened. "What in the world would she have to do other than be a wife and maybe a mother one day, Lord willin'?"

Gladdie cleared his throat again.

"Boy, you sure are coughin' an awful lot. You don't got one of them summer colds comin' on, do ya?" Pa asked.

"No, sir."

Seeing Gladdie so uncharacteristically nervous, Drusie decided to intervene. "Oh, Pa, we've got the most wonderful news. Archie wants me to go to Raleigh and make a record!"

Pa's eyebrows shot up. "A record?"

Ma almost dropped her spoon. "Well, that's somethin'!"

Drusie nodded. "Isn't it excitin'?"

Gladdie seemed to get caught up in the moment. A torrent of words rushed from him. "Archie heard Drusie play and sing today, and he wants to take her to Raleigh so she can cut a record. After that, they'll tour with a band and be known all over the country. Maybe even all over the world. Everyone will know Drusie's name and buy her records and pay money to see her play."

Ma gasped. "Imagine! Strangers payin' Drusie money for what we get to hear around these parts for free."

"Well, if that don't beat all." Pa tugged on his graying beard.

"Archie mentioned that I might make enough money to buy fine things, so he must be thinkin' my singin' is worth right much money," Drusie said. "But I don't want to live like one of them silent film stars. What I really want is for Gladdie to buy Mr. Goode's store. All I want to do is sell a few records, make enough money to help Gladdie buy the store, and then come back here and live."

Her parents knew about Gladdie's dream, so Drusie's announcement about the store was no revelation. Her new plans for a brief musical career were another matter. She could see by the quizzical looks on their faces that they were trying to sort out what her news meant for the family.

Ma recovered first. "You gotta leave home?"

"I don't want to leave," Drusie assured her. "I need to. I have to go with Archie to Raleigh. But I won't need to stay long. Hardly no time at all."

Pa remained unmoved. "Now hold on. He wants to take her to Raleigh?"

"He sure does," Gladdie confirmed.

Pa looked at Drusie. "What do you think of all this?"

Drusie folded the damp cloth. "I want to go with Archie Gordon to Raleigh."

"Now wait a minute. I don't think it's wise for you to go alone with a man to Raleigh—or anywhere else—when the two of you ain't married. Remember, the Bible says to avoid all appearance of evil." Pa studied Gladdie. "Cain't Drusie stay here at home where she belongs? The mountains are good enough for us. They should be good enough for her. I don't think she should go."

Ma spoke as she tended the fire. "But Zeke, I don't see why she cain't give it a try. Just because you didn't have a chance like this don't mean we should keep our daughter from tryin', does it? Besides, I don't know of no other way Gladdie can buy the store. Do you?"

Pa set his elbows on the table. "I won't argue that. And Gladdie, you know I think you're a mighty fine feller, and I don't want to stand in the way of you and Drusie havin' a good life. And ownin' that store would mean a good life for the two of you. I'm just saying it don't look right for a young lady to go travelin' on the road with a man."

"It will only be until we get to Raleigh," Drusie said. "If we leave well before sunup, we can get there without havin' to stop on the road for the night."

"Archie has a lot of female singers he manages. I know he makes arrangements for them to stay places that are safe for women," Gladdie said. "Then they'll be travelin' with the band."

"A bunch of men?" Pa scoffed. "I think she'd be much safer here with us. Don't you, Gladdie?"

Gladdie didn't answer right away, a sure sign he wanted to weigh his words. "I understand how you feel, but she'll be safe. I know there will be female performers other than Drusie goin' along. Like I said, sir, Archie has lots of girl singers he manages. He usually takes more than one band on tour at a time."

"He does, does he?" Suspicion hung in Pa's voice.

"It's all professional."

"Oh, Zeke," Ma interrupted. "If you would trust Gladdie to marry our Drusie, cain't you trust him to give advice on Drusie's future?"

He crossed his arms, but his cocked head showed he was still listening. "Well, you have a point, wife."

"Of course I have a point. Now this sounds like a good opportunity for Drusie. You know she cain't do nothin' around these parts but be a schoolteacher, and it don't look like Miss Hawthorne plans to marry anytime soon and give up her job. And besides," Ma continued, "you know I always wished I coulda made a dollar or two playin' music."

Drusie's mouth dropped open. "You did? Ma, I never knew."

"Child, you look like you're about to swallow a fly." Ma swatted her hand in Drusie's direction. "Now my little attempts at music warn't nothin'."

"Nothin'?" Pa protested. "Why, you was the best girl singer in the holler back in our day."

Ma looked over the fire. "That was a long time ago, Zeke."

"Oh, Ma, I've heard you sing. You can outdo me any day of the week."

"So what kept you from goin' on about makin' your dream come true, Mrs. Fields?" Gladdie wanted to know.

"You're about to marry one of the reasons," she responded. "I wanted to have children. And I wouldn't trade a one of my girls for all the money or fame in the world."

"Oh, Ma!" Drusie cried.

"Now, now, don't you say nothin'. I wanted to marry your pa more than anything, and I gave up my dream to do it. Not that it really was much of a dream. Back then, I didn't have no chance to make good in the city, and even if I had, I'm not sure I could have left home. I would have been too unhappy. And your pa wanted to work in the loggin' business, just like his pa before him. He didn't have no idea to own a store. And back then, makin' records warn't nothin' as easy as it is now, and show folk traveled by train." She smiled at Gladdie. "I don't see no reason why Drusie should give up her chance, especially to make such a big dream like yours come true, too, Gladdie. I think you'd make a fine storekeeper. You already make a fine clerk." She looked at her husband. "Ain't that right, Zeke?"

"Cain't deny it."

Ma looked at Drusie without flinching. "Gladdie seems to think it's a mighty fine thing for you to work with Archie, and if that's what he thinks, and since he's your intended, I think you ought to obey him. Preacher Lawson says we ought to obey our husbands. Remember when he said that?"

"I remember, Ma." Drusie felt girded by such encouragement. Surely God had used her mother to speak to her. It wasn't the first time. "What do you say, Pa?"

Pa rubbed his bearded chin. "Well, when you put it like that, I reckon I oughtta give you my blessing."

"Thank you, Pa!" Drusie embraced him.

"Thank you, Mr. Fields!" Gladdie rose from his seat and took Drusie by the hand. "Come on and let's tell Archie. We've got a lot to talk about."

"Hold your horses," Pa said. "There's somethin' else. A condition I have for you. And if you two don't go along with what I say, I cain't allow Drusie to go."

Chapter 4

Watching Pa as he sat still in his kitchen chair, Drusie felt as though she were a rock by the side of the creek, water rushing at her, unable to move. So Pa had a condition as to whether or not she could go to Raleigh and cut a record of the music of home. Now that it looked like Pa was about to throw a monkey wrench into her new plans, she couldn't help but feel disappointed.

What could the condition be? She tried to guess. Could he want Gladdie to marry her before she left? She suppressed a smile. Such a thought could make sense. After all, she'd never dream of taking her music to the world outside her mountain community except that Gladdie wanted to buy the store and she wanted to make enough money so that would be possible. Maybe Pa wanted to make sure Gladdie was tied to her right good before she made all that effort for him. Drusie trusted Gladdie, and if Pa said they had to get hitched before he would agree to let her go to Raleigh, Drusie wouldn't mind that at all.

Her heart reminded her of its existence by beating fast in her chest. She took in a breath. "What's the condition, Pa?"

He eyed Gladdie, then Drusie. "I want you to take Clara with you."

"Clara?" Drusie blurted. Her mind switched gears to cope with such an unexpected turn of events. Clara, going with them to Raleigh? To cut the record with her? Sure, Clara sang like a bird, but Drusie never thought about her sister even wanting to go.

"Yep." Pa nodded. "She sings real good. You two sound even better together than either one of you sounds by yourself. And havin' a sister along means you can look out for each other—just in case you find yourself in a situation you warn't meanin' to."

Gladdie interrupted with a protest. "But Mr. Fields, I won't let nothin' happen to Drusie. She means too much to me."

"You goin' along?"

"Uh, no, sir," Gladdie admitted, glancing at his feet and back to Mr. Fields. "I have to stay here and help my family."

"Well then," Pa said, "to my way of thinkin', you cain't help Drusie much if you're here and she's all the way in Raleigh. Now I don't mean no disrespect, son. I know you'd never set your mind to lettin' somethin' happen to her, but the outside world can be a mighty mean place where bad things can happen. Terrible

261

bad things. She needs protection. Now you say that your cousin has women travelin' with the band, but them women just ain't gonna look after Drusie the way her own sister would."

"I understand, sir." Gladdie's voice registered defeat.

"Well then, her sister needs to go, to my way of thinking, and there ain't nothin' you or Archie or anyone else can say to change my mind on that. So either both sisters go, or nobody goes. That's my final word." The way Pa looked right into Gladdie's brown eyes without flinching told Drusie that he meant what he said.

Anxiety clutched Drusie in her gut. What if Clara didn't want to go? Even more likely, what if Archie didn't want Clara to go along? Then Drusie's chances of helping Gladdie buy the store would be ruined. Mr. Goode would sell it to someone else, and they'd never have another chance. She didn't like debating with Pa, but this time she felt she had to kick up a fuss. She reached for an argument. "So you're gonna send Clara along and endanger her, too?"

"I believe in the old sayin' that there's safety in numbers. And Clara would look after you. And you'll look after her." He wagged his forefinger at her, shaking it on each word for emphasis.

She tried again. "I know that, Pa. I'll be so busy lookin' after her that I won't have time to sing."

When Drusie cut her glance to Gladdie, she noticed he rubbed his fingertips together. She figured he was thinking his way out of the situation, too. "Mr. Fields, I worry that if we insist, it might ruin Drusie's chances," Gladdie said. "Archie didn't agree to let another person come along. Travelin' is expensive, and she'd be another mouth to feed."

"And another mouth to sing, too," Pa pointed out.

"So do you think Clara would want to make a record?" Gladdie wondered aloud. "It's one thing to sing at church, but it's a horse of another color to sing on a record for the whole world."

"True. Why don't we ask her and find out?" Pa didn't wait for an answer before he hollered out Clara's name.

Ma stopped tending the pot of stew long enough to answer. "I sent her to fetch some water from the well. She's been gone long enough that she oughtta be back anytime now."

Pa rose from his seat and peered out the back door. "She's comin' on up here now."

"Maybe I should go help her," Gladdie said.

"Naw," Pa said. "She's got to learn to handle that bucket herself."

Silence fell upon them as they waited for Clara to struggle with getting the water to the house in a heavy wooden bucket. Drusie never minded when it was her turn to fetch water. She enjoyed walking outdoors, down the narrow path to

he well. The time alone gave her a few minutes to think and to enjoy God's creation. Her least favorite part of the journey was carrying the burdensome bucket
filled to the brim. Not splashing half the supply out onto the ground was the
trick to not making a second trip to the well. After many tries, Drusie became
skilled at carrying water without spilling a drop, something she took pride in.
Clara never did become quite so adept, and hence she complained whenever
it was her turn to do the fetching. But by walking slowly, she managed to keep
most of the water in the bucket.

Nervous, Drusie looked at the fire and contemplated stoking it while they
waited.

"Drusie," Gladdie asked, "would you mind fixin' me a glass of water?"

"Sure." She hurried to comply, grateful for the simple task. By the time she
was done, Clara had entered the kitchen with fresh water.

"Hey, Gladdie." She set down the water and glanced from Gladdie, to
Drusie, to Ma, and then to Pa. "What's the matter? Y'all look like there's bad
news brewin'. There ain't nothin' wrong, is there?" She paled.

"No, Clara. Nothin's wrong," Pa assured. "Sit on down." He nodded to an
empty chair.

She obeyed. "What is it, Pa?"

"Didn't Drusie tell you that she and Gladdie would be seein' his cousin
Archie today? The one that run off to Raleigh and has his own recordin' studio
now?"

"I remember Archie. Skinny and hardly old enough to think for himself
when he left here. So he made good?"

"Real good." Gladdie's voice was filled with pride.

"That's nice." Clara's posture relaxed. Obviously, she thought Archie's visit
had nothing to do with her.

Pa leaned forward. "How would you like to sing with Drusie, in front of
people, for pay?"

"For pay?" Clara laughed so hard she snorted. "Who'd pay us to sing?"

"Lots of people, accordin' to Gladdie's cousin Archie."

Clara turned serious. "What? You mean Archie wants me to sing? He has
the power to make such a big decision on his own?" She gasped, her voice showing a mixture of excitement and uncertainty.

"He sure does. He owns the studio and everything," Pa said.

"True, but everything ain't exactly set," Gladdie said. "At least, not yet. You've
gotten to be part of the deal if Archie plans to take Drusie."

Clara crossed her arms like a petulant child. "Care to explain?"

Drusie elaborated on the day's events. As she did, Clara went from lazing
back in her chair, displaying the interest of a schoolchild at the end of a two-hour
sermon, to leaning forward, mouth open and eyes wide.

"That's swell!" Clara said after Drusie concluded. "So Archie wants you to be a big-time singer, and with our humble mountain music at that." She shook her head. "Who'd've thought such a thing?"

"I know it's mighty amazin'," Drusie said. "So don't ya wanna go?"

"I don't rightly think I do."

Drusie's jaw slackened with disappointment. "But you got to, Clara! You just got to! If you don't, me and Gladdie will never get to buy the store."

"I know all about your dreams, and I'd like to help, but I cain't." She turned up her nose ever so slightly. "If I'm second fiddle, I don't want no part of this record business. I can stay here and be second fiddle to everybody else."

"I'll be happy for you to take the lead on some of the songs, Clara." Drusie set her hand on her sister's knee and held her gaze to show Clara her sincerity. "I'd welcome it. I don't need to sing so much that I don't have a voice left."

"Aw, come on, Clara," Gladdie prodded. "You and Drusie will have fun. You'll meet lots of people and have some cash."

"Cash money?" Clara shifted so that Drusie's hand fell from her knee.

Drusie leaned against the back of her chair. With Clara's renewed attentiveness, hope sparked.

"How much money?" Clara wanted to know.

Guilt marred Drusie's happiness. Remembering biblical admonitions about the love of money, she felt reluctant to use its lure as an argument to sway her sister, but desperation drove her. "Archie said somethin' to me about buyin' fine things."

"Fine things?" Clara's mouth hung open. "You mean, we can make that much money?"

Drusie shrugged. "I reckon."

Clara's eyes became dreamy. "I always have wanted to wear pretty clothes."

"Pretty clothes?" Ma objected. "Don't you think you got pretty clothes now?"

Clara turned her mouth into a sheepish line. "Yes, ma'am. You make me pretty dresses all the time. It's just that I can just imagine wearin' store-bought clothes every day."

"I don't suppose you can be blamed," Ma admitted. "You're young, and you can enjoy the finer things in life that we never had." She shook her head. "Imagine!"

"Clara won't have to imagine long, if what Archie says is true," Gladdie observed.

Clara rose from her seat and nodded once in a way that showed her mind was made up. "Okay. I'll go."

"Now money isn't everything," Pa cautioned. "If riches is what you want, maybe it's not such a good idea for you to go after all."

"Why else would I want to go, Pa?" As soon as the question left Clara's mouth, she twisted her lips and looked at her sister. "I know. You want me to keep Drusie out of trouble."

"That won't be hard. I don't plan on gettin' into trouble," Drusie assured her.

Clara cocked her head and pointed at her sister. "You better not. If I'm ever gonna be famous, I won't have time to look after you."

Pa's laughter filled the kitchen. "Then it's settled."

"Not quite yet, Mr. Fields." Gladdie wore a worried look that Drusie didn't like. "Like I said, my cousin Archie ain't agreed to your plan for two singin' sisters."

"I know it, Gladdie, but Clara deserves to make good in the city, just as Drusie does," Pa persisted. "So you tell your cousin if he wants Drusie, he has to take Clara, too."

"I'll tell him that, sir." Although he kept from frowning, disappointment etched Gladdie's voice.

Drusie kept her face unreadable. Pa never said it aloud, but he favored Clara. True, she was open about her emotions, filling the room with optimism whenever she entered and displaying cuteness even when disagreeable. Drusie was the serious, studious one—harder for people to get to know. Sometimes she wished she was more like her little sister. But God had fashioned them both for His reasons. Drusie had learned to live with their differences long ago.

Given their past history, she wasn't surprised that Pa had managed to turn her opportunity into one that would benefit her sister. Still, it would be nice to have Clara along. "Gladdie's right. Besides, Archie cain't decide nothin' without hearin' Clara sing." She motioned to her sister. "Come on. Pick up your fiddle and let's go to Gladdie's house. Archie's there now. You can audition, and he can tell us what he thinks."

"Is that okay with you, Pa?" Clara asked.

He nodded. "Makes sense to me."

Clara clapped, reminding Drusie of a little girl. "Let me put on my Sunday dress and clean up a little. It won't take me long, I promise." Without further ado, she exited.

Drusie could see from her level of intensity that she'd be dressed faster than a cow could swing her tail to shoo a fly.

Moments later, Clara emerged wearing a Sunday dress with a polka-dotted pattern that fit her form well, but not too tightly.

"You look nice," Ma said.

Clara patted her shiny light brown curls. "I hope so."

Without pause, Gladdie, Drusie, and Clara bid Ma and Pa good-bye and were on their way around the hill and past the hollow to the Gordons'. The walk back was more of a stride, and nothing that could be called romantic. This was a business trip.

"So," Clara asked, "do you think Archie will like me?"

"I don't see why not," Drusie assured her. "You were a pretty little girl when he left, and you're even prettier now." She lowered her voice, even though they were well out of earshot from the house. "I didn't want to say this in front of Pa, but I imagine Archie will start describin' you in terms of food as soon as he sets eyes on you."

Clara scrunched her eyebrows. "Food?"

"Things like 'dish' and 'tomato' is what he likes to say. I don't understand what he's talkin' about half the time, but he seems to think he's bein' nice. City ways—you know."

"I'll try to catch on," Clara said with a grin. "I just hope he thinks I'm pretty."

"You have to be more than pretty," Gladdie said, though not in an unkind tone. "You have to sing well enough for him to decide he wants to make a record with you. Archie is a businessman, and they don't like to lose money."

"I can imagine he don't."

"What do you think you'll sing?" Drusie asked.

"I don't rightly know." She paused to think. " 'Cindy' and 'Mole in the Ground' maybe."

"I can sing along with you on one so he can see how we do together," Drusie suggested. "Let's sing a hymn, too. He likes that."

"Okay."

They approached the Gordons' house, where Archie waited on the porch. Instead of rocking in a chair, he stood with one hand on his hip, looking at the horizon.

Clara stopped and took in a breath.

Drusie followed suit. "What's the matter?"

"N—nothin'. Uh, is that Archie?"

"Sure is," Gladdie affirmed.

Clara kept staring. "He's all growed up!"

Something in Clara's tone and sudden change in posture made Drusie nervous. If she decided to get a crush on Archie before she even spoke to him, Pa would figure that out right quick, and their trip would be doomed. "Now he's a big record producer, and we're just one of his acts—we hope. So don't go gettin' any ideas," Drusie hissed at her sister. "Come on." Drusie tugged on her arm, prodding her to resume walking.

Clara pouted but kept her voice low. "I ain't got no ideas. You're always thinkin' somethin' like that."

Drusie remembered how Clara liked to flirt with all the eligible bachelors but decided not to make further mention of that fact. Instead, she sent a silent prayer that the audition would go well. As long as Clara could concentrate on her singing and not too much on the brash redheaded man standing on the porch, surely everything would be just fine.

She hoped.

Chapter 5

Gladdie watched his cousin Archie stare at Drusie and Clara as they approached. Jealousy sparked through him until he looked more closely and saw that Archie wasn't studying Drusie, but Clara. He cut his glance to Drusie's sister and noticed she couldn't take her gaze from him, either. The idea made him uneasy. Archie was too much of a gentleman—and a businessman—to be forward with any of his singers. Still, Archie was a man who had an eye for the ladies, and Gladdie could feel tension emanating from him that hadn't been present until the moment the women came into view.

Lord, Thy will be done.

Gladdie wanted to elaborate on his prayer, but no words entered his mind. Everything had happened so quickly. What had started as a visit from Archie had turned into a business deal. Gladdie freely admitted that he had wanted Drusie to impress his cousin with her singing. He thought earning compliments from someone in the music business would make Drusie happy. That was all he wanted. All he ever wanted. Even his idea to buy the store was motivated by a desire to make a better life for them both.

As soon as Drusie showed up with her banjo, Gladdie realized from Archie's eagerness to hear her perform that auditioning Gladdie's fiancée was the real reason for the visit, not a family reunion. Archie was a businessman through and through, all right.

Conflicting feelings wouldn't leave Gladdie alone. He wanted to buy the store, and with Mr. Goode's retirement happening ahead of schedule, Gladdie could be required to come up with the money quickly. Too quickly. Drusie's success in the music business was the only way he could see that happening. But he didn't want to depend on his future wife to earn the money. To him, sending her out into the cold world didn't seem fair, no matter how much she wanted to go.

Gladdie left his own thoughts long enough to see that Archie gazed at Clara, who looked at him in return. He expected Archie to start talking about food, but for once, he seemed speechless. Gladdie cleared his throat. "Archie, do you recollect Clara Fields?"

Recognition flickered in his eyes. "I do! You're Drusie's little sister, all grown up?"

Clara looked him straight in the eyes before she decided to study the hem of her skirt in a demure manner. "That's me."

"You sure have grown up." Archie's voice had lost its usual brashness.

Drusie smiled. "That's just what she said about you."

Clara poked Drusie in the ribs. "Drusie!"

"There ain't nothin' wrong with what you said. It's just a fact."

Archie didn't take his gaze from Clara's face. "Yeah. It's a fact."

Gladdie wondered at the scene. Instead of his usual slang, Archie spoke in terms regular people could understand. For a moment, it seemed as though the old Archie he knew and liked had returned.

"It's—uh, sure nice to see you," Archie said.

"Why don't you sit down?" Gladdie suggested. "I have a reason for bringin' Clara to see you."

Gladdie's ma chose that moment to interrupt. "I thought I heard voices out here. Hello, Clara. My, you look pretty in your Sunday best. I always say the Fields girls are the prettiest around." She winked at Drusie, which made Gladdie feel proud and happy that his mother liked her.

"Today's special. Our Archie is home." Mrs. Gordon took Archie's chin in her hand and wiggled his clean-shaven skin with the affection of an aunt.

Gladdie remembered his responsibilities. "Could you let Pa know I'll be there to help in a few minutes?"

Ma cackled. "He's in a right good mood today. He said you can have the afternoon off this once."

"Well, hows about that?" Gladdie smiled. Realizing he didn't need to rush off to do chores left him feeling at ease.

"Supper will be ready shortly." Ma disappeared into the house.

"I would have offered to help, but she went in too fast," Clara said.

Gladdie tried not to smile. Enthusiasm for housework wasn't going to get Clara a husband; her pretty face would. "Ma can take care of supper. Besides, we need you out here."

"You do? Let's hear what's on your mind." Archie took a seat in a rocker.

Gladdie took in a breath before letting the words spill. "Mr. Fields said Drusie cain't go without Clara. He wants them to look out for each other."

Archie crossed his arms. "I see. He doesn't trust me, eh? Seems he'd know by now that a Gordon can be trusted."

"I know," Gladdie agreed.

"Please try not to let your feelin's get hurt," Drusie said. "Pa don't mean no harm. He just don't want nothin' to happen to any of us girls, that's all."

"I can respect that." Archie tapped his lips with his forefinger. "There's only one problem. I cain't afford to take you both."

Gladdie's emotions roiled at Archie's admission. He didn't want Drusie to leave home, yet she was so excited by the prospect of helping him make a better future for them both that he hated to see the opportunity slip away with such ease. But what could he do? "I reckon that's it, then."

"Wait," Drusie objected. "Clara's a great singer. She can sing with me. We sing together all the time, and most people seem to think she and I sound better together than apart."

"They do?" Archie's voice brightened, and he leaned forward in his seat.

"They do." For the first time since before they left the Fieldses' house, Gladdie's voice held a hint of optimism.

"Won't you give her a chance to sing for you before you make up your mind, Archie? Please?" Drusie begged.

"You got time, Clara?" Archie inquired.

"I sure do."

"Sure she does. She brought her fiddle." Drusie nodded to her sister. "Didn't you, Clara?"

"I sure enough did."

Archie rocked back. "Well, I don't have anything to lose by sitting here, enjoying the mountain air and the smell of biscuits baking, listening to the two of you harmonize. Why don't you sing me a couple of tunes? Clara, you sing a number by yourself, and then sing something for me with Drusie."

Without pause, the sisters played the tunes they had talked about earlier. Gladdie observed Archie's expression as they sang. His face went from unreadable to pleased.

After three choruses, they strummed the last note, and Archie clapped. "You're swell!"

"We are?" Drusie blurted.

"Don't sound so surprised. A star has to be confident," Archie reprimanded in a playful tone. He looked at the women and sighed, shaking his head. "I must say, you live up to your promise. I sure wish I could take you both."

Gladdie wasn't one to chastise others, but he felt a challenge was in order. "But Archie, you said you have plenty of money."

"Sure, I got plenty of salad. But it costs a lot to run a show, and I got to stay to a certain budget." He shook his head again, and he looked at Clara with—what? Longing?

Clara piped up. "I'll sing for free."

"Free?" Archie quipped. "That's a price made in heaven, but I can't let you do that."

"But you think we'll be successful, right?"

"Sure. I wouldn't cut a record with you otherwise. Even if you are the prettiest doll I've seen in a long time."

Clara averted her eyes coyly but got right back to business. "If we're that good, maybe Drusie will share her profits with me." She eyed her sister. "Would you do that, Drusie? There should be plenty of money to go around if we're as good as Archie says we are."

Drusie paused only for a moment. "You're right. It makes more sense for both of us to go and split the profits than for neither of us to go at all."

Archie cast Drusie a doubtful look. "Are you sure, Drusie? You're makin' a sacrifice not everybody would make."

"She's my sister. It ain't no sacrifice. You know she's doin' me a favor by goin' since Pa won't have it any other way."

"Okay then. Maybe I can see my way clear to give you a better percentage of the profits, then. Never let it be said I took advantage of you or anybody else."

Clara beamed. "So it's settled."

"Congratulations, Miss Clara Fields. You have just joined Mountain Music Records."

Clara shook his hand and held his gaze. "Why, thanks, Archie. This is the best thing that's ever happened to me."

"Yeah." His voice was soft.

Gladdie decided to break the spell. "Clara, I'm happy for you."

"Me, too!" Drusie embraced her sister.

"Now we just need a name for our twosome." Archie's businesslike tone had returned. "Got any suggestions?"

"I don't know," Gladdie said. "You're the professional."

"How about the Gospel Girls?" Clara suggested.

"But you'll be singing traditional mountain music, not just hymns," Archie pointed out.

The group bantered around several names.

"I know!" Archie snapped his fingers. "How about the North Carolina Mountain Girls?"

"Ain't that a mite long? Can anybody remember all that?" Gladdie wondered. "Might not be bad if we shorten it to the NC Mountain Girls."

Archie gazed at the sky. "The NC Mountain Girls." He paused. "Hmm. Not bad. Okay, let's go with that, then."

"Good. Now we can relax," Clara said.

"Relax?" Archie laughed. "You're just getting started. You've got to sign the contract." He reached into an inner pocket in his suit coat and handed Drusie some papers.

She read the contract as Gladdie and Clara peered over her shoulders. "Looks like a bunch of legal gibberish. I want Pa to sign for me."

"Them papers is nothin' but Greek to me," Clara said. "I want Pa to sign for me, too."

Drusie pointed to blank lines. "What's this for?"

Archie glanced at the lines. "Oh, those. That's to fill in the dates the contract is good for. I'll fill that in and let your pa initial it."

"How come it's a set time like that?" Gladdie asked.

"For everybody's protection. If things don't work out, it's easier to let the contract expire than to have to break a binding legal agreement," Archie said.

"Makes sense," Gladdie said.

"Fine with me." Drusie handed the papers back to Archie.

He returned the papers to his pocket. "I'll go see your father, and as soon as he signs, we'll begin. I have a tour in mind you can join. It starts a few days after I'm—*we're* scheduled to get back to Raleigh."

Drusie swallowed. "So soon?"

"The sooner the better," Archie answered. "Pack your bags. We're heading out tomorrow."

∞

After supper, Gladdie made a point of taking Drusie for a walk in the forest. They strolled along the narrow path they had covered together so many times before, stopping at familiar landmarks they could barely see as twilight fell.

Drusie paused at an ancient oak. Finding a heart with the couple's initials Gladdie had carved when they were in high school, she outlined the indentations with her finger. "Our own special tree. We still have the only initials carved on it."

"Remember the day I did that?"

"I sure do. It was May Day, and I was partners with Ben for the maypole dance."

"I never did like Ben much."

The sound of Drusie's laughter jingled prettily. "Mrs. Thomas set us together because he was so short and so am I. You know he always had eyes for Bobbie Sue."

"All I remember is I could hardly think about the dance, I was studyin' you so much and thinkin' about how I'd spent most of the mornin' carvin' out our initials. I didn't pay poor Hilda no mind."

"Don't worry. She was too busy flirtin' with Tab."

"Was she? I didn't notice." Gladdie placed his hands on hers and followed the motion of outlining the heart around the initials. Her soft hand felt so small and vulnerable under his. He wanted to protect her forever. How could he, when she was off to see the world without him?

Drusie didn't move her hand. "This here carvin' was quite a surprise. I didn't even know you had a hankerin' for me. Even though I know I sure had it bad for you." She stopped moving her hand long enough to give him a sly grin. "What would you have done if I'd said I didn't love you back?"

"Oh, I reckon I would have found some other girl with the initials D.F."

"Is that what you think?" A playful slap on the arm emphasized her point. "Who's to say I wouldn't have found somebody else with your initials?"

"He wouldn't have kissed you like this." Turning serious, Gladdie took her in his arms and caressed his lips against hers. He held her for all he was worth, letting the kiss linger so Drusie wouldn't forget his love for her. Judging from the way she relaxed in his arms and pressed her lips more urgently against his, he knew she would always remember him. "We'll marry as soon as you get back from your tour," he murmured between kisses.

"Do you mean that?" She peered into his eyes.

He held her more closely. "Yes. I ain't never meant nothin' more. I love you, Drusie. You understand me?" He broke off the kiss long enough to take a little box out of his trousers pocket. "I've got something here for you. I've been savin' money for it all along."

"Gladdie! I don't want you to spend your money on me!"

He shrugged. "Who else am I gonna spend it on?"

She looked into the little box. A heart-shaped pendant with the inscription I Love You glimmered against red satin. The pendant was set on a chain so thin it looked almost transparent. She gasped. "It's beautiful! Oh, I'll wear it always!"

"You better! Here, let me put it on you."

Drusie turned around and let him fasten the hook. The pendant hung daintily around her neck. "I love it! I'll sleep in it and everything!"

"You don't have to do that, as long as you don't forget how much I love you."

"I never will." She punctuated her promise with a sweet, tender kiss.

Gladdie would have kissed her back had they not been interrupted by someone clearing his throat. He turned to see Archie.

"So there you are. Sorry. I hate to break up the party, but your pa wants to see you, Gladdie. Right away."

Chapter 6

Gladdie wondered what Pa could want. Why had he sent Archie into the woods to find him? An ominous feeling visited Gladdie, but he tried to keep his voice light. "Sure, Archie." He took Drusie's hand. "Come on."

Archie shook his head. "He said he wants to see you alone. Sorry, Drusie. Gladdie, would you like me to walk her back to her house?"

"Sure." Gladdie swallowed. What could Pa want that meant he had to leave Drusie behind? He didn't like it. Not one bit.

"I hope everything's all right." Drusie's sentiment echoed his concern.

"It will be. Pray!" Gladdie blurted.

"I always do."

"At this rate, I'll even pray," Archie added. "Let's go, Drusie."

Gladdie approached his house with a sense of anxiety but kept putting one foot in front of the other until he heard Pa calling from the back. "There you are, Gladdie. Stay right there."

"Yes, sir."

Pa hollered out to the others that Gladdie had been found and to leave them be on the porch. Too fidgety to sit, Gladdie remained standing.

Soon his father appeared, looking fit and trim as always, his fine physique unable to be hidden by work clothes. Gladdie imagined he would look much like his pa if God allowed him to reach the age of forty-eight. So many years seemed a long way off.

"Sit down, son." Pa took a seat, and the tone of his voice demanded that Gladdie obey him.

"Yes, sir." Gladdie sat. "You wanted to see me?"

" 'Course I did. If I didn't, I wouldn't've called for ya." His eyes narrowed. "Now what's this I hear about you lettin' a woman earn your way?"

Hesitating, Gladdie didn't know what to say. The idea that Pa would object to their plans had never occurred to him. "Uh, is that what Ma told you?"

"No, but she did tell me you're plannin' to let Drusie go to Raleigh and sing to make money so you can buy the store. Is that right?"

"Yes, sir." Gladdie's stomach felt as though it was caught in a timber hitch knot.

Pa shook his head. "I'd've never believed such a thing if you hadn't've told me so yourself. That just won't do. Gordon men fend for themselves, and our womenfolk live on what we provide. If Drusie thinks she needs to live like a queen, she can make her own way, but you are not to take charity."

"Charity? I don't think of Drusie's singin' as charity. She's gonna be my wife." Seeing the hard look on Pa's face demoralized Gladdie. His pa had always been a stubborn soul, unwilling to accept help from anyone. Gladdie shouldn't have been surprised by his reaction, although he felt taken aback all the same. Gladdie reached for another argument. "I didn't ask her to go. She wants to go. Singin' in a band is her dream. Well, at least it is now that Archie's taken a mind to lettin' her and her sister form the NC Mountain Girls."

"So it was her idea to carry you. They even got a name for theirselves, huh?"

"Yes, sir." Gladdie hoped since the plans were already so far along that Pa wouldn't object further.

Gladdie's hopes evaporated when Pa shook his head again. "I wish them two girls the best, but all the same, I won't have people sayin' my boy had to take money from his intended like that."

He didn't want to argue with his father, but he saw no other way. "But Pa, how else am I gonna get to buy the store?"

"I've thought of that. I know you've had your eye to bein' a merchant for a long time now. Mr. Goode has been kind to you, even to the point of lettin' you have the day off so you could visit with Archie. Bein' exposed to the store like that, I can see why you got such an idea. And I think you'd be good at storekeepin', too. You got a head for figures, and people seem to like you right good."

Gladdie hadn't realized Pa had been paying so much attention to his hopes and dreams. The unaccustomed compliments from his pa, usually a taciturn man, pleased him. He took a moment to relish such golden words. "Thank you, Pa."

"Since you seem to have the ambition to make your dream come true, I think you have the determination not to waste money. So I have a plan." Pa leaned closer and lowered his voice. "Me and your ma, we got a few dollars saved up. I'll loan you the money. But you have to pay it back. With interest."

Gratitude, surprise, and excitement flooded Gladdie. "You—you'd do that for me?" He didn't recall Pa helping out his older brothers and sisters in such a manner.

"You're my son. Mebbe I'm gettin' soft in my old age. But you're my youngest, and time on this here earth is gettin' shorter and shorter for me with each passin' day. Experience has showed me that sometimes a man has to help his son out. But that don't mean all this is free. Like I said, you got to pay all the money back. If you don't, then the store's mine." Pa stood and extended his hand for a shake. "Deal?"

"Deal." Gladdie grasped his father's hand. "Thank you, Pa. I never would have thought you'd have enough money to help me out."

Mock insult covered Pa's face. "Why? Because we don't spend no more than

I make? We even manage to put away a few dollars every week. I'll bet a lot of them folks in Raleigh owe money to every merchant in town. They live high on the hog. We hill folk live simple and save up money for a rainy day."

"Maybe so." Gladdie grinned. "I'm gonna follow your advice, Pa, and save up my money, too. After I pay you back."

"You do that."

"Can I go tell Drusie now?" Gladdie paused and took in a breath. "You know what? This means Drusie don't have to leave after all! She can stay here, and we can get married right away!" He had to use all his restraint to keep from whooping and hollering.

Pa smiled. "You go right ahead. But don't stay too long at her house. You've got chores to do tomorrow mornin', and then we've got to go see Mr. Goode and make our offer."

They would be making Mr. Goode an offer! The idea made him dizzy with anticipation. Without delay, Gladdie took off for Drusie's. On the way, he met Archie.

"You're making tracks!" Archie observed. "What's your hurry?"

"I'll tell you as soon as I tell Drusie." Gladdie didn't stop. If he did, Archie was sure to pry the news out of him and try to talk him into letting Drusie go to Raleigh. "I'll tell you later."

Once he reached the house, Gladdie didn't knock on the Fieldses' front door but went in and hollered a greeting.

"Gladdie?" Drusie entered the parlor. "Whatcha doin' here? I warn't expectin' to see you again until mornin'." She grinned. "But I'm sure glad you're here. We hardly had time for a proper good-bye."

Gladdie rushed to her and took her hands in his. "We don't need no time for a proper good-bye."

"What do you mean?"

"We can get married right away!"

Drusie gasped, and Gladdie noticed that the moonlight streaming through the window caught her wide eyes. "Right away? Is that what you want?"

"Sure do."

She wrapped her arms around him. Setting her cool cheek against his, she spoke gently into his ear. "We can marry before I leave. Maybe Archie will stay another day or two and consent to be your best man. Clara will be my maid of honor." She broke the embrace and called her sister.

Clara responded by bounding in without pause. "I heard! Oh, this is keen, Drusie!"

"You eavesdropper, you!" With no accusation in her voice, Drusie hugged her sister.

"Wait," Gladdie said.

"Wait?" Drusie pushed away from her sister and looked at Gladdie as though he'd just suggested that Christmas was canceled. "I don't got no time to wait. I've got loads to do."

"You don't understand. Archie won't want to be my best man after what I have to say." Gladdie set Drusie down on the sofa, with Clara observing from a nearby chair. He told Drusie what had just transpired with his pa, omitting the prideful opinions he spouted about the Gordon men.

"So you can buy the store sooner than you thought," Drusie concluded. "You won't have to wait for me to earn the money. Oh, Gladdie, this is wonderful news!"

"And you know what this means, don't you?"

"Sure. We can get married now, just like you said."

"Yes, it does mean that," Gladdie agreed. "And somethin' else."

The smile disappeared from Drusie's face, replaced by curiosity. "What?"

"It means that you don't have to go to Raleigh after all. You can stay here and sing your sweet little heart out for me."

"Oh." Drusie dropped her hands from his.

"No!" Clara jumped from her seat in protest. "Drusie, you've got to go."

"But she don't need to go," Gladdie argued with fierceness even he didn't realize he felt. "We have the money for the store now. Don't you see, Clara? That's the only reason Drusie was goin' in the first place."

"You can still go," Gladdie pointed out to Clara. "It's just that Drusie don't need to go no more."

"Yes, she does," Clara whined. "Pa won't let either of us go alone. I've waited all my life for a chance to make good, and now I'm this close." She put her fore-finger and thumb a quarter inch apart.

"But Clara," Gladdie objected, "you didn't have no hankerin' to sing for pay before your pa came up with the idea."

"I know it, but now that I have the chance, I really want it. I want it real bad!" Clara exclaimed. "I cain't let anybody stand in my way now."

Clara ran to Drusie and took her by the shoulders. "Oh please, Drusie! You cain't let me down. Say you'll go. It won't be that long. No longer than you planned to start with."

Drusie's eyes lit with helplessness, and her posture slumped. "I don't know—"

"I do! You've got to go," Clara wailed.

Drusie turned to Gladdie. "I don't see no way out of it. You see for your-self how disappointed Clara will be if I cain't go. Not to mention, I'm sure Pa's already signed our contract. Please understand, Gladdie."

"But our plans—"

"I ain't gonna let nothin' happen to our plans," Drusie assured. "But if I don't go, and Clara loses her big chance all because of me, I'll never forgive myself.

And if you think about it real hard, you know years from now you'll never forgive yourself, either, if you keep Clara from goin'."

Gladdie tried not to glance at Clara, who no doubt would send him a mournful look if he did. He knew he wouldn't be able to stand it. "I don't like this," he murmured.

"I know," Drusie agreed. "Look at it this way. We can still use the extra money to set up our house. A store don't run itself without money. Why, I can even help you pay back your pa faster."

"I know. But I still don't like it. I don't like it one little bit."

Chapter 7

The next day before dawn, after excited and emotional farewells with their family, Clara and Drusie were headed out of the mountains toward the state capital. Drusie looked back at the only home she had ever known until it was out of sight, but Clara kept her focus on the road ahead—and on Archie. Drusie hadn't been surprised when her sister hopped into the front with Archie, leaving her in the back. But she had plenty of room and no desire to sit beside the record producer. Judging from the way Archie and Clara stole glances at each other from time to time, their initial attraction to one another hadn't ebbed.

Lord, help me keep Clara out of trouble.

If only Gladdie's love for her hadn't ebbed. Or had it? Couldn't he have stolen a few moments that morning to see her off?

Gladdie must be powerful mad.

Drusie slumped in her seat. Any excitement she once felt about the adventure had long since drained from her spirit. She could only hope—and pray—that time would heal Gladdie's anger. There was no other man for her. She had to come back to him. The sooner the better.

After they'd covered a few miles of crooked mountain roads, Clara took her attention from Archie long enough to look back at Drusie. "I'm sorry Gladdie didn't show up to say good-bye this mornin'."

"He took off a whole day to see Archie. Cain't expect him to live all the time like he ain't got no work to do." Drusie knew the excuse sounded puny, but she couldn't think of anything better to say.

"Maybe so." Clara's voice sounded unconvincing.

"Oh, it's all my fault," Drusie confessed.

"What's your story, morning glory?" Archie asked.

"Nothin'," Drusie answered.

"Oh, Gladdie got the money for the store from his pa, and now he's in a knot over us goin' with you," Clara explained to Archie. She shifted toward Drusie, draping her arm over the back of the front seat. "But don't you worry about that. Gladdie will come around."

"Sure he will." Archie barely slowed for a curve. "We'll be in salad days sure enough soon, and Gladdie won't regret letting Drusie go." He shrugged and glanced back at Drusie in the rearview mirror. "And if he does, well, you can keep all the money for yourself."

"I reckon that's your way of lookin' at things." Drusie tried to keep her voice from sounding too heavy, even though Archie's words didn't comfort her in the least. What was the use of having money if she couldn't share it with Gladdie?

Unwilling to dissect the past day's events further, Drusie stared out the window. The automobile seemed to fly by houses and trees. As they rode down a wide valley, she noticed that most of the trees in this part of the state were still green. Drusie had been hoping to enjoy the drive to Raleigh. She'd never been so far from home and wanted to see a different part of North Carolina at a pace where she could breathe in its beauty. But the way Archie drove, she wondered if they'd even get to their destination in one piece.

Later they passed the courthouse square in Burlington and followed the railroad line east. The drive lasted hour after hour, but since she was so enamored by the idea of seeing the state and because Archie sped along, the ride almost seemed short. Before she knew it, they had reached Raleigh.

Streets hummed with people who all seemed to have somewhere important to go. The buildings and houses were so close together compared to where she grew up that Drusie found herself feeling a mite closed in by it all. Many of the houses looked like mansions, but Drusie couldn't imagine being happy in any of them. How could anybody live in town, when some of the yards didn't cover as much as an acre? She held back a shudder. Excitement sparked the air, but Drusie longed for the solitude of home.

In contrast, Clara caught a flying bolt of energy before they passed the welcome sign. "Look at all the people! All the stores! Sunshine Holler sure does look slow after bein' here."

Archie chuckled. "You'll get used to it."

Clara eyed a woman wearing a fine wool coat trimmed in fur and a matching hat. "I hope we get to stay long enough for me to get used to it."

"I'm not sure I ever will." Drusie observed what looked like a near miss between two automobiles. Thankfully Archie's Auburn wasn't one of them.

"Where will we be stayin'?" Clara asked.

Drusie hadn't thought of that. Archie seemed to have the world at his command. His swaggering confidence never let up. Surely he had a plan.

He did. "I let all of my out-of-town canaries stay at Mrs. Smyth's Boardinghouse. She only accepts women boarders. I talked to her last week and told her I might be bringing her another lady. She's just set aside one room. You two don't mind sharing, do you?"

"Of course not," Clara said as Drusie nodded. "We share a room at home."

"Good," Archie quipped, "because you'll be sharing a room on the road, too." He glanced at Clara. "Feel like doing a little shopping before I take you to the boardinghouse?"

"Sure!" Eagerness colored her voice.

"Unless you'd like to grab a bite to eat first."

Clara shook her head. "I'm not hungry."

"Good. We can get started." Archie turned left at the next block.

Drusie noticed that Archie didn't seem to care much about her feelings. But then again, if she cared what boardinghouse they slept at, whether they ate, or what store they shopped at, she could always speak up.

Archie pulled in front of a store. ROSE'S FINERY was painted in lime-colored script on the front glass. "This is where I outfit all my stars. She keeps some inventory on hand for me, and she'll alter any dress you like to fit."

Clara clapped her hands, reminding Drusie of when she got a coveted doll for her sixth birthday. "A dress! I get a new dress already?"

He sent her an indulgent smile. "Maybe even two."

They headed into the shop, and moments later, Clara held up a red dress with silver and gold sequins sewn on the bodice. "I love it! Isn't it beautiful?"

Drusie inspected the garment. "I don't know. Isn't it a little low cut?"

"It won't show nothin'. I wouldn't wear nothin' I wouldn't want Grandpappy to see me in."

Rose, a gray-haired woman whose appearance hinted at youthful beauty, chimed in, "Your grandfather would be proud of you in this." She swept her hand in a motion toward racks of attention-getting clothes fit for any stage. "Any of my dresses here would do you proud." She aimed her forefinger at Archie. "That reminds me, Elmer's shirt is ready."

"Good. I'll see that he gets it."

"Will he need another one since you'll be on the road?"

"Not yet. But I might have to place an order for a new band member. That is, if I decide to hire a skin tickler," Archie mused.

"A skin tickler?" Clara asked.

Archie chuckled. "That's a drummer. I think you girls would sound fine with a harmonica and maybe a second fiddle. Even bass. I've got a man in mind who's good on bass and harmonica."

Clara took her gaze from the dress and concentrated on Archie. "You mean there's gonna be some men in the NC Mountain Girls Band?"

"Well, yes. But you two will be the stars. How could I have two beautiful girl singers onstage and not make them the center of attention?" Archie asked. "Especially if you'll be wearing that pretty dress, Clara."

Clara giggled and held up the dress. "You like it?"

"Looks good on the rack. How's about letting me see you in it? And you try on a dress, too, Drusie. If I'm fronting you canaries the money to buy these dresses, I think I'm entitled to see if they look good."

The last thing Drusie wanted was to let Archie ogle her in a fancy dress, but she realized he had a point. Rose had promised to alter the dresses if they didn't fit, and once they were on the road, sewing wouldn't be easy.

Moments later, each sister emerged in a sparkling frock.

Archie let out a low whistle. "You two look sweet. Not doggy at all."

"I agree!" Rose said with the eagerness of a clerk wanting to close a sale. She tugged at the sash on Clara's waist. "Looks like a perfect fit for you." She inspected the shoulders and waist on Drusie's frock. "You, too." Rose shook her head in disbelieving admiration. "You girls have perfect figures. You're lucky."

"I don't know about luck," Drusie observed. "We just do the best we can with what God gave us."

"And a fine job you do at that," Archie quipped.

Clara twirled. "I've never felt so wonderful as I do right at this moment."

"This is nothing. Just wait until you're onstage with adoring crowds applauding your every note." He nodded to the storekeeper. "Hows about another one for Clara, Rose? Oh, and Drusie, too."

Rose's eyes shone. "I have just the thing. A gold gown with sequins in neat little rows all along the skirt and sleeves."

"Sequins! They look fine on Clara, but for me?" Drusie hadn't given such a daring choice any thought. "I don't know. What do you think, Clara?"

"Oh, I would love for all my gowns to have sequins!"

Rose stood back and admired her handiwork. "They do show up well onstage."

"But do I have to be all sequined?" Drusie scrunched her nose.

Archie chuckled. "I thought you'd like to dress pretty."

Drusie shook her head and watched her sister try on one fancy dress after another. Clara enjoyed every moment of seeing herself and being admired in different outfits. Drusie settled for the only two she tried, happy to have those.

Later, Clara clutched her dress box to her chest as they rode to the boardinghouse. She wouldn't even let Archie put the dresses in the trunk of the car, saying she didn't want to let them out of her sight.

"I've never seen you so excited," Drusie commented.

"I've never been so excited. You don't seem thrilled at all, but I'm not gonna let that spoil my fun."

"Enjoy the fun all you like, because it won't last long. Now we have to work," Archie said. "First thing tomorrow morning we're going to the studio and record your songs."

⚭

Gladdie counted six pickled eggs that Mrs. Cunningham ordered, but his mind wasn't on his task. If only he hadn't let Drusie leave without telling her good-bye. He missed her, and the way they left things so uncertain left him longing to see her again. He wanted nothing more than to straighten everything out with her, to kiss her lips again, and to murmur into her ear how much he still wanted to marry her. But he couldn't. At least, not yet.

He handed the customer a mason jar containing the eggs. "Will there be anything else, Mrs. Cunningham?"

She ignored her child's plea for penny candy and counted the eggs. "Yes. One more egg."

Embarrassed, he took the jar she handed him and recounted them. "There sure is one missin'. I'm sorry."

"Sorry that Drusie's left, aren't ya? Cain't concentrate on a thing?" The matron's voice poured out in a sympathetic tone.

"Word does get around." He was glad the task of retrieving one more egg kept him from having to look at her.

"Yep. Fast around this place. Well, I hope she comes back. I'm sure she won't find no other man." One of the Cunningham tots pulled on her skirt. Mrs. Cunningham smiled and grabbed her package. "Put that on my bill."

"Yes, ma'am."

As she hurried out, Gladdie scratched a figure onto the ledger. He wished Mrs. Cunningham hadn't made such a suggestion. He hadn't thought that Drusie might start looking at city slickers with new eyes now that he'd been so mean to her.

Drusie, what have I done?

❧

The sisters spent a comfortable night at Mrs. Smyth's large house, yet sadness permeated Drusie. The reality of her decision had made itself evident. Now she'd give anything for a chance to turn back the clock just a few days, before big ideas about making money for Gladdie to buy the store got into her head. Then she'd still be home, planning to marry Gladdie. She would have been plenty happy no matter what, as long as she was Mrs. Gladdie Gordon. Now she was all alone, living a life she wasn't sure she wanted. And she had no one to blame but herself.

Soon Drusie was distracted by Archie's arrival. Clara brightened in his presence, but all Drusie could see was a long day of work ahead. In no time at all, Archie drove Clara and her into town and parked in front of a nondescript storefront. The tiny, dark studio was nothing like Drusie had imagined. Judging from Clara's lack of a smile, Drusie guessed she was disappointed in the dingy surroundings, too.

Still, the session ran without a hitch. Elmer, a fiddler, looked suave in his cowboy hat. The harmonica player, Al, was a dumpy man who showed them pictures of his children. The musicians seemed pleasant enough, and their demeanor soothed Drusie. Elmer and Al knew all the tunes Archie suggested, and after repeated practice, he deemed them harmonious enough to record. They were to play the song three times all the way through. Archie would make wax recordings of each set and decide later which was the best "take" to produce.

The sisters recorded an old ballad on one side and a gospel tune on the other.

"Good work! Like eggs in coffee." Archie rubbed his palms together. "You'll sound like a million bucks on the radio."

"The radio!" Suddenly Drusie felt nervous. She hadn't considered that people would be listening to them on the radio. All those faceless people sitting in front of boxes in their houses, playing music. What would they think of the NC Mountain Girls?

"Sure you'll be on the radio. How else will people get to know your music? Except for touring, of course. And you'll be singing on live radio, too. Our timing couldn't be better. You'll be joining our tour with the Country Bills and the Sweet Carolinas." Archie looked triumphant.

Clara jumped up and down. "How excitin'!"

For the first time in memory, Drusie wished she had failed. If they hadn't sounded good, then Archie would have sent them home. Against her will, Drusie remembered the other girls back home, with their covetous glances sent Gladdie's way. Sure, he loved only Drusie, but in her absence, would they try awfully hard to convince him to change his mind? Swallowing, she wished more than ever she could go home.

Gladdie, what have I done?

Chapter 8

A couple of days later, a caravan of cars met in front of Archie's house to hit the road for the first leg of the tour. The three groups formed a show. They had scheduled performances at radio stations, high school auditoriums, and churches in North Carolina towns. Drusie could only hope she'd be traveling slowly enough to observe the scenery. At least the first day looked hopeful with crystal blue skies and clouds that reminded her of the cotton puffs she kept on her dresser at home.

After suitcases and musical equipment were loaded into automobile trunks, Archie introduced the sisters to the members of the other bands, people they hadn't met during rehearsals. They had already met Al and Elmer, who would be playing backup for all of them. Homer, Orville, and Buford, the trio that called themselves the Country Bills, greeted them kindly but dismissed Clara and Drusie almost as soon as they were introduced. The two young women they approached afterward were a different story.

"June and Betty, I'd like you to meet Drusie and Clara." Archie nodded toward a voluptuous woman whose hair was dyed almost white. "They're part of the Sweet Carolinas."

Clara stood close to Archie. A little too closely, apparently. Drusie saw June's painted eyes shooting daggers at Clara, but Clara seemed too excited by the day's promise to notice.

"How long will you be tourin' with us, honey?" June asked Clara.

"As long as Archie says." Clara gazed at Archie with the adoring look of a schoolgirl fawning over a favored teacher.

"I hope you can keep up," June noted. "Archie works us all right hard. Don't you, Archie?"

Drusie sensed that June was trying to get some hidden message across to Archie, but he didn't seem to notice. He didn't seem to notice much of anything except how to get them going with as much efficiency as possible. With such a businesslike demeanor, Archie hardly seemed intent on intrigue, romantic or otherwise. Drusie could only pray she had misinterpreted June's hard attitude toward Clara.

⚭

Several days later, the caravan had traveled deep into tobacco country, although the fields lay bare since the leaves had long since been harvested. They had already performed five nights, twice on Saturday, and that night they were scheduled to perform at the county high school and had stopped at a motel on Route 1 long enough to dress before heading out to the school.

"Clara, have you seen my necklace?" Drusie asked.

"What necklace?" Clara responded.

"The gold chain Gladdie gave me. You know, the one with the little heart pendant."

"Oh, that. I don't know how anybody can lose anything, with us bein' more cramped than sardines in a tin."

"At least in this cottage, we ain't sharin' walls with anybody else."

Clara scrunched her nose. "True. In some of the places we stayed, I learned more than I ever wanted to about my band mates, hearin' every conversation through the walls." Combing her hair, she sighed. "I wish we was stayin' in better places."

"This ain't as high on the hog as you imagined, huh?" Drusie rifled through the compartments in her suitcase for the umpteenth time, hoping she might have missed her necklace. "Well, we ain't big stars that can waste money on highfalutin hotel rooms yet. Might never be."

"I don't know. People seem to like us right good. And Archie says he's happy with us." A dreamy look covered her expression. "Archie says after we finish up this tour, we might travel to even more places!"

"Imagine!" Drusie shut her suitcase. "I wonder where that necklace could be?" Her tone sounded as desperate as she felt.

"I don't see how you lost it since you never take it off."

"I do have to take it off when I bathe—and when we perform since it don't go with them fancy dresses you and Archie picked out."

Clara shrugged. "Maybe the clasp came open and you didn't realize it fell off. I'm sure it'll turn up."

"I don't see how I could have misplaced somethin' that important."

"There's no time to look for it now. We've got to be at the automobile in ten minutes." Clara set her comb in her purse and checked her reflection.

"You don't need to stare at yourself in the mirror all the time. You always look good," Drusie assured her.

Clara surveyed her sister. "You should look in the mirror more. Your lipstick is crooked."

Drusie inspected herself. Indeed, one corner of her mouth did appear a bit higher than the other. "I hate this old face paint. I cain't get used to it. And it feels so funny to have a coatin' of stuff on my lips all the time."

Clara laughed. "I kind of like it. This is the only time I can wear face paint without Pa callin' me a harlot."

"I don't know how crazy he'd be about us wearin' paint at all, even to sing.

Maybe especially to sing. I wish Archie didn't insist."

"It's just part of the business, Drusie."

"I'll be glad when this tour is over."

"I won't. I could go on like this forever."

They heard a rap on the dressing room door before June entered. "Archie says we gotta get a move on if we want to start the show on time."

"We're almost ready." Drusie decided to grab at the proverbial straw. "Hey, you ain't seen my pendant necklace by chance, have you? The one I wear all the time?"

June's gaze traveled to the hollow of Drusie's neck. "Sure haven't. You lost it?"

"Naw," Clara quipped, "she's just askin' dumb questions to see who'll give the smartest answer."

"Now, Clara," Drusie admonished her sister. As she turned her attention back to June, she saw her make a face at Clara but decided to ignore such schoolgirl antics. "I sure did lose it, and I'd be grateful if you could let me know if you see it anywhere. Can you ask Betty for me, too?"

"Sure thing. But right now, we'd better hustle unless we want Archie to dock our pay." She shut the door behind her.

"She took your necklace! I just know it." Clara snapped shut her compact.

"Oh, pshaw. I know you don't like June since she's got eyes for Archie—"

"So you noticed, huh?" Clara wrinkled her nose. "She hangs on to him like a cheap suit, but he don't pay her no mind."

Drusie blew out a breath. "You ain't here to make enemies. You're here to sing. Try to remember that. And remember somethin' else. Just because you don't like her none don't mean she's a thief."

"I know. I almost wish she was. Then Archie would have an excuse to kick her off the tour."

"You don't want that to happen. We're not famous enough to be headliners yet. We ain't able to fill an auditorium by ourselves."

Clara sniffed. "Well, maybe I can put up with her, then. Someday I'll be even more famous than her. I'm already prettier."

Drusie would have admonished Clara if she didn't know her sister well enough to realize she spoke at least partly in jest. She shook her head and watched Clara admire herself in the looking glass. She was definitely enjoying her newfound celebrity and the attention she gleaned from it. Watching Clara apply a fresh coat of red lip rouge, Drusie felt led to pray that Clara wouldn't let fame carry her astray.

❧

The week drew to a close, but no break was in sight for the tour. To Drusie, it seemed Archie had booked them in every town and venue possible. They were getting well known, though, and Archie said their record sales were up.

That wasn't all that was up. Drusie had caught Archie giving Clara a quick kiss on the lips, supposedly for good luck. The gesture had left Clara so disoriented that once they were performing, Drusie had to guide her through the second chorus of "When God Dips His Pen of Love in My Heart," a song they had sung since they were girls.

Drusie's feelings about Archie and Clara forming a bond were mixed. On the one hand, despite the age difference of a few years, they seemed to get along well, and she could see them working side by side as a married couple, in love with music and with each other. On the other hand, there was June. Jealousy sparked in her eyes whenever Clara entered the room. Even though she'd never seen Archie and June in any exchange that didn't involve business, Drusie had a feeling Archie was pushing June aside for Clara. She could only pray that Archie's feelings toward her sister were true and that the turnabout in romantic inclinations was part of God's plan. She didn't like June much, but she didn't want to see her heart broken, either. Drusie kept them all in her prayers.

∽

Gladdie swept the floor of Goode's Mercantile with energetic motions.

"You keep on like that and we'll have us a dust storm," Mr. Goode observed from behind the counter.

"I'm sorry. I'll try to be more gentle." He slowed his pace, knowing that he had gotten caught up in thoughts of the future and had started sweeping too rapidly as a result. He didn't want to admit how he couldn't wait for the day when Mr. Goode's name would be replaced with his own.

The shop bell tinkled, signaling the arrival of a new customer. Gladdie looked and saw two men he didn't know. They were dressed in the same style of suit that Archie wore. Tourists from out of town, no doubt.

He propped his broom against the counter and swiped his hands against his trouser legs. "Mornin', gentlemen. What might I help you with today?"

"Nothing, Gladdie," Mr. Goode said. "They're here to see me."

"Oh!" Gladdie retrieved his broom faster than a fly escaping a swatter. "Sorry," he muttered.

Mr. Goode tilted his head toward the men but kept his gaze on Gladdie. "We've got some business to tend to, son, so I'll be taking my friends across the street to the diner."

"Yes, sir." Gladdie wondered what could be so important that Mr. Goode, never one to spend an extra dime, would be treating strangers to lunch.

Mr. Goode eyed the display of sewing notions. "Now you go on and hold down the fort here. And in between customers, hows about you making sure the buttons are sorted? The Billings girls were playing in them today, and I suspect they misplaced some."

"Yes, sir."

287

Mr. Goode smiled and addressed his visitors. "He's a mighty fine worker, that one is."

"Looks like it," one of the men agreed. "He seems to be an asset for you."

Mr. Goode didn't comment but rushed the men out. Gladdie wondered why he never introduced his friends from out of town.

∞

An hour before the show, Archie rapped on the dressing room door. "Drusie! Telephone for you. Long distance."

She stopped powdering her face. "Long distance!"

"Long distance?" Clara echoed with equal surprise. "I hope nothin's wrong at home."

"Me, too."

"Don't blow your wig," Archie cautioned. "Just go to the business office and take the call. Then you'll have your answer."

"You have a point," Drusie conceded and hurried to the office. Archie showed her the telephone that was almost lost amid papers and a cup of coffee that still left its scent in the room. She picked up the heavy black receiver. "Hello?"

"Drusie?"

She could barely hear the disembodied voice that sounded like it came from another world, but the sweet tone was recognizable to her ears. "Gladdie! Is that you?"

"Sure is. You sound mighty winded. You okay?"

"Sure I am. I just had to run from my dressin' room to the auditorium's business office."

"Oh. I've been tryin' to reach you for several days now, but I couldn't never catch up with you. Y'all are movin' right fast through the countryside."

"We sure are. Is everything all right? I know this telephone call is costin' plenty. You callin' from the store?"

"Sure am."

"Mr. Goode will be dockin' your wages when the bill comes, then."

"I know it. But it's worth it," he assured her.

"Is everybody okay? Have you seen Ma and Pa?"

"They're just fine. Your ma was in the store yesterday, buyin' rickrack. I told her I'd be talkin' to you soon."

She leaned against the wooden desk. "Tell Ma and Pa I love 'em and miss 'em. Will you do that for me?"

"Sure will." He paused. "Drusie, I'm sorry about the way we left things."

She didn't hesitate. "Me, too."

"Really?"

"Really. I've been prayin' about it. You know, I wish I was there instead of here."

"I should've come to say good-bye to you the mornin' you left. I'll never let anything like that happen again."

"That's all in the past." She sighed. "I never should've gotten so greedy and gotten such big ideas in my head."

"You weren't greedy. You were just tryin' to help me. And I'll always love you for that."

Touched, she figured he planned to end the call there. But an intake of his breath told her otherwise.

"Will you come home as soon as the tour's over?"

"That's my plan."

"You won't let them city slickers charm you too much, will you?"

Drusie laughed. "City slickers? What gave you such a silly notion?"

"Oh, nothin'."

"Seen Edna Sue around lately?" she couldn't resist asking.

"She's been in the store once or twice. Why?"

Puzzlement in his tone and his nonchalant answer assured Drusie that if Edna Sue had set her sights on Gladdie in a big way, he still wasn't paying her any mind. "Just wondered."

"Oh, Bertha and Gertie said to tell you hello. They miss you in Sunday school class."

"I miss them, too."

"Drusie?"

"Yes?"

"I'd like it a powerful lot if you'd write to me."

She smiled into the receiver. "I will from now on, every day."

"I'll wait for the postman to come every day, then," he promised. "I love you, Drusie."

"I love you, too, Gladdie."

When she hung up, Drusie knew that once again all was right with her world.

The good feeling was shattered by Clara's scream.

Chapter 9

Drusie ran in the direction of the shriek and soon entered the door of their dressing room. Clara stood in front of her favorite dress that hung on a rack, waiting to be donned for the performance. Archie and Elmer hovered in the background, also having responded to Clara's cry of distress.

"What's wrong?" they all asked.

Clara picked up the hem of her red dress and held out the skirt for them to examine. "Look." Her voice caught on that one word, and Drusie realized that her sister could utter no more.

As soon as she viewed the skirt, Drusie could see why Clara had screamed. Holes about a half inch in diameter, encircled by brown rings, marred the fabric. "Looks like somebody burned your skirt with a cigarette."

Archie viewed the damage. "Whoever did this didn't just burn the dress. It's been attacked—viciously. There are even holes in the top."

Clara let go of the hem and wailed. "I cain't possibly wear this."

Archie groaned. "All that money down the drain."

Drusie suspected June was the culprit, but speculation would do them no good this close to showtime. She did note that June was nowhere around. No doubt she had busied herself with a fictitious errand so she wouldn't be nearby when Clara discovered the deed.

Clara dabbed a handkerchief at her eyes in an obvious attempt to keep tears from destroying the face paint she had applied. "My beautiful dress! What am I gonna do?"

"Simple. Wear the other one," Archie suggested. "You look beautiful in them both."

Clara nodded and took the other dress out of its garment bag. When they saw holes in that dress, too, everyone let out a gasp. This time Clara didn't bother to catch her tears. They streamed down her face.

Archie took her in a loose embrace. Drusie couldn't help but notice that the gesture didn't seem romantic. With witnesses, no doubt Archie planned it that way. "That's okay, doll. I'll buy you another dress."

"You can borrow mine tonight," Drusie said.

Clara brightened. "I—I can?" Just as quickly her smile evaporated. "But Drusie, you don't have but one dress, do you?"

Drusie remembered that she had dropped off her green dress at a local

290

seamstress's shop to have a ribbon reattached. The shop had long since closed. "That's okay. You can wear the fancy dress. I'll just wear what I've got on." She looked down at her red gingham dress. While clean, flattering, and serviceable, the frock didn't compare to anything with sequins.

"That won't look right, with one of you in sequins and the other in something so plain," Archie said.

"I don't care." Drusie's voice came out with more defiance than she intended. "We ain't gonna let nobody get us down. Somebody don't want Clara to go out there in her good dress, and she's just about succeeded. But I don't care if I have to wear rags—Clara's gonna look like a million bucks." Drusie crossed her arms and rooted her foot to make herself look as rigid as possible.

"You said 'she,'" Archie noticed. "You think you know who did this?"

"I have an idea—June," Clara said.

"June?" Archie laughed. "I don't think she'd do that."

"You don't, do you?" Elmer guffawed. "Then you don't know much about women, Archie. She's been madder than a bull in a pen ever since you brought Clara here."

Archie shot Elmer a dirty look. "Aw, June must have caught us in a honey cooler."

"Honey cooler?" Drusie queried.

Archie shuffled his foot. "You know—a kiss."

"So there's been more than one?" Drusie blurted.

"Never mind that." Clara's cheeks blazed, a sure sign that "honey coolers" had been the rule of the day with them.

Drusie wished she had kept a closer eye on her sister, but if Clara was determined to kiss Archie, Drusie could do little to stop her.

"Before we got here, were you and June a couple?" Clara asked Archie.

"No. As far as I'm concerned, she's just another canary."

Drusie turned to Elmer. "Do you think June had reason to think otherwise?"

"Aw, you see how women act around Archie. He draws the ladies like bees to honey. But I never saw him treat June different from anybody else. And if you don't believe me, I'll swear on the Bible."

"You don't have to go that far, Elmer," Drusie said. "Archie, you better not be playin' my sister for a fool."

"I'm not. I swear. You can bring me a Bible, too, if you want."

Drusie discerned more from Archie's plaintive expression and clear tone of voice than from his willingness to swear on the Bible. "Okay. But if you are, you'll be answerin' to our pa."

"Considering what a good shot he is with that rifle of his, I know I don't want to cross him." Archie's half grin conveyed levity, but Drusie knew he was serious. He drew his watch from his pocket and glanced at its face. "It's getting

291

late. Elmer and I had better take a powder so you girls can get dressed." With that, the men exited.

Clara gave Drusie a light embrace. "I'll never forget you for doin' this."

"I hope you'll never forget me anyway," Drusie joked.

Clara's gaze met Drusie's. "Are you mad at me for not tellin' you about Archie and me?"

"You was afraid I'd tell Pa and you'd have to go home, warn't you?"

"I was. Are you gonna tell him? Archie said if he found out, that would be the end of the tour."

"I don't care half as much about this tour as I care about you. Do you really think Archie loves you?" Drusie searched her sister's face. "I know we all grew up together, but Archie is a little older than you, and as adults you haven't known each other all that long."

"I do think Archie loves me. I—I know he does. But you know somethin'— I cain't think about marryin' him until his heart softens toward the Lord more. I think he got mad at God for takin' his parents so long ago, and he ain't been back to the Lord since."

"Nothin's too big to handle with God's help, but I can understand why a little boy would get mad and confused over such tragedy. But he's a grown man now, and it's high time he changed his outlook." Drusie stared at the wall but didn't think about the faded yellow paint. She could only feel sadness at Archie's loss and say a quick, silent prayer that his heart would change. Her prayer led her to express an idea. "Clara, maybe you can be the one to lead him back to God."

"I've thought of that." Clara looked down at her skirt. "And I've thought of somethin' else. I cain't kiss him anymore unless I plan to marry him. It just ain't right."

Drusie sent her sister a knowing smile. "I'm glad Ma and Pa don't have to be here for you to know right from wrong. I know if God wants you and Archie to be together, you will be. . .someday."

"I wouldn't tell this to nobody else, but I hope so. He hinted that he'd like to marry me someday, but I didn't do nothin' to take him up on his offer."

Drusie moved to give her sister a hug. "It'll all work out. You'll see. Now come on. We got a show to do."

Onstage later, Drusie couldn't help but feel self-conscious as she appeared in gingham while her sister shone in sequins. She surveyed the audience, even though she wasn't able to see much with spotlights flooding the stage and the people watching them sitting in relative darkness. She did eye a brunette in fur. The woman had been following them lately. She seemed to brighten whenever the men took to the stage. Drusie held back a smile. The men attracted quite a few female admirers.

Without meaning to, Drusie wondered how many male fans came to see them. She was glad she would never have to find out. Archie made sure they were protected from any bold men who might have been looking for more than an autograph.

Clara took to the spotlight like a duck to water. She couldn't remember when her sister had sung with a voice as pure and sweet. Clearly, onstage life suited her. She always approached each new performance with anticipation. Drusie, on the other hand, felt dread. Singing for the folks at home—her friends and family—was one thing. Entertaining strangers made her nervous.

Maybe I should let her be the star all the time.

Drusie made a point of observing June, who sat with her partner, Betty, along with the Country Bills, as they awaited their turn. At first the blond wore a triumphant grin when Drusie took to the stage in her plain dress. June's mouth turned into a red slash as soon as Clara appeared in her stage attire. June puffed with more vigor on her cigarette and glared at her competition. Yes, June was the culprit.

An unpleasant thought occurred to Drusie. She had no doubt that June was out to cause trouble. Could she have taken her necklace?

∞

Gladdie always made a point of arriving a few minutes before the store's opening, a fact Mr. Goode had said time and time again he greatly appreciated. As soon as Gladdie entered, Mr. Goode wasted no time in greeting him. "Gladdie, I've got some news. It's time for us to talk."

"Be right with you, sir." Gladdie hung his coat and hat on their customary hook with as much nonchalance as he could muster, contrary to his shaking hands and rapid heartbeat.

Not one for idle chatter or gossip, Mr. Goode never said he had news unless the message was important. Surely he was about to say that he planned to accept Pa's offer for the store and that Gladdie would soon be the owner. In his mind, he rehearsed one last time how he would assure Mr. Goode that he would do Sunshine Hollow proud and keep up the fine level of quality and service their customers had grown to expect. He still wasn't sure he could promise he wouldn't change the name of the store to reflect his ownership. Surely Mr. Goode would understand Gladdie's desire to tell the world he was finally his own boss.

In an uncustomary move, Mr. Goode sat by the potbellied stove and poured himself a cup of coffee. Normally he'd finished his morning beverage long before Gladdie arrived. "Have a cup?" Mr. Goode asked.

"No, thank you, sir. I had plenty at breakfast this mornin'." He didn't want to admit that he couldn't imagine drinking or eating anything at the moment. Anticipation had brightened his spirit but dulled his appetite.

"Sit down, son." Mr. Goode motioned to the empty oak rocker by the stove.

"Yes, sir." He obeyed even though he would rather have stood.

Mr. Goode took a swig of black coffee. "I suppose I might have summoned your pa in here, but I figured you and I could talk like men."

The admission made Gladdie's heart beat faster than ever. The mention of his pa could only mean one thing—that the store would soon be his. "I can relay whatever message Pa needs to hear. He knows he can trust me."

"I know it." The elder man took another swig slowly. A little too slowly.

Gladdie wondered why he was so reticent to relay welcome news. *Maybe he's just now realizin' how sad he'll be to leave the store forever.*

Mr. Goode cleared his throat. "I reckon you recall that not too long ago, a couple of men came here to the store and we all went out to lunch."

"Yes, sir. They were dressed in nice suits, the kind like my cousin Archie wears."

"I know they didn't look like they belonged here in these parts, and there's a good reason for that. They don't. They were here from out of town on business." He paused.

"Business?" A sick feeling visited the pit of Gladdie's stomach.

"Yep. They were representin' some buyers from out of town. Buyers of the store."

"Oh." Gladdie didn't know what to say. Surely Mr. Goode wouldn't sell the store out from under him. Not when he knew how much he wanted to go into business for himself. Yet when Mr. Goode stopped looking at him, Gladdie knew what had happened. He had accepted their offer.

"Gladdie, I know you and your pa thought I'd sell to you, and if you want to know the truth, I'd planned to. But none of us shook hands on the deal, so when this other offer came in, I had to take it."

"They're payin' a powerful lot of money, ain't they?" Gladdie's voice registered just above a whisper.

Mr. Goode nodded. "More than I know you and your pa could ever pay."

"But why? I mean, this here store is swell for Sunshine Holler, but it don't make enough money to impress people from out of town. Does it?"

"Well, they said that the people they represent want to live here now. They love the mountains and they have family here."

"What family?"

"I don't rightly know." Mr. Goode shrugged. "I reckon all will be clear before you know it."

Gladdie tried to digest what the storekeeper said, but disappointment clouded his reasoning. All he could do was fight back bitterness and anger. He tensed his hands against the chair rails to keep them from balling up into fists.

Mr. Goode leaned forward in his seat. "You know I think of you like a son, but I had to take the money. My daughter in Raleigh ain't rich, and she'll need whatever the sale of the store brings for the two of us to live. Trust me, she's grateful. And so am I."

"I understand," Gladdie forced himself to answer.

"I did look out for you. I told them you're a mighty fine clerk and that the new owners would be powerful foolish not to keep you on."

"Thank you." Gladdie knew the tone of his voice was like that of a little boy who'd gotten a doll for Christmas instead of a bike, but he couldn't muster much gratitude, try as he might.

"I know this is a disappointment for you and your family, and I'm sorry about that. But at least you still have a job. I'm sure they'll keep you on. And in these tough times, a job is somethin' to be grateful for." Mr. Goode finished his coffee and stood. "Now let's get to work."

Gladdie knew he'd seen all the sentiment Mr. Goode would be able to summon. He had to follow his orders. Having to tell Pa that Mr. Goode had sold the store out from under them was bad enough; he didn't want to tell him he'd lost his job, too. When he heard the news, Gladdie imagined Pa would call Mr. Goode a snake, but other than harbor ill will, there was nothing they could do. Nothing. And Gladdie knew the Bible forbade them even the luxury of hard feelings.

"Forgive us our trespasses, as we forgive those who trespass against us."

Yes, he would have to forgive Mr. Goode whether he wanted to or not. And he would. Surely Pa would, too. . .given time.

For once Gladdie felt glad Drusie was on tour. He wasn't ready to tell her yet that they'd have to find a different way to make good in Sunshine Hollow.

❧

"You girls sure pleased the crowd tonight," Archie praised Drusie and Clara after the show.

"Oh, Archie! Each show is even more excitin' than the last one," Clara proclaimed, looking up into his face. "I never get tired of singin' for a crowd."

"You wouldn't be just telling me that now, would you?"

"Oh no! I really mean it!"

Archie laughed. "I know you do. I was just jesting."

Elmer chose that moment to enter. " 'Scuse me for interrupting, but Al's feelin' mighty poorly. He don't look so good, either."

"I thought he looked a mite peaked this evenin'," Drusie observed.

Archie scowled. "He's been telling me he's under the weather, but I hoped he could hold on. I don't need him dropping out and gumming up the works."

"He cain't help it if he's sick," Drusie pointed out.

"Yeah, I know. Elmer, have you called a doctor?"

Elmer nodded. "There was a doctor in the house, and he says Al needs to go home. He's got pneumonia."

"Pneumonia!" Drusie said. "This is terrible!"

"You said it!" Archie blurted. "Elmer, can you see to it that Al's taken to the hospital? I'll get everyone here rounded up and see if I can figure out a way to get another harmonica player."

"Will we have to cancel the tour if we cain't find anybody?" Clara asked.

"No, but your sound really changes without a harmonica. Wonder who we can get now?"

Drusie didn't hesitate. "Gladdie is a great harmonica player."

"He sure is!" Clara confirmed.

"That's swell, but doesn't he work at a store?" Archie asked.

"Yes, but I can ask him what he thinks of joinin' us," Drusie offered. "He knows every song Clara and I sing even better than we do."

"I won't argue with you on that." Clara twisted a stray curl. "But won't that interfere with Mr. Goode trainin' him to take over?"

"Well, that's not a done deal yet," Drusie admitted. "The last time we talked over the telephone, Gladdie said that Mr. Goode listened to the offer he and his pa made, but he ain't accepted it as of yet. But once the store's sold, Gladdie will be tied to it right good. So I have a notion that him takin' a little break to join our tour for a week or two may be just the thing for all concerned."

"Snazzy," Archie said. "We can stay put while we get you girls new dresses and wait for Gladdie to catch up with us. If we play our cards right, we can make up the time on the road without havin' to cancel a performance. I can let the radio station know we need to perform in the afternoon instead of morning."

All that planning made Drusie dizzy, but she could see that Archie had confidence in what he said.

Archie directed his attention to Drusie. "Why don't you use the telephone in the office to call Gladdie first thing tomorrow? You should be able to catch him at the store."

∞

"You told Drusie you'd do what?" Gladdie's father was so taken aback that some of the slop missed the pig trough.

Gladdie made sure to be more careful with his bucket. He didn't need Pa fussing at him about the pig slop on top of everything else. At least he'd thought far enough ahead to break the news to Pa while they were busy with chores. With bucket in hand, Pa couldn't throttle him.

If he was going to be a man, he had to act like one. Straightening himself, he looked Pa in the eye. "I told Drusie I'm joinin' the band as a harmonica player. Don't worry. I won't run off and marry her or nothin'. I'll be a gentleman like all the Gordon men are."

"I ain't worried about that. I wonder if you're just runnin' away from your problems now that the store cain't be yours."

"I ain't tryin' to run away, Pa. I admit that nothin's been the same since I found out Mr. Goode took a better offer, but I wouldn't run away. Maybe the timin' of this whole thing with the band is God's doin'."

The two men headed for the gate, and Gladdie held it open for his pa. The men were quick to exit before any pigs took a notion to escape.

"So you cleared this with Goode already?"

"Yes, sir."

"And he didn't mind?"

"No, sir. I think he knows in his heart he done wrong. Or not exactly right, anyway."

Pa stopped so short that the bucket hit against his leg, but he didn't seem to notice. "Wonder who this mystery family is?" He snorted. "Probably them Moores."

"Hard to say, but I'd like to think they wouldn't do such a thing." Gladdie shrugged. "I reckon we'll find out from Zeb."

"Zeb? What's your brother got to do with this? I know he don't care nothin' for cipherin' and all the other work that goes along with keepin' shop."

"No, but he did say he'd like to take my place as clerk until I get back. I hope that's okay with you. Is it, Pa?"

They had reached the barn, and Pa motioned for Gladdie's bucket so he could store both containers in their proper places until feeding time rolled around again. "I reckon so. You boys have to make your way in the world, and I have to get used to the fact I cain't hold you here forever."

∞

A few days after Drusie placed the long-distance call to him, Gladdie caught up with the band. As soon as she spotted the familiar figure she loved emerging from a bus, Drusie ran to him. "Gladdie! I didn't think you'd ever get here!"

"It was a long ride, but here I am." He set down his suitcase and enveloped her in his arms.

His lips met hers in a kiss that seemed to melt the frigid air around them. Old feelings reawakened, their ardor reminding her all the more how much she had yearned to be near Gladdie and how glad she was that he had finally arrived.

"Enough, you two. We all know you're dizzy with this dame," Archie teased. "Need help with that bag, Gladdie?"

Gladdie broke the embrace slowly enough to let Drusie know he was sorry for the interruption. "Nope. I got it."

Archie started walking to the car. "Too bad you won't be seeing much of North Carolina. We're heading into Virginia and Tennessee on the next leg of the tour."

Gladdie picked up his bag and followed, along with Drusie. "Anywhere else?" he asked.

"Maybe Kentucky. Anywhere our music will be well received. This tour has helped get the girls known. Before long, we'll all be rich."

Gladdie touched Drusie's shoulder. "The longer you were gone from me, the less I cared about being rich. And I still don't care nothin' about havin' more than I need. I'm just glad we're together now."

"You'll be sick enough of each other with all the rehearsals and performances we have scheduled," Archie jested as he opened the trunk of his Auburn. "Gladdie, you need to run through the music with the band tonight and work in your part."

Gladdie tossed in his suitcase. "Fine. Has the other harmonica player gotten over what ails him?"

"He'll recover, but not before this tour is over."

"I'm sorry to hear it's gonna take so long for him to get well. I hate that my opportunity came at someone else's expense."

Archie shrugged. "I know it. But that's life."

"I reckon. Say, Archie, do you mind if I take Drusie out for a cup of coffee at the diner?" Gladdie cocked his head toward an establishment in sight of them.

Archie nodded. "Sure. There's time. June and Betty have a new number they want to go over, but after that I do need you to rehearse with the band. I know the girls are used to your playing, but Elmer needs to get comfortable with you, and you need to get to know him. Hows about I give you two lovebirds a half hour?"

"That's not enough, but we'll take it." Gladdie grabbed Drusie's hand, and they headed off for some time alone.

Chapter 10

Gladdie looked across the table at Drusie. With her eyes bright in excitement and her elated expression, she looked more beautiful than ever. They'd been apart too long.

A waitress carried a hot, open-faced roast beef sandwich and a ham dinner past them, sending enticing aromas their way. On the counter, slices of pie and pastries looked tempting under glass. He wished they had enough time for dinner, but he also knew Archie had to keep the band members to a schedule if they hoped to perform at the grueling pace he set for them. At least the coffee looked rich and smelled delicious. Sugar and cream added to the brew made for a tasty pick-me-up.

"And you know what?" Drusie was saying. "Archie never could get June to confess to burnin' holes in them dresses. Not that I blame her. He was plannin' to dock her pay—or worse. I just hope she got the idea of revenge out of her system and Archie's threats were enough to stop her."

"Judgin' from what you told me, she's mad as an old sittin' hen, all right. It ain't no fun to be thrown over for someone else."

"How would you know?" she jested.

"I don't know for sure, and I don't want to find out."

"I can tell you one thing; she'll never get to our clothes like that again. And I'm keeping an extra close watch on my money and jewelry."

"Why is that? She don't have nothin' against you, does she? Other than the fact you're Clara's sister."

"No, and I've always been nothin' but nice to her. But. . ." Drusie added an unnecessary spoonful of sugar to her coffee and stirred.

"What's wrong?"

She set her spoon on the plain white saucer that matched the cup. A tear escaped from the corner of her eye. "Oh, I was hopin' I'd find it before you came. I looked and looked and looked. Nothin'."

He knew what she meant. "The gold necklace."

She nodded, and tears came at a rapid pace. "I'm sorry."

He handed her his handkerchief and patted her hand. "Now don't you worry one little bit. I can buy you another necklace. Now that I'm in the band, I can buy you one soon. Maybe even one with a diamond."

"But I don't want a necklace with a diamond. I want the one you already

299

gave me. It means a lot to me."

"You still got me. Now that I'm here with you, you don't need to read 'I love you' engraved on a pendant. I can tell you myself, every day."

She patted her eyes. "Well, that's the best way to look at it, I reckon." She smiled.

"That's better. So you think not only that she burned holes in Clara's dresses, but that June's a thief in your midst, too?"

"It seems maybe so. Things turn up missin' from time to time."

Gladdie finished his coffee and set down the cup. "As much as y'all move around from place to place, it's no wonder things get lost."

"True. I just hope you're right. I have another story that beats that, though. Two weeks ago a show producer shorted us on ticket receipts."

"That's awful! How can somebody get away with that?"

"Archie tries to line us up with people who'll pay our fee ahead of time, but it's not always possible, apparently. He says sometimes we get involved with someone that ain't honest. There's not much we can do. At least we were just shorted and they didn't run off with the whole sum of admission money."

"True."

The waitress appeared again, and Gladdie accepted another cup of coffee even though Drusie declined. He wanted to linger and get the bad news out of the way. "Drusie?"

"What is it?"

"I have somethin' to tell you. I'm tellin' you now because I don't think you'll haul off and hit me in front of all these people." He looked around in an exaggerated manner.

"Haul off and hit you? You're a silly old thing. What's the matter?" She leaned across the table.

Her levity eased him. "First of all, I want you to know that I'll always be grateful to you for agreein' to sing in Archie's band so I could buy the store, even if Pa did end up comin' up with the money."

She reached over and took his hand. "I'd do anything for you. Thank you for lettin' me come out here with Clara. You haven't seen her yet, but she's blossomed under the limelight."

"And ain't got into much trouble?" he joked.

"Not too much. She and Archie seem to have found romance."

"They have? Well, how about that." He paused. "Come to think of it, I could sense somethin' in the air with them even before you left. You don't mind her gettin' involved with him, do you?"

"Not if it makes her happy. And after gettin' to know him, I've decided Archie's okay." She smiled. "But we've gotten off the subject, and the waitress is eyein' us like she'd like us to leave so somebody else can have this booth."

Gladdie cut his glance to the waitress. "Yeah. Right. Well, anyway, I've decided I don't want to keep shop all my life."

Drusie gasped. "You don't?"

"That's right."

"I don't believe it."

"I don't blame you. The whole story isn't as simple as all that. You see, the decision has been made for me. Mr. Goode sold the store out from under Pa and me."

"What?"

"That's right." Gladdie filled her in on all the details.

"Maybe the Moores will sell you their store," Drusie joked.

"If only." Gladdie let out a humorless chuckle. "You know what? This ain't what I thought I'd want—bein' out of a chance to own the store—but maybe it's what God wants. Why else would He let somethin' like that happen?"

"He does let things happen for a reason."

"I believe that, too."

"God works all for good." She squeezed his hand. "And now you're here. With me. Could we ask for more?"

"No. We sure couldn't."

∞

Four weeks later, Drusie knew that she had never been happier. For the first time since leaving Sunshine Hollow in Archie's Auburn, she enjoyed rising each morning in anticipation. Seeing Gladdie every day lifted her spirits. She knew she'd missed him while they were apart, but she didn't know just how much until they were together again.

"You look mighty cheerful," Clara noticed as they dressed for yet another performance.

"That's because I am." Drusie wiggled into her costume. "I'm enjoyin' singin' for folks a powerful lot more now that Gladdie's onstage with us. He gives me more confidence in singin' for folks I don't know."

"And I don't?" Clara jested.

"Sure, you help me a lot. More than you know. Sometimes I don't think I could've made it at all if you hadn't been here. And that's the truth," Drusie said. "And I have to say, I'm not as afraid of audiences as I used to be. I reckon I've gotten used to not knowin' nobody I'm singin' for."

"Not to mention, Archie's rehearsed us so many times I think I'm recitin' lines and singin' in my sleep."

Drusie laughed.

"I know you bein' happier has made Archie happy, too."

"There's only one thing. I'm gettin' tired of wearin' this stiff fabric. It's scratchy, too."

"But so pretty. And you know what Archie says. He says with the Depression on, people like to see singers wearin' pretty clothes even if they cain't afford to buy nice things for themselves."

"Like the men havin' to wear rhinestones and beads on their suits, huh?" Drusie grinned and shook her head. "Could you imagine them wearin' such getups anywhere else but onstage?"

"No, I cain't." Clara touched the hem of her dress. "But I sure do like my dress. It's even prettier than the one June burned."

"Now we cain't go around sayin' that even though we suspect," Drusie scolded. "After all, it ain't happened no more. Looks like whoever did it learned their lesson."

"Maybe, but if it was her, I wish she'd own up to it."

"She won't. The Hays Code might make sure everybody in the movies who's done somethin' wrong gets punished, but we ain't in no motion picture."

"It don't seem right. Why should she get off scot-free?"

Drusie shrugged. "I know it. But the Bible never promised us that everybody who does wrong will be punished here on the earth. She may look like she's gettin' away with somethin', but she ain't. At least, not in the long run."

Clara adjusted her bodice. "I reckon you're right."

"What we need to do now is pray that June finds the right man for her. If Archie was the right man for June, he never woulda looked at you twice."

"True." Clara nodded once. "And because you pointed that out, I think I will pray for her."

Drusie looked at the wall clock. "First we'd better get through this show."

"You're right. Time to get on out there."

Moments later, Drusie stood by Gladdie, waiting to go onstage. She eyed a now-familiar woman and tugged on his sleeve. "Who is that woman?"

He peered into the audience. "What woman?"

"She's sittin' on the second row, near the center. See? She's the brunette wearin' fur."

Gladdie spotted the woman in question. "She sure is familiar. Warn't she in the audience in several places in Tennessee?"

"Yes, and Virginia, too. And now it looks like she's followed us back to North Carolina."

Elmer interrupted. "Who you talkin' about?"

"This woman in the second row. She sure travels a lot," Gladdie said. "She's been followin' the band awhile now. Got any idea who she might be?"

"I—uh, why would you think I know?"

His stammering drew Drusie's attention. "You seem like you're a little slow to answer."

"I told you, I don't know."

Gladdie laughed. "So you say. Is she comin' to see you play every night?"

"You could do worse," Drusie said. "She's mighty pretty."

"Aw, come on. They're all here to see you and Clara. You're the stars."

Approaching from behind, Archie shushed them. "Stop your yammering. You're being introduced."

"He's right. We're on." Gladdie brushed Drusie's lips with his. The gesture never failed to send chills down her spine.

Drusie hung back as the band took to the stage and played a few chords of "Cindy." She and Clara were always introduced after that.

Archie placed his hand on the small of Clara's back and whispered something in her ear. Watching them, Drusie could only hope that he wouldn't break Clara's heart. She wanted her sister to have a real love, a love like she and Gladdie knew.

The rustle of a dress lured her gaze behind the couple. June's expression as she observed Archie and Clara held a mixture of wistfulness and resignation. Drusie had a feeling that June wouldn't be burning holes in any more dresses.

Soon their set was completed, and the sound of applause filled the air. Drusie lingered long enough to hear Gladdie play harmonica for the other bands. His music added texture to any act of which he was part.

She applauded wildly for him.

He met her backstage after the show.

"You thrive under that spotlight, don't you?" she said.

"I hate to admit it, because I don't want to seem like I think I should be the center of attention, but I do enjoy performin' for the crowd a lot more than I ever thought I would."

"That's because they appreciate you. But not as much as I do."

"They appreciate you. You were wonderful tonight. You're wonderful every night." He punctuated the statement with a kiss.

"You were even better." Drusie kissed him back. If only they were married. Traveling together had brought them some temptation they hadn't experienced at home under the vigilant eyes of their parents. Yet they knew they could trust each other. Both were too committed to God and a strong beginning for their marriage to go beyond a kiss.

"I wish we could marry right away," Gladdie mused.

"I know," Drusie agreed. "I wish we could, too. But you know it would break Ma's and Pa's hearts if we didn't marry in the same little church where they were wed all them years ago. And what kind of married life could we have on the road like this, anyway?"

They were interrupted by Archie. "That no good Burns."

"What do you mean?" Gladdie wanted to know. "Who's Burns?"

"Isn't he the show's producer?" Drusie guessed.

"He sure is. Or was—before he disappeared."

"What do you mean, he disappeared?" Drusie felt her heart sink in her chest.

Archie shrugged, a nonchalant motion that defied his face grown red with rage. "He up and left. No one seems to know where he is. At least, they're not willing to tell me."

"He's the stocky man wearing a cowboy hat and boots, right?" Drusie asked.

"Yes, that describes him. Have you seen him?" Archie's eyes took on a hopeful glint.

"Not since before the show. And I don't know where he would have run off to. I saw him takin' the ticket money, so it's not like our show was a flop," Drusie observed. "He—he did pay you our fee before he left, right?"

"That's just it. He didn't," Archie said. "Otherwise, I wouldn't care where he'd run off to."

"Drusie told me somethin' like this happened before." Shadows hovered over Gladdie's face as the stagehands dimmed the lights.

Archie started walking toward the dressing rooms. Drusie and Gladdie followed. "Yeah, but I had it on good word from one of my contacts that this guy could be trusted. I'll remember not to trust him again," Archie said. "I feel awful about it. I try to protect us, but we're out on our own in this world. From now on, our show is not performing for anybody until we're paid. And that's final."

"That's all you can do, Archie," Gladdie agreed.

"I hate having to punish the honest ones because of the ones who aren't so good."

"It's not your fault," Drusie said. "Don't beat yourself up. You do your best. And that's usually pretty good!"

"Yeah," Archie agreed.

Drusie took that as her cue to depart. "I know one thing. I've got to change out of this outfit. I'll let you know if I see Mr. Burns, Archie."

"Oh, one thing before you go," Archie said. "Speaking of seeing things, have either of you seen my mother-of-pearl cuff links?"

Gladdie and Drusie both shook their heads no. "When did you last see 'em?" Gladdie inquired.

"Last night, when I took them off to go to bed. I couldn't find them this morning, so I had to put on these other ones. Good thing I brought an extra set, even if I don't like them half as much." He shook his head. "I can't believe the thief has struck again."

"Maybe you just misplaced 'em," Gladdie consoled him. "Maybe you put 'em someplace different than you thought."

Drusie was sure June wouldn't be interested in cuff links. She hadn't been near Archie any more than necessary ever since the incident with the dresses, and Drusie had become convinced that June had given up on Archie.

"I just hope they turn up," Archie said.

"They cost a pretty penny, didn't they?" Gladdie asked.

"You shred it, wheat. And I'd better not catch anybody wearing them."

"I ain't wearin' your cuff links." Gladdie held his arms out for Archie to see. "I cain't afford shirts with no fancy cuffs. All my shirts button."

"I wasn't thinking of you, genius. You don't have a criminal bone in your body. But if you get any ideas about who might have made off with my cuff links, let me know." He made a quick exit.

"He sure is out of sorts about them cuff links," Drusie noticed.

"I would be, too, if I lost something that valuable. You don't think anybody made off with 'em, do you?"

"I sure hope not. If they did, they're in a heap of trouble with Archie."

◈

Two nights later they were getting ready to perform again when Drusie noticed that the woman in fur was back. She couldn't seem to take her gaze from Elmer. He caught the lady's eye once or twice during the performance as he played the fiddle and played the straight man for a few rehearsed jokes.

So the mystery woman does have a reason to be here!

Concentrating on the music, Drusie didn't have time to ponder anyone's romantic life except for that of each of the protagonists in her songs. But after the show, she hurried to the hole in the wall that passed for the dressing room she shared with Clara. All she wanted to do was change out of her sequined dress and into a plain skirt and simple cotton blouse so she could get back to the motel and sleep.

Just beyond her door, she noticed a couple hovering. Elmer and the mystery woman were deep in conversation. Drusie winked at him, but instead of a jovial smile and wink in return as she expected, Elmer looked shaken. The woman turned to peer at Drusie. Her mouth opened, giving her a stricken look, and she darted away. Drusie pretended not to notice that their behavior was strange. Yet moments later, as she changed her outfit, she couldn't help but wonder why the couple acted so distraught. Elmer wasn't married or entangled with any woman as far as she knew. Surely the mystery woman wasn't married. She hoped not. But why else would they have seemed upset at being spied?

Lord, if somethin' wrong is happenin' under our noses, please offer Elmer and this woman friend of his Your light to the right path. Show them their error and set them straight.

But what if she was wrong?

Lord, keep me from being a busybody. Amen.

Clara entered the dressing room.

"Hey, you're just in time to help me with this button that's so hard to reach."

Clara assisted Drusie. "You gotta be a contortionist to get dressed anymore.

Once I get rich, I'm hirin' a maid. Then I won't have to do nothin' I don't wanna do."

"Like dress yourself?" Drusie slithered out of her costume.

"Maybe." Clara grinned. "As long as I can shop, I'll be happy." Clara turned so Drusie could help her slip out of her garment.

"You don't need a maid. You got me."

"Not for long," Clara quipped. "Gladdie will have you home and in a family way before you know it."

"Clara! Must you?" Drusie felt heat rise to her face.

Her sister laughed. "Hey, you missed signin' autographs."

"I ain't worried none about that. The fans that really want my John Hancock will sure enough catch us on our way to the motorcar."

"But you won't be wearin' your gown." She grabbed a hanger. "And I won't be, neither."

"You know I don't care nothing about wearin' no gown." Drusie sighed and hung up her outfit.

"You seem mighty thoughtful tonight. What's wrong?" Clara asked. "Feelin' puny? I have to say, that bean soup I had for lunch didn't set well with me. I could use a glass of ginger ale to settle my stomach. You don't happen to have none, do you?"

"No." She took a stick of peppermint candy out of her purse. "Try this."

"Thanks. Well, if you ain't sick, then what's the matter?"

"Did I say anything's the matter?"

"You don't have to. This is me, Clara. Remember? I can see when you're slow."

"Oh, all right. Give me a sec." Drusie cracked open the door and peeped at the spot where she had seen Elmer and the mystery woman. Not locating them, she glanced around and saw no one in sight. The coast was clear.

"What's with the cloak and dagger stuff?" Clara hissed. "Who do you think you are, the Phantom?"

"No," Drusie responded in a loud whisper. She drew close to her sister. "I know it's none of my business, but I saw Elmer and that mystery woman in the fur coat, standin' by one of the dressin' room doors just now."   —

"So he knows her after all."

"Seems stranger he wouldn't wanna own up to it. It ain't like he's married."

Clara flitted her hand at Drusie. "Oh, you know how shy he is and how hard it is to have a private life around the band."

"True."

"If I was him, I'd be likely to keep it a secret, too. And I say good for him. He'd do good to land someone as pretty as that one is."

"Maybe. Maybe not. All I know is they acted awful strange when they saw that I was noticin' them. She shot out of there like a raccoon with a hound dog on its tail."

"Wonder why."

"I don't know. I just hope she ain't married or somethin'."

Clara opened the door wider to exit. "I hope not, too. I say he just wants everybody to mind their own business, that's all. But you're right. It sure ain't up to us to be busybodies about it."

Approaching, Archie interrupted. "What's none of our beeswax?"

Drusie held back a grimace. How did Archie always manage to run up on them right when they were talking about something important? "Nothin'."

"Aw, don't give me that. You two were talking about something. What's your story, morning glory?"

"We were just talkin' about Elmer's love life, that's all," Clara volunteered.

"What's the matter? Is he dizzy with a dame?"

"Oh, we might as well say. You won't let up until you know," Drusie said.

"That's right. If I ever decide to quit music, I could be a detective—a house peeper."

"We just noticed he was hangin' around the woman in the fur coat who comes to every show," Drusie elaborated. "I'm sure it's nothin'. Besides, I have somethin' more important to ask you. When are we going to end this tour? Soon?"

"End it? You can't mean that. You're doing so well."

"We do fine when the producers pay. Not so fine when they don't," Drusie noted.

"Yeah, well, I've taken care of that. Like I said before, from here on out, you don't sing until we get paid. And you'll be getting paid plenty over the next year."

"The next year?"

"Sure. Why are you acting so surprised? Your father signed you both to a two-year contract. You have to expect to work."

"But—but I had no idea I'd have to stay on the road that long. Gladdie and I will never marry at this rate."

"Sure you can. You can marry the next time you go home, in the church and everything. I'm not such a bad guy that I don't let my stars go home once in a while."

"But even if we did marry, what kind of life would that be for a newlywed couple?"

Archie shrugged. "If you love each other, you'll survive."

Chapter 11

With so many people around them, Gladdie hadn't spent much time alone with Drusie on the tour. But even a few sweet moments in relative privacy were enough to brighten his day. When they did manage to break away to a diner for a cup of coffee, he held those moments close to his heart.

They had been to a lot of diners—with and without the other performers—since Gladdie joined the tour. At first, eating out had been a treat, but now the diners, food, and even waitresses all seemed to look the same.

Drusie sat across from him in a nondescript booth. They were surrounded by what had now become familiar scents of diner food—gravy, vegetables cooked in ham hock, grits with butter, and beef cooked fork tender. Still, he longed for one of his mother's home-cooked meals.

"I sure will be glad when this tour is over. I'm thinkin' we shouldn't wait until spring to get married." He leaned closer to her. "Hows about we try for New Year's Day?"

"New Year's Day?" Drusie's expression hinted at vague disappointment.

Had Gladdie not known her so well, her lack of enthusiasm would have left him crushed. He decided to sweeten the pot. "Remember that jewelry store we passed on the walk over here?"

"Sure. What about it?"

"I noticed a weddin' band with orange blossoms on it. That band would look mighty pretty on your ring finger."

A smile touched her pink lips. "Yes, it would. But not yet."

"I know. We have to wait until New Year's Day."

The pained expression returned to Drusie's face. "If we want a settled life at home in the mountains, we got to wait longer than that. I just found out that Archie signed us up for two years' worth of tourin'."

Gladdie gulped. "Two—two years?"

Drusie's lips drooped. "That's a powerful long time."

"But how did he manage to do that without you knowin' about it?"

"Pa signed for us."

"But I thought he understood that we wanted to marry soon, and he didn't even seem all that excited about you goin' on the road to start with," Gladdie protested. "Why do you think he signed you up for such a long time?"

Drusie sighed. "I think he thought it was best for Clara. And I'm sure he figured we would make more money that way in the long run. To his way of lookin' at life, he must have thought the longer contract offered us more security. He always was one to look into the future and not take any chances. 'A bird in the hand is better than two in the bush,' he always says. Anyway, I don't know for sure. But whatever he thought, it's done now."

Gladdie understood. As long as the sisters lived under his roof, their pa would see to their affairs. It would be that way even if the sisters lived to be a hundred. Sure, city gals with big ideas might rebel against their fathers taking charge, but not Drusie. Since the cards had been played, everyone involved would have to work within the confines of the deal.

"I know he thought he was doin' what was best for you." Gladdie patted her hand. "I reckon he was taken in by Archie's smooth talkin', too. You know he can be persuasive. So try not to blame your pa."

"I know it. I keep rememberin' God's commandment to honor our parents. Pa's a good soul, but he can be a trial without even meanin' to. I know the Lord knows I don't mean nothin' disrespectful in that." She stared into her half-empty cup.

"I believe the Lord understands. I know I do." He shook his head. "That Archie. I imagine he wants to make as much money as he can while he can. After all, you always said you weren't plannin' to be with the group long. Do you still feel that way?"

"It's better with you here, but as long as we're on the road, I don't see how we can get married. Don't you care nothin' about our marriage plans?"

"I do. Why else would I be offerin' to buy you a weddin' band today? You know I do. I don't want to wait, either." He stirred two spoonfuls of sugar in his coffee.

"Archie did say we could get married now."

"Now? But I don't want our first year of marriage to be spent on the road."

"Me neither, but there ain't no other way without waitin'. Once the two years are up, I can make a home with you, Gladdie. A real home. Not just some slipshod, halfway doin's. I want to get up every mornin', early, and put on a white starched apron and fry you up some eggs for breakfast. I want to greet you when you come home every night from work. I don't care if that work is loggin' or farmin' or clerkin' at the store. I just want to be there for you." Her eyes took on a dreamy look, like she was watching a romantic movie with Gloria Swanson playing the glamorous leading lady.

"That does sound wonderful. Too wonderful. And contract or no contract, I'm gonna get you out of it." He placed some change on the table and rose from his seat.

Drusie followed suit and talked to him as they walked. "No, you're not. We cain't go against Pa. And what about Clara? She's blossomed since bein' on the road. I cain't take that away from her. And even though I dream of livin' in Sunshine Holler, life on the road ain't all bad."

"I know. But you don't want to be on the road forever, right?" Gladdie held the door open for her as they exited the diner.

"Well, not forever."

"Then you have to think of your own feelin's and not just Clara's. I know you never think of yourself, and in a lot of ways, that's good. But now it's time to. You cain't be Clara's keeper forever. Like you said, she's blossomin'. She's got Archie lookin' after her so close that nobody can get near her. She'll be fine."

"I think so, too, but Pa will be powerful mad if he finds out I left her. I cain't do it, Gladdie. I've got to stick to it—for the whole time. Pa will never let me go back on his word." She walked quickly to keep up with Gladdie's stride, holding her wool coat close to herself.

"That's right. It's his word, not yours. I don't think much of that. I was just plannin' on helpin' the band out until we went home for Christmas. I ain't comin' back for two years. Even though you're right—in some ways, it's kinda fun amongst all that hard work." They passed the jewelry store where the little wedding band shone through the window. He noticed that Drusie glanced inside, and he wished the store could be their destination.

He slowed his pace. "I want to wait for you, but it's hard. I've waited for you for years, since we was young'uns, and I'm tired of waitin'. We said we'd get married in the next few months, and now that your pa has signed you up to be with Archie forever and a day, I just don't know what to do. We don't need all this money you're making—or I'm makin'—'cept maybe to save up for the future, which is a good idea, I reckon. But we're simple folk. We don't need much money to live. I can work the farm and split the profits with Pa. Or I'll go back to my job at the store, even if I cain't own it."

"You don't want to do neither of them things and you know it."

"I'm the man here," he snapped. "You let me worry about how to make the money."

She flinched as though he'd slapped her. Maybe his retort did hurt. But she was saying hurtful things, too.

"I'm leavin' the band today. And that's final."

She didn't answer. Had she given in that easily? He didn't think so. Her silence seemed ominous. What was happening in that quick mind of hers?

As they approached the motel where the band was staying, Buford waved at the young couple.

"What's the good word?" Gladdie asked as soon as they drew close enough so there was no need to shout.

"Not much. I'm looking for my money clip. Have you seen it?"

"No," they both said.

"That's too bad. I had over twenty dollars in it."

"Twenty dollars!" Drusie clapped her palm against the base of her neck. Her mouth dropped open.

Gladdie let out a whistle. "That's an awful lotta money to lose."

Buford nodded. "You said it. You know, a lot of valuables have turned up missin' lately. What do you make of it?"

"I don't much like it. What else has turned up missin'?" Gladdie asked.

"Archie's cuff links, remember? And my necklace," Drusie said.

Elmer approached and interrupted. "What's the news?"

"My money clip is missin'," Buford informed him. "I don't reckon you've seen it, have you?"

"What would make you think I've seen it?"

"I'm askin' around," Buford said. "So much stuff has turned up missin'—a few dollars here and a few dollars there. Plus, one of the stage managers said he can't seem to locate his pocket watch."

"Is that so?" Drusie asked.

Buford nodded. "Turned up missin' just this mornin'. Seems mighty suspicious to me."

June and Betty joined them. "Say," Betty asked, "how come there's a party and nobody invited us?"

"Yeah," June added with mock derision.

"I wish we was havin' a party," Gladdie answered.

"We're tryin' to figure out who done took our stuff," Drusie elaborated.

"What stuff?" Betty asked.

As Buford explained, Gladdie glanced at June and noticed that her expression indicated she was as mystified as everyone else. Either she hadn't taken anything, or she could act even better than she could sing. Gladdie observed that Betty seemed stunned, too. He had a feeling Drusie's hunch about June being the thief was off. But if neither June nor her best friend and partner, Betty, knew anything about the missing items, who did?

Gladdie joined in the conversation. "I wonder who could be responsible. It could be almost anybody. We're around so many different people in so many unusual places, it will be almost impossible to find a thief."

"Unless he's in our midst," Buford said.

In his mind, Gladdie ran down the list of people he knew. "I wonder if it's that woman that keeps following us."

"You mean the woman wearin' the fur all the time?" Drusie asked.

"That's the one."

Elmer bristled. "Any woman wearin' a fur doesn't need to steal. Come on, Buford. I'll help you look for your money clip."

"Sure."

They walked away, and Drusie noticed that Elmer's steps were determined. "He sure seems upset," Drusie said.

"A little too upset about us suggestin' that woman, if you ask me," June remarked.

"I'll see if I can find anything. You girls wait here." Gladdie searched the automobiles parked on the patch of dirt that served as a parking lot. "I see Archie's car. He must be back from town. I'm goin' to meet with him now."

"And say what?" Drusie asked. "We ain't leavin' the tour."

"I know it. But I can give him a piece of my mind."

"I wish you wouldn't."

"Don't worry. I won't say anything we'll regret. And if I do, he can fire us."

Gladdie went to Archie's room and rapped on his door.

"Come on in." Archie stopped combing his hair when he saw Gladdie. "Oh, it's you." He motioned to the corner of the bed. "Siddown."

"I'll stand, thanks."

"Suit yourself. So did you have a nice break with your girl?"

Gladdie was in no mood for chitchat. "I have somethin' I need to tell you. I feel like you took advantage of Drusie real good, and I don't think much of that."

"Excuse me?"

"You know what I mean. She thought she was signed up for a year at the most. Never two years. That's forever."

"Not in show business. Why, that's just a start. I got plans for Drusie and Clara. Big plans. And you'll want to be there for the ride. You'll thank me later, Mr. Harmonica Player."

"I will, will I? Why, I have a mind to leave with Drusie tonight."

"Good luck with that. You're not their manager. Take it up with their pa if you don't like it. The deal is signed, sealed, and delivered. I have a carbon copy of the contract I can get out of my suitcase and show you right now if you don't believe me."

"Oh, I believe you. But I didn't sign anything. I'm doin' you a favor."

"You are—an expensive favor. But you're free to go. I can make do without you if I have to. But not Drusie. Or Clara. They're contracted to me, and they stay. Besides, the longer they stay on the road, the more famous they get. It's for their own good to stay."

"You mean for your own good."

Without warning, Elmer and Buford shadowed the door.

"What's the matter, boss?" Elmer asked. "We can hear you fightin' two doors down."

"This fight is almost done," Gladdie told them. "I have half a mind to tell you to keep your money, Archie."

He noticed Drusie and Clara loitered behind the men. Good. They could see he was serious. Gladdie reached into his pocket to search for the two dollars he liked to carry with him for emergencies. The rest of his money was back in his room. The amount seemed a small sacrifice to make a dramatic impact.

"Here you are. Drusie and I don't need you or your money!" He threw the dollars at his cousin. To his surprise, something clinked on the floor.

Archie gasped. He rushed to retrieve the shiny object. "Buford's money clip! And look—a twenty-dollar bill. What are you doing with this?" He glared at Gladdie.

Gladdie tensed. "I have no idea how that got there!"

Drusie spoke up. "You can believe him, Archie. I know Gladdie, and he's as honest as the day is long."

Gladdie threw her a quick smile.

"Must be a short day, then," Archie scoffed.

"How could you doubt Gladdie?" Drusie asked. "He's your cousin."

"He is, but I haven't seen much of him in years. Times are tough, and people change."

"Not Gladdie."

One of the roadies interrupted. "Of course you're going to take up for your boyfriend, Drusie. But we can't afford to have our things turning up missing." He looked at Archie. "What say we throw him out, Mr. Gordon?"

"It's Buford's money clip. Maybe we should see what he has to say about it," Drusie suggested.

"I'm running the show here. What I say goes," Archie responded. Then he nodded, but the motion was slow and bespoke sadness. "I never thought I'd see the day when I couldn't trust my own cousin. After all I've done for you, too."

"Wait!" Drusie protested.

Archie shook his head, glaring at Gladdie. "I've waited long enough to find out who the thief is around here. I would have given my eyeteeth for it not to be you."

"But this doesn't explain the items that were missing before Gladdie got here," Drusie pointed out. "Archie, I think you're too eager to solve this whodunit and too mad at Gladdie to see straight."

"Oh, I see straight, all right."

"If you were, you'd see that somebody's planted false evidence on me," Gladdie protested.

Archie chuckled. "You've been watching too many motion pictures."

"Maybe so, but I tell you, I ain't the one who took your stuff."

Archie eyed his cousin. "Are you planning on hiding behind your girlfriend's skirt and letting her make excuses for you?"

"No, I'm not hidin' anywhere. But I can see I'm no longer welcome here and everybody's wantin' to concoct any story they can to get rid of me. I know you don't believe I'm a thief."

"Now see here—" Archie protested.

"See here, nothin'. I'm leavin', that's what I'm doin'. I cain't stay where I'm not trusted."

"I don't blame you, Gladdie, but you gotta stay. You just gotta. All this will get cleared up. You'll see," Drusie objected.

Archie crossed his arms and surveyed his cousin. "You can walk to the bus station from here and catch a ride home."

Drusie tried to stop him. "But, Gladdie—"

"He's made up his mind, and if he doesn't want to be part of our show, so be it," Archie said. "I got enough problems without all this bickering. We've got a show to put on." He nodded to the band members. "Load on up. We've got no time to lose."

Gladdie tried to keep his face from displaying his distress. He had expected his own cousin to defend him and to respond to his threats by insisting that he stay. But clearly, Archie was too carried away by his emotions to see logic. The urge to argue struck him, but with Archie in such a foul mood, he knew there was no use. Even worse, he was parting from Drusie under a cloud.

Lord, part of this mess is my own fault. I shouldn't have been so stubborn and prideful. Now I'm about to lose everything I ever cared about. Please show me what to do.

"What's the holdup?" Archie interrupted Gladdie's thoughts. "You said you don't want to be part of our show, and the perfect excuse to get out fell right at your feet. So what's your complaint? Now scram."

Gladdie gave no answer except to go to his room and pack. Archie was hardly the voice of God, but for the time being, he offered the only direction he could hear.

Chapter 12

Onstage during the matinee show, Drusie heard applause but didn't absorb her success. She noticed Clara basking in the spotlight as usual. Obviously, she had put the day's drama out of her mind. Drusie envied the way Clara flitted about from hour to hour, not worrying about anything.

"And which of you with taking thought can add to his stature one cubit?"

The Lord's advice from the book of Luke popped unbidden into her head. Perhaps instead of envying her sister, she should follow her example of not worrying.

Still, Gladdie had gone against her advice and had ended up yelling at his cousin and saying regretful things. She had a feeling if the men hadn't been so fired up, Gladdie never would have tossed money at him and Archie never would have accused him of thievery and thrown him out on his ear. But the clock couldn't be turned back. Gladdie had been thrown out on his ear, and she had no idea where he was. She prayed he was safe. Or maybe he had talked Archie out of forcing him to leave. What if he was still safe back at the motel or, even better, watching her perform from a place where she couldn't spy him? If he was, she could make up with him. But what if he wasn't? She did know one thing—the music didn't have nearly as much texture without Gladdie's harmonica. Archie had talked a big game about being able to find another harmonica player with a snap of his fingers, but no such talent had materialized.

None of this would have happened if she had just stayed home. Drusie wished she could go back to the way things were, when all she had to think about, other than helping her mother put up vegetables and clean the house, was when she could be doing the same tasks as Mrs. Gladdie Gordon.

She watched Clara sing a solo of "See That My Grave Is Kept Green," a song she could perform well and which was always met with great applause. Clara would do just fine without her. At least she had prospered from their new situation. And from the looks of things, she had even found the love of her life in Archie.

Lord, I don't mean to be selfish, but did I have to lose everything so Clara could have everything? Help me to understand, and show me Thy will.

Clara's number ended, and they launched into "No Telephone in Heaven" before moving on to "Sunshine in the Mountain."

Drusie laughed and joked with her sister in a rehearsed act, performed so many times that she knew it better than her own name. For that she was grateful. Such familiarity gave her a sense of comfort, and the sounds of laughter and applause helped ease her mind, at least for a while.

As soon as they strummed the last note of their closing song, "Let the Church Roll On," Drusie took her bow and headed offstage. Archie caught her and made her linger to meet a few fans and sign autographs. Her favorite fans were the children. Little girls looked up at her as though she were a fairy-tale princess. If only that were true. She wondered if Cinderella ever got angry with Prince Charming.

As was expected of her, Drusie signed autographs until the crowd dissipated, but afterward she hurried to find Gladdie.

Outside the door, she almost bumped into Archie.

"Say, why are you making tracks?" he asked.

"I want to know where Gladdie is."

"You know where he is. He left, remember?"

"I wish you hadn't made him think he had to go." Noticing the night chill, she wrapped her arms around herself. "Both of you got way madder than you should have. I think you were too hasty."

"He's the one who decided to leave. Truth be told, I'm sorta sorry, but that's the way it goes."

"Maybe he's not too far from here. Maybe it ain't too late to tell him you've changed your mind."

"But I haven't. I realize you don't understand the ways of the world, as sheltered as you've been, but I can't afford to have discord on the tour. I'm in no mood to fight with you, either. So if you're smart, you'll drop the subject or I'll throw you off the tour, too. Clara can sing on her own."

Drusie knew he spoke the truth, but she also knew that Archie had taken a shine to her sister. No wonder he could act so brave about throwing her out.

Archie wasn't finished. "You may have saved some of your money, but it'll run out. When you can't find any food and you're out on your own, far away from home not knowing anyone, see who'll watch out for you then."

"People will know me as a singer. I'll find someone who can help me."

He ogled her, though his expression was devoid of passion. "You're a looker, but take away that sequined dress and you aren't any more special than any other broad on the street."

She wanted to tell Archie he couldn't scare her, but the look in his eyes told her she'd better not be too bold lest he keep a watch on her and foil the plans she had made while she'd strummed onstage. "Maybe you're right, Archie. What was I thinkin'?"

"You know I'm right." His posture relaxed.

"I'm off to bed."

"Don't you want to take dinner with the rest of us?"

She wanted to beg off but knew if she did, Archie would catch on that all still wasn't well. "Sure."

Dinner dragged, but Drusie maintained a happy face. She kept hoping against hope that Gladdie would show up at dinner, but as dessert arrived, she could no longer kid herself. He had left.

It was only hours later, after Clara was asleep, that she sneaked out into the night, determined to find Gladdie. She didn't pack much in her little bag, not even her sequined dresses. Where she was going, she wouldn't be needing them. Besides, Clara would be sure nothing happened to them. She would keep them safe for Drusie until she returned to fulfill the rest of her contract. She resolved to be gone as short a time as possible. After all, she couldn't go back on her father's word. That wouldn't be right.

The highway was lonely and dark, but she wasn't about to give up. Putting her thumb in the air with the boldness of the most hardened hobo, she walked and tried to hitch a ride back to her beloved mountain home. Once she got there, she would find Gladdie. She would convince him to return to the tour. Surely Archie would forgive him once they reunited. Then she and Gladdie could set their minds to thinking of how to prove the identity of the person who was really responsible for all the trouble.

∞

Gladdie stopped for a cup of coffee at a roadside diner somewhere in rural Lincoln County. He was grateful to find a diner of any description, since he'd seen nowhere else to eat for miles. He'd missed the last bus out of town, and since the town in question was nothing more than a signpost, he decided to hitchhike and get as far as he could before moving on to any new ideas. Except he had no new ideas, so he kept walking down the lonely road.

Money had never been in great supply for him, but his needs were simple. He had managed to save most of the money Archie had paid him to help on the tour. His guess was that he wouldn't see his last paycheck.

Upset that he would have to go home in defeat, without a job, and on the outs with a family member, Gladdie stared out the diner window. He thought about what a mess he'd made of his life, all because he thought Drusie could earn enough money to make his dream of owning a store come true. Then his dream went bust, and Drusie sang every night for strangers instead of living life at home with him, where she belonged.

Worse than anything else was that he left on bad terms with Drusie and he had no idea whether they'd ever make up. She'd been determined to keep to Archie's contract. Maybe she was right. And maybe she was right about wanting a more normal life than they could have on the road, with or without being married. Still, he couldn't help but be angry at her. Once again, she had chosen Clara and her happiness—and her obligation to her pa—over him. Maybe he should just let her rot. With stage lights as hot as they were, she'd spoil pretty fast.

His hardhearted thoughts upset him to the point that he couldn't eat his food, even though the grilled cheese sandwich—the cheapest entrée on the menu—tasted almost as good as his mother's. He knew why he was so angry at Drusie. He loved her too much.

Still watching the world go by, he noticed that every few minutes an automobile or truck passed, but otherwise no discernable activity occurred near the eating establishment. Gladdie wondered how they stayed in business. Then again, the dinner rush had long since passed.

An automobile turned into the patch of dirt in front of the diner. Gladdie watched as a grizzled old man disembarked from the driver's side. To his surprise, a young woman wearing a green wool coat emerged from the passenger side. The man's daughter, maybe?

He looked again and did a double take. *Drusie?*

What was she doing with a strange man out in the middle of nowhere? Unable to stop himself in spite of his earlier unkind thoughts toward her, he rose from his seat and rushed to greet her. He met her just in front of the door. "Drusie!"

She looked stunned. "Gladdie! What are you doin' here?"

The man who had brought Drusie intervened. "You know this here fella, young lady?"

"Yes, sir, I do."

"And everything's all right?" The man looked Gladdie up and down.

Drusie nodded. "I think so."

"I'll go on about my business, then, but I'll be nearby if you need me."

"Thank you, Mr. Davidson."

Gladdie shut the door behind them, and they watched the older man take a seat at the counter. Gladdie spoke in a low volume. "You sure make friends fast."

"Got to, when you're on your own. So what are you doin' here? I thought you was supposed to catch a bus."

"Couldn't. Missed it. What are you doin' here? I thought you'd told Archie you'd be singin' for him for the next two years."

"And I will. But first I had to be sure you were okay." She slipped into the booth. "And I really do want you to come back to the tour. Archie does, too, but he's too proud to admit it."

"Aw, Drusie."

"I know you was set up with that money clip. I think Elmer and that strange woman that hangs around with him have somethin' to do with everything that's missin', and I think we need to figure out how to prove it."

318

Gladdie grinned. "I'm glad you have faith in me."

"Of course I do."

He reached across the table and placed his hand on top of hers. "But how can I prove my innocence?"

"I don't hardly know. Cain't we put our heads together and think up a way? We've got some time if we ride back to where the tour is." A question occurred to Drusie. "So how did you get here if you missed the bus?"

"I hitched a ride with a farmer who dropped me off about a mile from here. I was wonderin' where I would stay the night, when I decided I'd just stay up and keep walkin'. Maybe someone else would be on the road, even if it's already past ten."

"Speaking of the time. . ." the only waitress, a plump redhead, interrupted. "Like I told your friend here, we're just about to close. We're open bright and early for breakfast tomorrow, though."

"Aw, cain't you spare her a little coffee? You got some left, don'tcha?" Gladdie asked. "I'll give you an extra good tip."

The waitress shrugged. "I reckon I can serve you, then. Only, you'll have to ignore me mopping the floor."

"I sure will." Drusie nodded toward the counter. "What about Mr. Davidson?"

She regarded the older man as though he were hardly visible. "Oh, him. He's like family. He's here all the time."

Gladdie fired off a question to Drusie. "So who is your friend?"

"Mr. Davidson? I'm mighty grateful to him for lettin' me have a ride. He said he can drop me off at a motel tonight not far from here. We were just stoppin' at this here diner for a pick-me-up. You know, maybe he'll let you ride with us. I don't see why not. There's plenty of room."

The waitress set down the bill. She stopped for a moment, looking at Drusie. "Hey, wait a minute. I think I've seen you somewhere before."

Drusie blushed.

"Have you just moved here?"

"Uh, no."

The pink-clad woman shifted her weight to one leg and eyed Drusie. "I know I've seen you somewhere before."

Gladdie couldn't resist prodding. "Are you a music fan?"

Stars seemed to sparkle in the redhead's eyes. "I sure am." She gasped. "Are you a singer?"

"Well, just for a little band—the NC Mountain Girls."

The waitress gasped even louder. "The NC Mountain Girls! Why, I saw you just a couple of days ago, up at the high school."

"That's right. That was us."

319

The plump woman squinted her eyes and put her head closer to Drusie's face. "Why, you're Drusie, aren't you? Your sister's name is Clara."

"I see you were payin' attention."

"Well, how about that!" She hollered toward the kitchen. "Lookie here, Jake! We've got ourselves a bona fide celebrity right here in the diner."

"You don't say?" A slim man wearing a stained white-bibbed apron came out to stare at Drusie. "Which one of you is the celebrity?"

The redhead whapped him with her towel. "It's Drusie. Drusie of the NC Mountain Girls. Remember? We saw them the other night at the high school."

"Oh, that's right."

She turned so fast that Drusie thought red hair would go flying. "Don't mind him. That night was one of the few we took off work. Usually we try to keep the diner open every day except Sunday. As soon as your show was over, we ran back here to reopen so we could serve the after-show crowd."

"Now Miss Fields is a big singer, Cindy Lou," he said. "She don't care nothing about how we run our business."

"Oh," Drusie countered, "but I find it fascinatin'."

"Well, aren't you sweet?" Cindy Lou smiled. "Sweet as pie. Speaking of pie, hows about I see if I can find a nice big slice for you? You look like you could put on a few pounds, and it wouldn't hurt you none. You like apple?"

"Sure, apple's fine."

Gladdie resisted the urge to search his pocket to be sure he had extra change for pie.

Cindy Lou disappeared into the kitchen, with Jake following behind.

"Ain't they nice?" Drusie whispered.

"Uh, yeah. They sure seem to be impressed with you. They didn't even say nothin' about me playin' the harmonica in the background."

"Oh, I should have said somethin'. Where is my mind? I reckon I was too flustered to think."

Gladdie dismissed the notion with a quick wave of his hand. "I don't care nothin' about that. Everybody knows I'm helpin' out Archie. My face ain't even on the placards. But that waitress recognizin' you and goin' all into a tizzy just shows how big a celebrity you're gettin' to be. Archie can make you such a big star that nobody will even have to ask who you are. They'll know you by your picture in them celebrity magazines."

"Pshaw. I don't wanna be in no celebrity magazine. I think I'd rather be just plain old me."

Cindy Lou interrupted. "Here you go, sugar. And a slice for you, too, mister." She set a piece of pie in front of Gladdie.

"Uh, I don't need—"

"Now are you turning down my home-cooked pie? I hope not, because I sure would be insulted if I thought that."

"Hows about me?" Mr. Davidson called. "Don't I get a piece of pie?"

"I can't give away the store, Frank." Cindy Lou shook her head. "He comes in here all the time. Hardly ever leaves a tip."

"I heard that. I won't leave no tip tonight, either, then."

"Fine. It's not like I'd notice, cheap as you are." Cindy Lou's teasing tone belied her criticism. Gladdie had the feeling if he himself lived close by, he'd come to this diner every chance he could.

Chapter 13

Mr. Davidson couldn't offer assistance since he planned to travel in the opposite direction. Even with Gladdie at her side, Drusie didn't like the idea of hitching a ride back from the diner, then trying to find the tour so late at night. Yet without an automobile of their own and with no bus station in sight, the couple didn't feel as though they had another choice.

"It's gonna be a long night," Drusie mused aloud. "If it warn't for Pa givin' his word that we'd sing for two years, I'd hightail it right back home and never look back."

"Don't worry. We'll pray together before we set off."

Drusie nodded.

Gladdie bowed his head. "Lord, keep us safe throughout this journey we're about to take, and help us be kind to others since we ain't in a good position right now. Mend discord, Father, wherever we may find it. And help Drusie and me remember we are a brother and sister in Christ so we can show the world Your heart. In the name of Jesus, amen."

"Amen," Drusie agreed.

Gladdie summoned Cindy Lou with a polite wave of his hand. "If you'd be so kind, we'd like our check, please."

"Check? No sir, it's on the house."

"That's mighty kind of you," Gladdie said, "but we cain't accept such generosity."

"Don't you worry. Tomorrow's customers will be glad I had to make some fresh pie." Cindy Lou winked.

"I thank you kindly," Gladdie said.

"Me, too," Drusie added. "That was some of the best apple pie I ever ate. Reminds me of my ma's."

"Either you really like your ma's pie, or you're terrible homesick."

Drusie smiled. "Both."

She and Gladdie rose from their seats.

Wind whistled against the building. "It's awful cold. Are y'all walkin'?"

"Hitchin' a ride," Gladdie said.

"How far are you going tonight?" Cindy Lou asked.

"Oh, about twenty miles or so. Ever heard of a motel called Sleepy Time?"

"Sure have. But I can't let you hitch a ride in this cold and in the middle of the night like this!" Cindy Lou looked toward the kitchen and shouted, "Jake!"

"Yep!"

"Our singers need a ride to the Sleepy Time Motor Inn."

Jake emerged, wiping his hands on an apron soiled with stains from the day's goodies. "All that way?"

"Now that's nothing," Cindy Lou said.

"Don't put your cook out on account of us," Gladdie protested.

"He's more than just a cook. He's my husband. And so if I want to get him to do something, it's my right, isn't it?"

"That don't mean I gotta do it," Jake pointed out, although his tone sounded good-natured.

Cindy Lou crossed her arms and shook her head, grinning. "I think you should take 'em where they need to go."

Jake shook his head back at her.

Cindy Lou stopped grinning. "They're good Christian people. I know because I saw them praying just now. Not to mention Drusie can sing a gospel song sweeter than anything I ever heard. They need our help, and it's up to us to do our part."

"Well, all right." He took off his apron to reveal a blue shirt.

"Oh, now you're being too generous. I mean it," said Gladdie.

"Now you let us be the judge of that. Besides, we don't have enough room in our house to put you two up for the night, and there ain't no places to stay nearby. So we sort of have to take you." Cindy Lou winked again.

"Well, if you insist. But we'll go only if you'll let us give you a little gas money."

"You can work that out with Jake. He handles all our money. Now I'll go pack you a little something to snack on for the trip."

Drusie shook her head. "Kindness like that can only be part of God's help."

"We'll just have to be sure we do good turns for folks in the future when we get a chance. I'll start now." Gladdie made sure to leave enough money on the table to cover Jake's gas and to thank Cindy Lou for her kindness. Though she had made the offer with no strings attached, he thought her kindness should be rewarded.

∞

Later, as they drove along the winding road in the dark, neither Jake nor Cindy Lou had much to say. That suited Gladdie. He was tired. He noticed that Drusie looked more than a little sluggish herself. Truly the day had been a trying one.

Jake pulled into the parking lot of the motel. "Here we are."

"I don't see none of the cars that belong to us," Drusie said.

"They must have gone ahead to the next place," Gladdie surmised. "Figures. Archie's always tryin' to make time on the road."

Gladdie snapped his fingers. "Wait! I think I heard Archie say somethin' about the next gig being in Southern Pines."

"We can get you there," Cindy Lou said.

Gladdie sent her a regretful smile and shook his head. "We cain't ask you to drive us that far tonight. We can just stay at this here place. We can get two rooms for the night and figure out how to catch up with the band tomorrow."

A rectangular structure with only a few rooms, the establishment was nothing but a roadside stop, convenient for tourists passing through the state or for singers looking for a place to lay their heads until they had to move on to the next stop. Still, automobiles filled almost every spot of the dirt parking lot.

"Hope they've got some rooms left. I won't leave you kids stranded until I know you've got a place to sleep."

"Thank you, Jake."

Gladdie hopped out of the sedan and made his way to the motel office. The place was dark, with no sign of life. He noticed a dirt road and realized it led to a plain house nearby. "I wonder if that's where the manager lives." He waved to Jake, Cindy Lou, and Drusie, then hurried to the front door of the white frame house and knocked.

After a few moments, a man wearing a nightshirt and hat answered. "We're closed."

"I know, sir, but I'd be mighty grateful if you could spare me and my girl two rooms for the night. We'll be stranded if you cain't."

"Stranded, huh?" He tugged on his graying beard and peered into the darkness. "Hey, I think I recognize you. Were y'all with those musicians traveling through here?"

"Sure are. I play harmonica, but my girl's the star. She sings."

"Well, in that case, I suppose I might be able to see my way clear to helping you out. There aren't many other places in these parts for you to stay at, so it's a good thing I answered the door. Don't always."

"Yes, sir."

"And by the way, you two are lucky I've got two rooms left. I wouldn't rent an unmarried couple just one."

"I don't call that luck, sir. I call it God's provision. And I wouldn't accept just one room for the two of us, either."

The older man's expression softened. "In that case, I don't mind so much having to get up in the middle of the night. Hold on a minute and let me get on some clothes."

Gladdie waited in the cold only a short time before the proprietor emerged and led him to the office. Gladdie detoured to the automobile and summoned Drusie. "We've got two rooms for the night. You can leave us in good conscience, Jake. We're mighty obliged to ya."

"My pleasure."

∞

Even though she'd been dog tired when her head hit the pillow, Drusie didn't sleep well. The metallic smell of steam heat mixed with stale perfume, cigarette smoke, dirt, mold, and body odor, as though previous occupants over the past thirty years had left their initials just as sure as they'd been carved on a sycamore tree. The sheets seemed clean, but they looked dingy. At home, her mother kept their sheets white and smelling of bleach, even if they were so thin a body could be seen right through them. Plaster walls, which she could discern thanks to the motel's lit sign, were once white but had yellowed from smoke and neglect.

The motel room was no worse than the band's usual digs. But it wasn't the sagging mattress that was keeping her awake; her thoughts were. It was the first night since they formed the band that Drusie had been away from Clara. She worried that her younger sister was all alone with no other woman she could call a friend or confidant. June hadn't pulled any fiery pranks since the dress incident, but then again, the jealous woman sensed that Drusie had caught on to her game. Without Drusie nearby, would June harass Clara? Drusie worried in spite of her earlier resolve. She realized that in her selfish pursuit of Gladdie, she had broken her promise to Pa that she would take care of her little sister.

Lord, forgive me. Please take care of Clara. And me and Gladdie, too.

∞

The next morning Gladdie didn't waste time before he knocked on the door to Drusie's room to awaken her. He wanted to catch up to Archie as soon as he could, and without a reliable mode of transportation available, he didn't think he could wait long lest they not catch the band before they moved on to the next town, wherever that might be.

"Comin'!" Her voice sounded chipper for first thing in the morning.

Gladdie smiled to himself. He looked forward to hearing that happy voice every morning for the rest of his life.

The door opened. Drusie stood before him, looking prettier than ever without her dark hair all dolled up and without a trace of face paint on her smooth skin. A crisp white collar peeked from underneath the top of her stylish green wool coat. He wanted to kiss her, but she barely threw him a glance. Clearly she was too preoccupied to think of anything beyond their journey.

"I'm ready, except I'd like a little breakfast. Do ya think there's anywhere to eat around these parts?"

"I saw a diner a few blocks from here when we passed by last night. But I don't know that we'd have time to get there and back before we have to check out. It's already past nine."

Drusie nodded. "We'll figure out somethin'."

A few moments later, Drusie and Gladdie soon stood before the office manager so they could check out.

"Where you young folks going after this? I don't see an automobile outside."

"We don't have an automobile, sir," Gladdie told him.

"You don't?" He scratched his head. "How did you get here?"

"We hitched a ride."

"Oh, I see." He handed Gladdie a few dollars in change. "Taking a bus somewhere?"

"I hope we can get to a bus station without too much trouble," Gladdie admitted. "We're tryin' to get to Southern Pines well before sundown."

"Southern Pines? Why, that shouldn't be any trouble at all. At least not for you. My wife is planning to go visit her sister in Fayetteville today. That's on the way."

"You—you are offerin' to let us ride with her?" Gladdie's voice sounded as bright as he felt. "That would be mighty kind of you, if you would. I'd be glad to give her some money for your gas."

The manager hesitated just a second. "That's all right. I remember what it was like to be young. Money's usually pretty tight. Fact, I know it's tight for you, hitching rides and staying here instead of some fancy place."

Gladdie and Drusie laughed.

"But 'Ain't We Got Fun?'" she asked, borrowing a song title.

"Living on love is a little easier when you're young than it is by the time you get to be my age," the manager mused. "Oh, by the way, I'm Oliver Dunbar. My wife's name is Bertie."

Gladdie introduced Drusie and himself in turn.

Mr. Dunbar tipped his head toward the closed door in the back of the office and shouted, "Bertie!"

From behind the door, Gladdie heard what sounded like the legs of a chair scraping against linoleum. He pictured the woman rising from behind a desk. Soon the door opened, and a wiry, gray-haired woman wearing rimless spectacles emerged. She was dressed in a pink outfit that looked better than the one his mother had for Sunday best. "You called?"

"This is Drusie and Gladdie. They stayed in our last two rooms last night. They were with that band before."

"Which one?"

"Oh, you know, the tour that just came through here. Several bands touring together, I believe it was." Mr. Dunbar didn't bother to conceal his irritation.

"Drusie and I are part of the NC Mountain Girls," Gladdie offered.

Mrs. Dunbar looked down her nose at him. "Humph. You don't look much like a girl to me."

Gladdie forced a laugh. "Drusie here's the main singer. And her sister Clara sings, too. I just play harmonica."

"He plays harmonica real good," Drusie said.

"I'm sure he does." She shrugged. "We have a lot of bands that stay here.

Sorry I didn't recognize you." She eyed them. "So you're the ones who woke us up?"

"Yes, ma'am," Gladdie apologized. "We're sorry."

"Happens all the time."

Mr. Dunbar nodded to Drusie and Gladdie as he kept his gaze on his wife. "They need a ride to Southern Pines."

Gladdie interrupted. "We can just get a ride to a bus stop if that suits you better, Mrs. Dunbar. Drusie and I don't want to trouble you no more than we have to."

"Now don't you worry," Mr. Dunbar said. "It's not out of her way." He looked at his wife. "You can take them along, can't you?"

Mrs. Dunbar assessed them as though they were tomatoes she considered purchasing at a farmers' market. Finally, she nodded. "You two don't look like criminals. And if my husband says you're all right, then you're fine by me."

Gladdie reckoned it took her long enough to decide that, but he opted not to make such a comment. After all, a free ride to the next stop was at stake. "I thank you mightily for your kindness, Mrs. Dunbar."

"I want to thank you, too," Drusie added.

She brushed off their gratitude. "Have you two had breakfast?"

"Now how do you think they've had breakfast if they don't have an automobile?" Mr. Dunbar snapped.

"I was just asking." Mrs. Dunbar's voice sounded testy. She turned her attention back to the young couple. "Can I fix you two a couple of ham biscuits?"

"That would be much appreciated," Drusie said.

"We would be mighty grateful, if it wouldn't be too much trouble," Gladdie added.

"No trouble at all. I've got to get on my wrap and fix your biscuits. Meet me out front in ten minutes."

Gladdie thanked Mr. Dunbar once more but hovered with Drusie near the door as they waited for their ride. Though not brutal, the weather was chilly enough that neither wanted to linger in the air any longer than necessary.

Ten minutes later, Mrs. Dunbar breezed to the front door and waved toward them in a motion to join her.

She had donned a surprising traveling ensemble. Gladdie had never bought a mink coat, but he was country enough to know real fur when he saw it. Her high-heeled shoes were well maintained and looked like they were made from real crocodile skin, as did her purse. Instead of the simple kind of hat his mother wore to church, Mrs. Dunbar wore a wide-brimmed hat tied down with a duster. In place of her spectacles, she wore heavy and unflattering old-fashioned goggles.

"I hope she can see with them things," he hissed to Drusie.

Mr. Dunbar quipped, "She can see just fine. Just uses her other glasses for reading."

Flushed with embarrassment at being overheard but feeling more confiden thanks to the assurance all the same, Gladdie didn't respond except with a ligh wave and to open the door for Drusie to walk out ahead of him.

He hadn't meant to stare as they walked to her automobile, but apparentl he had, as Mrs. Dunbar had a question for him.

"What you looking at, boy? Never seen a woman ready to hit the road?"

He made a point of looking at his shoes. "Uh, we don't dress so fancy wher I come from."

Mrs. Dunbar chuckled. "I don't know that this is so fancy, but my father gav me this hat and duster on the very day I got my first automobile in the year 1922 Bought it with my own money, I did. I wasn't married then. Mr. Dunbar and got married kind of late in life." She stared at a nearby tree but didn't appear t see it. She seemed instead to be somewhere else. "That car's long gone, but I'v had these gifts from Daddy ever since. Goggles have seen some years of good use, too. No sense in throwing out anything that's perfectly usable, I say."

"Yes, ma'am." Gladdie thought about his motel room and realized that th same philosophy applied there as far as the Dunbars were concerned. Judgin by their wear, the mattress and sheets hadn't been replaced since the year 1922 either.

Mrs. Dunbar inspected Drusie. "That feathered hat you got on won't las any time in the wind. You'd better take it off. I wish I had another duster to offe you, but I'm afraid I don't."

Gladdie looked up in time to see Drusie's eyes take on a concerned look "You mean, there will be wind?"

"Of course there will be wind. I have a brand-spanking-new Chevrole Phaeton five-passenger convertible. When my friends ride with me, nobody ha to endure a rumble seat." Mrs. Dunbar led them to a dark green vehicle with it cream-colored top left in the down position. "Isn't this a beautiful automobile?"

Gladdie marveled at the large white walls on the tires. "She sure is, ma'am. He shot Drusie a look. Now he could see what Mr. Dunbar did with his money i lieu of spending it on making the motel look better and feel more comfortable.

If Mrs. Dunbar caught them exchanging glances, she didn't let on. "M Dunbar gave Polly—that's what I named her, Polly—anyway, he gave Polly t me for my birthday last week. I'm not going to tell you which birthday it was but I can say I've enjoyed celebrating my twenty-ninth year a number of times Anyway, I haven't had much call to drive Polly yet. I'm excited about traveling along on the open highway." She patted the car. "You are, too, aren't you, Polly?"

Drusie shivered. "I don't mean any disrespect, Mrs. Dunbar, but ain't it mite chilly to be drivin' with the automobile's top down?"

"Pshaw!" Mrs. Dunbar swished her hand at them. "I can't believe young people today are such weaklings. A good shot of brisk air will do you good."

Gladdie wanted to note that wind didn't whip right through fur like it did wool, but he decided he'd better not agitate the only person offering them a free ride to Southern Pines.

Mrs. Dunbar looked at her left hand as though she'd forgotten she held a paper sack. Without missing a beat, she gasped. "Oh, I almost forgot—your ham biscuits."

She handed Gladdie two biscuits and Drusie one. None of the biscuits held much in the way of meat, but they would do for a light breakfast. "Thank you," Gladdie said, along with Drusie. He proceeded to board the automobile.

"No, you don't." Mrs. Dunbar's voice cracked through the brisk air.

Gladdie stopped. "Don't what, ma'am?"

"Don't dare get in my automobile with food of any kind. I don't want ham grease all over my seats and floorboard."

Gladdie wanted to quip that the chance of their getting any grease from ham with her biscuits was slim, but he held his tongue.

"I'll wait while you two eat." She hopped behind the wheel and sat, looking as happy as anybody Gladdie had ever seen.

Standing in the cold to eat wasn't comfortable in the best of circumstances, but the dry biscuits made the catch-as-catch-can breakfast all the worse. Gladdie took small bites of his portion, wishing he had a glass of water, but getting a drink of any description wasn't convenient and would only delay the trip. Drusie ate slowly as well, apparently not enjoying her meal, either. Yet he knew she would never express a complaint about anyone's generosity.

"You enjoying your biscuits?" Mrs. Dunbar called from the front seat.

"We appreciate you for sharing your food with us," Drusie answered.

"Thank you mightily," Gladdie added.

Gladdie encountered a feeling of relief when Mrs. Dunbar didn't fish for compliments. At least he wouldn't have to figure out how to keep from telling her a fib.

"Here." Mrs. Dunbar handed them each a handkerchief. "Wipe off your hands."

They did, and without delaying a second longer than it took for them to position themselves in the backseat, Mrs. Dunbar started the engine, hit the gas pedal, and took off out of the dirt lot, setting the automobile on the road.

Gladdie watched Drusie hold on to her hat as the motor roared. Every time Mrs. Dunbar met another vehicle, she beeped the horn and waved. Obviously the act of driving invigorated her. She lifted her head high and stared straight ahead. Though he could only see her from the back, he could tell from the way her cheeks puffed out that a little smile decorated her face.

Gladdie noticed Drusie shivering, so he put his arm around her. Holding on to her hat, she snuggled closely to him. Gladdie mused that the scene would feel romantic except that they were both freezing.

"I grew up in New England," Mrs. Dunbar yelled to them. "This is such mild weather. Hardly ever get a decent snow around these parts. Sure do miss the snow."

The last thing Gladdie wanted to see was snow. "Yes, ma'am!"

She glanced at them in the rearview mirror. "When do you kids plan to get married?"

Gladdie missed what she asked and responded to her mutterings. "I'm sorry, ma'am?"

"You didn't hear me, eh? That's just like a man."

"I'm sorry. I really didn't hear you."

She shouted louder. "I said, when do you plan to marry Drusie?"

"Uh, maybe you should ask her," Gladdie shouted.

She swerved to avoid a cat in the road. Gladdie held on to the back of the front seat for dear life with his free hand, and Drusie held closely to him.

"If we ever get out of this automobile alive, we should get married right away," Gladdie whispered in Drusie's ear. "Pa always said life is short. Ours might be shorter than we thought."

Drusie giggled, and Gladdie tightened his grip on her.

The near miss with the cat didn't deter Mrs. Dunbar's interrogation. "That's not a firm answer. Don't you have a date, missy?"

"Not yet," Drusie answered.

Gladdie wondered if she meant that or if she was just being polite to Mrs. Dunbar.

"Well, you'd better get one." Mrs. Dunbar let go of the wheel with one hand and wagged her finger in Drusie's direction. "My first boyfriend escaped me by promising to get married. But he ran off before he kept his promise. Skunk!"

"I'm sorry," Drusie answered.

"I'll never let that happen to you." Gladdie nuzzled her neck, relieved that Drusie had taken the pressure off him—and his voice since shouting was straining it—to field questions.

"Stop it. You're tickling me," Drusie teased.

"Maybe if I'd let the skunk nuzzle me, I'd be married to him now," Mrs. Dunbar shouted, then switched topics. "So where did you say you need to go?"

Drusie looked at Gladdie, and he could see in her eyes she was tired of shouting. "Southern Pines," he yelled.

"What's in Southern Pines?"

"Hopefully my cousin. He's supposed to be at a concert tonight."

"A concert? What kind of music?"

"Mountain music."

"Oh, I should have figured, with you being called the NC Mountain Girls."

Mrs. Dunbar scrunched her nose. "I don't mean no harm by it, but I don't know that I'd like that music very much. A bunch of hillbillies blowing into a jug? No thanks."

Gladdie opened his mouth to retort but stopped when he encountered Drusie's elbow in his rib cage.

"Everybody has different tastes," Drusie yelled. "That's why God gave us different kinds of music."

"I suppose you have a point. Not that you seem so much like hillbillies or anything. It's just that my tastes run more toward classical. So where is this hillbilly concert?"

Gladdie responded, "I don't rightly know."

"You don't know?" They had reached the edge of town, forcing Mrs. Dunbar to slow the automobile.

To his relief, now Gladdie could answer her without yelling quite so loudly. "We usually perform in high school auditoriums, but not always. Sometimes we perform in churches."

"I don't have all day to hunt. My sister doesn't like me to be late for lunch."

"We don't want to make you late. You can drop us off anywhere you like and we'll find our way."

"No, I won't, either. I can't leave the two of you stranded with that luggage. What did my husband get me into?"

Gladdie pointed to a street sign where someone had attached a piece of paper. "Say, that looks like an ad for the concert. Can you stop?"

Mrs. Dunbar brought the massive machine to a halt by the curb. "You want to get out and look?"

Gladdie nodded and leaped out of the car. He memorized the information on the sign before returning to the car.

"What did it say?" Drusie asked.

"It says we're supposed to be at Our Redeemer Church at eight tonight. Says it's a gospel concert."

Drusie nodded. "Those are my favorites."

"Mine, too," Gladdie agreed.

Mrs. Dunbar ignored their comments. "I know where that church is. Do you want to go this early? If the concert isn't until eight, I doubt anyone's there yet."

Gladdie eyed a diner and wondered how long it would take them to walk to the church. "How far is it from here?"

"A few blocks." Mrs. Dunbar studied the sign. "Say!" She turned and looked at Drusie, then to the sign, then back. "Is that your picture on that sign?"

Drusie blushed. "Sure is, ma'am. To tell the truth, I'm surprised my picture's still on the ad."

"I'm not," Gladdie noted. "It's only been two days, and even if it had been two months, Archie wouldn't want to spend the extra money printin' up new flyers until the old ones was gone."

"True."

"Two days since what?" Mrs. Dunbar asked.

"It's a long story," Gladdie answered.

"It always is, isn't it?" Mrs. Dunbar studied the ad. "Well, I'll be! Drusie, you really are a headliner, just like Gladdie said."

"Yes, ma'am."

"How about that? Sometimes show people tell tall tales, so I had my doubts you were much of a celebrity. But that really is you." She studied the ad again and looked back to her young female passenger. "Although I did have to look close to recognize you. I must say, the picture flatters you."

"I have on a right smart amount of face paint in that picture, ma'am."

The older woman studied Drusie. "Hmm. I see the difference. I suppose you don't look half bad at that. You should wear lip rouge all the time."

As Mrs. Dunbar searched her purse, Gladdie whispered in Drusie's ear. "I think you're prettier without it."

Drusie blushed and smiled.

Mrs. Dunbar handed Drusie a piece of paper. "Here. Let me have your autograph."

Gladdie held back laughter. Mrs. Dunbar had been snobby about their music until she realized Drusie was a lead singer in a popular band.

"I'm sorry about what I said earlier about your music," Mrs. Dunbar apologized as she took the paper from Drusie. "I really do prefer classical, and I think singing three hymns in church every Sunday is enough gospel music to endure for the week. But I should have kept my opinions about your hillbilly music to myself. Why, you don't look like hillbillies at all. Not much, anyway, I don't suppose."

"That's fine," Drusie answered with her usual sweet spirit. "Maybe now you'll give us—and our mountain music—a chance."

"Maybe I will." She looked at Gladdie. "I didn't see your picture on the placard."

"I'm not a member of the band, ma'am. At least, not anymore."

"Oh." She slipped the paper into her purse and snapped it shut. "Well, I wish you two lovebirds all the best. Maybe I will try to catch you in concert the next time you come to town."

"I hope you do," they said in unison.

As he watched Mrs. Dunbar drive off, Gladdie was almost sorry to see her go. But he hoped he would never have to take such a harrowing ride again.

Chapter 14

D rusie and Gladdie went into the diner and warmed up with coffee. They lingered but couldn't hold a booth forever, so they ventured outside, taking their time and moving with slow determination. With nothing better to do, they spent the afternoon window shopping. This was no small feat, since at his insistence Gladdie carried both of their suitcases. They paused in front of each storefront for a time, with Gladdie setting down their baggage at each stop.

Drusie could feel tension mixed with anticipation when they neared a jewelry store. Some of the rings boasted stones that were very big, much bigger than Drusie ever wanted to wear, no matter how famous she became or how many songs the band recorded. The more she got out in the world, the more she realized that all that mattered to her was Gladdie. Mrs. Dunbar let her first love get away. Drusie didn't want that to happen to her.

They stared at mannequins dressed in the latest styles. Drusie couldn't help but dream of herself dressed in the rose-colored suit and matching hat displayed in one window. The man's dark blue suit next to it looked sharp, too. She imagined Gladdie turning heads in such an outfit. She longed for a night out, regardless of what she would be wearing. She missed the church socials and her friends back home. Life on the road didn't offer too many breaks for any of the band members. She guessed that some of the tension and backstage drama had much to do with everyone being plumb worn out.

"What do you think we should say to Archie when we see him?" Gladdie ventured.

Drusie didn't answer right away. "I don't know." She strolled to the next window and focused on yet another display. Natural mink fur trimmed a beige suit. She noticed that the fur was punctuated with darker brown hairs that gave it texture. Not that she cared, but studying it helped her to concentrate on thinking about how to get Gladdie back in Archie's good graces.

"I think the world and all of Archie, but he can be a vexation at times."

"And from the looks of things, we just might have him as a brother-in-law, too."

"Clara's that far gone, huh?"

"I'm afraid so. I would have rather seen her set her sights on a stronger Christian, but I cain't make decisions for her. Besides, I don't think she'll consent to marry him until he gets closer to the Lord."

"Wonder when that will be." Gladdie's voice was tinged with regret.

"Soon, I hope." She sighed. "He's made my sister happier than she's ever been. We all grew up together. You know what she's like. She's always loved attention, and she's never had a chance to wear pretty clothes, at least not the fancy clothes Archie puts us in to sing onstage."

"I wonder if your pa would mind if he could see you."

"I don't think he'd mind. Even under the spotlights, nobody can see through them. And I wouldn't agree to wear anything low cut. I'm glad Archie didn't insist."

"Well, you do sing gospel songs," Gladdie pointed out.

"True." Drusie sighed. "Archie has invested money in us. I feel kind of guilty about that, even though I do think he took advantage of us just a little bit." She looked at Gladdie, unable to hide her distress. "I'm sorry to have to say that about your cousin."

"How Archie behaves ain't your fault. No point in lyin' about it to spare my feelin's. I'm sorry things didn't turn out the way we thought they would."

"It's all my fault," Drusie said. "I didn't know what I was gettin' into when I first wanted to play for Archie. I just knew I liked to sing and that my friends and family thought I was right good. When Archie agreed, you could've knocked me over with a feather. I mean, it's one thing for your ma to say you sing good, but it's a horse of another color for a man like Archie to like what you do."

"I know it." Gladdie picked up their suitcases. By resuming a slow pace to the next window, he encouraged Drusie to keep moving. "Don't you never think you're no good at singin'. I think you can live the rest of your days out knowin' that people—all kinds of people—think you sing good. Even if all this turns out bad, you've had a chance not everybody gets. And that is to live out a dream that a whole lot of singers would've given their eyeteeth for." Gladdie set down their luggage.

Drusie peered into the hardware store window but didn't take much interest in a wheelbarrow and a sign promising that seed orders for spring planting would be taken starting January. "You're right. Archie did give me a chance not many girls ever get. I'll have to thank him for that, no matter what."

Tired of staring at the wheelbarrow, she edged away. Gladdie picked up their suitcases and they walked toward the corner, planning to stroll through the residential section. They had the address and knew the road would lead to the church where the bands were scheduled to perform that evening. The waitress at the diner had told them they'd have to pass through a few blocks of houses before they'd find a small white church on the corner of Fifth and Elm. Gladdie kept pace beside her.

Lord, thank You for sending us sunshine and not much of a breeze so we don't freeze to death.

Drusie noticed a large residence on a lawn that looked like it would take a lot of upkeep. Maybe being rich had its advantages, but Drusie couldn't imagine herself in charge of a big home like the one they were passing.

"You'd like a big house like that one day, wouldn't you?" Gladdie mused.

"Naw, I was thinkin' just the opposite. I reckon I'll always be a little mountain girl."

"That's why you're so popular singin'. People see you're genuine, and they like that. When you sing a song, they know you mean it."

"I'm glad you think that. Sometimes I wonder, I get so tired. I thought singin' would be an easy way to make some fast money. And I suppose in some ways, it is. I have grown to like performin' for the crowds." Drusie sighed. "But you know somethin'? Goin' here, there, and yonder with the band has taught me somethin' important. Entertainers are paid to make what they do look easy. They have to look like they're havin' the best time in the world, singin' their hearts out night after night after night. They have to make it look like they've only sang their songs once or twice, not a hundred times, so many times they're sick of every tune. Some nights, I wish I never had to hear a banjo play again. But until you fell out with Archie, I kept goin'. For Clara. And so we could have us a nice little nest egg."

"I'll always love you for that." He sent her the crooked grin she knew and loved.

"And I'll always love you, too." To keep from getting too sentimental in public, Drusie changed the subject. "There's the church."

"Sure looks like it. It should be unlocked. We can go into the sanctuary and rest and pray."

"That's a fine idea. Hey, how are we gonna handle this situation with Archie? We've been together all day, and even with all our prayers, I don't sense a firm answer from the Lord on what to do about this, exactly. Have you?"

"No."

"We still ain't come up with a way to prove Elmer and that strange woman are to blame for all the missin' stuff. I reckon even our brains together are a mite puny."

Gladdie laughed. "Maybe so. But not as puny as all that. I've been thinkin', maybe it's not up to us to prove nothin'."

"Say what?"

"I know it sounds odd, but I mean it. I've been thinkin' and thinkin', and I just don't feel right about tryin' to prove anything about Elmer. I don't think it's my place, somehow."

A phrase from Romans popped into Drusie's head. " 'Vengeance is mine; I will repay, saith the Lord.' "

As they approached the church, Drusie's stomach tied itself into a knot when she noticed Archie's automobile parked out front in all its cream-colored glory. "They must be early."

"Must be. But I don't think that should keep us from prayin'." He stopped, and they took a moment to ask the Lord for the right words. As soon as they did, Drusie felt stronger. She sensed that Gladdie did, too.

The band was unpacking in the sanctuary. Archie was off by himself, talking with two men Gladdie hadn't seen before. He watched his cousin pat one on the shoulder and wondered who they were.

"Archie! I'm back!" Drusie called to him. She touched Gladdie's arm in silent instruction for him to hold back on his greeting, thinking it wiser for her to see Archie first since he was a little less angry with her than he was with Gladdie. At least, she hoped.

Archie didn't hesitate to turn his head toward the sound of her voice. He smiled and, excusing himself from his new companions, broke off from them and headed toward her. "Well, well, well! You decided to come back, I see. I knew you'd miss being onstage and all the accolades. Not to mention the pretty dresses. You made the right decision." He crossed his arms. "I hope you realize this means I'll be giving you a 10 percent pay cut. I can't have my canaries running off on me and then thinking they can just come back anytime without paying the piper—or should I say, the fiddler."

"I don't care nothin' about that. How's Clara?"

"She's swell. Why wouldn't she be? She's done a stand-up job without you."

"Oh." Drusie couldn't help but feel a touch of disappointment.

"Oh, all right," Archie admitted. "She bawled all night after the show." He shook his head and stared at the peak in the sanctuary.

Drusie felt Gladdie's presence nearby. "Hello, cuz."

Archie's posture became rigid, and his expression darkened. "What are you doing here?"

"I came here to be with Drusie." Gladdie pointed to his chest. "But I demand an apology."

"Sure. Have it your way," Archie said. "I'm sorry. There—is that enough?"

Gladdie looked as shocked as Drusie felt. "That was easy," Gladdie said.

"Too easy," Drusie said.

"Okay, I admit it. Your innocence was proven for you. June is missing her earrings. And I know one thing, if anybody had reason for taking her stuff, it was you. Or Clara, and she had plenty of people stand up for her saying she couldn't have taken them."

"That's a relief. I'd hate for Clara to be accused of wrongdoin', especially with me gone." Drusie knew how much Archie wanted Clara on the tour at any cost, but she refrained from expressing the sentiment.

Archie nodded and elaborated. "June was wearing them when you left, and hey disappeared last night after the show." In an uncharacteristic motion, he stared at his wing-tipped shoes and shuffled his feet. "Truth be told, I knew you didn't take anything, Gladdie. I was just so steaming mad about everything that's happened that all I could see was red. I was looking for an excuse to throw you out, and I took it." He looked back at Gladdie. "So I guess I should say I'm sorry I flew off the handle last night. I do want you back in the band." He extended his hand. "Deal?"

Gladdie accepted his hand. "Deal. But if I'm ever accused of wrongdoin' again, I expect you to take up for me."

"Will do."

One of the men to whom Archie had been speaking interrupted. "Mr. Gordon, we're ready."

"Okay, go ahead." Archie introduced the men to Gladdie and Drusie as a duo, the Rustling Rangers.

The taller of the two stared at Drusie and snapped his fingers. "Hey! Aren't you one of the NC Mountain Girls?"

"Drusie Fields." She extended her hand, which the man accepted.

"Bill Richards, ma'am." He tipped his cowboy hat. "And this here's my partner and brother, Milton."

"Nice to meet you both."

"Uh, are you going to listen to us play?"

"I'd like to."

Milton let out a whistle. "I didn't know a celebrity would be listening to us audition." Milton and Drusie shook hands. "Now I think I might be a little nervous."

Drusie laughed. "I'm nothin' much. I'm just a mountain girl who loves singin' and listenin' to good music just like anybody else."

Gladdie watched the exchange as he hovered in the background. The longer Drusie stayed a celebrity, the more he became accustomed to being shunted aside while Drusie accepted accolades. He was glad God hadn't made him a proud man. His pa never would have let his ma take over like that.

"Okay, enough booshwashing," Archie prodded. "I don't have all day. I've got a show to put on. Let's hear you."

"Sure thing." Bill nodded to his partner, and the Rustling Rangers struck a few chords of an old mountain hymn. Even though the playing caused the people in the sanctuary to stop and listen, their expressions approving, the men had sung only half a verse before Archie stopped them.

"What else have you got?"

Both men stopped playing mid-note and shook a bit. Bill was the first to regain his composure. "We got plenty." He mumbled something to Milton, and they began a song Gladdie had never heard with a melody that possessed a bluegrass feel. Archie let them sing up to the chorus before getting them to move on to the next tune. The dance went on through several songs, including two hymns. Through it all, Archie didn't show any reaction.

"Well?" Bill asked, clutching his fiddle as though it might break if Archie's opinion wasn't favorable.

Archie looked at Drusie and Gladdie. "What do y'all think?"

"I think they're good," Drusie said. "Better than good—I think they're grand."

"Good enough to cut a record?"

"More than good enough."

Archie looked at the men, whose faces had relaxed with relief. "Are you from around these parts?"

"No. We're from Clarksville, Virginia. We drove to Raleigh to see you, but the studio was shut tight as a drum," Bill explained. "We waited until the next day, and then finally one of your men, Harry, opened up shop. He listened to us and said we were good, but he couldn't help us. You had to make the decision. But he said you were on the road and wouldn't be back for a spell. He told us you'd be here tonight. I don't 'spect he thought we'd drive all this way to find you, but we did. I appreciate you for giving us a chance like this, Mr. Gordon."

"Persistence can often outweigh talent, although you've got plenty of both," Archie said. "If you had said this was your hometown, I'd have guessed that everyone would be rooting for you strong. But since no one around here knows you—that's right, isn't it? No one knows you?"

"That's right."

"Well, I see you went to a lot of trouble to secure an audition with me," Archie said, "and that means a lot. That shows me that you have the determination to make it in this business. So I have a proposition for you. Will you play a few gospel songs before the NC Mountain Girls go on tonight and see how you do with the audience? If they like you, I'd be leaning toward offering you a chance to record."

"We'll take that chance, Mr. Gordon!" Bill exclaimed. "Thank you mightily. We appreciate it an awful lot."

"That's fine. You two fellows go ahead and practice. Showtime's at eight sharp. I don't like to keep my audience waiting."

"Yes, sir, Mr. Gordon. We won't keep them waiting. No, sir." The men hurried out of the sanctuary.

"Looks like you've made someone else's dreams come true," Drusie remarked.

"That's what I do. I make dreams come true." Archie's smile bespoke the smugness of control.

"You will let them make a record if the audience likes them, won't you, Archie?" Gladdie asked.

"Of course I will. They don't realize it, but I'd give them a contract anyway. I figured I might as well give the audience a bonus. Publicity will do everyone good." Archie winked. "Now you better get hopping, Drusie, and get that dress on. Your blue one, since this is a church. Showtime will be here before you know it."

Drusie found Clara in the dressing room, standing in front of the mirror, making sure every hair was in place. "Clara?"

She spun to face Drusie and put her hand on her chest. "Don't scare me like that!" Her eyes widened. "What are you doin' here?"

"I'm here to fulfill my contract. Is that okay with you?"

"Okay? It's better than okay!" Clara ran toward her for a hug. "I'm so glad you came back. Don't you ever leave me again without sayin' somethin' first. So what happened?"

Drusie shared the story of her adventure.

"That's really somethin'." Clara shook her head. "I'm so glad you're safe and sound and back here where you belong."

The sisters embraced once again, and Drusie's heart felt warmer.

∞

Archie proved to be right. Time did fly, and the show went even better than they expected. For churches, Archie always suspended his usual rule of advance payment, opting for donations. As promised, a love offering was taken, and Gladdie helped man the booth where they sold copies of their recordings.

Drusie came up to them after signing autographs.

"How did you like that? All those people loving you?" Archie asked.

"I always enjoy when people like my music."

"Keen. We're just getting started making real money." Archie rubbed his palms together. "This is going to be some kind of take tonight."

Gladdie interrupted. "I don't know. These people probably don't have a lot of money. I just hope they enjoyed the music."

"That's why you're not a businessman, Gladdie. You have no acumen for money."

"Whatever you say, Archie."

The promoter tapped Archie on the shoulder. "Boss, I've got to speak with you."

Gladdie didn't like the look on his face, and judging from Archie's concerned expression, he didn't, either.

"What's the matter, Earl?"

"The love offering. It's gone. All of it."

Chapter 15

Stunned by the news of the missing money, Drusie, along with everyone else, looked at Archie. He looked even more shocked than when they found the burned dress.

"What do you mean, the love offering's gone? That just can't be," Archie said.

"It can be, and it is. I'm sorry." The deacon's voice was low in volume.

Drusie glanced at Gladdie, who stood beside her. Upset, she instinctively reached for him. He clasped her hand in his and squeezed it in a way that gave her comfort.

Archie wasn't so easy to console. "Did anybody ask the head deacon about this?"

"Yes, and he said he gave the money to a brown-haired woman who said she was with you."

Drusie couldn't help but pounce on the description. "Was she wearin' fur?"

"Fur? Not at the time, no."

"Oh." Drusie felt a little foolish.

"But she did have on a red dress that looked like somethin' you'd wear to a nightclub instead of a church, and she was tall."

"That sounds like her," Gladdie mumbled.

"Sounds like who?" Archie asked.

"The woman who's always around Elmer."

Archie groaned. "I hate to say it, but that does sound like her. But we can't be sure. I sure hope it's not her. Elmer's been with me a long time. I trust him like a brother. I'd hate to think he's gotten himself dizzy with a dame that isn't walking the straight and narrow." He snapped his fingers. "Maybe somebody in the audience took it. Yeah, that's it."

"I'd like to think a stranger made off with the money, but I doubt it. Remember, we did put on a gospel concert tonight, and I imagine we attracted mainly church people," Gladdie said. "Besides, I didn't see nobody actin' suspicious anytime after the offerin' was taken."

"And even if we could question anybody," Archie pointed out, "they've all gone home now. We'd never find them."

One of the older deacons approached. "I'm really sorry this happened, Mr. Gordon. I'm embarrassed that something like this could happen at our church.

We have gospel groups singing here all the time, and this is the first time this has happened."

"I believe you. But can you help us? Can you describe the woman you gave the money to, other than the fact she was tall, wearing a fancy red dress, and had brown hair?"

He thought for a moment. "Well, I can tell you that as soon as she took the money, she stuffed it in her purse and put on a fur coat."

"A long, dark fur?" Archie's voice rang with defeat.

He nodded. "It was the only fur I saw here tonight. She stuck out like a sore thumb, because most of the people around these parts can't afford such luxury. I'm sorry, Mr. Gordon. I guess I should have asked more questions," the deacon apologized. "But I mean, she was dressed so nice, like a motion picture star, and wearing that fur and all. She acted like she was in charge, so I assumed she was since she said she was with the band. Why, I thought maybe she might have been your wife."

"It's not your fault. We'll get the money as soon as the band member she hangs out with shows up. I'm sure it's all a mistake. He'll set things right," Archie answered.

"Hey, I heard the money's missing," one of the stagehands complained, approaching from behind. "If this keeps on, I'll be going in the hole working for you, Arch."

Mutters of discontent rippled through the tour members.

Archie waved his hands in a soothing motion. "Hold on. We'll get our money back as soon as we find Elmer. Go on now and let's get the gang together, and then we can all get paid and sleep better tonight."

"I hope so," June sniped.

Soon the band members were gathered, except for one.

"Where's Elmer?" Gladdie asked.

"I don't know. I couldn't find him," Archie admitted.

"I don't know where he is, either," Gladdie said. "I hollered into the men's dressing room, and I thought everyone would show up like usual. I don't know why he wouldn't."

"Maybe he's with his girl," Clara guessed.

"I wish he'd show up." Archie's tone indicated his impatience. "Now that he's not here for the meeting, I have a feeling something's rotten in Denmark. Does anybody around here know where he is?" Archie scanned the faces around him.

No one had a good answer.

"I remember seein' that woman who always hangs around him," June noted.

"I saw her, too," Betty said. "Boy, oh boy, that coat she had on was sure swell."

"Sure was," June agreed. "She was in the audience tonight. Second row center, as usual. I can't help but wonder if she's got something to do with it."

"Could be," Gladdie said. "When they're together, somethin' always turns up missin'. I'm thinkin' back, and every time a trinket or money gets lost, that woman has been with him that day."

Drusie thought for a moment. "You know somethin', you're right. I always was more than a mite suspicious of that woman, but I didn't have her pegged as a thief."

Waves of agreement sounded among the tour members.

"Of course I'm right," Gladdie joked before turning serious. "Only this time, I wish I was wrong."

"Maybe you're still wrong," Archie said. "But if you're not, don't worry. Elmer's still around here somewhere and we'll expose him. If he's guilty, I suspect that for now he's playing it cool and not running since he's a band member."

"True," Betty said, "but he should have shown up to the meeting if he didn't want us to suspect anything."

"You've got a point. Let's go see if we can find him and his girlfriend. Gladdie, you look inside. I'll see what I can find out in the church yard." Archie nodded to the women. "Clara and Drusie, Betty and June, you split up into pairs and look at all the places that just the women have access to and see if you can spot the dame."

"Sure thing," they all agreed.

"Maybe we should split up one by one and cover more ground that way," Drusie suggested.

"I wouldn't," Clara said. "What if she's got a gun?"

"A gun? I hadn't thought of that." Drusie's throat grew dry. She swallowed, but it didn't help much. *Heavenly Father, please don't let anyone get harmed in all this mess.*

"Be careful," Gladdie whispered in her ear.

"You, too."

Drusie and her sister looked through the church but didn't see the fur-clad woman. "She's a slick one," Drusie said, surrendering the search after exploring every Sunday school room that had been used by the women to change clothes.

"We cain't give up. She's got to be here somewhere."

"No, she doesn't. She may be long gone by now. I would be if I was her."

"But she cain't be far from Elmer, and he's due to play again with us tomorrow night."

"True," Drusie conceded.

Without warning, they heard a man shout in the sanctuary. "Stop right there! We've got you surrounded."

Drusie rushed up narrow wooden steps, with Clara following right behind her. They reached the top of the stairs just in time to see Elmer rushing out of the church. Gladdie ran behind him. Drusie and Clara ran to the entrance. They watched as Gladdie caught up to Elmer.

"Hey, what's all the fuss about?" Drusie heard Elmer say.

The men stood in a huddle and talked. Drusie noticed Elmer's facial expression change from disbelief to anger, then sorrow.

Gladdie broke away from them and approached the sisters. "Looks like that woman took Elmer for a ride. He thought she was interested in him, but apparently she had planned this all along."

"What?" Clara and Drusie said at once.

The shake of Gladdie's head conveyed his sadness. "That's right. Elmer thinks she must have been the one who took all our things. I don't know that he's all that surprised. I reckon he's overheard people talking about his girl for quite some time and he didn't want to believe she could do anything wrong. But I can see how sorry he is. He told me now he understands why she didn't want anybody to know they were seeing each other. She had planned this big take all along, it seems."

"How sad." Clara's eyes misted.

"It is sad. His heart is broken."

Drusie took Gladdie's hand. "Oh, I'm so glad we didn't try to pin this all on Elmer. I would have felt just awful, even though that woman was connected to him."

"Me, too."

"At least they know it warn't us."

"Yep," Gladdie agreed. "At least some of us are havin' a happy endin'."

Chapter 16

The next day, everyone was anxious for news. Drusie longed for the return of her little gold necklace, especially since it was worth much more to her in sentiment than it would ever bring in money. She had a feeling the woman had sold everything long ago.

"No luck, Drusie," Archie told her. "They did catch her, though. She was trying to get as far away from here as she could—with another man, to boot."

"Poor Elmer," Drusie couldn't help but say.

"I know it. And poor us. She pawned everything. Even if she had saved the tickets, we don't have time to go find everybody's stuff. I can't even take a break long enough to find my cuff links. They didn't hold any sentimental value. I left my father's watch at home. That's the only jewelry that means anything to me. As for the cuff links, well, it's a good thing I was able to buy another pair almost identical to the ones that were stolen." Archie held out an arm and showed them a shiny cuff link of gold inlaid with mother-of-pearl.

"Lucky you," Drusie said without much enthusiasm.

Archie shook his head. "I'm sorry you got a tough break, kids."

"I've got all the time in the world. I still want to find my necklace," Drusie countered.

Archie's sympathy proved temporal. "You might want to, but you won't be able to. You don't have time. You're still under contract to me."

"And so is Elmer?" she couldn't help but ask.

"And so is Elmer. He was a dupe. He's learned his lesson about trusting a pretty face too soon."

Drusie remained silent. She could imagine the hold the woman in fur had on Elmer.

"This has just been too much excitement. I don't know what I would have done if you hadn't been here, Drusie." Clara embraced her sister. "I'm so glad you're back for good! I missed you so much when you were gone."

Drusie laughed. "It warn't that long, but I missed you, too."

"I have a feelin' you're desperate enough to take me back, too, Archie." Though Gladdie's tone sounded light, Drusie knew he wasn't jesting.

Archie laughed. "I'm that desperate—if you'll come back, that is."

"Good. I got ya right where I want ya."

"You sound like a hardboiled gunsel in a gangster film," Archie replied

344

"Where's your Chicago typewriter?"

"I ain't no gunsel. I'm a G-man. And here's my Chicago typewriter." He pretended to spout off bullets at Archie with a Thompson machine gun.

Archie placed his hand on his chest and pretended to collapse.

"Boys!" Clara chastised. "We sing songs. We don't make gangster movies."

Drusie laughed, glad that the tension of the past few weeks was shattered and the easy camaraderie they once enjoyed had returned. "Okay, Gladdie, what's your big idea?"

"Archie's gonna love it." Gladdie rubbed his hands together. "How about you lettin' me manage the NC Mountain Girls? Then you can be free to go back to the studio and cut records with more acts. Maybe you can go on another tour yourself."

Archie didn't even contemplate the idea. "No can do, pal-ly. I'm not leaving Clara." Archie gazed at Clara with unmistakable love in his eyes. "But I tell you what. To make it up to you and Drusie for me flying off the handle and letting you go—and because you're a great harmonica player—not only can you stay with us for the rest of this tour, but you can have a job with me as long as you want."

"Well, it ain't as good as managin' the band. You really mean what you say, right?"

"Sure I do. I'm not in the habit of saying things I don't mean."

"I'll stay on one condition."

Archie raised his arms in mock surrender. "How many conditions have you got?"

Gladdie laughed. "Not so many. I want me and Drusie to marry soon—over the Christmas holiday. And now that Drusie's takin' a likin' to performin', and I have, too, I do want us to stay for a while. But I also want us to have enough time to have a home life while Drusie keeps her contract with you."

"You want to have your cake and eat it, too," Archie said.

Gladdie crossed his arms. "Yep."

"You drive a hard bargain. I'm proud of you, Gladdie." Archie emphasized his sentiment with a pat on Gladdie's back. "I think you've finally learned how to be a good businessman."

"What do you think of that idea, Clara?" Drusie asked, even though she could guess the answer. Clara's face looked rapt with anticipation. She didn't want to leave the music industry—or Archie. Gladdie's solution was perfect.

"What do I think?" Clara's eyes widened. "Why, I didn't know my opinion counted for nothin'."

"I don't know why you'd say that. You're one of the stars," Archie noted.

"I don't need to be the star of the show. I like singin' with my sister better."

Drusie sniffled, trying to hold back her emotion. She never expected Clara, who loved attention more than anything else, to say that she'd rather share the spotlight with her than keep the accolades of audiences to herself. Perhaps the worldliness of playing music for money hadn't gotten to her little sister as much as she suspected. *Thank You, Lord, for being there for Clara when I was gone.*

"I have one more favor to ask you, Archie," Gladdie said.

Archie crossed his arms. "You're a good businessman, but I have my limits, even when it comes to my own cousin."

"I know. But we got this one comin' to us. Can we have a week off at Christmas instead of the two days you had planned for us? Drusie and I talked about gettin' married on New Year's Day."

Archie opened his mouth to protest.

Gladdie raised a palm to stop him. "You have to admit, even that doesn't leave much time for a honeymoon. And I know you don't have no concerts lined up that week. I wouldn't ask you to disappoint our payin' fans by cancelin' out on them. All you had for us to do was make another record. Cain't we do that later?"

"I don't know. We've got to strike while the iron is hot," Archie argued. "Do you have to get married over the holiday? Can't you get married anytime? There's a church in every town. Most of the time, you got your pick of places to get married in."

"But I want Ma and Pa and everybody else to be there," Drusie said. "Even though I don't need no fancy weddin'."

"Yeah," Gladdie agreed. "I want to go home so Drusie and I can be married by Preacher Lawson. He's been our pastor ever since I can remember, and I cain't imagine bein' married by anybody else."

"Me neither," Drusie concurred.

"Oh, all right. But only three days. We've got to cut more records now that everybody's excited about your songs and askin' about where to get the platters. You might be famous now, but they'll forget you all too soon if you disappoint them."

"But we ain't askin' for much time," Gladdie pointed out. "Just a couple of days."

"A couple of days? That's not much time to put on a big shindig worthy of celebrities." Archie ticked off the list on his fingers. "The music, flowers, getting your dress made, food, the invitations. . . I don't see how all that can be planned in such a short time."

"But I don't want nothin' like a celebrity would have," Drusie said. "I just want a simple day."

"I want what she wants," Gladdie agreed.

Archie lifted his palms in surrender. "Okay, kids. It's your day."

Epilogue

As planned, the wedding took place on New Year's Day at the little church in Sunshine Hollow where the Fields family had worshiped for several generations. Pastor Lawson officiated at the ceremony. Gray clouds concealed the sun but not enough to threaten rain or snow. Friends and family surrounded Drusie and Gladdie. Drusie never remembered being happier.

Just as the tour ended, Archie had taken them to a fine store in Raleigh so they could choose dresses. Both men had traveled to a haberdashery down the street to be fitted for brand-new suits. She'd already seen Gladdie in his dark blue suit that made him appear dapper in a more subdued way than his lively stage garb. He looked like a model in a magazine ad aimed at a busy executive. She would have married him while he wore old dungarees, but she sure was glad he'd look dashing in their wedding photograph.

Drusie had bought a knee-length green dress for her wedding day, choosing a lovely shade that complemented her dark hair and fair skin, in honor of new beginnings and the season of Christmas.

"You've never looked lovelier," Clara told her.

Drusie didn't want to brag, but she knew her sister spoke the truth. She could feel warm happiness radiating from her face.

Remembering their family as they made ready for the wedding, Drusie and Gladdie had paid train fare for everyone to join them in Raleigh, where their parents and sisters chose apparel they'd wear as participants. Ma adored her mauve-colored dress with touches of lace. "Too good for me," she'd said, but her ecstatic expression told them otherwise. Pa looked dandy in his new suit, even though he did complain about having to wear a tie. Her sisters looked lovely in pink. As she gazed upon her family, Drusie smiled with so much pride her cheeks hurt.

Drusie and Gladdie waited as the wedding photographer set up a scene with a decorated archway to frame the newlyweds and their wedding party.

"Everything's so beautiful, Gladdie." Drusie let out a sigh.

Gladdie gazed into her eyes. "For the first time in my life, I have enough money to treat you right, and I'm gonna do it. Just you wait until you see where we're headed for our honeymoon."

"Where are we goin'?"

"I'll never tell." Gladdie grinned at his new sister-in-law and Archie.

"Especially in front of these two."

Drusie grinned and swatted at him with her bouquet of six red roses that they had ordered from the new owners of Goode's store—relatives of the well respected Simpsons—especially for her day. They came all the way from a florist in Greensboro.

"Now don't ruin your pretty flowers before we get our pictures taken," Clara teased.

"I know. But now I won't be able to think of anything else but tryin' to guess where we'll be goin' after this."

"Won't you tell her, Gladdie?" Clara prodded.

"Oh, all right. I'll tell you where we're goin'—Washington, D.C."

Drusie took in a breath. "All that way?"

"Yes, all that way. Don't you want to see the monuments?"

"Sure, but—but we don't have time."

Gladdie caught Archie's glance long enough to wink. "We do now. The time off is Archie's present to us."

"Yeah. But don't take too long."

"Always the businessman," Gladdie remarked.

"I don't care what you say; I cain't think of a better gift." Drusie sighed. "So much happiness today. We'll be back on the road all too soon."

"You regret becomin' a celebrity?" Archie asked.

Drusie thought for a moment. "Nope. Cain't say that I do."

"I'm glad to hear that," Archie said. "But I have to say, since being around you again, I remember the simple pleasures of home. And the love of God. I've forgotten Him lately, and I think it's time for me to get closer again."

Clara gasped. "Do you really mean that, Archie?"

"Sure do."

Clara beamed.

Drusie's heart warmed. With Archie's heart softening, maybe one day he would be her brother-in-law. She had a feeling Clara wouldn't mind one bit.

The photographer summoned Archie and Clara, along with the rest of the wedding party, for pictures.

Drusie watched everyone pose and smiled. "Just think of how much things have changed for us in so short a time."

"Ain't it the truth. I think it's been for the better," Gladdie observed.

"Me, too. Because of you and your grand ideas, I was able to take the music of home to other people, so they could enjoy what we know. I'll always be grateful to you for that."

"And I'll always be thankful to you for wantin' to sing so our future can be secure. I never imagined I'd be playin' harmonica in the band."

"Me, neither. I'm so glad Al is all better now and can play for Bill and Milton."

"Yep," Gladdie agreed. "Now Archie's runnin' two tours at once. It's unbelievable how his business keeps growin'."

"Unbelievable? I'm not so sure. Archie wants his bands to put on lots of gospel concerts, and the Lord blesses that, I think."

"I think so, too. And just look at how I thought my life was over when the Simpsons bought the store, but now everything is better than ever. The Lord always is full of surprises, isn't He?"

"Amen. Without Him, I couldn't have lasted a minute on the road. And He gave me my voice to start with."

Gladdie squeezed her. "That's what I love about you, Drusie. You never forget the real Source of life. You'll make me a fine wife forevermore. I can only pray that I'll be the husband you deserve."

"You'll be that and so much more, Mr. Gordon."

"I'll do my best, Mrs. Gordon."

"Mrs. Gordon. Imagine! I'll be Mrs. Gordon forever. Mrs. Gladdie Gordon." She sighed the way she always did when she watched one of her favorite motion pictures end happily.

Mr. Gladdie Gordon squeezed her shoulders, making her feel protected. "Do you think you'd ever be happy just livin' here with me and not singin' for the public?"

His query took her by surprise. "What does that mean?"

"I mean, will you leave tourin' behind when we have babies?"

"In a heartbeat!"

He beamed. "We'd better not say nothin' about our future plans to Archie. He won't like that much."

"Maybe he doesn't, but I do." Drusie lifted her mouth to Gladdie for a sweet kiss. When his lips met hers, she knew once and for all that they would be making beautiful music together for the rest of their lives.

TAMELA HANCOCK MURRAY

Tamela lives with her husband and their two daughters in Virginia. Tamela is a Christian romance author and has written several Bible trivia books. She is also an agent with Hartline Literary Agency. Tamela enjoys spending time with her family and friends and researching her stories of love and life in small towns. Hearing from her fans makes Tamela's day! Visit her Web site at www. tamelahancockmurray.com.

A Letter to Our Readers

Dear Readers:

In order that we might better contribute to your reading enjoyment, we would appreciate your taking a few minutes to respond to the following questions. When completed, please return to the following: Fiction Editor, Barbour Publishing, Inc., P.O. Box 719, Uhrichsville, OH 44683.

1. Did you enjoy reading *Blue Ridge Brides*?
   ❑ Very much—I would like to see more books like this.
   ❑ Moderately—I would have enjoyed it more if _____
   _____

   _____

2. What influenced your decision to purchase this book?
   (Check those that apply.)
   ❑ Cover   ❑ Back cover copy   ❑ Title   ❑ Price
   ❑ Friends   ❑ Publicity   ❑ Other

3. Which story was your favorite?
   ❑ *Journey to Love*   ❑ *The Music of Home*
   ❑ *Corduroy Road to Love*

4. Please check your age range:
   ❑ Under 18   ❑ 18–24   ❑ 25–34
   ❑ 35–45   ❑ 46–55   ❑ Over 55

5. How many hours per week do you read? _____

Name _____

Occupation _____

Address _____

City _____ State _____ Zip _____

E-mail _____